Praise for
The Pharaoh's Daughter

"A story I have waited for, *The Pharaoh's Daughter* throws light on one of the Old Testament's most enigmatic—and least lauded—figures. With gorgeous prose and painstaking research, ancient Egypt comes alive. This poignant story is a fascinating look into the early life of Moses and the time of King Tut. Poetic and fiercely compelling, this is Andrews's finest yet."

—TOSCA LEE, *New York Times* best-selling author of *Iscariot*

"What a delight! I loved sinking into the treasures of Egypt, with all the lush and fascinating detail that Andrews skillfully brings to life, in this behind-the-scenes imagining of a familiar tale."

—TRACY HIGLEY, author of *Pyramid of Secrets*

"Inspired by the scriptures, Mesu Andrews brings the ancient world to glowing life!"

—R. J. LARSON, author of *Prophet*

THE
PHARAOH'S
DAUGHTER

Books by Mesu Andrews

In the Shadow of Jezebel

Love in a Broken Vessel

Love's Sacred Song

Love Amid the Ashes

THE PHARAOH'S DAUGHTER

A TREASURES OF THE NILE NOVEL

MESU ANDREWS

WATERBROOK
PRESS

THE PHARAOH'S DAUGHTER
PUBLISHED BY WATERBROOK PRESS
12265 Oracle Boulevard, Suite 200
Colorado Springs, Colorado 80921

All Scripture quotations are taken from the Holy Bible, New International Version®, NIV®. Copyright © 1973, 1978, 1984, 2011 by Biblica Inc.™ Used by permission of Zondervan. All rights reserved worldwide. www.zondervan.com.

This book is a work of historical fiction based closely on real people and real events. Details that cannot be historically verified are purely products of the author's imagination.

Trade Paperback ISBN 978-1-60142-599-7
eBook ISBN 978-1-60142-600-0

Cover design by Kristopher K. Orr; cover photography by Kelly L. Howard

Published in the United States by WaterBrook Multnomah, an imprint of the Crown Publishing Group, a division of Random House LLC, New York, a Penguin Random House Company.

WATERBROOK and its deer colophon are registered trademarks of Random House LLC.

Library of Congress Cataloging-in-Publication Data
Andrews, Mesu, 1963–
    The pharaoh's daughter : a treasures of the nile novel / Mesu Andrews.
        pages cm
    ISBN 978-1-60142-599-7 (softcover)—ISBN 978-1-60142-600-0 (ebook) 1. Bible. Old Testament—History of Biblical events—Fiction. 2. Egypt—Kings and rulers—Fiction. 3. Moses (Biblical leader)—Fiction. I. Title.
    PS3601.N55274P48 2015
    813'.6—dc23

                                            2014043266

Printed in the United States of America
2015—First Edition

10 9 8 7 6 5 4 3 2 1

To my daughters, Trina and Emily. You are my heroes.

Acknowledgments

Thanks to my agent, Karen Ball, who guided me through a new contract process, and to the great folks at WaterBrook Multnomah—you are amazing. To Shannon Marchese, my senior editor: *The Pharaoh's Daughter* is richer, fuller, and more complete because you saw Anippe's soul before I did. To Amy Haddock, my marketing director: from our very first meeting, your energy and commitment to trying new things inspired me. (And you make the best chocolate-chip cookies EVER!) Thanks to the design team for the fabulous cover—more than I could have asked or imagined. Publicity and Sales teams, you are my hands and feet, and . . . WOW, you cover a lot of territory. "Thank you" isn't enough for all you do to get my book into readers' hands. A special thanks to Stuart McGuiggan, who was instrumental in bringing me to WaterBrook Multnomah. I owe you a cup of coffee, sir!

Our gracious God has surrounded me with a tribe of generous people, who gave of their time, talents, and resources to help me complete this book. Thanks go to Suzanne Smith, research librarian at Multnomah University, for trimming my research time in half by collecting books and articles on topics I requested. I'm so grateful to Phil and Pam Long for the use of their mountain cabin for those writing retreats in God's glorious creation. And to my three critique partners—Meg Wilson, Velynn Brown, and Michele Nordquist—I couldn't do this writing thing without your love, encouragement, and fantastic editing.

Finally, to both my spiritual and earthly families—thank you. My prayer team, BFF Team, my parents, and our kids—you pray for and encourage me through every panicked e-mail and plot roadblock. My incredible husband endures not only the ups and downs of my writing journey but also edits the full manuscript at least three times in its various forms. He's my rock, my hero, my biggest fan. I love you, Roy Andrews.

EGYPTIANS

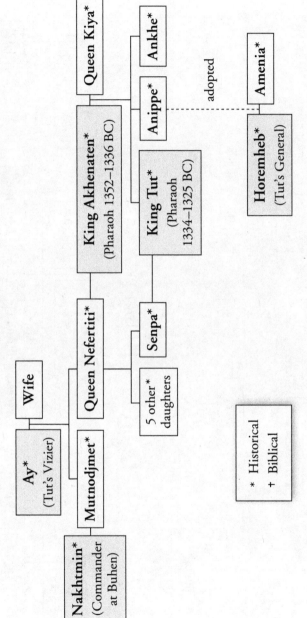

Nakhtmin*
(Commander at Buhen)

Ay*
(Tut's Vizier)

Wife

Mutnodjmet*

Queen Nefertiti*

King Akhenaten*
(Pharaoh 1352–1336 BC)

Queen Kiya*

5 other* daughters

Senpa*

King Tut
(Pharaoh 1334–1325 BC)

Anippe*

Ankhe*

Horemheb*
(Tut's General)

Amenia*

adopted

* Historical
† Biblical

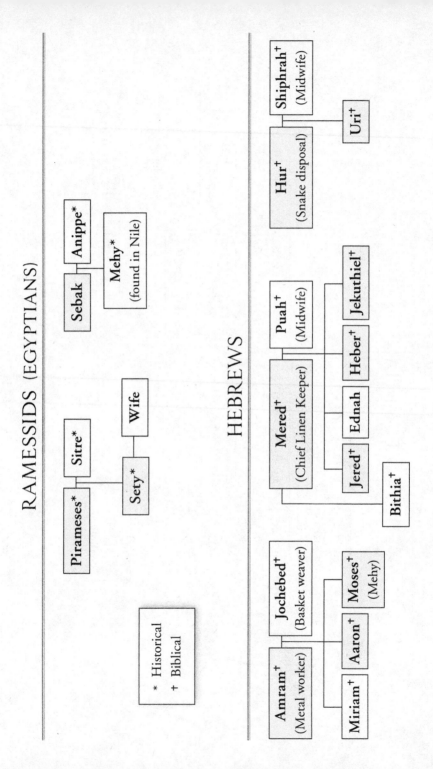

RAMESSIDS (EGYPTIANS)

HEBREWS

* Historical
† Biblical

Pirameses* — Sitre*
Sety* — Wife

Sebak — Anippe*
Mehy*
(found in Nile)

Hur† — Shiphrah†
(Snake disposal)   (Midwife)
Uri†

Mered† — Puah†
(Chief Linen Keeper)   (Midwife)
Jered†   Ednah   Heber†   Jekuthiel†
Bithia†

Amram† — Jochebed†
(Metal worker)   (Basket weaver)
Miriam†   Aaron†   Moses†
(Mehy)

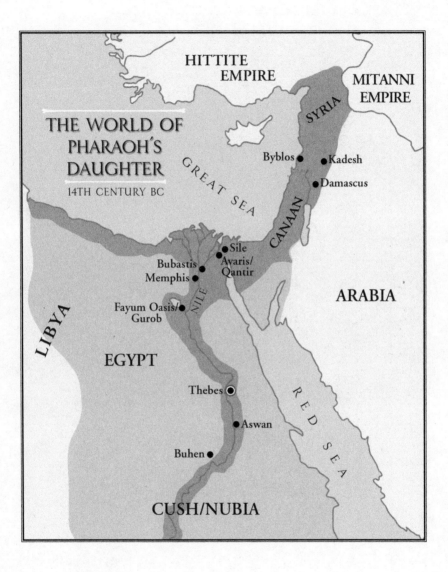

THE WORLD OF
PHARAOH'S
DAUGHTER

14TH CENTURY BC

HITTITE
EMPIRE

MITANNI
EMPIRE

SYRIA

GREAT SEA

Byblos ● ● Kadesh

● Damascus

CANAAN

● Sile

Bubastis ● Avaris/
Memphis ● Qantir

ARABIA

LIBYA

Fayum Oasis/
Gurob ●

NILE

EGYPT

Thebes ◉

RED SEA

● Aswan

Buhen ●

CUSH/NUBIA

NOTE TO READER

Ancient Egypt is a fascinating and challenging world to describe. Writing about it is sort of like drinking water from a fire hose. Information is everywhere! Some accurate, some simply ridiculous. Lists of pharaohs differ. Legend contradicts legend. And their gods—even ancient Egyptians disagreed about their gods.

How does one write a historically accurate story with such divergent information?

I began with the unalterable Truth of God's Word. The *Author's Note* details my process for making historical choices for the story, and the rest is plausible fiction—a story of what *might have happened* to Pharaoh's daughter. If at any point the story deviates from Scripture, it's unintentional—and I ask your grace and forgiveness.

The names and themes of this book are complex—as Egypt itself is complex—but stick with it, dear reader. Let the story unfold within your heart and mind. Walk with me among the bulrushes of the Nile and into the unsuspecting life of Pharaoh's daughter.

PROLOGUE

The royal linen closet is a dark hiding place, but I'm a big girl—almost five inundations old—so I'm trying not to be afraid.

I wonder . . . is it dark in the underworld? Was Ummi Kiya afraid when she and the baby inside her crossed over this morning?

The priest ordered me and my little sister to the birthing chamber. Ankhe is only three. She wouldn't go.

The priest was angry, so he came to our chamber and grabbed Ankhe's hand. "You must see the beauty of Tawaret—goddess of childbirth!"

Instead, we saw Ummi Kiya's blood poured out on the straw under her birthing stool. Her light-brown skin was white as milk. The midwives pulled out a baby boy, but he was as gray as granite.

The angry priest wasn't angry anymore. He knelt before Ankhe and me. "Anubis, god of the underworld, has stolen their breath. I'm sorry."

I ran from the birthing chamber, screaming, before Anubis could steal my breath too.

I've been hiding a long time because Anubis might still be hunting. He knows my name, *Meryetaten-tasherit*. It's hard to understand, but I'm called a *decoy*—named after Queen Nefertiti's daughter Meryetaten to confuse Anubis should he prowl the palace grounds. If I stay in this linen wardrobe all day and night, perhaps the dark god will take the Great Wife's daughter instead.

Nefertiti, the Great Wife, hates me because Abbi Akhenaten loved my mother. Ummi Kiya was his Beloved Wife, and she gave him a son—my brother, Tutankhamun.

Pharaohs like sons, but Abbi Akhenaten doesn't like daughters. He frowns when my sister Ankhe and I enter the throne room. Maybe it's because of Ankhe's tantrums.

Ummi Kiya said Ankhe's *ka* is troubled like Abbi's. He throws tantrums too, but because he's pharaoh, he doesn't get in trouble.

My legs hurt, and my tummy's rumbling. I don't want to stay in this dark closet anymore. But the linen robes hanging around me smell like Ummi Kiya—lotus blossoms and honey. Who will love me now that she's gone?

My brother Tut will. He's only six, but he protects me. He checks my bed for scorpions at night and makes his tutors teach me the same lessons he's learning. We learn about Hittites and Nubia, and we try to write hieroglyphs.

Ankhe is too little for lessons, and she doesn't know about love either. Will she ever love? Or will she be like Abbi Akhenaten and live forever with a broken ka?

I hear footsteps. Someone is coming. My heart feels like horses racing in my chest.

"Mery?"

Someone's calling me. I think I know that voice.

"Mery, *habiba,* I know you're in there."

A little light shines in, and I peek through the robes at a kind woman's face. Her cheeks are plump and round, her smile warm like the setting sun.

"You know my ummi," I say.

"Yes, I was Kiya's friend. Do you remember my name, Mery?"

She offers her hand, but I scoot behind the robes into the corner of my wooden shelter. Her smile dies, and I wonder if she'll unleash Anubis now that I've been found. I hear a sound like a wounded dog—*it's me! I must stop crying!*

"Mery, I'm sure your ummi Kiya's heart measured lighter than a feather on Anubis's scale of justice. She is waiting for us both in the afterlife, but she would want you to trust me now."

I can't stop shaking, can't speak. I can only stare at this woman whose smile is gone and whose eyes are now filling with tears. Is she angry? I don't remember her name, but I know she's the big general's wife. Will she call the army to kill me?

"Your abbi Akhenaten has given you to General Horemheb and me. You are our daughter now."

She reaches for me again, but I slap her hand away. "No! I want Tut!" I bury my face in my hands and pray for Anubis to find me. *Take me to Ummi Kiya!*

"Mery. Mery!" The general's wife is kneeling and bent into the closet, shaking my shoulders. "Tut will stay with you. We're all staying here at the Memphis Palace together. Your brother, you, me, and General Horemheb. You will be with Tut as you've always been." She strokes my hair and doesn't seem angry that I yelled.

Slowly, I look at her. "Did Abbi give Tut away too?"

"No, little habiba. Tut is prince regent. He will always be Akhenaten's son, but all Kiya's children will remain under General Horemheb's protection in Memphis. Because the general and I have no children, Pharaoh gave you as a precious gift. You are now our daughter. I hope this pleases you."

She cups my cheek and looks at me the way Ummi did. Maybe she could love me a little. "What is your name, lady?" I ask.

"I am Amenia. Would you like to know the new name General Horemheb has chosen for you?"

I suck in a quick breath and scoot to the edge of the wardrobe, surprising my new ummi. "I get a new name? Anubis will never find me if I have a new name!"

Chuckling, Amenia stands and helps me to my feet. "You will be called *Anippe*, daughter of the Nile. Do you like it?" Without waiting for a reply, she pulls me into her squishy, round tummy for a hug.

I'm trying not to cry. Pharaoh's daughters don't cry, but her soft, warm arms make me feel so safe. Maybe Amenia could be my new hiding place instead of the dark linen closet.

My tummy is growling again.

"You must be hungry after being in that wardrobe all day." Amenia kisses the top of my head and gives me a little squeeze before letting go. "We must present you to your abbi Horemheb before our evening meal."

"What about Ankhe? Will she come with us to meet our new abbi?"

Amenia loses her smile. She holds my shoulders hard. "Anippe, do you trust Abbi Horemheb and me to do what's best?" Her voice makes me shiver.

"Where is Ankhe?"

"Ankhe is safe, and she will always be your little sister, but she will not meet General Horemheb."

After another kiss on my forehead, Amenia smiles, and we start walking through the tiled hallway to meet my new abbi.

I try to stop at Ummi Kiya's chamber, but Amenia pushes me past. So I keep walking and don't look back. Like the waters of the Nile, I will flow.

PART 1

These are the names of the sons of Israel who went to Egypt with Jacob, each with his family: Reuben, Simeon, Levi and Judah; Issachar, Zebulun and Benjamin; Dan and Naphtali; Gad and Asher. The descendants of Jacob numbered seventy in all; Joseph was already in Egypt.

Now Joseph and all his brothers and all that generation died, but the Israelites were exceedingly fruitful; they multiplied greatly, increased in numbers and became so numerous that the land was filled with them.

—EXODUS 1:1–7

1

Then a new king, to whom Joseph meant nothing, came to power in Egypt.

—Exodus 1:8

FOUR YEARS LATER

Anippe dipped her sharpened reed in the small water jar and swirled it in the palette of black powder. Her scroll had only one stray drop of ink— one less drop than Tut's—and she was determined to best her big brother. She drew a second water symbol, adding it to *bread, water, basin, box,* and *owl,* to finish her brother's name: T-t-n-k-h-m-n. Leaning to her left, she peeked at Tut's progress. Her letters were much clearer, and he now had three stray ink drops.

"Very good, Anippe." The tutor peered over her shoulder, his breath reeking of garlic and onions. "Your writing is almost as precise as the divine son's."

Tut smirked, and Anippe rolled her eyes. "Thank you, revered and wise teacher." Maybe his vision was blurred by the cloud of his stinky breath.

"My letters are just as good!" Ankhe shouted from across the cramped classroom. She slammed her reed on the small, square table and began tearing her scroll into pieces. "You spend all your time with Tut and Anippe."

The tutor grabbed his willow switch, and Ankhe turned her back in time to save her face from the lashing. "If I spend more time with you, Ankhe-Senpaaten-tasherit, you will likely be whipped more often. Is that what you wish? You will show me respect in this classroom, and you will act like the daughter of a god."

Tears stung Anippe's eyes, but she blinked them away. Daughters of gods didn't cry. The tutor had never used his switch on her, but she didn't wish to test him. She reached for Tut's hand under the table, silently begging him to intervene. The divine son was never punished.

"Oh wise and knowing teacher, let us resume our lesson." Tut raised one eyebrow, seeming much older than his ten years. "If I am to rule Egypt some-day, I must understand why some vassal nations have betrayed Pharaoh Akhenaten and pledged allegiance to Hittite dogs. Our eastern border is at risk if I can't control buffer nations between us and our greatest threat."

Anippe gaped at her brother. He remembered nations and territories as if they were written inside his eyelids.

The tutor issued a final glare at Ankhe before returning to a stool beside his favored pupil. "Very astute questions, son of the good god Akhenaten, who is king of Two Lands and lord of all. The Hittites are indeed our greatest east-ern threat, a military machine with iron weapons, but we must also beware the Nubians in the south. They pose as loyal servants to Egypt's king, his officials, and our military, but you must never trust a people not your own."

Anippe slipped away from the table, certain the tutor was lost in his topic, and slid onto the bench beside Ankhe. Her little sister was still whimpering, head down. When Anippe tried to smooth her braided wig, Ankhe shoved her hand away.

Like always.

Ankhe hated discipline, but she didn't like to be loved either. Soon after Ummi Kiya's death, Tut told the grownups that *all* Pharaoh Akhenaten's chil-dren should be tutored, and he tried to have Ankhe at the same table—between her older brother and sister. But as she grew, her tantrums became worse. Sometimes even the switch wouldn't stop her. So the tutor moved her to a sepa-rate table.

Separate. That was what Ankhe would always be, no matter what her siblings tried.

Anippe saw welts rising on Ankhe's back under her sheer linen sheath, marks from the tutor's switch. "I'll ask Ummi Amenia for some honey to put on your back."

"She's not my ummi." Ankhe picked up her reed and dipped it in water and pigment. "They didn't adopt me."

"But Amenia still cares for you, Ankhe." Anippe wanted to hug her, but she'd tried that before. Ankhe hated hugs. She hated to be touched at all.

The sound of soldiers came from the hallway, spears tapping the tiles as they marched. This sounded like more than the two guards who always stood at their doorway. This sounded like a full troop. Tut looked at Anippe, afraid, and Anippe grabbed Ankhe's hand. Her little sister didn't pull away this time.

General Horemheb appeared at the doorway, his big shoulders touching the sides and his head too tall to enter without ducking. He looked scary in his battle armor—until he saw Anippe and winked.

She wasn't afraid anymore. Her abbi would protect her against anything. He'd loved her and spoiled her since the day Amenia introduced them.

But when he saw Ankhe, his face turned as red as a pomegranate. He scowled at the tutor. "Why is my daughter seated with the little baboon? You have been told to keep them apart."

Before the tutor could answer, Abbi Horemheb grabbed Anippe's arm, lifted her from the bench, and landed her back on the stool beside Tut. Anippe's eyes filled with tears. Abbi was always rough with Ankhe but never Anippe—never his little habiba. She sat straight and tall beside Tut, blinking her eyes dry, trying to be the princess Abbi wanted her to be.

When her abbi returned to the doorway, Anippe noticed two other people standing with the soldiers—a beautiful lady and Vizier Ay. Abbi Horem hated the vizier. Maybe that was why he'd lost his temper.

Who is that pretty woman with them? The woman wore a long, pleated robe, fastened at her shoulder with a jeweled clasp. Her braided wig fell in layers with pretty stones woven through it on gold thread. Anippe studied her face. She looked familiar, but she wasn't one of Amenia's friends who visited the Memphis Palace.

Vizier Ay took three steps and stopped in front of Tut and Anippe's table. "Pharaoh Akhenaten has journeyed beyond the horizon. The priests have begun the customs of Osiris."

Tut straightened and hid his shaking hands under the table. He was quiet for a while, breathing as if he'd run a long race. When his breath came smoothly again, he said, "The good god Akhenaten will cross the night sky and warm us with the sun each day." His voice quaked. He was trying hard to be brave, but Anippe knew how much Tut loved Abbi Akhenaten. The weight of Egypt now rested on her brother's slim shoulders. "When do we sail for the burial ceremony?"

Vizier Ay tilted his head and smiled, as if Tut had seen only five inundations. "We have much to discuss with you, divine son, but first I would have you meet your new wife."

"Wife?" Tut squeaked and then peered around the vizier at the woman. Anippe's big brother withered into a shy boy. He motioned for General Horemheb's approach and then beckoned him close for a whisper. "I have no need of a wife, Horemheb—not yet."

Abbi Horem leaned down, eye to eye. "Divine son and beloved prince, a young king needs three things to rule well: a teachable ka, wise advisors, and a good wife." He tilted his head toward the pretty lady at the door. "Senpa is your good wife. Ay and I are your advisors. And you have demonstrated teachability. You are both humble and powerful. I am honored to bask in your presence, most favored son of Aten."

Tut's throat bobbed up and down, perhaps swallowing many words before the right ones came to mind. A bead of sweat appeared on his upper lip while everyone waited for him to speak.

"How old is she?" Ankhe blurted out the question Anippe wanted to ask but didn't. Tut's eyebrows rose, clearly awaiting an answer.

Abbi Horem's face turned red again, and he slammed his hand on Ankhe's table. "You will be silent unless asked to speak."

Ankhe raised her chin in defiance but didn't say another word.

Vizier Ay guided the pretty woman toward the table where Tut and Anippe sat. "Divine prince, meet your wife, Ankhe-Senpaaten. She is your half sister—daughter of Akhenaten and Nefertiti. You may call her *Senpa*."

Anippe stared at Nefertiti's daughter. All their lives, they'd been warned of Nefertiti's evil. Now Tut must marry one of her daughters? How could they ask it of him? Senpa was beautiful, but she was ancient—at least twenty inundations, maybe twenty-five. How could a ten-year-old be a husband to a twenty-year-old queen?

Anippe shivered and earned a stern glance from Abbi Horem.

Vizier Ay cleared his throat and nudged Senpa aside. "Divine son and ruler of my heart, we have many details to discuss regarding the burial ceremony and your coronation. Perhaps you, in your great wisdom, could dismiss your sisters to Amenia's chamber to plan the wedding festival?"

"Yes, you may go." Tut's voice sounded small.

Anippe wanted to stay, but Abbi Horem was already instructing a contingent of guards to escort them to Amenia's chamber.

"Wait!" Anippe's outburst quieted the room. "If it pleases my dear abbi, I would ask one question." She stood and bowed to her abbi, using her best courtly manners to gain his pleasure before asking what burned in her belly.

"You may ask it, my daughter."

Lifting her chin and squaring her shoulders, she tried to speak as a king's sister—not as sister to a crown prince. "Will Ankhe and I remain here at Memphis Palace with Tut and Senpa after their marriage?"

Vizier Ay laughed, startling Anippe from her composure.

Abbi Horem turned her chin gently, regaining her attention. "No, little habiba. Tut will remain here at the Memphis Palace with me and Vizier Ay. However, Senpa, Amenia, you, and Ankhe will relocate to the Gurob Harem Palace with the other noblemen's wives and children. The king's officials visit Gurob several times a year. You'll enjoy helping in the linen shop and have many little girls to play with."

Anippe worked hard to keep her smile in place, but her heart felt ripped in two parts. First Ummi Kiya and now Tut? Would the gods take away everyone she loved?

She bowed slightly to her abbi and then reached for the scroll on which she'd drawn Tut's name—a memento of their last class together.

The tutor blocked her path, hand outstretched. "I'm sorry, Princess. I can't let you keep that scroll."

"But why? I—"

Ankhe jumped to her side, grabbed the scroll, and hid it behind her back. Abbi Horem snatched it away, gave it to the tutor, and raised his hand to strike Ankhe. Anippe stepped between them, halting the general's hand.

Grabbing Anippe's shoulders, he shook his head. "You protect her too much, habiba. She must learn to behave as a princess." He hugged her tight and kissed her cheek. When he stood, towering above Anippe and Ankhe, he addressed them both. "You can no longer write your brother's name in hieroglyph. He is now divine, and his name is sacred. Only royal scribes may write the six-part name of a king within an oval cartouche. Now, my guards will escort you to Amenia's chamber with Senpa."

Anippe obeyed without argument. She looked over her shoulder as they left, wondering when Tut would become a god. This morning they'd laughed and teased and even raced from their chambers to the schoolroom. She'd almost beaten him. Surely a god could run faster than a girl.

Tut sat utterly still, expressionless, listening to his advisors. Perhaps that was what a god looked like—empty.

Anippe made sure Ankhe was behind her and then followed the beautiful daughter of Nefertiti down the open-air corridor to the women's chambers. Losing herself in the sound of chirping birds and sandals on tile, she breathed in the smell of lotus blossoms as they passed a garden pond.

Like the waters of the Nile, I will flow. I am Anippe, daughter of . . . Horemheb and Amenia.

2

*With cunning they conspire against your
people; they plot against those you cherish.*

—PSALM 83:3

FIVE YEARS LATER

Anippe lingered in half-lucid sleep, dawn's light as vexing as a knot in her loom. Gurob's Harem Palace was nestled in Egypt's marshy Fayum, gloriously still before daylight. Only the sound of a lark's distant trill and mosquitoes' constant humming nibbled the edges of Anippe's consciousness.

"Daughter, get up. Hurry, you must get dressed." Ummi Amenia shook her shoulder. "Your brother summoned you to the Throne Hall—immediately."

"What's so urgent?" Anippe bolted to her feet, causing her head to swim. She closed her eyes and reached for the bed, but Ummi yanked her back to her feet.

"No, don't sit down. You must get dressed." Shuffling her toward the clothing baskets and pegs, her ummi continued honking like a mother goose. "Take this robe to the maid. She's waiting in the courtyard to apply your paints." Ummi Amenia draped a freshly pleated gown over Anippe's arm, then turned her shoulders and gave her a little shove. "I'll bring the new linen sheath. You must look perfect this morning."

"Why must I look perfect for Tut?" Growling under her breath, Anippe looked longingly at her younger sister, who still lay quietly on her back, wig hanging neatly, head suspended by the carved turquoise neck rest. "Why wasn't Ankhe summoned to see the king? Why does she get to sleep until midday?"

Ummi Amenia nudged Anippe toward the adjoining courtyard. "You sound like a six-year-old, habiba. You're a grown woman now. Fourteen-year-olds don't whine."

Anippe stopped midstride and turned, arms folded. "Why am I a grown woman when you want me to do something, but I'm acting like a little girl when I want something?"

Chuckling, Amenia cupped Anippe's cheek. "My habiba, Pharaoh Tut has a special edict that will prove you are grown. Now, please, let our maid dress you." Her tenderness quieted Anippe's complaints, and she pecked her ummi's cheek with a kiss, surrendering to the inevitable.

They continued beyond four papyrus-shaped pillars into their private courtyard, where their Nubian maid waited beside an embroidered couch. The morning sounds of birds and frogs and breeze-swept palms distracted Anippe while the maid began her practiced ministrations.

Anippe lifted her arms to give up her sleeping coverlet and receive the sheer linen robe over her head. The sheath came next, draped under her right arm and over her left shoulder, with a gold and turquoise clasp at the base of her throat. Anippe lifted her long spiraled wig so Ummi Amenia could affix the *menat* to counterbalance her heavy gold and gemstone collar. Dressing complete, the three women moved in concert to prepare for the finishing touches. While Anippe reclined on her couch, Ummi Amenia reached for the basket of bracelets, and the maid gathered her pots of ointments and paints.

This Nubian had served Amenia, Anippe, and Ankhe since they'd arrived at Gurob five years ago. She spoke little and smiled much. Her eyes sparkled from within, though Anippe couldn't imagine how a slave could be happy.

With the first stroke of malachite beneath Anippe's bottom lashes, Ummi Amenia cleared her throat. "Your Abbi Horemheb has returned from the Hittite battle."

Anippe bolted upright, nearly toppling the pot of malachite paste from the maid's hand. "Why? Was he injured? Are the Hittites invading?" For months they'd heard only of Egypt's losses, and the general never left a battle unless summoned.

Calmly, Amenia pressed Anippe's shoulders back against the couch and with a single nod instructed the Nubian to resume her duties. "Your abbi Horem is unharmed. He arrived late last night, and he's waiting to see you in the throne room with King Tut."

Momentary delight gave way to dread. Anippe would soon see the two men she loved most, but what could be urgent enough to bring her abbi home? "Why would Abbi Horem come to the Harem Palace? He hates women's gossip, and he's never enjoyed the king's annual hunt in the marshes."

Ummi Amenia's slight hesitation spoke louder than her words. "He's come to see you, habiba."

Anippe's eyes remained closed, submitting to the maid's practiced hand, but her insides began to tremble. "Have I done something to displease him, Ummi? Are *you* angry with me?" Fear coiled around her heart. They'd adopted her years ago. Had they tired of her?

"No one is angry with you, habiba. You are our treasure." Amenia rested a quieting hand on her arm. "And because we treasure you, we must protect you and provide a husband for you."

Anippe swallowed hard. Ummi had spoken of providing a husband before, but each time Anippe had laughed and teased Ummi Amenia toward another subject. This morning felt different.

She heard a shuffle beside her and opened her eyes. Ummi Amenia crouched on the maid's stool, her face hovering near.

"Do you trust Abbi Horem and me to do what's best for you, daughter?"

Swallowing the lump in her throat, Anippe could only nod. Seeming appeased, Ummi relinquished the low stool to the maid once more. Anippe gratefully hid behind closed eyes and remembered the last time this kind woman asked her, *"Do you trust us to do what's best for you?"*

Amenia had crouched in front of the royal linen closet on the day Ummi Kiya died, coaxing Mery into her arms. *Meryetaten-tasherit.* The name had taunted Anubis and filled her with fear every day of her life—until General Horemheb and Amenia gave her a new name.

Would a husband change her name too? Would he love her like Abbi Horem and Ummi Amenia had?

Anippe's heart nearly stopped. *A husband will expect children!* Panic started in her belly and rose into her chest, tingling and burning. Ummi Kiya's lifeless eyes and the baby's gray body raged in her memory.

A soft linen cloth dabbed Anippe's cheek. "Habiba, you mustn't cry. You've always known we would make a good match for you someday. This marriage is for your protection—for the protection of Egypt's Two Lands." Amenia's gentle voice unleashed more tears. "Shh, now. No more tears. Your maid will paint your lips and cheeks while I dry your eyes."

Anippe drew in a deep breath and exhaled slowly, then pouted her lips for the maid's expert application of red ochre. Ummi dried her eyes, taking care to remove whatever remained of the smeared malachite.

While the maid painted Anippe's lips, she forced herself to think of anything but childbirth. *Did Ummi say this marriage would protect Egypt?* Surely Abbi wouldn't match her with a foreign prince in some treaty and send her far away. Tears threatened again, but she swallowed back the emotion. Ummi was right. She'd always known the day would come when she would be forced to marry.

With freshly painted lips, Anippe formed her question. "Please, Ummi. Tell me why Abbi Horem returned from battle to order this marriage and how my wedding feast will protect Egypt's Two Lands."

Anippe sensed a commotion beside her and opened her eyes. Amenia had taken the paints from the maid and commandeered her stool. "Please awaken Ankhe and dress her in the chamber. I'd like to speak with Anippe alone."

The Nubian bowed and obeyed, hurrying out of the courtyard. Anippe sat up on her couch, and Amenia lowered her voice to a whisper. "The Hittites are not our only enemies, habiba. One of your Abbi's messengers intercepted suspicious correspondence between Vizier Ay and Commander Nakhtmin in Nubia."

Anippe had heard of Nakhtmin. "The same commander that's marrying Vizier Ay's daughter? The women of Gurob have talked about nothing but the wedding festival since the inundation. Perhaps the correspondence was about their upcoming marriage."

Amenia stroked her cheek with a good-natured grin. "Women speak of wedding festivals, habiba. Viziers and commanders do not. Vizier Ay seeks control of Commander Nakhtmin's Nubian slave army. If Ay coordinates a rebellion, Egypt is divided, and Tut's reign is over."

"He wouldn't dare!"

"Powerful men crave more power, and Vizier Ay is more dangerous than the Hittites right now, so your abbi Horem returned to the Gurob Palace to protect your brother from an enemy he doesn't yet recognize."

Amenia pressed Anippe's shoulders back against the couch. Anippe closed her eyes for the final touches of kohl around her eyes. She lay quietly for several heartbeats, considering the broader scope of life and death and the part she'd play in Egypt's history.

"Who is my husband, and how will our marriage bring peace?"

"I would rather your abbi Horem introduce him to you. But know this, daughter. Your abbi loves you and has chosen the man best suited for your future—and for the future of Egypt."

Anippe heard the clattering of paint pots and applicators as Ummi Amenia replaced the items on a silver tray. "Almost done. Sit up, habiba. Let me put on this gold-braided headband." She fitted a hammered-gold weave over Anippe's wig and held up a polished-bronze mirror. "What do you think?"

Anippe stared at her reflection. Long braids punctuated by gold beads were accented by the golden headband resting above her brow. Deep green malachite danced beneath her sandy brown eyes, and perfect kohl bands extended from her upper lids to her temples. "You painted my eyes like yours, Ummi. I look . . . grown up."

"Today, you become an *amira*, Anippe." Amenia's voice was gentle but firm. "From this day forward, you will have your own home, your own estate, your own husband."

Morning light dimmed to gray, and Anippe fought tears again. "Me. An amira."

"Your groom is waiting for you in the throne room with King Tut and your abbi Horem."

"Has General Horemheb made a match for me too?" Ankhe came running from their adjoining chamber and knelt at Amenia's feet. "I'm only two years younger than Anippe." Hope glistened in her eyes, breaking Anippe's heart.

Gently but firmly, Amenia cupped Ankhe's chin. "No, child. General Horemheb is not your abbi. We've allowed you to live with us because Anippe is your sister, but it's up to your brother Tut to make a marriage match for you."

The familiar cloud settled over Ankhe, and she cast an accusing glance at Anippe. *Betrayer!* Her eyes held the same look every time Abbi Horem hugged Anippe and each time Amenia spoke a tender word. Though Anippe had no part in the decisions that formed their lives, Ankhe blamed her—and yet clung to her.

"Perhaps I can talk to Tut and ask him to make a match for you too, sister," Anippe said.

Ankhe rolled her eyes and stomped back to the chamber, flopped on her bed, and covered her head with the sheet.

Ummi Amenia turned Anippe's chin, demanding her attention. "Ankhe will adjust. You must hurry to the Throne Hall."

They exited through the courtyard gate, then wove through the maze of harem apartments in silence until they emerged into a pillared corridor. Dawn's glow lit the limestone palace walls, and Anippe marveled at the sun god Re. How did he sail his sacred barque through the dark waters of night to bring them a new day every day? If she were a priest or a king, she would sacrifice an extra offering this morning. Did Ankhe see the same sunrise? Could she rise from her bed and find something for which to be thankful?

Beyond these walls, government officials slept in summer villas, while a peasant village readied its wares for another day of trade. Surrounding the sea of humanity was the Fayum's lush green marshlands—home to Egypt's big-game animals. Lions. Hippos. Wild oxen. Once each year Pharaoh arrived to free the noblemen from their civilized cages to hunt wild beasts.

Late each summer, noblemen left the Memphis Palace, where Egyptian men ruled the nation, and journeyed to the Gurob Harem, where Egyptian women ruled the men. The harem housed most of Egypt's royal women, related by blood or marriage to the king and his advisors. Their linen workshop produced the finest cloth in the world, its quality and quantity outpaced only by Gurob's gossip.

Silence had escorted them to the end of the long corridor, and Anippe grew weary of the sound of squeaky leather sandals. "Ummi, can't you tell me anything about the man I'm going to marry?"

Ummi Amenia stopped at the threshold of the mosaic-tiled hallway leading to the Throne Hall and gathered Anippe's hands in her own. "Your abbi Horem has chosen one of his best soldiers as your husband. King Tut is torn between your abbi Horem's desperate measures and Vizier Ay's deception." She released Anippe's hands, straightened her spine, and assumed an unfamiliar coolness. "You decide who to trust with your future."

Amenia walked away, leaving Anippe to walk the mosaic-tiled corridor of the Throne Hall alone.

3

The products of Egypt and the merchandise of Cush . . .
they will come over to you and will be yours.

—ISAIAH 45:14

Anippe approached the Nubian guards at the throne-room doors, trying not to stare at their ebony chests glistening in the morning heat. Like most Medjay warriors, these guards wore leopard-skin loincloths, carried two-cubit-long flint-headed spears, and wore bands of beaded necklaces representing battle kills. These guards were inexperienced—only two beaded strands—but they were no less terrifying than the king's personal guard.

With a deep breath, Anippe mustered her courage, remembering Abbi Horem's assurance. *"The only thing fiercer than a Medjay's fury is his loyalty. Medjay friendship in life is Medjay friendship in death."* They opened the heavy cedar doors as she approached, and she hurried through.

The heavy doors slammed shut behind her, echoing in the expansive hall constructed to resemble Pharaoh's luxury barque. The ceiling reached as high as the ship's expansive sail, white linen fluttering down from papyrus ropes draped pillar to pillar. The room itself measured from doors to throne the exact length of his ship from helm to rudder, and the blue faience tiles on which supplicants approached their pharaoh reminded all that King Tut—like the Nile—was Egypt's life giver.

Six men stood at the opposite end of a long crimson carpet—all staring at her. Two Medjays guarded her brother, Tut, from behind his elevated throne, while Vizier Ay waited at the carpet's threshold. Abbi Horem stood across from Ay with a handsome soldier, clearly the man she was to marry.

Utterly still and painfully flushed, Anippe was sure her heart pounded hard enough to bounce the gold and turquoise clasp on her chest.

A steward's voice boomed behind her, nearly startling her out of her sandals. "Enter, Princess Anippe, into the presence of the good god, King Tutankhamun, strong bull, pleasing of birth, one of perfect laws, who pacifies Upper and Lower Egypt, who wears both crowns and pleases the gods, great of the palace of Amun, lord of—"

"Enough!" Tut crashed his flail against his armrest. "Leave us."

Anippe glanced over her shoulder to be sure no one else lurked. The steward slipped out the door, and she was suddenly alone at the far end of the crimson carpet.

Tut swatted his flail against the armrest again. "Come, Anippe. We have important matters to discuss."

She bowed in deference, swallowing what she would have said five years ago—before he was a god. *He must be in one of his moods again.* Tut had been especially volatile since his wife and half-sister, Senpa, miscarried their first child while visiting nobility in the Delta. He'd ordered his queen to recuperate at Gurob, where their sisters and Amenia could minister to her weary body and grieving ka—that part of every human that lives forever.

As Senpa shared details of her painful loss, Anippe battled memories of Ummi Kiya's death and the baby brother that never drew breath. Senpa had been nearly full term when her travail began while at the Delta estate of Qantir. Hebrew midwives tried but couldn't save Senpa's baby girl, a baby too malformed to survive. With quiet sobs, she'd spoken of the pressure a king and queen feel to produce an heir. Amenia had hoped to calm her. *"You're both young,"* she'd said. But even Anippe knew a king wasn't pleasing to the gods until his wife bore a son.

Anippe tried to make her feet move toward Tut's throne. They wouldn't budge.

Her brother almost looked like a god today, seated on his gilded throne, wearing the double crown of Egypt's Two Lands. His eyes were painted with kohl—the sign of Horus a bold stripe toward his temple and a downward curl toward his cheekbone. Pharaoh's golden collar—inlaid with rubies, lapis, and jasper—gleamed around his neck. But it hung like a millstone on his dark brown shoulders. She ached for him, for the children they once were.

Abbi Horem walked toward her, arms open, breaking the awkward silence. "Come, my treasure. Welcome your abbi home."

She hurried to his familiar warmth and safety, snuggling into his chest—caring nothing about her eye paints or his perfect white robe. "I've missed you, Abbi. Why can't you come home more often?"

Abbi Horem set her upright and held her shoulders, looking hard into her eyes. "When I am at war, I stay at war; and when I am at home, I am fully yours."

Tucking her under his protective wing, they approached King Tut together. She didn't dare look at the handsome soldier, but she could feel his gaze on her.

Vizier Ay nodded politely when she and Abbi Horem halted beside him at the edge of the crimson carpet. Ay was as old as the general but quite handsome for his age. Many in the harem found his dove-colored eyes appealing. Anippe found his light eyes eerie and believed the tall, slender vizier to be a jackal in fine linen. His gaze roamed her form freely, making her shiver.

Repulsed, Anippe stepped toward the throne, head bowed. "Life, health, and peace to the divine son of the great god Horus. I have come as you commanded, most revered brother Tut. How may I serve—"

"Tell her, Horemheb. Tell my sister why you took your best soldier from a crucial battle in order to plan her wedding."

She glanced up and saw a sheen of sweat on Tut's brow, his jaw muscle dancing. Why was he angry at Abbi Horem? Did he disapprove of the man Abbi had chosen?

Abbi's expression was more than battle weary. Fighting Hittites for ten months could account for fatigue, but his countenance revealed a deeper agony. "As you wish, my king." He cast a burning glare at the vizier before softening his gaze for Anippe. "It is time for the House of Horemheb to unite with the House of Rameses."

He nudged the officer forward, joining his hand with Anippe's.

The House of Horemheb? Before Anippe could ponder the statement further, the soldier's large hand engulfed her own. She looked up and found his eyes devouring her. The strength of his bearing moved her back a step.

Abbi Horem gripped her arm and moved her close again. "Anippe, my treasure, this is your husband, Commander Sebak. He is my best officer, Master of Horse, and he is honored among the great Ramessid military family." He turned a threatening glare at the vizier. "Sebak and his Ramessid guards will protect you at his estate in the Delta."

"In the Delta?" Anippe jerked her hand away. "But I don't want to live in the Delta. I want to stay in Gurob with Ummi."

She saw the Master of Horse raise an eyebrow but couldn't tell if he was amused or angry. She didn't care.

"Mery." The quiet name from her past stopped her like a slap. Tut hadn't called her *Mery* since Abbi Horem adopted her.

She bowed her head, letting the ebony spirals of her wig hide her gathering tears. "Yes, my king?"

"You will do as General Horemheb commands." His tone was suddenly resigned, the anger gone. Why? What had changed?

Anippe dared lift her eyes to the god on the throne and saw the same blank expression that shadowed Tut's face on the day he married Senpa. "Our lives have never been our own, sister. Horemheb has always protected us—me on Egypt's throne and you, when he adopted you and named you *Anippe*." He paused, staring hard at Horemheb, and finally nodded what seemed like silent gratitude before returning his attention to Anippe.

"Honored daughter of General Horemheb and beloved sister of the good god King Tut—I proclaim Sebak, commander of the Ramessids, is your husband this day. The royal family will attend the wedding feast at Sebak's Avaris estate in the Delta upon the completion of the king's royal Fayum hunt." Then, leaning forward to address Sebak, Tut's eyes narrowed, sharpening the sign of Horus. "Commander Sebak, Horemheb's fears for Anippe may be unfounded, but she is not only his treasure—she is Pharaoh's beloved sister. Protect her or die."

Anippe wanted to scream, *No! I don't know this man, and I don't know the Delta!* But she remained silent, an obedient daughter, sister, woman.

Sebak stepped closer and placed a possessive hand at the small of her back. "It is my honor and pleasure to protect Anippe, great god of the Two Lands. Every Ramessid in the Delta will see that she is safe at Avaris." His voice rumbled low, and his intimate touch sent a surge of fear through her.

Anippe knew little of the Delta except that it contained Hebrew slaves, grain fields, and Egypt's fiercest soldiers—the Ramessids. And Senpa's baby had died there.

She peered up at the giant beside her and looked into his warm brown eyes. They sparkled and laughed. Could eyes laugh? Perhaps not, but the lazy grin on his face was infuriating.

He reached for her hand, cradled it like a fragile glass bead, and placed a tender kiss on her palm.

Fire raced up her arm. She snatched her hand away, and her breaths came in short, quick gasps. Was it the commander's nearness or Tut's rising anger?

The king glared at his vizier. "General Horemheb left the battlefield because he believed you were a threat to my sister. I'd like to assure him this is untrue, but how can I, when I hear rumors of your conspiracy with Nakhtmin in Nubia?"

"I am as loyal to you as I've always been, great and mighty son of Horus," the vizier protested. "My messages to the commander in Nubia were to arrange my daughter's marriage. I, like General Horemheb, feared for my daughter's safety here at Gurob and took steps to safeguard her from those loyal to the general."

"Those loyal to the general?" Tut's voice squeaked like a boy becoming a man. "Is no one loyal to King Tut anymore?" His words echoed in the near-empty hall, a reminder that Tut was Amun-Re, god of the sun on earth.

A shiver crept up Anippe's spine. Tut had been acting more like Abbi Akhenaten lately—impulsive, easily agitated—all signs of an unbalanced *ma'at*. The seasons, the sun and moon, justice, truth, and relational harmony hinged on the divine equilibrium of the earthly *Lord of Ma'at* seated on Egypt's throne.

As Anippe's concern mounted, Tut breathed deeply, crossed the golden crook and flail against his chest, and stared into the distance. She could almost see him return the balance of ma'at.

"General Horemheb, do you have proof that Vizier Ay has been involved in any treasonous activity?" Tut asked.

"Vizier Ay has amassed too much influence in southern Egypt. By marrying his daughter to Commander Nakhtmin, he secures military allegiance with the Nubians in Cush and purchases goodwill for every southern trade route to the Red Sea. The whole Nubian army is at his disposal, which means my family—and your throne—is at risk should he decide to raise a rebellion."

Ay began shaking his head, smiling, mocking. "All unfounded accusations, my king."

Tut raised an eyebrow at Horemheb. "Proof, General. Have you any proof?"

Anippe waited for Abbi Horem to produce the messenger Ummi Amenia had mentioned—or perhaps the papyrus scroll his soldiers had confiscated. To her surprise and disappointment, Abbi Horem's shoulders slumped, and he began massaging the back of his neck. She felt her stomach tighten into a knot.

"The soldier who carried messages between Ay and Nakhtmin met with an untimely accident on one of his missions, my king. I believe it was no accident, but I cannot prove it." Abbi leveled a sharp gaze at the vizier and then returned his attention to Tut. "I have never lied to you, good god and divine son of Horus. You are the beat of my heart and my life giver. You must believe me. This man is deceiving you."

Tut held his gaze for several heartbeats, but Ay's nervous laughter invaded the silence.

"A gripping speech, General, but how can I be held responsible for every soldier that meets with an 'untimely accident'?" He spread his hands before the king, penitent. "My every act is done in the name of the good god, King Tut, and for the greater good of our united Two Lands. I don't deny communications with Commander Nakhtmin. He crushed a Cushite rebellion, and together we've successfully increased trade routes through our southern border, importing more gold, precious stones, and spices than ever before. Is it any wonder I wished to match him with my daughter?"

The vizier lost a measure of his good humor when he turned on Abbi Horem. "Tell us, General, how many Canaanite vassal nations have your

Ramessid troops recaptured from the Hittites? Have you neutralized their threat to Egypt's trade routes or secured our eastern border?"

Abbi's fiery temper fizzled, and Anippe's stomach twisted. She hadn't realized the Hittites threatened their major trade routes. Tut didn't appear surprised by the accusations, but he was certainly feasting on the vizier's honeyed tongue.

And Ay had more honey to offer. "Did the general report his glaring defeat at Amqa and the Hittites' rapidly growing forces?"

Sebak slipped his arm around Anippe's waist, moving her away from the general and vizier. He pressed his lips against her ear and whispered, "This just became dangerous."

When she saw her brother's expression, Anippe was thankful for Sebak's concern.

Abbi, too, must have recognized the danger. "I've sent messengers with regular reports to King Tut, keeping him apprised of the Hittite situation. Our good god Tut knows I fight only for him—and would die for him."

"Your loyalty is touching, but it won't save Egypt if the Hittites block trade on both land and sea." King Tut looked every bit the angry god. "Why would you deceive me about the Amqa defeat, Horemheb?"

Abbi Horem went to one knee. "My beloved and mighty king, I have *never* deceived you. I received word of Vizier Ay's repeated messages to Nubia soon after the Amqa defeat, and I had to act quickly to secure your life and Anippe's future. Don't you remember the extra guards I sent to the Memphis Palace for your protection along with the messenger telling of my plans for Anippe's marriage?"

"I remember the messenger said nothing of defeat or a burgeoning Hittite army!" Tut slammed his flail against the armrest again, and everyone fell to their knees, heads bowed. His tone was barely controlled rage. "Vizier Ay has assured us his messages were to arrange his daughter's marriage. What assurance can you give, General, that Anippe's marriage isn't simply a distraction to conceal news of defeat?"

Vizier Ay was the first to gather his courage and lift penitent hands. "Perhaps the general didn't want to alarm our king prematurely." He stood then, taking on a conciliatory tone. "You see, mighty king, every nation the Hittites conquer adds to their military strength because they force the opposing troops to serve them to build their army. They defeated the Mitanni kingdom, then swept into Syria, captured the Phoenician coastline, and are now pressing into our Canaanite vassal states. Our general undoubtedly has a plan to stop the Hittite war machine." Ay stood, towering over Horemheb, who remained on his knees before Pharaoh. "Tell us, General, can you stop the Hittite war machine, or is Amqa the first of many defeats?"

Anippe held her breath, waiting for Abbi Horem's anger to erupt. Instead, he rose slowly and met the vizier nose to nose. "Do you think you can counsel me on the Hittites? Are you a war-torn general who mixes blood with beer after a battle? No, Vizier. You play with wooden soldiers and clay swords. I refuse to discuss military strategy with you."

"General." Tut's voice intruded on the advisors' private war. "You will discuss your plan to re-conquer Amqa with both Vizier Ay and me. How can I trust either of you when you won't trust each other?"

The Throne Hall grew deafeningly still, the silence trumpeting Tut's authority. Finally, he spoke to the newlyweds. "Anippe and Commander Sebak, you may rise."

Sebak helped Anippe stand, his calloused hands somehow gentle on her oiled and scented skin.

"Commander Sebak, you will escort my sister to her chamber. After this short meeting with my advisors, we begin the Fayum hunt. I'm tired of talking. I want to kill something—something with four legs, preferably, not two."

Anippe cast a worried glance at Abbi Horem and back at her brother.

Tut winked at her. "I'll return the general safely to Amenia if your new husband promises he'll ride in my chariot for the hunt. I get to chase lions and wild oxen once a year, and I think Sebak can improve my luck. If I miss the beast with my arrow, perhaps Sebak can snare it with his bare hands."

Sebak smiled and bowed. "Anything my king commands." He gently touched the hollow of Anippe's back, nudging her toward the door.

"Snare it with his bare hands?" The same hand so tenderly placed on her back? With each step, Anippe's panic grew. She'd only just met her husband,

and they expected her to leave Gurob forever to live in his Delta estate? That meant only a few days left at Gurob. Her family would accompany her to Avaris for a feast and then leave her alone. Alone—in the Delta—with Hebrews and goats and Ramessid soldiers who snared beasts with their bare hands?

"Wait!" Anippe fled back to the throne and clutched Tut's feet. "Please, son of Horus, mighty of birth, good god and just ruler of the Two Lands, please let Ummi Amenia and Ankhe come with me to Avaris. Please don't exile me to the Delta without my family."

Tut's fingers strummed the spirals of her wig, and she looked up to see his tender smile. "Would you feel better if I sent Ankhe with you?"

Relief washed over her like a wave. "Yes, brother, and Ummi too."

His smile died, and he slid from his throne and lifted her to meet his gaze. In a whisper, he confided, "Amenia must return to the Gurob Harem. Horemheb needs her here to—" His words seemed to drown in whatever worries lay behind his eyes. "We must trust the general's judgment on this." He brushed her cheek and resumed his throne and his regal bearing. "Ankhe will remain in Avaris after the wedding festival as my sister's handmaid."

"What? My handmaid? No, she's our—"

Tut's expression—hard as granite—stopped her. He was the god-king again. "Ankhe refuses to act like royalty, Anippe, so she'll live like peasantry. Perhaps a Ramessid taskmaster can teach her respect where others have failed."

How could Anippe face Ankhe with the news? She'd promised to intercede with Tut about a marriage match, but she'd forgotten, and now it was too late. Consigned to servitude, Ankhe would feel betrayed once more. Anippe stood like a pillar, feeling guiltier than ever.

"Anippe, my treasure." Abbi Horem appeared beside her. "The divine son of Horus has given you in marriage to the man I've chosen. Sebak is your husband now, your family. He's a good man." Abbi Horem led her back to Sebak and placed her hand in his again, and the big man's fingers closed over it.

She refused to look up. How she wished for her bronze mirror so she could set her features in Tut's empty stare. Resignation. Obligation.

Removing her hand from Sebak's grasp, she smoothed her linen sheath, sliding both hands down the curves of her form. Finally, she lifted her gaze to meet her husband's.

The warm brown eyes of a giant welcomed her. His lips, parted slightly, seemed poised to speak but fell instead into that same lazy smile she'd seen before. He wore the short, tightly-curled wig of a military officer, and around his neck hung the coveted Gold of Praise—the highest achievement in Pharaoh's army. How had he distinguished himself? Tut must favor him to bestow such a gift.

Beneath that gold collar lay the muscled chest of a soldier. Bronze arms with leather bands tensed under a sheer linen shirt—the quality of cloth matching that of Gurob's workshop. Might he have a sister in the harem?

Without permission, he tilted her chin up. "May I escort you now?" Mischief played in his tone, and for a moment she considered slapping him.

"What is my name, now that I'm your wife?" she asked instead.

He tilted his head, brow furrowed. "I will call you Anippe, but our servants will call you 'Amira.'"

Another name. Without answering, she turned and hurried toward the doors. *Like the waters of the Nile, I will swell and flood and rage. I am Anippe, Amira of Avaris.*

4

[The Egyptians] made [the Israelites'] lives bitter
with harsh labor in brick and mortar and with
all kinds of work in the fields; in all their harsh
labor the Egyptians worked them ruthlessly.

—EXODUS 1:14

Mered stepped outside Avaris's bustling linen workshop, inhaling the cool evening air. Harvest would begin in a few short weeks. He leaned against his favorite palm tree and watched a gentle night breeze stir the weeping willows down the hill by the Nile, promising relief after a brutal summer's heat. There'd been no breeze, and the Nile's flood had measured lower than he could ever remember.

"Get back to work, linen keeper." The estate foreman appeared, slapping his cudgel into his palm. "You may dress like an Egyptian, but don't forget you're a slave."

Mered stared at the weapon, his answer a whisper. "I must coordinate with the bakery and brewery for the wedding feast." He hadn't been beaten in years. The guards saved their physical brutality for the unskilled workers. The craftsmen received a different kind of torture. "Master Sebak ordered festival bread baked in clay molds of his patron god, Seth, and special recipes of beer."

"Why would Master Sebak tell his chief linen keeper of these special wishes and not me? I'm his estate foreman."

The foreman's look was threatening—a jackal's face with a long snout and close-set eyes. Why had he come to the linen shop tonight? Ramessids seldom interfered with Avaris's best-selling commodity.

Mered chose his words carefully. "Master Sebak understands the estate foreman has more important matters to attend to th; said I shouldn't bother you with mundane details." M(the foreman chewed on a papyrus stalk, rolling it fr to the other. Perhaps he looked more like a cow than a jacκ..

"Go on, then. Get to the bakery and brewery, but this wedding κa. be perfect, Hebrew." The foreman strolled away in the rising moonlight, and Mered released the breath he'd been holding.

He looked over his shoulder to be sure the foreman wouldn't hear. "This wedding feast will be perfect," he whispered, "but not because of your threats." He would do it for Master Sebak.

Mered had grown up serving as apprentice to his father in Avaris's linen shop, which was connected to the main villa by a tiled path. Young Sebak, tired of his studies, had often sought out Mered for sparring with wooden swords. When disease swept through both Avaris and the neighboring Qantir estate, killing nearly half the Ramessid dynasty, it was Mered who comforted young Master Sebak after his parents' deaths.

The night breeze lifted Mered's shoulder-length hair, refreshing him. He ran his hand along the jagged trunk of their favorite palm tree. He and Master Sebak had spent hours talking beneath this tree after Master Sebak's parents died. They talked about everything that summer. Slavery. War. Women. Life—and death. And they still shared a close bond—as close as an Egyptian and Hebrew could have.

So it didn't matter that Mered hadn't been home for two days or that his body ached and his mind was muddled and begging sleep. Master Sebak's wedding feast would be perfect because he was a good man who deserved to be happy.

Mered walked back into the linen shop and through the main villa to get to the estate's bakery and brewery. After dark it wasn't safe to prowl the grounds because of the jackals and hyenas. He'd weave through the garden and then through the villa's kitchen instead.

The bakery and brewery slaves would still be hard at work. No doubt they hadn't been home in two days either. Perhaps Mered would check the granaries while he was on the south side of the villa. His friend Hur was in charge of

ɡ and snake disposal. The villa cats kept the rats and vipers controlled
ɩ enough for Master Sebak, but he was a soldier, gone most of the time.
With a new amira coming to live at the villa, perhaps Hur should do a thorough inspection.

The smell of freshly baked bread and fermenting mash told Mered the bakery and brewery were as busy as his linen shop. He heard some sort of clay vessel crash to the tiled floor. Then came shouting, a *thwack*, and a scream. His stomach knotted. Ramessid guards hovered in the bakery and brewery, eager for samples, their constant presence a looming threat to the slaves. Nervous hands made slippery fingers, and Ramessid whips were ever ready to lash.

Mered rounded the corner to an all-too-familiar sight. A Hebrew woman cowered beneath the watchful eye of a Ramessid guard, trembling as she picked up the pieces of a broken bread mold. The baker lived a few doors down from Mered in the craftsmen's village, but this woman lived with the other unskilled laborers on the plateau between Qantir and Avaris.

"Dead-man's land" was what the unskilled Hebrews called the elevated fields and mud pits connecting the neighboring villas, where they barely survived in mud-brick long houses. Avaris and Qantir shared the slaves who lived on the plateau and divided equally the products of their labor.

A few Hebrews were deemed messengers between estates, beaten if they couldn't transfer a scroll from Avaris to Qantir in the time required to serve and eat a meal. Many unskilled slaves worked fields of grain, vegetables, vineyards, and fruit trees. Others tended flocks and herds of cattle, sheep, goats, and pigs. When slaves were punished, they were sentenced to the mud pits. Day after day of mixing, molding, drying, and carrying the building blocks of Egypt. All of it occurred in the muddy, desperate world overlooking two pristine Egyptian villas.

The woman picking up the clay pieces was one of the fortunate unskilled slaves. Though she lived on the plateau, she was shuffled between the villas and gardens of Qantir and Avaris for menial tasks. The unlucky women worked their short earthly lives in dead-man's land under the constant abuse of hungry, hot, and weary Ramessid guards. Since both Master Sebak and his uncle Pi-rameses, the master of Qantir, were soldiers and seldom in residence, lower ranking family members managed the slaves—men of lesser distinction and even lower character. They treated the Hebrews no better than they treated pack animals.

Mered turned away and decided to visit the brewery first.

The open corridor and cooler evening air provided welcome relief. Mered inhaled deeply, clearing his head. Life would be better when Master Sebak returned. His intolerance for slave abuse spread quickly when he thrashed a guard nearly to death last year after finding a Hebrew maid beaten and cowering in the garden. Ramessid guards, though never kind, were at least restrained while the master was in residence—but how long could it last? Would Egypt's fiercest warrior sleep in a warm bed with his young wife while his men continued to fight the Hittites?

El-Shaddai, please give my master a nice, long respite. If not for his sake, for the sake of Your people, Israel.

Torches in their metal wall shafts lit the sandstone path as Mered passed the hive-shaped granaries. Wishing he'd brought a stick to stir the path in front of him, he kept vigilant watch for rats and vipers near the grain. He didn't want to surprise a cobra tonight.

The scent of soured mash drew him. A few more steps, and he entered the bustling world of Avaris's brewery. Unlike the bakery, which used petite clay bread molds, the brewery dealt in huge vats of crumbled bread, fermented at different stages, poured through giant sieves, and flavored in huge bowls with dates, nabk-berries, and pomegranates.

The chief brewer spied him as he entered the door. "Mered, come sip the latest batch." A rotund man and happier than any Hebrew should be, the brewer almost certainly sipped the latest batch too often.

"Thank you, but no. I've come to make sure we'll have a hundred large amphorae of Master Sebak's favorite beer for the feast."

"Of course. Of course." The brewer wrapped one arm around Mered's shoulders and rubbed his chin with the other hand. "Now, which is Master Sebak's favorite beer?"

Dumbfounded, Mered opened his mouth, but no words came. How could the chief brewer forget the master's favorite beer?

"Bahaha! I'm only playing, Mered." The big man slapped his knees, thoroughly amused.

Two Ramessid guards slammed their clay cups on a low-lying table, sloshing the remains, and then hoisted themselves to a swaying stance. "Brewer, get back to work. Linen keeper, why are you distracting this man? He has very important work to do." Slurring every word, the guards walked toward them in much the same approach as a slithering snake.

The brewer suddenly sobered and leaned close. "I'll have a hundred amphorae of Master Sebak's dark date beer for the feast. You worry too much, my friend. Go home to your pretty wife before these guards beat us for entertainment."

He shoved Mered toward the door and let out a booming laugh. "The next batch of honey beer is ready for tasting. Would you two fine officers give your approval before I dare offer it to Master Sebak?"

Mered hurried out the door and down the hallway, past the granaries and bakery, without stopping for breath. He'd have to thank the chief brewer for that rescue when they saw each other in the craftsmen's village.

The chief Hebrew overseers were housed with the skilled craftsmen in a special area of the estate. Six mud-brick long houses had been built north of the villa and down a slight hill, along the banks of the Nile. Ramessid guards seldom visited the craftsmen's village—unless one of the skilled Hebrews needed discipline. The guards were forbidden to harm the craftsmen for fear that production of jewelry, beer, or linen might decrease. Instead, guards tortured skilled craftsmen through their families—making wives, children, or even parents pay for the craftsmen's errors.

Mered was breathless by the time he returned to his linen shop, but crossing the threshold was like entering the safety of a womb. The steady rhythm of the weavers' wefts and warps echoed his heartbeat. Unskilled laborers hummed in time, striking flax stalks with wooden mallets to separate the fibers.

His workmen had labored nonstop since Master Sebak's surprise visit with General Horemheb. News of the wedding had revived them all with purpose and joy. Master Sebak was different from other Ramessids. Kinder. More just. His personal loss and pain made him more generous with slaves who endured hardship daily, and each one agreed that the master had endured life alone long enough.

Mered shouted above the rhythmic beat of busy hands. "Skilled craftsmen, go home for the night and get some rest. Unskilled, remain till morning. I'll send a new group at dawn to relieve you."

The designers, weavers, and bead workers halted their projects and congregated at the north door. "Mered, are you coming?"

A moment of decision. Should he stay to supervise or sleep a few hours? The brewer's words echoed in his memory. *You worry too much, my friend.* His sleeping mat beckoned him, and the thought of his wife's warm body urged him toward the door.

"Yes, I'm coming."

His wife, Puah, had been gone the morning Master Sebak summoned Mered to the linen shop at dawn to announce his wedding plans. Puah kept strange hours now that she'd been assigned as assistant to the Ramessids' chief midwife, Shiphrah.

Mered's heart squeezed a little, wondering how the midwives felt about the king's return for Sebak's wedding. When Pharaoh Tut last visited the Delta with Queen Senpa, Shiphrah and Puah had been woken in the middle of the night to attend the queen's premature birth pains. Puah had cried for days afterward, reliving the heartbreak of the stillborn baby girl. Did his wife know Queen Senpa was expecting a second child and would soon be returning for the wedding?

A group of thirty craftsmen left the north door of the linen shop. Those in front and back carried sticks and torches to ward off night beasts. Hoping to distract himself from the dangers of their journey, Mered squeezed a young weaver's shoulder. "Are you almost finished with the amira's wedding gown? I saw your progress. The design is exquisite."

The weaver's eyes were wide with fear, his back as rigid as the stick he held to ward off jackals. "It should be finished by the time the royal barque arrives, my lord."

My lord. Mered hated when his brother Hebrews treated him like an Egyptian master. "You need not call me '*my lord.*' I'm simply Mered." He patted the weaver's shoulder, hoping to infuse a measure of peace, but saw that his attempts were simply prolonging the young weaver's discomfort.

Mered slowed his steps, allowing the weaver to join those with whom he felt more comfortable. The group ahead began shouting and waving their sticks and torches, giving wide berth to a small knot of hyenas feeding on a kill at the side of the path. The four scraggly hunters scattered as the humans approached, and Mered held his breath. Would they find animal or human prey ahead? The Ramessids had been known to throw a dead slave to the night beasts for a snack.

The craftsmen walked past an antelope's remains, and Mered heard others sigh with the relief he felt. A familiar loneliness crept into his bones, making his weariness unbearable.

Please, El-Shaddai, let my Puah be home. With her, he could forget Egyptians and Hebrews and hyenas. He could simply leave his day behind and love her.

Four craftsmen, including Mered, split from the group and climbed a low rise to the first mud-brick long house. A narrow alley separated the first two long structures, the front doors of the first long house facing the back wall of the second row of long houses. The structures were a honeycomb of rooms, doorways, and walls. When one family needed more space, they knocked out a wall and added a doorway to another room. When an elderly couple no longer needed a place for children, a growing family accessed more of the structure.

Mered arrived at his door halfway down the long house and paused outside to remove his sandals. Dust coated his feet and ankles even after the short walk home. He could feel the grit between his teeth, in his hair and eyelashes. Harvest season would stir more dust, and just as it became absolutely agonizing, the life-giving inundation would flood the Nile, bringing muddy relief to their dusty world. But until the mud came, they lived, breathed, and ate dust.

Mered wiped his feet and legs. He blew the dust from his sandals and left them outside the door, donning the cloth slippers Puah required inside their home. A grin curved his lips. If El-Shaddai blessed them with children, she'd have to set aside her obsession with cleanliness.

Mered peeked around the rough-spun linen curtain hanging across their doorway. As his eyes adjusted to the lamplight in their single room, he saw Puah crouched over the cook fire, her back turned. Why was she still awake? Glancing left, he noted the curtain pulled across the doorway leading to their neighbors' rooms. The family whose rooms opened into their space must be settled for the night.

And then he heard Puah's soft whimpers.

Mered crossed the room without a sound, his mind grasping at ways to comfort his grieving wife. Had Puah helped deliver their neighbors' third child while he'd been gone? He'd dreaded the day they'd have a newborn on the other side of that curtain—not because of inconvenience or annoyance, but because his wife's empty womb would ache unbearably.

He scuffed his feet on the reed mat as he approached, trying not to startle her.

Puah wiped her cheeks before turning to greet him and donned a forced smile. "Mered. I didn't think you'd be home tonight. Is the wedding dress finished for the amira?"

He reached for her hand, helping her to her feet. Burying his fingers in her coarse brown hair, he stared intently into eyes that shunned his gaze. "I don't care about the amira's dress. I care about my wife, who thinks she must hide her tears when I come home." She tried to pull away, but he captured her cheeks between gentle hands. "Puah, talk to me. Did Jochebed have her baby?"

She shook her head. "No, but she's had false labor all day. It won't be long."

She closed her eyes and grew still. Tears seeped beneath her lashes, and her knees crumpled, sending them both to the floor. Mered held her as waves of grief escaped on silent sobs. What could he say that hadn't already been said? He wanted children too, but talking about it only seemed to upset them both.

"Puah, we've been married only two years. You're still young—only seventeen. We must give the Lord time to work."

"But He's already worked in every other wife my age. What if I'm barren like Sarah or Rachel?"

"Sarah and Rachel gave birth to children of promise, remember? What if God is simply waiting for the proper time to give us a child—as He did with Sarah and Rachel?"

"You're not listening to me." She buried her face in his chest, unleashing a fresh torrent.

Mered pulled her closer, rubbing her back for reassurance. "I am listening. I hear your heart. You want to be an ummi." She nodded her head but didn't speak. "But I need you to listen to me as well. Have you considered God may delay giving us children because of His mercy rather than wrath or vengeance?"

At this she looked up. "How is it merciful to deny me a child?"

Her knitted brow and pout made her even more beautiful, nearly distracting him from his perfectly reasonable argument.

"What if you and Shiphrah attend the birth of a wife of a Ramessid and her baby dies? What if she decides to take our child in return for the loss of her child?" Even in the dim lamplight, Mered saw Puah's face pale. "It's heartbreaking to be childless, my love, but are you prepared for the heartbreak of bearing a slave child?"

"Do you think that's why neither Shiphrah nor I have children? El-Shaddai closed our wombs to protect us?" She began shaking her head, tears flowing in earnest again.

"I didn't say that, Puah."

"I don't want to be a midwife then. I want children, Mered. I want your children. I want a family."

"Shh, my wife. Shh." He gathered her into his arms again, wishing he could infuse her with the peace he'd found in El-Shaddai but knowing she must seek Him for herself. "We have no choice, Puah—not you as a midwife, nor me as Chief Linen Keeper. Our lives are not our own. We belong to El-Shaddai—and Master Sebak."

5

[Pharaoh] said to his people, "The Israelites have
become far too numerous for us. Come, we must
deal shrewdly with them or they will become even
more numerous and, if war breaks out, will join
our enemies, fight against us and leave the country."

—Exodus 1:9–10

Anippe hurried toward the double doors to escape her husband, but Sebak's long, steady strides kept pace, and his relentless hand on her back nearly set her aflame. She stopped at the doors, head bowed, refusing to acknowledge his presence but waiting while he reached for the latch.

He peered beneath her spiraled wig with that infuriating smile. "When I open this door, I will escort you. If you try to run, I will carry you."

How did he know she planned to run back to her chamber? Was he a diviner or a soldier?

The Medjays on the other side of the door swung it wide open, and Anippe resumed her hurried pace—not a run exactly, but a walk that would prepare Sebak for tonight's hunt. She refused to be an easy catch.

Only four steps into the chase, Sebak's arm encircled her waist and her feet left the mosaic tiles. He stopped, holding her against his muscled chest with one arm, openly appraising her flushed cheeks. "Are you frightened of me specifically or of men in general?"

Her mouth, as dry as the Eastern Desert, couldn't form a single word, let alone a coherent sentence. He bent as though to set her feet on the tiles but then slipped his other arm beneath her knees, cradling her in his arms. He walked leisurely toward the harem corridor, carrying her as if she were as light as a feather.

Her neck and cheeks felt as if she'd been in the sun too long. What was she supposed to say? Or do? She'd never really talked to a man—other than Tut or Abbi Horem or her old tutor. She kept her head forward, hiding her cheeks with the spiraled wig, and fidgeted with her gold and turquoise clasp.

"You've no need to fear me, Anippe. I've been chosen to protect you, not harm you."

He stopped, and her heart skipped a beat. What was he doing? Looking right and left, she saw nothing but palm trees, palace walls, and scurrying servants in the long portico leading to the apartments.

"Why did you stop?" She looked into the most handsome face she'd ever seen.

"I wanted to see your eyes. They're beautiful, you know. Like the sand at my Avaris quay." He kissed her forehead.

She held her breath. He began walking again, and the pillars began to tilt. Anippe realized she'd forgotten to breathe. This man had completely paralyzed her. Was this love? Her stomach was in knots, her hands were sweaty, and her chest had butterflies fluttering inside. *Oh Lady Hathor, goddess of love—kill me now if love is more painful than this.*

"Anippe, are you all right?" Sebak's stricken expression told her she must somehow have voiced her torment. He bent to one knee and seated her on his other. "Say something, please." His huge, callused hand brushed her cheek, concern tugging the stray hairs between his eyebrows down toward his nose.

Tears choked her. Sebak had been nothing but kind. He deserved an answer. "I'm a little afraid of you, but mostly I'm afraid of living in the Delta without Ummi Amenia. I won't know anyone except Ankhe after the wedding guests leave, and I've never had Hebrew slaves—only Nubians."

His warm brown eyes caressed her, soothing her. "General Horemheb has promised I can remain with you in Avaris for at least two months before I return to battle." He strummed the spirals of her wig, causing the gold beads to clatter. "You will be Amira of Avaris, and our Hebrews will serve you as well as any Nubians. My slaves are hard workers, and they serve me willingly."

"But what will I do at Avaris? Here at Gurob, I work in the linen shop, designing patterns for the weavers and even weaving some of the cloth myself."

Sebak reached for her linen sheath and rubbed the silken cloth between his fingers. "My Chief Linen Keeper is weaving your wedding dress as we speak, and it will make this sheath look like a rag."

Indignant, she grabbed her sheath from his grasp. "I'll have you know this is the finest linen Gurob produces."

He chuckled and with a single finger traced a line from her shoulder down her arm, to her thigh, and across her knees. "And I'll have you know that Avaris produces the best linen in the Delta—perhaps in all of Egypt—and you now command the slaves in that shop, Amira. My Chief Linen Keeper, Mered, is anxious to please."

Anippe's breathing grew shallow, her mind muddled. How could she think with him so near, his touch so intimate? She leapt off his knee, turned away from Sebak, and smoothed her robe. "What happens when you leave after two months? I'll be alone, and you'll go off to war and forget you have a wife." She didn't run this time. She lingered. Waiting—like prey hoping to be snared.

His presence loomed behind her. His hands slid around her waist, and he pressed his lips against her ear. "I am your husband forever, Anippe. I've had no wife before you and will have no woman besides you. General Horemheb has entrusted to me his greatest treasure, and I will prove worthy of his trust—and yours." He moved aside her spiraled wig and placed a tender kiss at the bend of her neck.

Knees weak, Anippe closed her eyes and let the sensation carry her into her future. She was married. To this soldier. And he seemed wonderful. Could it be?

She felt a tap on her nose and opened her eyes to her husband's amused grin. "Should we go to your chamber now?"

For the first time, Anippe was in no hurry to see Amenia and Ankhe. She'd really prefer Sebak carry her in his strong arms forever, holding her close and whispering sweet promises. "Would you like to carry me again, or should I walk?

Her fierce warrior laughed—a rolling rumble from deep in his belly. "Your abbi warned me you were unpredictable."

"Did he mention stubborn?"

"I think he called you determined." Sebak looked into her eyes again as if searching for something hidden. "I look forward to knowing everything about you, Anippe."

She tucked her chin, cheeks flaming again, and began walking. Did he plan to take her to his chamber tonight? Maybe she should have listened more closely all those times Ummi Amenia tried to talk to her about a woman's wedding night.

Gathering her courage, Anippe forced the words from her throat. "Will I leave Ummi Amenia and Ankhe's chamber tonight?" Her voice quaked despite her efforts to calm it.

Sebak kept his pace slow, letting the morning breeze anoint their journey through the pillared walkway. "You'll remain with Amenia until our wedding feast at Avaris." He walked a few more steps in silence, seeming thoroughly content to enjoy the breeze and listen to birdsong. "Would you like to know our travel plans and how I intend to honor my bride?"

"Yes, please." She edged a little closer as they walked. Her shoulder brushed his arm, and he slid his hand around her waist. Possessive. Protective.

"I've ordered harem servants to collect your belongings and load them tonight on a supply ship. They'll leave tomorrow, since towing the larger boat will require double the travel time of a royal barque on the Nile's low waters. You and your family will follow on the king's barque after the hunt and should arrive about the same time as your personal items."

"But what if I need my—"

"Only pack the robes and jewels necessary for the journey." He stopped and turned her to face him. "Once you arrive in Avaris, all your needs will be met, my wife. Your abbi Horem and I stopped at my estate on our way here. My Hebrew craftsmen have already begun working on your wardrobe and jewelry. As I said before, your wedding gown will be the most beautiful in Egypt."

"I thought Hebrews were shepherds and farmers, not skilled craftsmen."

The words sounded insulting, and she regretted them immediately. "I'm sorry. I didn't mean . . ."

Sebak laughed and brushed her cheek. He replaced his arm around her and began their leisurely stroll again. "My Hebrews were nomad royalty who have lived in the Delta longer than the Ramessids. They came to Egypt hundreds of years ago because of a famine in their land of Canaan. They and other Canaanites formed the Hyksos race and settled in the Delta. Have you heard of the Hyksos?" He lifted an eyebrow, no doubt expecting her to swoon at his wisdom.

Most women weren't educated, but Anippe's lessons with Tut's tutors were suddenly quite valuable. "Of course. The Hyksos ruled Egypt for centuries—until Pharaoh Tuthmosis III drove them out."

Sebak's booming laugh floated on the morning air, joining the happy sounds of harem women at work. "Correct, Amira." He leaned over to kiss the top of her head as they walked. Anippe's heart fluttered. "But Pharaoh Tuthmosis didn't drive out the Hyksos by himself. He enlisted the aid of my military family—the Ramessids—who dwelt among the Hyksos and knew their weaknesses. We expelled them from Egypt—except one stubborn clan, the Abiru, or Hebrews as they're called today—and Pharaoh showed his gratitude to my Ramessid ancestors by offering them estates.

"The Hebrews, however, grew so quickly in number, wealth, and power, that the next pharaoh feared they'd leave Egypt and share their wealth and power with our enemies. He remedied the threat by again enlisting the Ramessids—this time as slave masters—to disperse the twelve clans of Hebrews among various estates in the Delta."

Sebak stopped walking, and his hand fell from her waist. Anippe waited for more of the story, but he folded his arms across his chest and lifted his eyebrows as if waiting for her response.

Puzzled, she couldn't hide her annoyance. "What? Why did you stop?"

After acknowledging two Nubian guards, Sebak nodded toward her chamber door. How had they arrived so quickly?

He reached for her hand, cradling it like a treasure. "Avaris will be your kingdom, Anippe. When our months of marriage communion are over and I return to battle, you will rule our villa and our Hebrews. You will be Amira." He leaned over and brushed her lips with a kiss. "You will remain Sister of Pharaoh, Daughter of Horemheb, but now you are Wife of Sebak—and I will love you, Anippe. You will be happy as Amira of Avaris."

Anippe's knees felt like water, and she stumbled back when he released her hand. Steadying her, he chuckled and motioned the guards to open the chamber door. His hand pressed the small of her back, making her feel protected and treasured. They entered together, linked by this single touch.

"Good morning," Amenia greeted them as they entered, setting aside her embroidering.

Ankhe was seated at her loom near the courtyard but stood when Amenia held out her hand, summoning her for introductions. Anippe's heart raced at the sight of her little sister. She'd almost forgotten the terrible news she must deliver.

Anippe took a deep breath. "Ummi Amenia, may I present Commander Sebak, Master of Horse, Ramessid nobleman of the Delta—my husband."

Sebak bowed deeply, and Ummi Amenia touched his wig, giving permission to rise. "Congratulations, Commander, on your promotion and your new bride."

"Thank you, Amira Amenia. Please know you are always welcome at our Avaris estate."

"Avaris?" Ankhe's face drained of color. "Anippe can't leave me. She can't go to Avaris." Without waiting for answers, she fled from the courtyard through the same gate Anippe had used earlier.

In the awkward silence, Amenia stood gazing at the floor. Anippe felt Sebak's hand leave her back, their connection broken. She turned, hoping to explain Ankhe's outburst, her life of pain, her need for love and patience.

Her husband's face was hard as granite. "I see now why your brother made her your maidservant. She'll require strong discipline to serve among the Hebrews at my villa." He leaned down, kissed Anippe's cheek, and marched out of the chamber.

"Your maidservant?" Ummi Amenia breathed on a whisper, as if fearful the gods might hear.

"How will we tell her, Ummi? She can't know that it was Tut who decreed it." Tears brimmed at the thought of another rip in her little sister's heart.

Amenia opened her arms, inviting Anippe into their restful embrace. "Well, at least she'll be with you. I'll tell her. Ankhe won't like it, but she'll do it because it means she stays with you."

In the warmth and safety of her ummi's embrace, a sudden realization struck Anippe with blinding horror. She pushed away, stricken. "If Abbi Horem fears my life is in danger at Gurob, how can you live here safely?"

Amenia's features seemed a battlefield of their own. Compassion fought sadness. Anger wrestled resignation. "You are Horemheb's future, little habiba, and I am his past. My role is to remain at Gurob Harem, discovering noblemen's schemes through their wives' chatter, while you and Sebak give us grandchildren to provide for our afterlife." She patted Anippe's cheek, love glistening on her own cheeks. "We all must dance to the music of the gods, Anippe— even when the song is a dirge."

"But Abbi Horem loves you—"

"Of course he loves me," she said, reaching for her embroidery and resuming her seat on the wooden stool. "But sometimes love requires sacrifice, habiba. Now sit down with me while we wait for Ankhe to return from her tantrum."

6

Anippe leaned against the third-level rail of Tut's royal barque. She was covered head to toe with rough-spun linen to keep dust from coating her. Towing had commenced two days ago, when the Nile split into seven branches north of Memphis, the water level little more than a creek. Oars were used only while docked from dusk to dawn to brace the barque upright in the shallow waters. Weary oarsmen had begun towing at dawn, using papyrus ropes bigger than Anippe's arms. She'd left her bed and the cabin she and Ankhe shared the moment she felt the ship's movement, watching every step that dragged her farther from Gurob.

Avaris was normally a two-day journey at the height of inundation, but during *Shemut*—the four months of harvest—the Nile was at its lowest cycle. Today began the fourth—and final—day of their journey, but Anippe would rather be sequestered in a ship's tiny cabin with Ankhe than forced into a family she'd never met.

The Ramessids. Violent. Ruthless. Their women remained in the Delta, never mingling with noblemen's wives at the Gurob Harem. They were a lofty bunch—men and women alike—a strange breed of grandiose savage.

But Sebak hadn't seemed that way. Strong, yes, but kind and thoughtful. Her only concern was his introduction to Ankhe and the wary eye he'd kept on her since.

A cabin door slammed behind her. She didn't need to turn to know it was Abbi Horem. They'd met at dawn every morning of the journey at this very spot.

"Good morning, my treasure." Abbi's gravelly voice betrayed his sleeplessness. "I'm ready to get off this cursed ship."

Anippe looped her arm with his, squeezing until he grinned. They began their stroll down the steps to the middle level. Mornings had become a special time to break their fast together while waiting for the others to join them. They'd talked of Ummi Amenia, the Hittites, and Tut, but today she needed to know about her husband.

"Tell me about Sebak, Abbi." She gripped the handrail as they eased down the four steps. "Why did you choose him from all your soldiers?" She needed to know why the man she respected most chose this particular Ramessid.

They arrived on the middle-level deck and sat on opposite cushions beside a low-lying table. Abbi Horem signaled a Nubian to serve their meal. "Sebak's abbi was a good friend and a valiant commander. He died too young from a senseless plague and left Sebak and his young uncle, Pirameses—also my good friend—to manage the twin estates of Qantir and Avaris."

He gazed into the distance, perusing the sun-dried fields along the riverbanks. His head moved in rhythm with the heaving of the towmen. "On the battlefield, Sebak is fierce as Seth, god of darkness. His men call him *Seth reborn.* But in devotion to his troops—his family—only Pharaoh possesses more integrity, more peace. Sebak is a gentle giant, habiba, and he will be loyal to you till death."

She reached across the table to grasp his hand, warmed by the description, but his expression changed, his eyes sharp as a flint knife.

"But never betray him—or me." Anippe tried to ease her hand free, but her abbi held tight. "Your husband demands your loyalty, Anippe, as do I. You'll become his eyes and ears at Avaris when he returns to battle. I've placed you in Sebak's hands, and you must stay with him and honor him—no matter what happens."

Rattled, she couldn't think how to respond. Why the sudden intensity? Thankfully, two servants arrived with their meal, and Abbi released her hand to steal a slice of cucumber before it reached the table. While slaves delivered silver goblets of grape juice and moon-shaped bread with a baked-egg center, she pondered her abbi's words.

The Sebak she'd come to know during the past few days could never be Seth reborn. Seth, the god of chaos and darkness, killed and mutilated his own brother. Sebak could never be capable of such carnage—on or off the battlefield. Everything she'd seen in her husband proved Abbi Horem's first description true. Sebak's ma'at was balanced. Justice and truth walked before him as naturally as the sun greeted the moon. She'd have no trouble being loyal to him and Abbi Horem.

A bowl of stewed dates wafted the sweet scent of cinnamon upward, soothing her tension, untying her tongue. "Abbi, I'm not a betrayer, and I will honor the husband you've chosen for me. You and Ummi Amenia have been my only family, and I would never . . ."

The niggling concern she'd felt at news of the Amqa defeat mingled with Abbi's final plea. *"I've placed you in Sebak's hands, and you must stay with him and honor him—no matter what happens."*

Tears filled her eyes, and she reached across the table and gripped Abbi's hand. "Just because I'm Sebak's wife doesn't mean you can die in battle. Ten husbands cannot replace you. Those filthy Hittites—worms of the underworld—can't get the better of you. You are General Horemheb, Prince Regent of the Two Lands, my abbi Horem . . ."

Her pent-up emotions strangled her final words, and tears dripped into her stewed dates.

Abbi Horem squeezed her hand and then dragged his cushion to Anippe's side of the table to cradle her under his arm. "Oh, my little warrior, there's not a Hittite born that can best me. Now, either cry harder and provide more water for the Nile, or dry your tears and let's eat." He chuckled and wiped her eyes with a linen cloth he drew from his belt.

She gave him a playful shove and pulled the steaming dish of dates closer. Whatever had sobered his expression earlier seemed washed away with her tears. He attacked his bread and dates like a starving soldier, and they settled into amiable silence.

The sun had risen over the eastern hills, and the ship rocked in rhythm with each heave of the oarsmen's ropes. The sailors marched on shore alongside the barque, heeding the pilot's commands in perfect rhythm. "Left, right, *pull!* Left, right, *pull!*"

The pilot's command brought an especially solid heave, jiggling the scoop of dates off Abbi Horem's bite of bread.

Anippe giggled and prodded Abbi Horem from his annoyance. "Here. Follow me." She held her bread poised over the stewed dates, waiting for the ship pilot's command. With the next "Left, right, *pull,*" Anippe mimicked, "Tear, dip, *chew.*" And then shoved a hunk of dripping goodness into her mouth. Chewing like mad, she hurried to tear the next morsel and ready it for dipping. "Tear, dip, *chew,*" she said with her mouth full, laughing, chewing, and swallowing at once.

They kept pace and were soon a laughing, chewing, silly mess with date juice streaking their chins. Neither heard Ankhe and Amenia descend the steps.

"Well, I'm glad your husband sailed on another ship," Amenia huffed. "I'd be humiliated if he saw either of you like this."

Abbi Horem fairly leapt from his cushion, grabbed Amenia's waist, and kissed her soundly—smearing date juice all over her freshly painted face. Ankhe rolled her eyes, but Anippe giggled, loving the way her parents had always shown their love so freely. Would she and Sebak openly show their love to their—

Her stomach roiled at the thought of children. Heart racing, palms sweating, she felt the dates rumble in her gut. She could never have children. Never.

Abbi Horem released his wife and chuckled. "Today, we celebrate our daughter's marriage, Amenia. We're enjoying our last day of fun before we must be proper."

He bounced his eyebrows, and Amenia's stuffy armor crumbled. She licked her lips, tasting the date-juice deposit of Abbi's kiss. "I'll have some of that, please—in a bowl."

Ankhe sullenly perched on the cushion beside Anippe. "I want grapes."

Her three simple words drained the joy from Abbi Horem's face.

Anippe recognized his gathering storm and waved over a servant, who had emerged from the galley. "Do we have more grapes aboard? Pharaoh's sister desires grapes to break her fast."

"The *handmaid* of Pharaoh's sister desires grapes." Horemheb sat on the cushion directly opposite Ankhe, his gaze burning a hole through her.

Ankhe stared at her sandals. Anippe wished for a moment's peace, but life with Ankhe was like towing a ship up the Nile. Every step an effort. Each advance resisted.

"I believe I'd like grapes too," Amenia said, trying to appease. The servant bowed low and eagerly disappeared behind the galley curtain.

Ankhe's eyes pooled with tears in the silence. Amenia had spoken to her about Tut's decision before they left Gurob. She'd ranted and raged, but what could anyone do? Why not accept it and make life better? But not Ankhe.

"I'm just as much a child of Kiya as Tut and Anippe. Why must I serve as Anippe's handmaid?" Ankhe asked.

Abbi Horem released his frustration on a sigh. "You have refused every effort to train you in the ways of royalty, Ankhe. Instead of more beatings or a life in Gurob's slave quarters, the merciful god Tut gave you to Anippe as her handmaid."

"Merciful?" Ankhe blinked tears over her bottom lashes. "Tut isn't merciful. He hates me as much as you do."

"I don't hate you, Ankhe-Senpaaten-tasherit."

Ankhe winced at Abbi Horem's use of her full name.

"I simply wish you would rise above Pharaoh Akhenaten's weaknesses— but I see no divine spark in you." Abbi leaned over the table, a handbreadth from her face. "You will always be *tasherit*—your only purpose to save Senpa, should Anubis come prowling."

"You never gave me a chance. You never changed my name." Ankhe's tears streamed down her cheeks.

"Abbi, please." Anippe laid her hand on his arm, pressing for his attention. "Why don't you give Ankhe a new name—like you gave me? Perhaps then—"

"No, enough about Ankhe." He pulled his arm away and glared at his wife. "You see, Amenia, she's done it again, this girl. She steals all the attention for herself and ruins Anippe's happy day." He poured out more complaints while the girls exchanged sorrowful glances.

Anippe's heart broke for her sister, but what could she do? They were both in a prison, Anippe locked in Abbi Horem's perfect approval, Ankhe in his perfect disdain.

Perhaps when Anippe was Amira of Avaris, she could give Ankhe a respectable title, and they could repair their damaged relationship.

Amira of Avaris. She still wasn't sure what it entailed, but perhaps it could be a new start for both her and Ankhe.

Abbi Horem and Tut had alerted Anippe when the king's barque approached Avaris just before dusk. Ankhe had accompanied her into their cabin to dress her in fine linen and apply her paints and jewelry. Now Anippe sat in seclusion. Waiting.

She heard footsteps on the deck outside her curtained doorway—heavy steps with a determined stride. *Sebak.*

Anippe held her breath and stood up. The curtain snapped aside.

Her husband's expression was priceless. She'd never felt so beautiful, so adored, so cherished. Sebak approached as if she were Persian pottery and might break. He lifted her hand and kissed her palm, sending fire through her body.

"You are radiant." He spoke in a whisper, affirming the sacred moment.

She ducked her chin, unable to answer, but forever grateful to Ankhe for her skills with paints and jewels.

Sebak tilted her chin up so she would meet his gaze. Anippe saw that his eyes danced with delight as he asked, "Are you ready to come home?"

Anippe swallowed the lump in her throat and nodded, fighting tears. *Home.* Would Avaris ever feel like home?

He held her hand as they took their first steps but then stopped abruptly.

Seizing her waist, he pulled her close and swept his lips over hers—never touching—only a breath between them. "I won't taste those ochre lips until after the feast."

He released her, panting—or was it her breathing she heard?

"Wait for me on the deck," she said, voice gravelly. She cleared her throat and added, "I need a moment."

Sebak nodded, letting his hand trail down her arm before stepping back through the curtain.

Anippe smoothed her pleated robe, trying to gather her wits. This man left her senseless. Heart pounding, sweat glistening, she inhaled and then blew out her breath slowly. "You are the Amira of Avaris, Anippe," she whispered to herself. "Act like it." She stepped into the cool night air to join her husband.

The remnant of the evening sun glinted off Sebak's Gold of Praise collar; his smile was equally bright. He wore wide gold bands on both wrists and had exchanged the short kilt of a soldier for the longer, pleated *shenti* of an estate master. A fine linen shawl billowed from his shoulders, tied at his narrow waist.

"Does my appearance please you?" he asked, lifting his arm to escort her, and Anippe wondered if she'd spend her whole life breathless.

"Very much." She placed her hand above the gold band on his wrist and allowed him to lead her around the corner of the barque's deckhouse.

There, gleaming in the last rays of golden sunset, was Avaris—and it halted her. Lifting her hand to cover a small gasp, she felt her fingers tremble.

"It's beautiful." Her heart escaped on a whisper, her relief palpable.

The marshy landscape of Avaris reminded her of Gurob. Papyrus lined the sandy banks, with weeping willows bowing feathery branches over the water. A multitude of slaves and soldiers lined both sides of a dusty path leading up a distant hill toward a crowning limestone villa. King Tut and Queen Senpa had already begun their ascent with guards and musicians leading the way, while Abbi Horem and Ummi Amenia waited on the quay to accompany Sebak and Anippe. Ankhe stood with the other servants on the barque.

"So, you're pleased?" Her husband's voice was small, and he touched her hand, drawing her attention. "I want you to be happy here, Anippe."

How could a giant sound like a child? Startled at his vulnerability, she grasped his hand. "I'm happy when you are with me."

And it was true. If she could forever see her reflection in his eyes, she would never fear again. If she could always live in his embrace, she would never yearn for another.

But what would happen when he asked her to bear a child? What would happen when he returned to battle? What then . . . what then?

"Come, wife. Let me introduce you to your new household."

7

*The more [the Israelites] were oppressed, the more
they multiplied and spread; so the Egyptians came
to dread the Israelites and worked them ruthlessly.*

—Exodus 1:12–13

The Hebrews had raised their hearts and voices to welcome Master Sebak and his bride when they disembarked Pharaoh's royal barque. Even King Tut, seated on his gilded palanquin on six Medjays' shoulders, had glanced over his shoulder to see the source of the ruckus. Master Sebak strutted as if he were the king of Egypt, his new bride at his side.

Mered chuckled at the memory. Sebak had been as nervous as a schoolboy when he'd docked his ship at midday to finalize preparations for the royal family's arrival. True to his character, when the work was done, he'd permitted every Avaris slave—skilled and unskilled—to gather at the quay and welcome the royal guests. A grand entrance before the main event.

Mered hid behind an acacia tree in the villa's garden entry, vicariously enjoying the wedding feast. The meal was long past. Musicians played a lively tune while dancers swirled veils around half-drunk guests. The dark date beer had been much appreciated. Mered must congratulate the brewer.

Sebak's young bride was lovely—Amira Anippe, they would call her—and she looked like the goddess Isis in the wedding gown Mered had designed. It was the sheerest *byssus* sheath his shop had ever made, the Avaris symbol woven proudly into the selvage. The pleated sheath draped over an equally sheer gown with gold thread and precious stones sewn into the pattern of a palm tree—the Egyptian tree of life. The new amira had gasped when Mered presented it to her.

"Masterful," she'd said. Sebak had squeezed Mered's shoulder with approval—praise worth more than ten weeks' allotment of grain.

"Don't you have a wife at home?" A low voice startled Mered, and a strong hand whirled him around.

"Master Sebak." Mered bowed deeply, ashamed of his spying. "Forgive me. I was . . . I wanted to see . . ."

A deep chuckle drew his gaze. "Get up, Mered. I'm not angry with you."

Relief washed over Mered, and the joy on Sebak's face emboldened him. "Your wife is beautiful, my lord. I pray El-Shaddai's blessing on a long and happy life together."

His master received the words graciously, as he did each time Mered mentioned his God.

Returning his attention to his bride, Sebak sighed. "She is beautiful, isn't she—and it emanates from within, my friend." His features clouded, and he nodded in the direction of his uncle, master of neighboring Qantir. He and Pirameses had been rivals since their fathers died, leaving the boys neighboring estates. "Not like Pirameses's young wife. That woman poisons everything she touches. Our estates are too close to keep the wives apart, but I don't want her tainting Anippe's inner ka."

Mered nodded his agreement but wasn't sure how he could help keep one amira from influencing another.

"Anippe plans to stay busy by using her design and weaving skills in your linen shop, my friend. Perhaps she'll be too busy to learn the bad habits of Qantir's amira."

Startled at his master's candor, Mered wasn't sure which topic to address first—the Avaris amira in his workshop or the Qantir amira's bad habits. He chose the safest. "I look forward to introducing the amira to our linen processes as soon as she's ready, my lord." In truth, he cringed to think of any Egyptian in his workshop, but he would try to be hospitable.

"Good. Good." Sebak clamped a hand on Mered's shoulder. "Anippe will come to trust you as I have, Mered. And if she feels comfortable in your workshop, she'll spend less time in Qantir picking up bad habits from Pirameses's wife."

Mered knew the bad habits included entertaining traveling merchants and disposing of slaves as if they were fleas on a dog. *El-Shaddai, guard our amira's heart and give the Hebrews favor in her eyes.*

Sebak stood mesmerized, gazing at the wedding feast. "Isn't she stunning, Mered?"

"She is, my lord, and she seems quite taken with you as well."

He turned, eyes bright. "Really? Do you think so? Because I think I love her." The words tumbled out, seeming to surprise even him. "Can it be love when we met only a few days ago?"

"A heart follows no rules, my lord. My wife and I grew up together and were betrothed as children, but our love grows deeper each day."

"I want to protect her, spend every moment with her. Her face fills my dreams, and her body beckons me—"

"Yes, well . . ." Mered cleared his throat, cutting off additional descriptions of his master's passion. "Whether you love the amira now or a year from now, you'll enjoy exploring every new experience with your wife."

"And I am ready to explore." Sebak grabbed Mered's shoulders and shook him with delight. "It's time. Go home to your wife, my friend, while I take mine to our chamber and—how did you say it?—*'enjoy exploring every new experience.'*"

Mered watched his master return to the feast, passing the dancing girls and their floating veils as if they were old maids in rags. He greeted the men's table first, bowing deeply to King Tut and offering lavish praise on his successful hunt in the Fayum—two wild oxen, a lion, and a hippo. Sebak offered only a curt nod to Vizier Ay, noticeably aloof toward Egypt's governor. The groom then bowed to his uncle Pirameses, master of neighboring Qantir. He was Sebak's nearest relative, and because he was higher on the family tree, decorum dictated respect—though Pirameses and Sebak were nearly the same age. Pirameses extended his well-muscled arm, and Sebak gripped his arm, forearm to forearm—even tonight a test of wills. The two men were flint against flint, casting sparks whenever they were in the same room. A silent exchange, and Sebak moved on to his father-in-law, General Horemheb.

The groom knelt before Anippe's abbi, and the room fell silent. "I am honored to guard your greatest treasure. Know that I will cherish her and protect her with my life, General."

Sebak bowed his head, and Horemheb placed a hand on his head. "May the mighty Isis, goddess of magic, marriage, and motherhood, bless your marriage and visit your chamber this night." He winked at his wife, Amenia. "So that many grandchildren provide for my future."

The guests exploded in celebration, and the young bride tucked her chin, appropriately shy. Musicians resumed their melody, and the dancers whirled and spun at the edges of the room. Queen Senpa nudged Anippe to her feet, and the bride's handmaid seemed moved to tears—not overly sentimental, but rather unsettled. The girl stepped into the shadows, removing herself from the celebration, and watched with a granite expression.

Sebak approached the women's tables, hand extended. "Come, my love. It's finally time to live as husband and wife." As Anippe reached for his hand, he swept her into his arms, and carried her from the main hall.

Her mother, Amenia, reached for her Hathor-shaped sistrum—a percussion instrument of two oxen horns with bronze discs strung between them—and struck it on beat, jingling in rhythm behind them. One of the guests commented that her training as a chantress in the temple of Amun-Re granted her the right to accompany the newlyweds to their chamber and offer her blessing.

Mered didn't understand Egyptian gods and symbols and legends, but neither did most Egyptians. Only the pharaoh and temple priests made sacrifices, and most noblemen added their own color to the legends. Egyptian peasants endured ever-changing stories of the gods, depending on which version best served the current political powers.

At least El-Shaddai was unchanging—though many Hebrews had given up hope of His ancient promises. Abraham's God hadn't spoken to a child of Israel since the days of Joseph.

But Mered knew He existed. The stories of Abraham, Isaac, and Jacob were too vivid, too exact—the people too flawed and God too merciful—to be illusion. Someday El-Shaddai would speak again, and Mered would be ready.

The fading sounds of celebration drew him back to the feast. This night of love made him hungry for his own bride, Puah. While wedding guests lingered, Mered slipped through the north garden gate, snagged a torch, and picked up a stray stick before walking into the night. Jackals and hyenas couldn't keep him from his wife tonight.

Anippe watched Ummi Amenia over Sebak's shoulder. Amenia rejoiced in her chanting, seeming lost in the rhythm of her jingling sistrum. Sebak's stride matched her tempo, gently rocking Anippe in what should have been a calming sway. But her heart pounded as the sounds of celebration dwindled in this distant hallway. It seemed they'd walked forever. How big was the villa? Anippe shivered, her nerves getting the better of her.

"Are you cold?" Torchlight reflected in Sebak's eyes—and concern, always concern for her.

"A little."

"I have extra robes in my chamber for you." He kissed her forehead. "You won't be cold long." His eyes were hungry, promising more than robes to keep her warm.

At the end of the long hallway, he turned right, where a suite of four doorways were clustered and Ramessids guarded each one. Dressed in bronze-studded leather breastplates and kilts with leather girdles, these soldiers stood at strict attention as Sebak halted before the first door. "You may open for my bride."

Ummi Amenia's chanting ceased as did her sistrum's beat, and the Ramessid opened the chamber door without comment or a glance at his commander.

Sebak placed Anippe's gold-and-jeweled sandals on the tile. She wasn't sure her shaky legs would hold her, but Amenia cupped her elbows and held her gaze.

"You are daughter of Horemheb, sister of King Tut, and now wife of Sebak." Amenia placed a hand on the big man's forearm, drawing him into their circle. "Love each other well. Trust each other only. Give to each other always."

She turned and hurried away before Anippe could cling to her.

Anippe began to tremble.

Sebak laid his hands on her shoulders, and she jumped as if he'd stabbed her. Sliding his hands down her arms, he pressed a whisper against her ear. "Shh, habiba. I won't hurt you."

She looked through the open door to the waiting chamber. Dimly lit with only two small lamps, the darkness meant to swallow her. Paralyzed with fear, she commanded her body to move, but she could think only of what tonight could mean. *Pregnancy. Childbirth. Death.* She'd barely tasted love, and now she must die?

Still measuring her fate, she was again swept into her husband's arms and carried to the future she both longed for and mourned. Beyond the dimly lit chamber was an attached private courtyard, revealing the clear night sky. Sebak shoved the heavy cedar door closed with his foot.

Anippe's heart hammered. "I should go back and check on my sisters. Ankhe was crying, and I saw Queen Senpa wince when she reclined at the table. Truly, she grabbed her belly. If something happened to the baby while she was here, I couldn't forgive myse—"

He covered her mouth with a kiss, hungry at first, but then he gently pulled away. "I will never hurt you, Anippe. No need for tears."

His words both reassured and startled her. She hadn't realized she was crying.

She nodded, still shaking, and then closed her eyes, sending a river down her cheeks. He curled his arms, drawing her into his chest. Instinctively, she wrapped her arms around his neck, holding on to the one who was ripping her away from all she held dear. This man she didn't know but who promised safety—the man who was about to place her life in grave danger.

"I'm frightened."

He buried his face in the bend of her neck and whispered, "I know." He carried her up two steps and past a curtained partition, laid her on his feathery-soft mattress, and knelt beside her on the floor. "I will cherish you." He lifted her hand and kissed her palm. "Tonight." And kissed her wrist. "And tomorrow."

Fire shot through her veins, and a single oil lamp illumined the lazy grin she loved.

"May I join you on the bed now?" he asked.

Suddenly finding it hard to breathe, hard to think, and impossible to speak, Anippe simply nodded. She would check on Ankhe and Senpa in the morning. She would even meet the underworld gods in childbirth. Nothing could smother the ecstasy of this night as Sebak's wife.

8

Frantic knocking at the door awoke Anippe. Before consciousness fully dawned, a rough hand slammed over her mouth, pinning her to the bed.

Sebak hovered over her and slipped the hilt of a dagger into her hand. "Stay in bed and be silent until I find out who's at our door. My Ramessids and Hebrews would never disturb my wedding night." His voice was a whispered growl, sending a chill up her spine.

Anippe had never held a dagger, but her husband seemed to think a dagger should accompany his simple question at the door.

"Who's there?" In the waning moonlight, he donned his robe and drew another short sword from a belt hanging by the door.

"I need to speak to my sister." Ankhe's strangled whisper beckoned Anippe, but Sebak's glare stifled Anippe.

"My wife is not to be disturbed in our chamber, and you will answer to me in the morning." Sebak jabbed the short sword at the door, and it stuck there, rocking in the wake of his fury. Was this the Seth reborn that Abbi Horem described? Silence lingered, and Anippe's breaths came in short quick bursts.

"Senpa is losing her baby." Ankhe's voice was flat. "We should send for the midwives."

Sebak's shoulders slumped. He yanked the door open and pulled Ankhe inside. "Who else knows?"

Anippe dropped her dagger and ran to embrace Ankhe, who explained through tears. "Senpa told Amenia she wasn't feeling well during the feast, but she started cramping after she and Tut were alone in their chamber. Tut summoned Amenia to attend her until the midwives arrive, and then he told me to go and get them." She released her sister and turned to her new master. "Please, Sebak. I don't know how to find the midwives."

"You will address me as Master Sebak, and you have lost valuable time coming to our chamber to find midwives. Why not ask a Hebrew serving maid in your sleeping chamber or any of the Ramessid guards along the way?" He stepped forward, backing Ankhe toward the door. "You are a servant, Ankhe-Senpaaten-tasherit. You will do as you're told, or you'll feel the foreman's strap." He stormed out of the chamber, slamming the door behind him.

Ankhe turned misty eyes toward her sister. "None of the Hebrews will speak to me because I'm your sister, and I'm afraid of the guards." Anippe tried to embrace her again, but Ankhe shoved her away. "I don't want your pity." A single tear leapt over Ankhe's bottom lash, her chin lifted in defiance.

Anippe's frustration soared. What did Ankhe want from her?

She grabbed her little sister's hand and started toward the door. "Come. We'll find a housemaid to summon the midwives. You and I will help Amenia make Senpa comfortable until they arrive."

"No!" Ankhe ripped her hand away. "I can't go near Senpa."

"What? Why not?"

"I'm Ankhe-Senpaaten-*tasherit*—the decoy for Senpa. If Anubis comes to claim Senpa for the underworld during her miscarriage, that jackal-faced god might take me instead."

Anippe wiped weary hands down her face. "Ankhe, I understand your fear, but think about our sister. Senpa is alone in this strange place, and she needs us." She reached for Ankhe's hand, pleading.

"Think about me. No one ever thinks about me." Pulling away, Ankhe reached for the door latch. "If these chamber guards will order a house slave to take me to the midwives, then you and Amenia can help Senpa." Without waiting for Anippe's approval, Ankhe flung open the door. "Your amira has instructions for you."

The four large Ramessids standing outside the suite of chambers mirrored Anippe's surprise. Gathering her courage, the new amira tried to sound imposing. "Find a Hebrew that can lead my sister to the midwives."

"As you wish, Amira." One of the guards turned without further prompting, and Ankhe hurried from the chamber to follow.

Anippe realized she had no idea where to send messages of Senpa's condition. "Ankhe, where is King Tut?"

On her way down the long hallway, Ankhe shouted over her shoulder. "Ay and Horemheb are consoling him in the main hall. Tut blames himself for Senpa's miscarriage, making her sail on that wretched barque during unlucky days this month."

Anippe noted the chamber guards' raised eyebrows and cringed at her sister's indiscretion. Not only had Ankhe used familiar names for all of Egypt's top leaders, but by dawn the whole villa would lay blame for Senpa's miscarriage at Tut's feet. Would Ankhe ever learn to hold her tongue?

Avaris's new amira stood at her chamber door, feeling almost as ridiculous as her tactless sister. She had no idea where guests slept at Avaris. Where was Senpa's chamber?

"May I escort you to the queen's chamber?" The chamber guard beside her door nodded slightly, respectful and kind. "This way, Amira."

He extended his hand toward a side hallway leading to a pillared portico that appeared to connect more rooms on another wing. She'd barely walked ten steps when she heard Senpa's heart-rending cries.

"I can find the chamber from here. Thank you."

"As you wish, Amira." He bowed and turned to go.

"Wait, what's your name, Ramessid?"

"I am Nassor, Amira."

"Thank you, Nassor. I will mention your kindness to Master Sebak."

He offered his thanks with another nod and a slight smile before turning to go. Anippe followed the groans to the last chamber on her left. She pushed open the door and found Amenia leaning over Senpa's coiled form.

"You must try to relax, dear one. Your baby wants to enter this world before crossing over to the next, and we must help it make the transition." Amenia dabbed Senpa's sweaty brow with a wet cloth.

"May I help?" Anippe took the cloth, and Senpa immediately clutched Anippe's hand to her cheek.

"Thank you for being here." Before Senpa's words ended, another pain seized her, drawing her knees to her chest.

Amenia placed a cloth between Senpa's teeth and coaxed her to bite down when the pain grew unbearable. "Better the cloth than your bottom lip." She smoothed the expectant mother's fine hair, made sparse from years of royal wigs. At twenty-seven, Senpa was still young enough to bear children but considerably older than Tut's fifteen years. If she didn't produce an heir soon, the king would likely take another wife.

The cycles of Senpa's pain seemed endless. Anippe dabbed her brow with each new wave, and Amenia chanted the sacred songs of Amun through the relentless struggle.

Finally a soft knock, and two women entered, both dressed in sand-colored, rough-spun linen. One carried baskets filled with clay jars and bundles of herbs, while the other carried a birthing stool.

"Good evening, my queen," said the older of the two. Her tone and manner were fluid and gentle, like the Nile during *Peret*—when the water returned to its banks and sowing began. "I'm Shiphrah, and this is Puah, my assistant. We've come to ease your pain and deliver your baby."

Ummi Amenia helped Senpa to the birthing stool, giving the midwife room to examine her patient. When another pain gripped the queen, Shiphrah grimaced and then whispered instructions to her assistant.

Puah was younger, beautiful, and capable. Her hands worked feverishly, pouring a drop of this, adding a sprinkle of that, crushing leaves of something else. Without a word, she handed the potion to Shiphrah, who lifted Senpa's head and helped her drink.

"I'm sorry we meet again under these circumstances, my queen. This is the same blend as last time. Your cramping will increase for a time to ensure a complete delivery and help prevent infection." She cradled Senpa's shoulders even after she'd finished drinking, her affection for the queen seeming genuine.

"I understand . . . I remember." Senpa buried her face in the woman's chest.

Anippe covered a sob, aching for her sister's loss. How could she bear losing two babies?

When the contractions increased, Anippe huddled in the corner and watched in horror as her sister's body expelled the living treasure the king and queen yearned for most. With a final push, Senpa's body went limp, and the room grew deathly still.

"Senpa?" Ummi Amenia, seated behind her on the stool, shook her shoulders.

No response.

Anippe whimpered, unable to stifle her panic. "Not Senpa! Not Senpa too."

"Lay her on the mat. Over here. Puah, grind more giant fennel—now." Amenia and Puah jumped to obey Shiphrah's commands. "Amira Anippe, please help get her on the mat."

Shaken by her new title, Anippe lunged to help Amenia drag Senpa's body to the reed mat, while Puah ground the fennel into powder and mixed it with sweet wine.

"Here," Puah said, handing the cup to Shiphrah.

The chief midwife cradled the queen's shoulders again, lifting the potion to her lips. "Queen Senpa, you must wake up and drink this wonderful wine. Come, now. Come on."

Senpa sputtered and then gulped, dribbling the wine concoction down her chin, while the other women cried with relief.

Anippe returned to her place in the corner, watching the others tend to Senpa. Childbirth, the cruelest deception of the gods. The priests had said it was a beautiful offering to the goddess Tawaret, but it was vile and bloody and torturous, and Anippe would never bear a child—if she could avoid it. Her wedding night with Sebak had been near rapture, but if it led to this, she'd shave her body and serve in the temple of Amun. Could she serve as priestess though she'd been spoiled by a husband? Priests would allow anything if offered enough gold.

"Amira? Amira?" Puah's voice shook Anippe from her reverie. "You should tell the king."

Anippe stood, realizing that Shiphrah and Amenia were frantically working over Senpa again. She looked ashen, eyes closed, body still. A pool of blood lay around her.

"Is she dead?"

"No, but . . ." Puah bowed her head.

"But?"

Seeming reluctant to speak, the assistant midwife fixed her eyes on her dusty sandals. "The next few hours will determine her fate. We will pray."

Pray? Why pray? If Tut was a god, why couldn't he save his babies? "You can pray all you want. I'll report my sister's condition to Pharaoh."

Anippe fairly ran from the room, driven out by undying images of dying women. Senpa lying so still. Ummi Kiya's empty eyes staring at a distant corner. Why were the realities of childbirth the expectation of her gender?

Through the columned portico she ran and then down the long hallway. The morning sun streamed through the windows as she hurried toward the main hall. Would the men still be there, or had they moved on with their day? Hunting, perhaps? Sword drills or archery practice—while the women faced life and death and surrendered lost dreams?

She entered the main hall doorway and saw her brother. Slumped over the low-lying table, King Tut's face was buried in his hands. No wig or *wereret*— the crown of Egypt's Two Lands. Vizier Ay leaned over him, whispering. Both men looked up at the sound of her frantic breathing.

"What news?" her brother asked. Hope in the face of hopelessness.

She swallowed hard and walked the longest fifteen steps of her life. Kneeling on a cushion opposite him, she grasped his hands. "Your baby girl was too young to survive and was taken by Anubis before her first breath. Senpa lost a lot of blood. The midwives say we can only wait and . . . pray."

The outcry she expected never came. Perhaps her brother had truly become divine. Instead, he spoke with utter calm. "Vizier Ay, your reasoning rings true—even if General Horemheb disagrees. The Hebrews have become too numerous and have skewed ma'at in the Delta. The gods deny me children—specifically male children—so I deny the Hebrews any male infants until Queen Senpa produces my heir."

Anippe shuddered and released her brother's hands. "What are you saying?"

"All Hebrew newborn boys will die." His eyes stared through her to a place she could not see. Surely, he was a god—no human could care so little about other lives.

Anippe cast an accusing glare at Vizier Ay, realizing this must be another of his schemes. This edict would eventually diminish Delta slaves, but more importantly, it would stir Hebrew unrest and demand increased military patrols, leaving fewer Ramessids to fight Hittites—and monitor Ay's activity in the south.

"Summon the midwives, Anippe." Tut's eyes pierced her soul. "They will be the instrument that restores health to my wife's womb, harmony in Egypt, and ma'at in King Tut."

Mered watched silently as his master groomed his seventh horse that morning. The stable boy stood at strict attention, currycomb at the ready, but Sebak needed the therapy of horseflesh beneath his hands. After the young master lost his parents, Mered often found him in the stables at dawn, his cheek pressed against a stallion's side, his gentle whisper soothing both man and beast—as Mered had found him this morning.

A villa slave had summoned Puah before dawn, saying Queen Senpa was cramping and needed help immediately. Master Sebak's grief told Mered the cramping had worsened—the king and queen had lost another child.

Pounding footsteps scattered Mered's thoughts. General Horemheb marched toward them from the villa as if to battle.

"You must warn the other Ramessids, Sebak. Ay has poisoned the king's mind against your Hebrews and commanded the midwives to kill all newborn slave boys. Ay said doing so would restore Tut's lost ma'at and heal Senpa's womb." Horemheb crossed his arms over his chest, stretching the leather bands on his biceps. "I think it'll make your Hebrews more unruly and drain our already stressed military resources."

"Puah?" Mered spoke his wife's name without thinking, drawing both soldiers' attention.

"Yes, Puah was one of the midwives." The general stepped closer, examining Mered as if he was judging horseflesh. "Who is she to you, and why are you—a Hebrew—pretending to be Egyptian?" His hand moved to the hilt of his dagger. "We kill Hebrews who try to escape."

Sebak stepped between them. "Puah is Mered's wife, and he is my Chief Linen Keeper. He wears our workshop's finest robes to display quality to traveling merchants. If his wife is in danger, Mered's mind is on his wife. Without Mered's attention, the linen shop suffers. Without Avaris linen, Delta trade declines."

General Horemheb's face was set like stone as he eyed Mered from the top of his Egyptian-cropped hair to the hem of his pleated linen robe. The only things missing were a wig and face paints. "You will follow me, linen keeper—now."

The general whirled toward the villa, and Sebak nudged Mered forward, falling in step behind them. Was he being arrested—or worse?

Within moments they arrived in the villa's main hall, where General Horemheb approached King Tut. Mered fell to his knees, while Master Sebak towered above his right shoulder. Vizier Ay stood at Pharaoh's right, with Puah and Shiphrah beside him, their faces streaked with tears.

Mered cautiously peeked up and saw Puah's face brighten when she saw him but fade the moment Pharaoh spoke.

"Why have you returned, Horemheb? I've made my decision, and it's firm. You'll not change my mind." Tut reclined on the cushion where he'd celebrated the marriage feast last night. "You're the one who taught me to seek ma'at at all costs, Horemheb. Ay has simply suggested killing male Hebrew babies as an efficient method to achieve it."

Horemheb stepped forward and fell to one knee, head bowed. "Oh great

Pharaoh, one of perfect laws, who pacifies the Two Lands; Lord of all, who wears crowns and pleases the gods; Ruler of Truth, who pleases his father Re—your will is my command, and I am your obedient servant. I have not come to argue but to help balance the counsel of your wise vizier. As you say, ma'at is only achieved when our king hears both sides of an argument."

Tut's eyes narrowed, and he leaned over the low-lying table. "Like uneven water jugs on a shoulder bar, the Hebrews in our Delta have unbalanced Egypt's Two Lands. By their deaths, we will balance the nation—and Senpa will bear my son."

Mered gulped, thankful to be hiding his expression with a bow. How could the king speak of life and death when he'd seen so little of it in his fifteen years?

"And Queen Senpa will bear a fine son, oh good god." Horemheb's voice was gentle, sincere. The change of tone was like a slap, and something akin to shame averted Tut's gaze as the general continued. "If it pleases my king, may I introduce Mered, Commander Sebak's Chief Linen Keeper and husband of Puah, the midwife." Sebak nudged Mered, who maneuvered on his knees to flank Horemheb.

"Why would I care to meet a Hebrew slave?"

"Because this is the man who will comfort his distraught wife after she kills Hebrew baby boys. Mered is the overseer of the second most productive linen workshop in Egypt. How will the chaos of mass killing affect your Delta linen production? And if the slaves should try to rebel, the Ramessids would, of course, quash the rebellion—but at what cost? Must I assign greater military resources to Delta settlements when I need every available soldier to fight the Hittites?" He bowed his forehead to the tiled floor. "Please, my king, listen to me. Can't you see that Ay is trying to unsettle your ma'at, not restore peace—"

Tut slammed both hands on the table and stood. "It's you, Horemheb, who unsettles me."

Everyone collapsed to their knees, bowing in the crushing silence. Only the desperate panting of the grieving king echoed in the room. "Rise," he said in a low growl.

Every supplicant stood, but no one dared speak. Silence drew into awkwardness.

Finally, Tut addressed his general again. "You view Egypt through the wary eyes of a would-be king, but Vizier Ay sees Egypt's king and his would-be heir. You protect Egyptian linen, but you've forgotten to defend Egypt's king." The young king struggled against his emotions, his cheeks quaking. "General Horemheb, Commander of Egypt's Armies and Prince Regent of the Two Lands, I see another more worthy of this throne. I hereby revoke your—"

"No!" A woman's high-pitched cry sliced the air. Amira Anippe emerged from the hall and fell at Tut's feet. "Please, incarnate Horus, healer of the Two Lands, and beloved brother of my heart. I beg you to wait until your grief has passed. Don't change a decision in darkness that you made in light. You and I watched Abbi Akhenaten rule Egypt with emotion and whim, but you have ruled with wisdom and forethought. Senpa needs you now. Let your strong leaders—General Horemheb and Vizier Ay—tend your nation while you tend your queen."

Mered heard only heavy breathing and silent yearning in a room filled with Egypt's future.

King Tut strummed his sister's spiraled wig, offering her a sad smile. He kissed her cheek and stood, turning his attention once more to his prince regent. "General Horemheb, you will leave my presence tonight. Return to battle the Hittites, while I tend my wife and rule my nation. You remain prince regent until I have an heir." He glared at the midwives. "And I'll have an heir as soon as you fling every male Hebrew newborn into the Nile. Now leave me." Turning to Ay, his features softened. "The vizier will accompany Senpa and me to Memphis when the queen regains strength to travel."

Shiphrah and Puah hurried out of the hall, and Mered furtively touched Sebak's arm to beg leave.

The king must have noted the motion, for he barked, "All of you—get out."

Mered needed no further prompting. He fairly ran to his wife, who had already fled to the garden on their way home. "Puah, Shiphrah—wait."

Both women turned, eyes red-rimmed, tears streaming down their cheeks.

Puah ran into her husband's arms, while Shiphrah stood quaking beside them. "How can we kill the very lives God gave us to deliver? If we disobey Pharaoh, we die; but if we sin against El-Shaddai, we suffer Sheol forever."

Mered gathered Shiphrah into his arms as well, and the three formed a tight circle of grief.

"I can't kill a baby," Puah whispered, "I can't." She buried her sobs in his chest.

Heartbroken, Mered held both midwives, praying silently for their strength and wisdom. *El-Shaddai, how can You let this happen? Protect Your people, Israel.*

Startled by a hand on his shoulder, Mered whirled to see Sebak and Anippe looking almost as distraught as the Hebrews. "My lord," Mered began, "I was just . . . I . . . may I escort Puah and Shiphrah home before returning to the linen shop?"

"Of course, Mered. Take them back to camp and stay with Puah if she needs you—"

"Wait." Anippe wriggled away from the master's protective arm. "I could go with them, Sebak, and get instructions from Shiphrah on how to care for Senpa while she's here."

Sebak appeared as confused as Mered felt. "The midwives will care for Queen Senpa. An Egyptian amira doesn't stroll into a slave camp, my love. It simply isn't done."

Mered watched the amira carefully. She acquiesced, allowing Sebak to corral her waist, but she wasn't satisfied. Her sharp glances and fidgeting fingers told Mered this amira wanted to follow the midwives for more than instructions on Queen Senpa's care.

Master Sebak cleared his throat, gaining Puah's and Shiphrah's attention. "You two must begin now to obey the king. Every male newborn from this moment forward goes into the Nile. I'll send the first regiment of soldiers this afternoon to take a census of all Hebrew children. We will enforce this—even in the skilled craftsmen's village." He looked at Mered then, their roles as slave and master never more distinct than in this moment. "I'm sorry, my friend."

9

Everyone lies to their neighbor;
they flatter with their lips
but harbor deception in their hearts.

—PSALM 12:2

Anippe walked in Sebak's shadow through the garden, past the empty main hall, and down the hallway toward their bedchamber. He hadn't spoken or touched her since they left Mered and the midwives. Nassor, the Ramessid at their doorway, saluted him and pushed open their cedar door. Sebak pressed the curve of her back, encouraging her to enter first.

"Thank you, Nassor," Anippe said as she passed.

Ankhe was waiting beside a tray of grapes and honeyed dates, goat cheese, and various nut-breads. She kept her head bowed but gave no sign of retreat.

"Get out," Sebak growled.

Ankhe stepped forward, intense and defiant as she'd always been with Abbi Horem.

"Thank you, Ankhe." Anippe moved between her sister and husband, guiding Ankhe toward the door. "I'll call for you after Sebak and I have finished our meal." She raised her eyebrows, hoping to communicate the wisdom of surrender.

Ankhe left quickly but not quietly. The door slammed, and Sebak turned on Anippe, sparks like a flint stone in his eyes.

"I will not tolerate her disrespect. She needs the strap, Anippe, and I will administer it so she'll never need it again." He grabbed her shoulders and pulled her close. "It's the most merciful thing to do, my love. She's like a wild mare unwilling to be broken. She must learn—"

Anippe pulled her husband's head down and kissed him into silence. His anger channeled into passion, and for a moment, she thought he'd consume her.

"Wait, wait, please." She pushed him away.

Like a man awakened from deep dreams, he opened his eyes and focused on the face held between his hands. "I waited twenty-one years to take a bride—and so I took her. In my life I must wait for kings and generals and armies to reach terms. Why must I wait for my wife?" He wasn't angry—yet—simply anxious. Like a little boy begging for honey cakes.

How could she tell him he must wait because she was terrified of bearing his child? The women at Gurob Harem spoke of herbs and leaf packs to prevent a man's seed from bearing fruit, but she must get to the midwives to obtain the items.

"I must go to Senpa," she said. "You gave the midwives permission to return home, and Amenia was with her all night."

She saw desperation in his eyes. And then came the anger.

He swept her aside. "I'm going to the stables."

The door slammed shut behind him, and Anippe was alone. Abbi Horem would return to battle today. Tut, Senpa, and probably Ummi Amenia would return to Memphis as soon as Senpa was well enough to travel. Anippe would be left in this strange villa enduring a selfish sister and a good husband with a bad temper.

She sank onto her feather mattress and sorted out her options. They were few. If she tried to speak to the midwives while they tended Senpa, someone in the villa might overhear her request and tell Sebak.

"Never betray him," Abbi Horem had warned. A cold shiver shook her in the midday heat. Sebak had wanted to give Ankhe the strap for disrespect. What would he do to his wife for cheating him out of an heir?

Ankhe. A new thought launched her from the bed. Ankhe knew where the midwives lived because she'd summoned them for Senpa. She could lead Anippe to the slave camp to speak privately with Shiphrah and Puah.

"An Egyptian amira doesn't stroll into a slave camp," Sebak had said. She did if no one knew she was Egyptian. Anippe's and Ankhe's skin was lighter than most Egyptians because Ummi Kiya was a princess from the Mitanni

kingdom, given to Abbi Akhenaten as a treaty bride. Their daughters both inherited Kiya's sandy-brown eyes and brown hair, rather than Egyptian dark browns and blacks. Without fine linen, a wig, and face paints, Anippe could pass for a Hebrew—at least for a little while.

She hurried to the gathering area of her chamber and rang the Hathor-shaped chime, summoning her maid. Ankhe arrived grim faced and squint eyed.

"You can pout all day about Sebak's temper, or you can join me on an adventure." Anippe watched Ankhe for the slightest sign of consent.

"What adventure?"

"Find rough-spun Hebrew robes for both of us. We'll remove our cosmetics. No wigs either. We need Hebrew women's head coverings too. They'll help hide our thin hair. You're taking me to the midwives."

"Why should I?"

"Because, like it or not, you're my handmaid, Ankhe."

The sisters stood locked in a stare. What thoughts whirled behind Ankhe's eyes? Rage. Rebellion. Bitterness. These were the only emotions Ankhe seemed capable of feeling.

Anippe squeezed her eyes shut, hating herself for what she was about to say. "If you help me deceive Sebak, you'll rob him of a child."

She opened her eyes and found Ankhe smiling. The glee on her sister's face was nauseating.

"And if I refuse to help you?" Ankhe asked.

"If you refuse, I'll let Sebak train you with his strap."

Ankhe lifted her chin defiantly, considering the ultimatum, but she showed no sign of surprise or disgust at Anippe's blatant manipulation. Anippe was sickened by it. She'd become everything she hated about Egyptian royalty—conniving and controlling.

But she did it for love. She adored Sebak. Why place her life at risk—their days on this earth together at risk?

"I'll get the Hebrew robes and head coverings while you remove your paints," Ankhe said, eyes sparking with mischief. "I'll do anything to disgrace your pompous husband."

Anippe watched Ankhe go, and a wave of foreboding washed over her. For the first time in her life, she needed Ankhe and must rely on her discretion. Would their secret draw them closer, or was Anippe a fool to trust a girl who seemed incapable of caring for another?

Mered sat alone at the table in their one-room home, listening as his wife shuffled baskets, rearranged clay pots, and poured out her pain. Though married only two years, he'd known her all his life, and this woman needed to work while she ranted.

"I won't do it. I'll die before I'll kill another living soul. And a baby? Who does King Tut think we are? Midwives don't kill babies. We witness their first breath of life, that's what we do. And furthermore, who does King Tut think he is—taking the sovereign decision of life and death into his mortal hands? Yes, I said mortal. A pharaoh is no more divine than my right—"

"I couldn't agree more." Anippe's voice brought Mered out of his chair.

"Amira." He nearly knocked over the table as both he and Puah fell to their knees, faces in the dust, arms extended. "My wife and I apologize if we offended—"

"You may rise." Anippe's presence filled their small room, but . . .

Trying not to stare, Mered glanced repeatedly at his master's new bride and her handmaid—neither wearing paints or fine linen or wigs. They looked . . . well, thoroughly Hebrew. Their complexions matched Puah's olive tone.

"May we offer you pomegranate wine or gold beer?" Puah stepped forward, nudging Mered aside since his voice seemed to have left him. "I'm sorry we have no grape wine or dark beer to serve your taste."

"Thank you, no. My sister, Ankhe, is the handmaid who summoned you and Shiphrah to attend Queen Senpa. Do you remember Ankhe?"

Mered watched his wife nod tentatively, her trembling fingers laced together at her waist.

"Good, then you know how we found your home. I'm not here to cause trouble. I simply need your help—but you can't tell Master Sebak."

At that moment, Mered's world shifted. Deception had come to Avaris, and its name was Anippe. He took a step toward her, palms upturned, pleading. "My amira, Puah and I are happy to help you—always—but Master Sebak loves you and would do anything for you. He's told me so himself."

Tears pooled in her eyes. Her jaw set like Aswan granite. The epitome of an inner clash. "What I do, Mered, I do to ensure a long and happy life with my husband. Your only role will be to periodically deliver a package to me from Puah. In return, I'll double your grain and cloth allowances and give you a larger dwelling."

He bowed, careful to keep his tone humble. "Thank you, Amira, but we're quite content. Our master has always been generous." He waited, hoping he hadn't offended the woman who held Sebak's heart in her hand.

"Return to the linen shop, Mered—now—while I speak privately with your wife."

He shot a panicked glance at Puah, who studied her hands and refused to meet his gaze. Mered kissed her temple and hurried out, squeezing past the amira's sister, who blocked the doorway.

"Remember, Mered," Anippe said as he reached the threshold, "complete secrecy. Your wife's life depends on it."

He stumbled through the door and down the path toward the villa, torn by love for his wife and loyalty to his master. Who was this young bride who'd stolen Master Sebak's heart and brought Egypt's chaos to Avaris? Sebak had avoided political turmoil by focusing on his career, but now royalty shared his bed and threatened his slaves. *El-Shaddai, hear my cry. Protect us from the schemes of our new amira.*

Anippe's heart was in her throat as Mered left his home. She'd never threatened a slave and never spoken so rudely to a man. Puah stood across from her, mirroring Anippe's posture. Hands clasped tightly in front to steady their shaking. But Anippe was the instigator—and the amira—and she must take the next step.

"Puah, I need your help. Can we sit down and talk?"

The midwife motioned Anippe toward the table, offering their single chair. "Please, sit there. I'll get you something to drink, and maybe some dried fish or dates." Puah kept her head bowed, nervously shuffling through baskets. She grabbed a clay pitcher and spilled water onto the dirt floor around three clay cups, her hands trembling too violently to pour.

Ankhe loomed by the door, but Anippe walked over to the frightened midwife and guided her to the lone chair. "Puah, please. Come talk with me."

Puah sat, hands folded, head bowed. "I won't kill Hebrew babies. I won't."

Anippe crouched before the young woman, capturing her gaze. "I'm not here about my brother's edict."

"Well, your brother's edict is my whole world."

The anger reflected in Puah's unshed tears revealed a tough side Anippe respected. "Perhaps we can improve each other's worlds." She stood, towering over the Hebrew for her next revelation. "I refuse to endure what I witnessed in Senpa's chamber this morning, and you're going to ensure I don't have to."

Puah's head shot up. "I can't promise you'll never miscarry. Only El-Shaddai gives the breath of life."

"You can make sure I don't get pregnant, Puah. The wives at Gurob Harem used a poultice for their interludes with traveling merchants. It always worked."

"Nothing always works, Amira. Only a barren woman is sure she'll never conceive." Puah's voice had gone flat. She began tracing random figures on the table.

"But you know of this poultice? You or Shiphrah could provide the ingredients and teach me to use it—without Sebak knowing?"

The midwife's hand stilled on the table. "How long will you refuse to bear his child?"

Anippe's cheeks burned. Why did she feel shamed by a Hebrew midwife's question? "How long will you refuse to kill Hebrew babies?"

Puah laughed without mirth and resumed making circles with her fingers on the table. "Grind together dates, acacia-tree bark, and honey to make a paste, and then coat a wadding of sheep's wool with the concoction. Insert it shortly before . . ." The midwife met Anippe's gaze. "Now, how will you improve my world, Amira? Can you keep Hebrew babes alive—while we keep your womb dead?"

10

*And because the midwives feared God, he gave
them families of their own.*

—EXODUS 1:21

THREE MONTHS LATER

Anippe stared at the ceiling in dawn's pink shadows and wiped her
cheeks, defeated by the sleepless night—her last night to feel Sebak's
warmth beside her for who knew how long. She removed her neck rest and
rolled to her side, laying her cheek against her outstretched arm, careful not to
crease the spirals of her wig. She couldn't let Sebak awaken to a rumpled, puffy-
eyed wife on his last morning at home.

When had she fallen in love with this honorable and gentle man?

His temper hadn't flared since those first days of marriage. The gods must
have conspired against their happiness. What other explanation could there
be? Senpa's miscarriage. Tut's ridiculous decree. Abbi Horem nearly replaced as
prince regent.

But two weeks after Senpa's miscarriage, the royals left, and though
Anippe missed her family, she was relieved when Ankhe's disposition improved.
She clung to Anippe in their aloneness, which translated to Sebak as long-
overdue respect. He seemed pleased, and the sisters were closer than they'd
been since childhood.

Anippe watched the slow rise and fall of his chest as he slept. He was beautiful, rugged, flawlessly flawed. Long, black lashes fringed almond-shaped lids.
His nose turned slightly at a knot halfway down, where it had been broken in

battle. A scar intersected his right brow. They'd been married only three months, but she couldn't imagine life without him. She'd dreaded his return to battle since the day she married a soldier.

Dread became reality today.

A messenger from Abbi Horem had arrived yesterday while Anippe and Sebak lounged in the garden. Dusty and weary, he had demanded to speak with Sebak immediately—and privately. They disappeared into the villa. Anippe waited only moments before seeing the messenger hurry away toward the Ramessid barracks. When Sebak returned to his couch in the garden, his whole countenance had changed.

"General Horemheb has recalled me to duty, habiba." He spoke matter-of-factly into the distance. "I leave tomorrow."

"Tomorrow? Why so soon? Where are you going?"

Slowly, he turned his head, appraising her with empty eyes. Her gentle husband was gone. "I go when I'm called, and you must never ask where."

She reached for his hand, and he recoiled.

"I'm going to the stables for a while." He towered over her, jaw flexing, breathing hard. "I'll meet you in our chamber for the evening meal. We'll talk more then." Looking away, he wiped both hands down the length of his face and expelled a long sigh before returning his attention to her with a softer voice. "I'll be better then."

Anippe could only nod, fighting the tears clawing at her throat as he walked away.

She had discovered a horrendous truth yesterday. Sebak's heart was hers, but his mind and body belonged to Egypt.

Tears threatened again this morning as she watched him sleep. Why was she so emotional? *Lady Isis, goddess of motherhood, please don't play tricks with me.* Anippe had used Puah's poultices faithfully and had given herself to her husband freely. In return Anippe had interceded with her husband on behalf of the midwives, and the Ramessid troops swept only the unskilled village for newborn Hebrew males. Granted, it was only partial protection from Pharaoh's edict.

Had Puah also provided only partial protection in her herb bundles? *Is that why my red flow is a week late in coming?* Her interrupted cycle had not gone unnoticed. Sebak, eager for children, had been counting the days.

Nightmarish visions of Senpa and Ummi Kiya played in Anippe's mind, while fresh tears slid across her nose and into her braided wig. The man softly snoring beside her was the best man she knew. To raise his child would be a privilege, a feat that would surely make her ka feather-light on the eternal scale of Anubis.

But why risk death and separation from Sebak, when they could adopt as Horemheb and Amenia had done? Truly, she loved children, and since taking steps to prevent conception, her arms had ached all the more to hold a child of her own.

But I'm protecting Sebak and myself from the separation of death. The argument sounded reasonable in the dark shadows of her mind, but in the light of day it was deceit—betrayal—plain and simple.

As if sensing silent turmoil, her husband stirred. His waking filled the room with life as his head turned in the carved turquoise neck rest. The lazy grin she loved lit his sleepy face. "Are you watching me?"

Without warning, he rolled over and pinned her to the bed, enveloping her with his arms, his scent, his love.

"I'm memorizing your face before you leave me . . ." Her voice broke, and the tears started.

She tried to turn away, but his elbows trapped her wig in place while her face slid left. Her eyes were suddenly cloaked in darkness and her right ear framed by the elegant black tresses.

Sebak roared with laughter and snatched off her wig, burying his kisses in the ticklish spot on her neck.

She felt absolutely naked but couldn't stop giggling or push him away. "Stop! Please, stop."

Before she could utter more protest, he silenced her with a kiss—playful at first, then slow and gentle. When he pulled away, she clung to him, pressing her cheek against his to hide her ugliness.

With one arm, he held her. With the other hand, he removed his own wig. Curiosity drew her eyes upward. Her gentle giant was completely bald, the skin hidden by his wig several shades lighter than his face and neck. He was radiant, handsome, confident—hers.

"You are the most beautiful woman in the world to me, Anippe." He stroked the thin hair atop her head, examining, adoring. "You need no wig or paints to please me. You need only be honorable, faithful, and loving to our children."

He kissed her again, but she couldn't mock him by returning his passion. How dare she imagine her heart weighing favorably on Anubis's scale?

She pressed against his chest, and he rolled aside. "Come, my love," she said. "We should prepare our candles to take to the quay for today's Feast of Lotus."

His wounded expression nearly drew her back. "Tell me again why we chose today as the Feast of Lotus."

She replaced her wig and scooted off the bed. Donning only her sheath, she scurried into their sitting room before he could retrieve her. "We didn't choose today for the feast, remember? You chose to celebrate the first day of inundation with your send-off to battle." Anippe heard her husband rifling through baskets in their bedroom behind the partition. "What are you looking for?" she asked.

He peeked his bald head around the dividing curtain. "I should wear my uniform today, but I can't find my cudgel." Gone before she could suggest where a stray cudgel might hide, Sebak continued his frenzied search, while Anippe nibbled on the fruit they'd shared after their meal last night.

He'd returned from the stables in much better humor, as the husband she knew. The man she loved. They feasted on marinated goose with cucumber yogurt sauce and roasted lamb seasoned with garlic and onions. Fresh fruits and vegetables were sparse, and they ate mostly dried dates and figs, since harvest season had passed.

Sebak had dangled a dried fig, and as she opened her mouth to receive it, he had whispered, "Are you carrying my child?"

The night had been perfect until that moment. Thankfully, he dropped the fig into her mouth, giving her a few moments to chew and think of an answer.

After a swig of honeyed wine, she forced her features into a seductive pout. "It's too early to tell, habibi."

He placed his hand on her stomach and whispered against her cheek, "Perhaps we should celebrate the Feast of Lotus tomorrow with the new year. As the inundation waters bring fertile silt from the south to nourish our land, perhaps an offering of lotus candles at the Avaris quay will ensure fertility in the amira's womb."

"But I thought we'd spend your last day alone together." She kissed him deeply, pressing her will. "I don't want to share you with the whole estate."

He groaned but pulled away. "Wait right there." Hurrying to the door, he flung it open and spoke to the Ramessids on duty. "Nassor, summon the estate foreman. He knows I return to duty tomorrow, but I've decided to celebrate the Feast of Lotus as a good-bye gift for the whole estate. The foreman will need to get the chief baker and brewer to work all night, and craftsmen to fashion the silver lotus candleholders."

"Yes, my lord. Right away." Nassor and another Ramessid marched into the darkness, while the other two remained.

Sebak slammed the door, delight in his eyes. "It will be wonderful. We'll make the day about celebration and new life—not about good-byes and—"

Death. He'd stopped before the word tumbled out, but Anippe's face must have revealed her horror.

Rushing to her, he had swept her into his arms and buried his head in the bend of her neck. "We will sing for the lotus tomorrow and carry our candles to the Nile, dreaming of the day I'll return to you. But know this, habiba. You are my dream, and I will hold you in my heart every moment I'm away."

"Found it." Sebak appeared from behind their bedroom partition, triumphantly bearing the knotty-wood cudgel. Blood still stained its surface.

Anippe turned, wiping away tears, and rang the Hathor-shaped chime. The sooner Ankhe brought their morning meal, the sooner they could take candles to the quay and return to the cocoon of their private chamber.

Mered and Puah walked hand in hand toward the Nile, following friends, family, and Egyptians toward the Avaris quay. They walked slowly. Puah's queasiness had subsided but hadn't completely disappeared during the past few weeks. Her belly was rounding like a lovely little melon, and they prayed daily for a daughter.

How could any Hebrew hope for a son while the threat of Pharaoh's edict still loomed?

Puah had counted thirty baby boys in the craftsmen's and unskilled's camps. Fearing God more than Pharaoh, neither midwife obeyed Pharaoh's edict, but Ramessid guards cast three newborns into the Nile. Though the slave camps mourned their loss, the twenty-seven baby boys spared brought some measure of solace.

Gossip among the camps said Master Sebak had forbidden Ramessid death squads in the craftsmen's village. No one knew for sure, but Mered believed the master was simply too enthralled with his bride to order regular Ramessid inspections of both camps.

The amira also seemed too distracted to visit the linen shop. Mered wasn't at all disappointed she stayed away. His only contact with Anippe had been in his home—when she threatened his wife.

He still prayed for the young amira—that she would cease her deception. He obediently delivered Puah's small baskets to Ankhe on the first day of each week, placing the bundles on his desk and waiting for two sacks of grain to mysteriously replace them. Mered knew nothing of midwifery, so he dared not guess the contents. But of one thing he was certain—his wife's life depended on it.

"Where's your candle, my friend?" Master Sebak swatted Mered's back, nearly tumbling the linen keeper down the dusty hill to the quay.

Regaining his footing, Mered chuckled. "I don't need a lotus-shaped silver pot to carry my prayers to El-Shaddai. He knows my dreams no matter what shape they take."

The amira peeked around her husband's large frame. "Then why do you and Puah even attend our lotus feast?" Her painted smile did little to mask the bite in her tone.

Puah squeezed Mered's hand, warning him to tread lightly. Neither of them had seen the amira since the day she visited their home. "We come to honor Master Sebak and pledge our loyalty to you, Amira, while he's away."

"Humph." She turned away, her cheeks and neck growing crimson.

"Thank you, my friend." Sebak placed a hand on Mered's shoulder. "And thank you, Puah, for taking care of the women on both estates. My wife has kept me distracted . . ." Sebak noticed Puah's swollen abdomen and looked as if he'd swallowed a bad fig.

An awkward silence ushered them partway down the path until Mered couldn't stand it any longer. "We estimate she'll deliver during the first month of sowing season." He lifted an eyebrow. Would Sebak mention the king's edict?

"Congratulations, my friend." Master Sebak's gaze searched the gathering crowd at the shore, and then a slow smile shone as bright as the midday sun. He gathered Anippe in his arms and kissed her gently. "You have a heart of gold, my wife. Mered, you should thank your amira for her kindness."

Confused, Mered glanced at Puah for clarity, but she looked as puzzled as he felt. "Of course. I do thank her . . . but for what exactly?"

Sebak lowered his voice, glancing around to ensure he wouldn't be overheard. "Anippe asked that I discontinue patrols in the craftsmen's village. My guards have enforced Pharaoh's edict only on the unskilled plateau between Avaris and Qantir." He gazed at Anippe adoringly. "You knew Puah was expecting and wanted to save their child, didn't you?"

"Well, I . . ." Anippe ducked her chin, speechless.

So the rumors were true. Master Sebak had ordered patrols only in the unskilled village. But how had Anippe discovered Puah's pregnancy? Even Mered's linen workers were only now discovering she was expecting.

"We're very thankful, Amira." Puah leaned forward, capturing Anippe's gaze. "I hope someday to be as helpful when you need my service."

Sebak's eyebrows shot up, and he slid his arm around his wife's waist.

"Perhaps the gods arranged our meeting today, Puah. Anippe thinks it's too early to be sure, but I may have an heir by harvest."

Puah's color turned to limestone gray. She tried to swallow several times before answering. "You must be very pleased."

Sebak was utterly ecstatic, seeming oblivious to Puah's discomfort. "When should you examine her to be sure there's a child? How should she proceed? Should she rest more? Eat certain foods?"

Mered noted veiled fury in Anippe's eyes and interceded before she exploded. "Perhaps Puah could visit the villa and discuss the ways of women with the amira later." Placing his arm around Puah, he tried to comfort while lightening the mood. "Master Sebak and I could stomach talk of war and livestock better than the stories Puah tells me after a birth."

Both men chuckled, while the women stewed in their separate pots. Mered had no idea what trouble boiled between them. Surely Puah would tell him if it was serious.

Puah stopped abruptly, causing the sea of candle-toting worshipers to flow around the two couples. "If the amira is pregnant, Master Sebak, how should Shiphrah and I send news to you? Will anyone know your whereabouts?"

Anippe turned her back, covering her face. Sebak's joy fled, and Mered sensed this had been a topic already discussed by the newlyweds. A topic of great pain.

"No one in Egypt can know my location—at least, not right now. Perhaps later. Perhaps when . . ." Shaking his head, the master turned to embrace his wife. Whispering, coaxing, he kissed her forehead and drew her into an embrace so tender, Mered felt like an intruder.

Whatever faults Anippe had, she had quenched the loneliness in Master Sebak's heart and loved him well. For this alone, Mered would stem his disdain and serve her faithfully. "What about the messenger that came yesterday to deliver your orders from General Horemheb? Could he become your designated courier to and from Avaris?"

Anippe's head popped up from Sebak's consuming embrace, and she stared at him with doleful eyes. "Surely Abbi Horem could assign one messenger to carry news to all Delta estates. That messenger could check for personal up-dates from Mered before leaving Avaris." She stroked his cheek. "Please, Sebak. No one would have to know."

Mered's heart twisted. *No one would have to know.* More deception.

"You must promise never to ask my location, Anippe." Sebak held her shoulders. "I will not risk lives for the sake of a child."

Anippe laid her head on Sebak's chest and glared at Puah. "Nor would I willingly risk a life for the sake of a child."

Confused, Mered looked to his wife for answers, but Puah's head was bowed, her fingers laced into white-knuckled fists. Anippe had spoken a hidden message, but what? She was angry with Puah, but why?

A meaty hand clamped down on Mered's shoulder. "It's a worthy sugges-tion, Mered." Sebak whirled him around, and they resumed their walk toward the quay. "I'm sure when General Horemheb hears he has a grandchild on the way, he'll be happy to spare one messenger to exchange that and other vital news with the Delta."

11

The Lord saw how great the wickedness of the human race had become on the earth, and that every inclination of the thoughts of the human heart was only evil all the time. . . . So God said to Noah, . . . "Make yourself an ark."

GENESIS 6:5,13–14

A nippe lay on her bed, waiting for Ankhe to bring her midday meal. Sebak had been gone for two days, and she'd left the chamber only once—to find Ankhe when she didn't answer the chime. Anippe rolled off the bed and lumbered into the sitting room, spying the new water clock that had been delivered soon after Sebak's skiff sailed from the quay.

Anippe dipped her finger in the slender-mouthed vase, barely skimming the water's surface. Her only visitor each day was a priest of Seth, who tended the clock. The temple of the patron Ramessid god was housed at Qantir but shared by both estates. Avaris focused on production rather than religion and boasted a thriving bakery, brewery, oil press, winery, linen shop, metal shop, ceramic shop, and a dozen other skill-based workhouses. Qantir, according to Sebak, housed a temple among other pomp and fluff.

A veritable army of Sethite priests filled every water-clock vase on both estates at precisely the same time each day. A small hole in the bottom of each vase slowly released a small amount of water by which one could track the hours of the day. Anippe examined the level of the water—her only proof that time at Avaris did not stand still.

She suspected the priests' regular visits to her chamber served a dual purpose since the water clock appeared the day after Sebak's departure. The priests presented regular offerings to the dread god of darkness, and they no doubt expected a frightened young widow, now alone in her villa, to increase her offerings.

Had they forgotten she was General Horemheb's daughter? They would receive their monthly allowance of gold and grain and no more.

Days were endless without Sebak, and nights were torture. Already the sound of his laughter and the memory of his touch were fading. When the chief laundress attempted to wash her bed sheets, Anippe chased her out of the chamber with Sebak's dagger. One good scrubbing with natron, and her husband's musky, masculine scent would be lost forever. No. She would wrap herself in his sheets and shirts and memories until he returned to her.

A quick knock preceded the cedar door's opening. Ankhe entered without permission—again. She placed a fruit-laden tray on the low-lying table and poured two glasses of date beer—a sweet nectar that had rounded Ankhe's figure considerably. "I'm glad to see you're out of bed. Life does not end because one man goes to war. People are asking if you're with child."

"What? Why would they ask such a thing?"

"Sebak may or may not have mentioned the possibility before he left. Regardless, wagging tongues like to paint pictures, and Avaris is a mural."

"And what strokes are you adding with your brush, sister?"

"I tell them they'll find out soon enough."

Anippe stomped back toward her bedchamber, shouting over her shoulder. "I suppose we'll all find out soon enough."

"But you must stay out of that bed. If you're with child, you need the exercise. If you're not, let's go down to the Nile and enjoy these first days of inundation. The water has reached the first mark on the water gauge, deep enough to bathe."

But Anippe didn't care about the Nile or water gauges. She had the bed in her sights, though the sun still hung low in the east, and she was ready for a nap.

A stain on the bed stopped her.

Ankhe, running to catch up, nearly knocked her over. "What? What's wrong?" She peered around Anippe's shoulder. "Well, I guess you're not with child after all."

Anippe could only stare, thoughts conflicted, emotions raging. She wasn't pregnant—was that good or bad? It was good, definitely good. So why was she crying? She wiped a stray tear from her cheek and tried to stem the tide—to no avail.

Ankhe stood before her, hands planted on her hips. "I thought you'd be happy. All I've heard since the day after your wedding is 'I don't want a baby. I'm terrified of birth.'" She pointed to the blood-stained sheet. "The gods heard your prayer."

"There's a difference between not wanting a baby and not wanting to give birth, Ankhe." The truth was, the moment Anippe realized she might never have a baby, she wanted one all the more. "Didn't you see how excited Sebak was when he left, believing I might be carrying his heir?"

Ankhe's smile sent a chill down Anippe's spine. "Yes, and I wish I could be the one to tell him he has no heir—and he never will."

"How can you hate him, Ankhe? He's been kind to you these past months."

"I hate anyone who tries to take you from me, Anippe. You are mine." Her expression grew dark. "You'll always be mine." Without awaiting a reply, she walked toward the bed to strip the sheets.

Anippe swallowed the lump in her throat, unsure how to respond to a swift and unfamiliar fear. Something in Ankhe was changing, something gray becoming black. How could Anippe control Ankhe's dark moods—protect her but also keep her from hurting others? And how could Anippe tell Sebak he had no heir? She looked again at the blood-stained sheet, felt the ache of her empty arms. *Lady Hathor, goddess of love, how do I keep my husband's love and fill my longing for a child without bowing to Tawaret, the awful goddess of childbirth?*

With arms full of dirty bed sheets, Ankhe crossed the room toward the Hathor chime to call for the estate laundress.

"Stop," Anippe said. "We're not washing those sheets." Confused, Ankhe dropped the sheets on the floor, ready to argue, but Anippe silenced her with a raised hand. "We'll tear the sheets into the rags I need this month, but mention it to no one. I'm staying in my chamber. Let the wagging tongues of Avaris keep wondering if their amira is with child."

Mered had watched every station of the moon through the single window of their one-room home, trying to erase the images of dead infants floating in the Nile. Master Sebak had been gone a week, long enough for Ramessid guards to sweep through the unskilled camp, sending countless infants to their watery graves. Did they kill only males? Who would dare challenge the guards without Master Sebak here to protect them?

As if the images in his mind weren't terror enough, Mered had listened to their neighbor's three-month-old son howl incessantly through the night. Jochebed had given birth only days after King Tut's edict and had successfully hidden their son all these weeks. Thanks be to El-Shaddai, the hyenas and jackals had howled all night with him, masking his cries. But dawn's glow would send night beasts to their dens. How would Jochebed and her husband, Amram, hide their wailing child then?

"I think he's quieting down." Puah reached for Mered's hand and drew it to her trembling lips in the predawn darkness. "Perhaps he's worn himself out and will sleep all day. I don't know how Jochebed can continue weaving baskets and keep the baby hidden. Miriam has been helpful, but with the inundation floods beginning, Miriam must help dig canals in the fields—"

The all-too-familiar screaming swelled, and Mered saw lamplight illumine a silhouette in the curtained doorway.

"Mered? Puah? Are you awake?" Jochebed's voice was a desperate whisper from the adjoining rooms.

Mered tugged Puah close. "We'd have to be dead to sleep through that."

"Yes, Jochebed." Puah shoved him and climbed off their mat to meet her friend at the doorway. "What do you think is troubling him?"

Mered sat up, evidently a sign to the rest of the family they could enter. Amram stumbled in, bleary-eyed. Daughter Miriam and little Aaron followed close behind him.

Content to let the women handle the baby, Mered left the sleeping mat and stirred the embers of the cook fire. "Who wants barley gruel?"

"Me. I'll help." Miriam was five or six, the perfect little mother. She went straight to Puah's sack of ground grain and measured out two clay cups for the pot. "Should I go to the river for fresh water?"

Mered chuckled at her eagerness. "Let's not visit the crocodiles yet. They don't go to sleep until the sun rises."

She busied her little hands, seeming oblivious to her newest brother's piercing cries.

Mered added more dung chips to the fire, building the flame, before hanging the pot of water-soaked grain over the spit. The baby's screams intensified, raising the hairs on the back of Mered's neck. He whirled on the adults huddled behind him. "Can't anything be done for the boy?"

Poor Jochebed's face twisted, and a torrent of tears fell from her eyes. Puah set her fists at her hips and turned on Mered like a hungry jackal.

"Jochebed and Amram have kept this child hidden for three months without a peep from that baby boy. And you demand silence when he has one night—one night—of torturous pain?" Her fury moved him back three steps. "Look at him, Mered. Can't you see him pulling his little legs up? His belly hurts. Why don't *you* do something for the boy?" She turned on her heel and marched back to comfort the grieving mother.

Amram looked his direction with a sympathetic gaze that said, *"You'll learn, son."*

"He's right. Mered's right." Jochebed sat in their lone chair, her own tears anointing the crying child. "We can't keep him any longer. The Ramessids finished at the unskilled camp yesterday. They're sure to come here since Master Sebak lef—" She shook her head, unable to voice the truth they all knew.

Amram took the boy from his mother, his gnarled hands trembling as he cradled the child in the crook of his arm. Jochebed was Amram's second wife. He was well past the age of most fathers, but these were his first children.

Jochebed offered Amram the baby's little clay waste pot, always kept close at hand, but he refused it. Flustered, she sputtered and fussed. "Well, at least cover him with this piece of cloth, or he'll anoint you without warning."

The boy screamed louder in the unfamiliar arms of his father. Amram, like most Hebrew men, left babies to be raised by their mothers.

"El-Shaddai has not left me alive this long that I should witness my son's murder. Jochebed, get one of your baskets." In his fifth decade, Amram knew his own mind, and he was one of the finest metal workers in the villa. The old man's hands were as steady on gold and silver as his heart was on El-Shaddai. When his wife stood gawking, he raised his bristly gray eyebrow. "Get a papyrus basket, wife—one with a lid."

Confused, the others waited in silence, the baby's hoarse cries the only sound. Jochebed disappeared behind the dividing curtain into their adjoining rooms, and within moments returned with a sturdy papyrus basket—handles on each side and a lid.

She tentatively placed it on the table but stood between it and her husband. "What do you intend to do with our child, husband?"

Amram's eyes pooled with tears. Little Aaron and Miriam, seeming to sense the tension, clung to their father's legs. Amram lifted his face toward heaven and closed his eyes, sending tears streaming into his long gray beard. "When El-Shaddai saw that every inclination of the human heart was only evil all the time, He said to Noah, 'Build an ark coated with pitch, to sail on the floodwaters, and I will save you and your family with you.'"

Mered felt a shiver skitter up his spine and heard Jochebed gasp. *Floodwaters.* The Nile began flooding the day Sebak left. Surely, Amram didn't intend to make an ark of that basket and . . .

Silence. Complete, throbbing silence. The babe was still for the first time in hours, eyes heavy with sleep in his father's arms. Jochebed buried her face in her hands and wept.

It had been four hundred years since God's presence had moved among the tribes of Israel, but in the single room of this mud-brick long house, El-Shaddai had spoken—by silencing a baby's cries.

Even the children recognized something special was about to happen. Miriam and Aaron stood with wide eyes, staring at their little brother.

"Will he build an ark like Noah?" Miriam whispered.

Amram tried to answer, but his cheeks quaked with barely controlled emotion. Puah muffled her sobs in Mered's chest as he looked into the children's innocent faces.

"No, Miriam," Mered said. "This basket will be your little brother's ark. We must cover it with pitch so it will float, and the Nile will be the floodwaters that carry him to safety."

He looked up at Amram and Jochebed, grasping at hope. "Maybe a traveling merchant will find him, or perhaps he'll sail all the way to a port on the Great Sea." If God could stop a baby's cry, surely He could steer a pitch-coated basket.

Miriam's little brow furrowed, red lips in a pout. "Well, we'd better wait till the sun rises to put him in the river—make sure the crocodiles are sleeping."

If the thought wasn't so terrifying, Mered might have applauded her quick wit. Crocodiles. Hippos. Sea snakes. These were only the animal dangers. What about the Nile currents? Ship traffic? And the most obvious hindrance—Ramessid lookouts stationed at estates and military fortresses along every shore.

Amram gathered Jochebed under his free arm, still holding his sleeping babe tenderly. Huddled together as a family for the last time, they talked quietly, planned, even laughed.

Mered's heart broke. He and Puah returned to their sleeping mat, sitting with their backs against the outer wall, the low light of dawn streaming through the window above them. Mered tucked his wife against his side and rested his cheek atop her head. "What will we do if our baby is a boy, my love?"

Puah remained silent for several heartbeats, but when she looked up, tears filled her eyes. "Perhaps our son, too, will float away in an ark to a faraway land and live a healthy, happy life."

"Perhaps." Mered pulled her close again, wishing he could believe it—praying their own child was a girl.

Anippe discovered the true benefits of being an amira during the days of her red flow. Remaining sequestered in her spacious chamber and private courtyard, she ordered her Hebrews to connect a walkway and bathhouse to one of the canals branching off the Nile. During the inundation, the Delta became an oversoaked cloth with every wrinkle and crease filled with life-giving water. The Avaris villa and its buildings stood on high ground, but the cool, soothing Nile rose to Anippe's threshold like a welcome suitor.

The constant chanting of Hebrew slaves at work had nearly driven her mad, but Anippe watched from her sitting room, cloaked in shadows, while the slaves finished the last tiles on the walkway and placed pillows in the bath-house. Even in her foul humor, she recognized the favor of the gods. The slaves were finishing now—the walkway and private bathhouse complete on the very day she would present her cleansing offering to Lady Hathor.

Perhaps Ummi Amenia had been right all these years, lauding the impor-tance of Lady Hathor's cleansing ceremony. *"After your days of seclusion, you must thank Lady Hathor, goddess of love, for the end of your red flow and then ask that she continue to flow through you—now with love for another."*

"But my lover is gone," Anippe whispered to no one. "Will Sebak still love me when he no longer thinks I bear his child?"

Puah's herb bundles accused Anippe from her embroidery basket. She'd hidden them there with the certainty that her strong soldier would never shuf-fle through needles and thread. Had she been wrong to deceive him? Surely her kind and gentle husband would never have demanded she bear a child despite her fear. Or would he? *"You need only be honorable, faithful, and loving to our children."* Clearly, his love hinged on her childbearing.

A quick knock, and her chamber door was flung open. Ankhe bent her knees to enter, balancing a large basket on her head with one hand, carrying a silver tray with the other.

Fruit, cucumbers, and an amphora of wine precariously slid to the edge of the tray. "Take this," Ankhe said. Anippe jumped to obey, and Ankhe lowered the basket, showcasing its contents. "Three sacks of grain, two bundles of dried figs, thirteen raisin cakes, three hins of barley beer. The priests of Seth will be furious that we're sending a portion of their offering to Lady Hathor's temple in Dendara."

Anippe set the tray aside, glaring at her sister. "The priests receive an offering—meaning I offer it to them. Besides, what can they do to me? Refuse to fill my water clock?"

She rolled her eyes, and Ankhe giggled—an unusual sound, like a rat's sneeze.

Anippe studied her. "Why are you so happy?"

Sobering, Ankhe plucked a date from the fruit tray and began nibbling. "I'm glad you're not pregnant, and I'm happy for a private bath. Those stupid Hebrew house slaves try to make me feel like one of them, but I'm not. I'm Pharaoh's sister." Her passion rose with each word, bulging her neck veins.

An uncomfortable silence fell between them.

"I'm sorry, Ankhe."

Her sister lifted stormy eyes. "I shouldn't have to be your handmaid, Anippe. You could change this."

"I can't. What if Tut found out I released you against his command? We'd both be punished—perhaps lose our lives." Did she believe that, or was she as guilty as the others of pressing Ankhe under her thumb? Regret seized her, and words slipped out before she considered their impact. "What would you do if you were no longer my handmaid?"

Ankhe's eyes brightened. "I would lounge by the river with you. We could talk of travel and marriage, and we could curse the old hens at Gurob."

Pity surged when Anippe heard Ankhe's dream world. "How can we speak of travel when we've only been to Memphis and Gurob? How can we speak of marriage when I've known a husband for three months and you've never married?" She reached for Ankhe's hand. "Even as amira, I must be productive. Wouldn't you like to spin or weave? Maybe work in the gardens? Let's find something you enjoy but maintain the title of handmaid should Abbi Horem or Sebak return from battle unexpectedly."

Ankhe removed her hand from Anippe's grasp and stared into the distance. Anippe waited, hoping for some kind of response—confirmation, disappointment, even a temper tantrum. Silence stretched into loneliness.

Finally, Ankhe painted on a smile and assumed a pleasant air. "Let's take our bath. You bring the scented oils for the ritual. I'll bring the fruit and wine."

Anippe watched her go, a sense of dread creeping through her. Ankhe had stored up too much anger in her short life. If a spark ever caught fire, her rage might be unquenchable.

12

*Then Pharaoh's daughter went down to the Nile
to bathe, and . . . saw the basket among the reeds
and sent her female slave to get it.*

—EXODUS 2:5

Mered made sure his morning duties took him near the river. He'd
check the retting process of the flax—ensuring his workers removed
every seed head with rippling combs before stalks were soaked. Avaris flax was
planted, harvested, processed, and spun in shifts so that every step of the pro-
cedure was occurring at all times. A delicate process, to be sure, but not nearly
as delicate as the one he'd witnessed this morning before leaving for the day's
work.

Jochebed had chosen her best papyrus basket, large enough to carry her
son. She and Amram coated it with tar and pitch to make it seaworthy, as God
had instructed Noah to coat the ark generations before. They wrapped the
babe in specially woven red-white-and-black-striped cloth to represent the
Levites—their clan of Jacob's descendants.

Amram had gathered them all together and pronounced his blessing: "Let
this child be wrapped in the promise of Israel. He is a son of Levites, son of
Israel, the son of Isaac, the son of our father Abraham. We place him in this ark
on the floodwaters—in the hands of God Almighty."

Jochebed had then placed the basket under one arm and taken Miriam by
the hand. She had planned to set the basket afloat near the craftsmen's village,
where it would float past Qantir and to the Great Sea, but Mered's flax harvest-
ers had already begun work along the shoreline—their slave drivers too alert to
set Jochebed's basket a sail. Mered had watched the weary mother search for a

secluded spot, walking, walking, walking . . . until she passed the quay. Miriam followed her, pretending to help harvest reeds for basket making.

Mered had lost sight of them in the bulrushes south of the villa. He was certain Jochebed and Miriam could invent an excuse for their presence near the villa, but he'd searched in vain for a floating pitch-covered basket on the Nile. *Please, El-Shaddai, protect the babe who must now sail past Avaris and Qantir to the Great Sea.*

The sound of wooden mallets hitting stone brought Mered back to the moment. Glancing upriver, he noticed additional guards posted near the amira's new privacy wall. Hebrew laborers had gossiped about the secluded bathhouse connected to the master's private chambers. No one had seen the amira since Master Sebak left—not even the workers. Some said her mind was addled. Some said she suffered morning sickness and would birth a Ramessid heir before harvest. Mered simply prayed her guards didn't notice a lone papyrus basket floating by.

He walked along the riverbank, checking water gauges for his report to the king's tax collectors. Yet all the while he kept hoping to see the small basket sailing past. *Oh please, El-Shaddai, hide the small vessel from Ramessid guards and reveal it to traveling merchants or foreign royalty.* If El-Shaddai could create the heavens and the earth, if He could give Abraham a son at age one hundred, surely He could shelter a tiny ark with such precious cargo.

Mered greeted the villa slaves as he walked among his linen workers along the shore. House slaves were seldom released to visit their families in the skilled or unskilled camps, so on days like this, Mered tried to station family members close to each other so they could at least complete their tasks side by side.

With his mind so thoroughly distracted, he meandered too close to the bulrushes and planted his left sandal in the deep black mud. He bent to retrieve the mired sandal and glimpsed a disturbance at the corner of Anippe's private wall.

"Lord God, no."

It was little Miriam. Guards running toward her and shouting. Ankhe appeared from behind the new privacy wall and yanked the girl into seclusion, leaving the guards stunned—and retreating back to the shore.

"Get out!" Ankhe screamed at the guards. "This is the amira's private bath-house, and no one comes past this wall. You'll feel your captain's strap if you come a step farther."

"But the girl." One of the Ramessids reached for the little Hebrew's arm, and Ankhe reached up and slapped him. Startled—then enraged—the soldier drew back his fist.

"Hit Pharaoh's sister and die, Ramessid."

The guard hesitated. "What do you mean '*Pharaoh's sister*'?"

"I am King Tut's and Amira Anippe's sister—fallen out of favor—but I assure you they will feed you to the crocodiles if you lay a hand on me."

Anippe watched from the edge of the wall, staying hidden in the bul-rushes. Ankhe had more courage than a hundred Ramessid soldiers.

The big guard shoved Ankhe. "Get behind the wall and take the Hebrew brat to Pharaoh's real sister." He trudged toward shore in the waist-high water, and called over his shoulder, "The next Hebrew we keep for sport."

Ankhe spit at his back and grabbed the little girl's arm to keep her head above water.

Anippe steadied the basket and moved back toward the bathhouse, giving Ankhe room to come around the privacy wall and introduce their little in-truder. She heard a baby's cry from inside the basket and peeked inside.

Before she could inquire of the girl as to the basket's contents, she heard Ankhe scolding her. "Why are you playing in the bulrushes? Don't you know you could be eaten by crocodiles? Or worse, attacked by those soldiers?"

"Ankhe, she's frightened enough without your screaming. Bring her over here." The girl had obviously followed the basket.

Anippe removed the lid for more than a peek. Black ringlets covered the baby's head. Pink cheeks and gums glistened as he wailed his disapproval. Real tears rolled from tightly pressed lashes, and she nearly wept with him.

"It's a Hebrew boy, Anippe." Ankhe's flat tone proclaimed more than the obvious.

A Hebrew male *infant*. He should have been cast into the Nile weeks ago.

Months ago. Shiphrah and Puah should have killed him. If Anippe was loyal to her brother, she should drown him right now.

Anippe discarded his rough-woven Hebrew cloth and placed his naked body next to hers. Skin to skin, he nestled into her heart—and his crying ceased. Cooing. Quiet. Peaceful. He snuggled into the bend of her neck, and she felt his warm breath, steady and strong.

Life in her hands. Given by the gods. Without birthing pain. But with its own kind of danger.

She squeezed her eyes closed. Could she keep him? Deceive the whole world? Abbi Horem's warning screamed in her memory, "*Your husband demands your loyalty, Anippe, as do I.*" But wasn't she being profoundly loyal to give Sebak an heir while eliminating her risk of childbirth? She would love this child and make him Sebak's heir. It was the will of the gods.

"No, Anippe." Ankhe's wary voice shattered Anippe's dream.

"What do you mean, *no*? Don't you see, Ankhe? Hapi, goddess of the Nile, has given us this gift. Our faithful offerings have finally produced some worth."

Ankhe's disbelief was mirrored by the little Hebrew girl's awe. She openly appraised Anippe's bare form. "You're so . . . so . . . smooth."

Her innocent comment loosened even Ankhe's pinched expression. Considering Hebrews were quite hairy by nature—even their women—a fully shaved Egyptian would seem quite a wonder. "I suppose I am smooth, aren't I?"

The girl nodded, riotous curls bobbing. Droplets of the Nile perched in her hair, remnants from Ankhe's splashing. The sun's rays made them glisten—as bright as the hope in her eyes. "Shall I get one of the Hebrew women to nurse the boy for you?" Her round brown eyes were identical to the baby's. She was probably his sister.

"You will not get a wet nurse." Ankhe shoved the girl aside and lunged for the baby, but an ummi's instincts emerge quickly.

With a stiff right arm, Anippe seized Ankhe's throat—while her baby rested peacefully near her heart. "The girl asked *me* the question." Seeing her sister's mouth gape but draw no air, Anippe released her and turned to the little Hebrew. "Yes, go. Ask Puah the midwife to accompany you and a wet nurse to the villa. Do you know Puah?"

The little girl nodded and smiled, revealing two missing front teeth.

"All right. Bring Puah to the villa, but don't tell anyone why you've come. Ankhe will meet you at the main entrance."

Without hesitation, the little girl splashed into the bulrushes, ready to face the guards again if she must. "Wait," Anippe shouted. "Not that way. You may leave through my chamber. There is a big guard named Nassor beyond the door. He won't hurt you if you tell him the amira is expecting you to return with the midwife."

"Yes, Amira." She bounced out of the water, hurrying up the path.

Anippe returned her attention to Ankhe—who stood like a withered lily, rubbing the red marks on her throat. "Look at me, Ankhe."

Ankhe raised her gaze, jaw flexed, chin defiant. "Yes, Amira? How may your lowly handmaid serve you?" Her tone conveyed anything but service.

"You will rejoice with me that the Nile god, Hapi, gave me this child. I am Anippe, *daughter of the Nile,* and now the Nile has given me a son." She studied the perfect babe in her arms. "You will become Sebak's heir, little one, and I will be the Amira of Avaris forever."

"But that's not who you are." Ankhe's cheeks bloomed bright red. "You're Meryetaten-tasherit, firstborn daughter of Kiya, a trick of the Great Wife Nefertiti to protect her daughter. You're a mockery, a lie."

"No, Ankhe. That's who I was." The infant fussed, sensing her tension. Anippe began to sway, calming him and herself. "Now I am this boy's ummi."

"If you keep this child, our brother will kill it—and then kill you."

"Our brother will never know. Neither will Sebak or any of our house slaves. Only you, me, and three Hebrews."

"How do you know the Hebrews won't betray you when Sebak returns?"

"The slaves don't want this child murdered any more than I do. Who do you think placed him in this basket? They've hidden him for months—look at him. He's not a newborn."

Ankhe smiled like a hungry jackal. "And why do you think they set him adrift today, Amira?"

Anippe had no answer. Why would they place a child in crocodile-infested waters when they'd successfully hidden him for so long? Her confusion fed her sister's triumph.

"The Ramessids swept dead-man's land last week, and this week they begin inspecting the Hebrew craftsmen's houses." Ankhe sneered. "Can't you smell the rot?"

"Rot? What are you talking—" The realization nearly buckled Anippe's knees. She'd smelled decay but assumed it came from the kitchens or rotting animals. Looking at the water surrounding her, she panicked and started to rush toward shore.

"Anippe, Anippe, don't worry." Ankhe strolled toward the bathhouse, arriving on shore with the boy's basket in tow. "The river's floods swept the bodies downstream quickly. I haven't seen one since yesterday."

Anippe covered a sob and tried to soothe the baby, who was crying again after her mad dash toward shore. She looked at Ankhe's cool demeanor. Was she a monster? How could she speak so casually of such horror? "What's dead-man's land?"

Ankhe turned and pointed to the hill overlooking the villa. "It's that huge plateau above us, where most of your Hebrew slaves are worked to death by numbskull Ramessid guards. The unskilled slaves live and work up there in the fields and mud pits. Most die before they're forty—from little food and much abuse."

"How do you know all this, Ankhe?" Anippe's gentle sway had calmed the babe, but her calm fled when she saw a slow, sinister grin crease Ankhe's lips.

"I know this because I eat and sleep with house slaves, but my living arrangement is about to change. Isn't it, sister?" She reached out to touch the baby's curly hair, but Anippe pulled him away. Ankhe's expression turned cold. "I refuse to keep your secret unless . . ."

Anippe knew what Ankhe wanted. "I already told you, I can't free you. Tut specifically ordered you into servitude. We would both be punished if anyone discovered I'd restored your royal status."

Ankhe didn't flinch. "I will become your son's tutor. It's not spinning or weaving, but it's *productive*. And I'll live in a chamber beside you instead of the servant's quarters." She stepped toward the babe again, a silent threat that moved Anippe back. "These are not requests. This is the price of my silence."

Anippe laid her cheek against the baby's downy-soft hair. He was so warm, so sweet, so alive. Sebak needed an heir. She needed a baby. Most important of all, this baby would likely die if she sent him back to the Hebrews. She glanced at Ankhe again, who still waited for her answer. Ankhe was selfish and impulsive, but she'd never hurt anyone. Perhaps she would enjoy caring for a child.

"It's settled then," Anippe said. "I'll find a different handmaid, and you'll begin helping me raise my son. When he's ready, you'll be responsible to teach him as we were taught by Tut's tutors."

Genuine surprise stole Ankhe's smug expression. "How will we convince people he's Sebak's child? Your husband has been gone only a week, and this baby is already months old."

"You said the servants already think I'm pregnant. I'll stay in my chamber, courtyard, and bathhouse until just before harvest. We'll say I'm overwhelmed with nausea at the slightest odor, or I'm too vain to be seen with a rotund figure. Let their wagging tongues paint whatever picture they like."

"But in six months that boy will look even less like a newborn—and even as he grows, he'll always be taller, bigger, stronger than his age should allow."

Anippe looked down at the curly headed babe, whose arms were already pudgy and healthy. "His abbi Sebak is taller, bigger, and stronger than most men." She wrapped his chubby hand around her finger and cast a pleading gaze at her sister. "Ankhe, if we can keep his identity hidden for three or four years while he's with his wet nurse—"

"Three or four years, Anippe? Where will you hide him for three or four years?" Her voice squeaked, signs of an oncoming tantrum. "If you send him back to the Hebrew camp, the Ramessids will find him, and if you move him into the villa, everyone will know you have a baby—a week after you looked thin and beautiful, walking to the quay with your husband for the Feast of Lotus." Her last words were delivered on a shout, and Anippe looked right and left, wondering how many dozens of slaves and guards heard her rant.

"I assume by your objections you'd rather continue as my handmaid and forget this ridiculous scheme?"

Ankhe's eyes narrowed, and she ground her words through clenched teeth. "No. I would rather be your son's tutor."

"Good." Anippe tugged her finger away from the baby's grasp and reached for Ankhe's hand. "Come, sit with me on the cushions. Bring the baby's basket."

Reluctantly, Ankhe followed, dragging the dripping basket behind her. Her groaning drowned out the Nile's rushing waters as they settled beneath the three-sided bathhouse.

"We're going to make this work, Ankhe. Your rant gave me an idea."

"I'm glad I could serve you, Amira."

Anippe met her sister's mocking with patient calm. "We could make the wet nurse a house slave and move her into the chamber beside mine. Remove her from everyone and everything she knows while she nurses my son for three or four years."

Ankhe lifted a skeptical brow but didn't immediately refuse. Progress. "What if the war ends and Sebak returns to find a Hebrew child as his heir?"

Anippe traced the damp curls on the baby's head, considering her answer carefully. "You know many children don't survive their first three years, Ankhe. And who knows how long the war will go on?" She swallowed the lump in her throat, refusing to imagine the worst for her son or her husband. "I won't send word of my pregnancy to Sebak until we know how the war is going. I just think this baby is destined by the gods to be mine." Lost in the deep pools of his brown eyes, Anippe caressed his cheek and counted his fingers and toes.

"Babies cry. What if he cries?" Ankhe reached over to tickle his belly.

"I've heard infants crying in the villa. I know some of the house slaves have babies."

Ankhe sighed. "Three, and they're exasperating."

"Perfect. We'll move the wet nurse today, and Puah can visit me regularly to give the appearance I'm under a midwife's care." She hugged Ankhe, scrunching the baby, causing him to fuss. "Here, take him."

Thrusting the babe into Ankhe's arms was pure genius. Anippe could see the walls around her sister's heart crumble as his little hands reached for the shiny gold beads at the ends of her braids. The hard creases in Ankhe's forehead relaxed, and her pinched expression eased to—well, almost a smile.

"Perhaps by the time Sebak returns from battle, he'll see what a fine job you're doing as his son's tutor and make a marriage match for you with a Ramessid soldier." The words were out before Anippe had calculated their impact.

Ankhe's eyes glistened, and her cheeks shaded pink. "Do you think Sebak would really make a match for me?"

Heart thudding like chariot horses, Anippe forced a smile, hoping to instill more confidence than she felt. "Of course, he would. You're my sister."

Seeming satisfied, Ankhe began jabbering at the baby, fawning and cooing like a doting aunt.

Anippe tried to steady her breathing, panicked by the magnitude of her increasing deceptions. *Oh mighty Hapi, protect this gift of life offered up from the Nile, for if my deceptions are discovered, not even Pharaoh will protect me.*

13

The name of Amram's wife was Jochebed, a
descendant of Levi, who was born to the Levites
in Egypt.

—NUMBERS 26:59

Too weary to lift his arms, Mered braced his elbows on his desk and lowered his head to remove the white linen wrap he wore. He'd endured a whole day's summer sun to watch the amira's private wall but never saw little Miriam escape. Had Ankhe taken her to the amira? Turned the girl over to chamber guards? He pressed his sweat-soaked linen against weepy eyes, grieving the precious child who'd helped him cook gruel this morning.

"Linen keeper, why aren't you working?" The estate foreman's voice cut through him like a knife.

Startled, Mered stood, knocking over his stool. "I've supervised my outdoor slaves all day." He nodded toward the fading sunlight. "I needed to check some figures before going home." Why was the foreman here anyway? Ramessids never invaded his shop.

"Well, you're not going home yet. The amira sent me to tell you she wants two papyrus scrolls so she can draw designs for your weavers." Mered noted crimson rising on the foreman's neck and kept a wary eye on his hand, which fidgeted with the cudgel on his belt. "I don't know why I'm suddenly the amira's errand boy, but you've been told."

Mered bowed promptly. "I'll deliver the scrolls tonight—immediately." He heard the man's sandals retreat and then raised his head to watch him waddle from the shop. Short and wide, the estate foreman likely hadn't walked from one side of Avaris to the other in years. He was most definitely not an errand boy.

So why send him? And what stirred the amira's sudden interest in design?

Mered rubbed the confusion from his weary face and grabbed two blank scrolls. He didn't care about the amira or the foreman. He cared only about getting home to Puah and checking on Miriam's parents. They'd surely discovered the child missing by now, and perhaps he could offer some details of her disappearance—though his news would not be comforting.

"Good night, all." He waved to the night workers as he left. They'd be towing, hackling, and roving flax fibers in the dimly lit workshop till morning, when the weavers and bead workers returned to resume their intricate projects in daylight.

His sandals tapped on the tiled pathways between buildings as Mered hustled to complete the errand and walk home before dark. Trekking down the craftsmen's village hill at dusk was even more dangerous during inundation. Crocodiles sought higher ground when the rising Nile left its banks, and mother crocs were especially protective of their newly hatched young.

Passing through the garden, Mered noticed the blue lotus blooms already beginning to close for their night's slumber. Like skilled craftsmen, they'd revive at dawn, warmed by the sun's strong rays, to share their elegant beauty. Mered inhaled deeply, capturing a whiff of their lingering fragrance.

He turned down the long hallway leading to the villa's private chambers, a worrisome thought only now starting to bloom. What if the amira's summons was a trap? Mered's feet slowed as his heartbeat quickened. And why had she sent the estate foreman with the message?

Stopping short of the residence hallways, Mered stared at the two blank papyrus scrolls in his hands, plagued by a more practical question. Did she even have a scribe's set of reeds and pigment to write with?

He measured the fading rays of sunlight in the hallway's high windows. Frustration rose as the sun fell. He must get home to explain about Miriam.

A few more hurried steps carried him to Master Sebak's private chamber. Ramessid guards glared at him as if he was a pesky rat in the granary.

He held up the scrolls. "I'm delivering these to the amira."

The largest guard pounded his sword hilt on the amira's door, and the handmaid Ankhe peeked through a narrow opening. "It's about time you got here, linen keeper. Come in." She opened the door wider, revealing a dimly lit chamber.

Mered remained firmly rooted in the hall, extending the scrolls across the threshold. "I've no need to see the amira. You may give her these scrolls—"

The guard grabbed the back of his neck and shoved him through the door. Mered stumbled in behind Ankhe, his eyes adjusting to the darkness. Tapestries hung like curtains across the open-air courtyard, making the few lamps in the master's chamber seem like stars in a midnight sky.

"Follow me." The amira's sister walked toward the partitioned bedchamber, but Mered held his ground.

"I'll leave the scrolls on the table and go." He bent to deposit them on the low-lying table, refusing to be lured any further into whatever game the amira—or her sister—might be playing.

"Mered? Bring the scrolls into the bedchamber." Puah's voice. Why was his wife in the amira's bedchamber?

Rushing past the lamp-toting sister, Mered breached the partition to find his wife standing over Anippe, who looked pink-cheeked and healthy on her puffy mattress. Fire stirred in his belly, and he threw the papyrus on the bed. "Here are your scrolls, Amira. May I take my wife and go?" Mered reached for Puah's hand, which she offered, but then she ducked her head.

Anippe's kind expression turned cold. She reached for the blank scrolls—intentionally slowly—and unrolled the first, then reached for the second. She was in no hurry to answer a slave.

Anippe peered around Mered, searching in the dim light behind him. "Ankhe, why don't you tell the linen keeper why I summoned him?"

He'd rather know what happened to Miriam. He'd rather hear that the amira's deceptive ways were behind her.

Instead, he glared at Anippe while the handmaid spoke. "Master Sebak trusted you, and my sister thought she'd bring you into her confidence. She is with child, and your wife will care for her in the months leading to the delivery—but Anippe will remain sequestered in her private chambers."

Mered's shoulders sagged, his anger doused with shame. Master Sebak's young bride had turned to him for support, and he'd failed her—failed Sebak. *El-Shaddai, forgive me.*

Anippe cast the scrolls across the bed, splayed open. "I wanted to draw designs since I won't visit the linen shop until after Sebak's heir is born." Her fiery gaze burned a hole in him. "Perhaps it was an inconvenience for you to bring the scrolls. Perhaps another Hebrew would manage the linen shop more efficiently."

On his knees before her last word was spoken, Mered was shaken to the core. "Please, Amira, forgive me. I'm not myself. I was in a hurry to get home tonight because I saw my little friend Miriam disappear behind your private wall today. Her mother, Jochebed, is a dear friend—"

"You saw Miriam enter my bathhouse?" Anippe's anxious tone stopped Mered's pleading.

He watched the three women exchange concerned glances, feeding his dread. "Please, can you tell me what happened to the girl?" he asked.

The amira's stare was a silent threat that lingered into awkwardness. "I'm taking the girl as a house slave," she said finally. "She pleased me."

Ankhe's eyes bulged. "Anippe, that's not what we discus—"

The amira silenced her with a lifted hand and addressed Mered again. "You, linen keeper, will return to your shop and work through the night for your insolence. Your wife, Puah, will bring the girl to the villa immediately."

Mered's heart raced. *Puah? Walking to the village alone at dusk?*

Anippe smiled like a jackal. "I'm not without mercy, Mered. Puah can bring Miriam's ummi to serve at the house as well. We'll find some use for the woman." Without warning, her expression turned to granite. "Now get out."

Anippe's heart was in her throat as Ankhe escorted Mered past the bedchamber partition to the door. It all made sense. The striking resemblance between Miriam's and the babe's eyes. Miriam returning with a wet nurse so quickly. Jochebed was Miriam's mother—and the baby's. Anippe rubbed her temples, doubts haunting her. What if Jochebed refused to give up her son at weaning time? And what about Mered—if he'd seen Miriam disappear behind the wall, had he seen the basket? He didn't mention it. Surely if he'd seen the basket, he would have inquired. He certainly wasn't shy about expressing his concerns. The chamber door slammed shut, and Puah jumped, reminding Anippe of her presence.

Ankhe appeared moments later. "Well, I think that went well. Puah didn't have to lie to her husband, and the estate foreman knows you're working on linen designs while sequestered."

She picked up a scroll and rolled it up, securing it with the leather tie. "Perhaps the household won't think their amira is completely mad."

Anippe heard Puah sniff and noticed the woman wiping her cheeks. Perhaps she'd been too hard on the midwife's husband. "Go get Jochebed and Miriam, Ankhe."

With an indignant snort, her sister marched out of the chamber to retrieve the baby, the wet nurse, and the girl who had been waiting in the bathhouse. Alone now with Puah, Anippe could explain her decision to keep Mered at the shop tonight.

"Thank you, Amira." Puah wiped away more tears, and Anippe's confusion mounted.

"Why are you thanking me?"

"You could have ordered me to return home with your secret and lie with my silence or lie outright to Mered." She sniffed, wiping her nose on a small piece of linen from her belt. "My husband can't abide deceit. At least now he knows, but I didn't tell the lie."

Anippe cringed at the woman's twisted gratitude. "I know I'm placing you in a difficult situation, Puah, but I'll reward you well if we succeed."

The midwife smiled through her tears. "I need no reward, Amira. I'm a slave. I do as I'm told."

Ankhe arrived holding Miriam's hand, and Jochebed followed, carrying the baby boy. Miriam bounced over to Puah, and Jochebed laid the babe in Anippe's arms.

"You're the boy's ummi, aren't you," Anippe said.

Crimson crept up Jochebed's neck. "I was his mother this morning, but you're his ummi now." She bowed and clasped her trembling hands.

Anippe traded a doubtful glance with Ankhe. Could they risk Jochebed's attachment? What if, after nursing him for three years, she tried to steal him away or worse—tried to reveal the truth?

"I should be going." Puah planted a kiss on Miriam's head.

Unaware that she was now Anippe's house slave, Miriam ran to her ummi Jochebed and clutched her waist. "I love you. Good-bye. I'll see you when you're done being a wet nurse."

Jochebed knelt and steadied Miriam's shoulders, an unnatural peace settling over them. "You be a good helper for Puah. Take care of your father and brother while I'm gone. When I come home, life will be as it has always been."

Somehow, the woman's words soothed Anippe's fears. "If you recognize this baby is truly *my* son, Jochebed, both you and Miriam may stay and serve in the villa."

Miriam clapped and bounced, and Jochebed let happy tears flow. "Thank you, Amira. Thank you."

Ankhe rolled her eyes. "How can they be happy about being prisoners until your ruse is over?"

Miriam ceased her celebration. "What's a prisoner?"

If Anippe wasn't holding her new son, she would have pitched a vase at Ankhe's head. She scooted to the edge of her bed and stood near the little girl, who had wide innocent eyes and lots of questions. "A prisoner is someone forced to stay somewhere they don't want to be."

"Like the Hebrews?"

Jochebed clamped a hand over her daughter's mouth. "No, Miriam." She bowed her head. "Please forgive her, Amira. Sometimes she doesn't think before she—"

"Miriam, you must learn to think before you speak." Anippe didn't want to be cross with the girl, but lives were at stake. "The baby from the basket is now my son, but no one can know I found him in the Nile. Do you understand? We must let everyone think I'm pregnant and that this baby came from my own body. You will stay in the chamber next door with your mother while she nurses my son."

Miriam struggled from her mother's grasp. "But who'll take care of father and Aaron?"

"I will, little one." Puah knelt to meet Miriam face to face. "Mered and I will take good care of Amram and Aaron while you and your mother serve in the villa. But remember, you mustn't tell anyone why you're here."

The little girl bobbed her head and bounced her curls. If innocence and beauty were rewarded, this girl would win a prize. Hopefully her discretion would develop with age.

"All right then." Puah turned again to Anippe. "I'm sorry, Amira, but I really must go. It's already dusk, and since Mered won't be able to walk with me—" She covered her mouth, stricken. "I didn't mean to accuse . . . or complain. You had every right to discipline—"

"Yes, I had every right, but I sent Mered to the linen shop because I was hiding Jochebed and Miriam in the bathhouse." She lifted her brow to make the point. "I commanded him to work through the night because of his insolence."

Puah bowed and nodded. "I understand." She fidgeted with her belt and waited.

Anippe noted the last shades of sunset and felt a twinge of guilt that she'd kept the midwife so long. "Ankhe will instruct Nassor to escort you home." She turned to Ankhe. "Make sure he takes at least two other guards with him. I can't have my midwife eaten by jackals or hyenas."

Puah grinned, and Anippe felt a moment of connection with her. Could they ever be friends? What an odd thought.

"Thank you, Amira." Puah bowed and then walked toward Jochebed, offering a meaningful glance. Their hands met and then released slowly as they parted. A tender and silent good-bye between two women who obviously knew the depths of friendship. What were their lives like in the Hebrew camp, away from Ramessids and masters and fear?

Little Miriam yawned, her mouth almost swallowing her face, and then growled as she exhaled.

"Miriam." Jochebed seemed mortified. "Don't be rude."

Anippe chuckled but admired the Hebrew mother's diligent training. "Perhaps it's almost bedtime."

"Yes. She and her little brother, Aaron, sleep and rise with the sun."

A shadow of grief crossed the woman's face at the mention of her son, and Anippe suddenly felt guilty for destroying this family. "I'll pay you, Jochebed, for your service. I'll send extra rations of grain, wine, oil—whatever your husband and son need while you're gone."

Jochebed drew Miriam into an embrace, her face fairly beaming. "Thank you, Amira, but there's no need. You've given me Miriam."

"Well, regardless, I'll begin the extra rations tomorrow."

Miriam yawned again, quieter this time, but still reminding Anippe the child needed sleep.

"You two will sleep in my sitting room tonight," she instructed. "Tomorrow, we'll spend the day at the bathhouse." Smiling at the babe in her arms and then at Miriam, she said, "You can help me take care of the baby while we're hidden away by the Nile, and when we return to the chamber tomorrow evening, nice slaves will have made a doorway through my bedchamber wall." She pointed to a space on the other side of her bed, where an entry would be made joining the next chamber. "Then, you and your mother can visit the baby and me without having to pass by those Ramessid guards in the hallway."

"Just like at home with Mered and Puah." Miriam clapped and giggled.

Anippe turned to Jochebed for clarification. "Our family's rooms share a doorway with Mered and Puah's room in the long house." Jochebed bowed and nudged her daughter to mirror her respect. "Thank you, Amira, for taking such good care of us." When she lifted her head, she looked longingly at the baby. "Would you like me to take him for the night?"

The chamber door slammed shut, and Anippe heard voices. "Ankhe?"

A young Hebrew woman appeared carrying a newborn. Ankhe followed, wearing a smirk and carrying a basket of clothes. "I thought I'd make a quick adjustment to our plan, sister—like you did by inviting Miriam to stay."

Anippe looked down at the Hebrew boy in her arms and then back at her sister. "What have you done, Ankhe? Will you tell the whole villa and get us both killed?"

Ankhe's Hebrew woman suddenly looked terrified, but her sister wore a triumphant grin. "Anippe, meet your new handmaid, Ephah. Since you've been slow in the past to keep your promises to me, I selected Ephah to replace me as your handmaid."

"Ankhe, this wasn't part of the plan. Why would you choose a handmaid with an infant—a male infant?"

"I chose her *because* of her son. She's been hiding him in our slave quarters for a week." She wrapped her arm around the girl's shoulders. "We made quite a stir when we left, making sure all the house slaves knew we were moving to chambers on the master's wing because the amira is with child and will be learning to care for an heir."

"But what if the guards try to throw him into the Nile?"

Ankhe rolled her eyes. "You're the Amira, Anippe. Tell the guards you saved this male to practice holding the waste pot for Sebak's heir. Use your authority. Bluff if you must." Ankhe retraced her steps toward the chamber door and lowered her voice. "I'll sleep in the private chamber across the hall. Ephah and her babe will share the chamber with Jochebed and Miriam so that either baby's cry will sound natural, normal, unremarkable. They must simply make sure the two brats don't cry at the same time." Ankhe folded her arms across her chest, daring Anippe to argue.

Was this the new normal—Ankhe thinking she could manipulate and command whenever she pleased? Anippe massaged her temples again and took a deep breath. Better to choose her battles. "It's a good plan, Ankhe. Thank you." Anippe examined Ephah from head to toe, taking in her raised chin and narrowed eyes. "Ephah and Jochebed will remain in my chamber tonight with the children. I can't have them walking out the door with two baby boys, and I dare not keep one in my chamber and risk him crying out."

Ephah glared at Ankhe. "You said I'd sleep on a down-stuffed mattress tonight."

Anippe tried to hide a grin. It was good for Ephah to learn quickly not to trust Ankhe. "Ephah, you and Jochebed can use cushions from the bathhouse to make beds on the sitting-room floor."

"All right then," Ankhe said on her way to the door. "Don't wake me in the morning."

When the door closed behind her, Jochebed hurried toward the pitcher of water. "Let me get clean water for your bedtime bath, Amira."

"No, Jochebed." Anippe held her new son in one arm and stilled Jochebed's fidgeting with the other. "My new handmaid will do that. You and Miriam should make your beds."

Ephah jerked the pitcher from Jochebed's hand. "Will someone at least hold my baby while I work?"

"Of course, child." Jochebed's tender words were wasted on the maid. Ephah thrust her son at the older woman and disappeared behind the servant's partition. Jochebed turned to Anippe. "She'll get better in time. Women are sometimes emotional after a birth."

Anippe looked into Jochebed's kind eyes and then down at Miriam's bright smile. The gods had given her a son from a loving family. For this she was truly grateful. Only one question nibbled at the edges of her heart. How could she ensure their silence when their service was no longer needed?

14

So the girl went and got the baby's mother. . . .
So the woman took the baby and nursed him.

EXODUS 2:8–9

SIX MONTHS LATER

Master Mered, I've got the amira's designs for you." Miriam skipped across the sandstone tiles of the linen shop, waving two scrolls and initiating chuckles from every worker she passed.

Mered received the scrolls with a frown, glaring his scoffing workers back to their tasks. Cupping her chin, he captured her gaze. "Miriam, remember what we talked about? There's no need to call me 'master.' I'm a Hebrew slave just like you and the others."

"Yes, but you don't dress like us. Why is that?"

Mered heard snickering from behind the vertical looms. He'd lived with ridicule for his Egyptian style—even suffered an occasional brawl—but his workers generally understood why Master Sebak required it of him. "I dress this way because I must sell linen to Egyptian and foreign traders, but my heart and soul are dedicated to El-Shaddai. The Lord doesn't judge a man by his hair and clothes but by his thoughts and deeds."

"Will El-Shaddai judge King Tut for being so mean?"

"Shh." Mered grabbed Miriam and covered her mouth. He whispered against her ear, "You must never say such a thing. Not all Hebrews are loyal to our people, Miriam, and if an Egyptian hears you've spoken against their king, it's death for you and your family." He released her and saw tears welling in her eyes. Pulling her back into his arms, this time to comfort her, he laid his cheek atop her head. "I'm just trying to protect you, little one. These walls have ears."

"Well, these walls tell me the king is coming to Avaris."

"What?" He pushed her away again. The poor child no doubt felt like laundry on a river rock. "Where did you hear this?"

"A royal messenger brought a message to Amira Anippe this morning, saying King Tut wants to be here when her first baby arrives. His barque arrives tomorrow."

Mered's mind began to spin. Anippe's child was still a month from term. Would the king stay in Avaris that long? Would the amira come out of seclusion to greet him?

"Master Mer—" Miriam clamped her hands over her mouth as if reining in wild horses.

"You can call me simply Mered."

"All right. Simply Mered." She giggled but then sobered, her little brow wrinkled with concern. "When King Tut comes, will he make the guards throw Puah's baby into the Nile?"

Mered pressed his fists against his eyes, trying to erase images of infants' bodies rushing among the waves, decayed along the banks, half-eaten by feasting crocodiles. The Ramessid patrols had continued their gruesome task after Sebak's departure. Shiphrah and Puah still refused to kill the boys, making sure they were absent at the moment of birth—usually waiting outside the doorway in case of complications.

But Puah couldn't be absent at the birth of her own child, and they were most certainly not throwing their son into the Nile—or setting him adrift in a pitch-covered basket. Had Amram's youngest son lived? Mered shook his head and rubbed his face. How could a boy in a basket be saved when God let so many others perish?

"Mered, are you crying because Puah's baby is a boy?" Miriam patted his forearm, stirring him from his thoughts.

He released a deep sigh and stared into those deep pools of innocence. "No, Miriam. Puah will have a girl. We will have a daughter."

She rested her elbow on his desk and sighed. "Well, that's good. Maybe you should tell the amira, because she seemed worried Puah might have a son."

Mered turned on his stool and gathered her into his arms. "And why might the amira think Puah would have a son?"

"Because Shiphrah sent word this morning that Puah was having birth pains, and the amira said she'd pray to her gods that Tut wouldn't throw the baby in the Nile."

Mered leapt from his stool, sending it skidding across the tiles, and raced from the linen shop without a backward glance. Why hadn't Shiphrah sent for him? Down the hill toward the craftsmen's village he ran, stumbling more than once. Perhaps rolling down the hill would be faster.

He passed a herd of pigs, scattering a few, which earned him the ire of the herdsmen. He wound his way through a group of slaves on their way to weed another field. This year's inundation had left the Delta's soil rich and black, growing grain to record heights, ripe and full. He passed it all with fresh awe at El-Shaddai's creative wonders.

"My wife is having a baby!" Mered shouted, receiving more than one strange look as he rounded the corner of the first long house.

But then his joy drained away, and his heart nearly failed. Huddled near his doorway, a knot of old women blocked the entrance, while toddlers played all around them. His legs turned to water but somehow carried him home.

A woman near the back of the crowd noticed his approach. "Oh Mered. Your darling Puah will bear your child by evening—perhaps a little later." Her pink-gummed smile nudged aside his overwhelming fear.

"Is she well? May I see her?"

"Oh, a husband should never see his beloved bearing their child. If that man is kind, he would never touch her again. If he is wicked, he would despise her baser instincts." She elbowed his midsection. "You go back to the workshop. Let Shiphrah take care of your Puah, and let us old crones take care of the little one."

Mered rose on his tiptoes, trying to see beyond the gray heads clogging his doorway, but it was no use. Puah was safely sheltered within the bosom of womanhood, and he was an intruder here. He would do as he was told and return to the workshop—but he would discover all he could about the king's visit.

El-Shaddai, please let my child be a girl.

⁂

Anippe paced in her chamber, wearing a groove in the tiles between her bed and the courtyard pillar. "We must stop him. Tut can't come to Avaris until after I've given birth."

Ankhe rolled her eyes. "Anubis will sprout wings and sing Hathor's love song before you give birth, sister."

The young handmaid, Ephah, giggled, and Anippe shot her a glare that would have killed a meeker soul. Ankhe had become Ephah's protector, and the girl had become almost as lazy as the king's younger sister.

Ankhe shook the unfurled papyrus delivered by the messenger that morning, royal seal still dangling. "Our brother won't wait for his visit. This scroll was sent from Bubastis yesterday."

Anippe growled, hating that Ankhe was right—again. Her sister had become more arrogant since moving into the private chamber across the hall from Anippe.

"We'll tell Tut you're ill and forbid him to enter your chamber for fear of rousing the gods' displeasure," Ankhe said.

Incredulous, Anippe stopped her pacing. "Ankhe, we do not forbid King Tut to do anything. Besides, he's Horus incarnate—son of Isis, who is the goddess of healing. Not even a wheezing cough or weeping sore would deter the great Pharaoh."

"Well, if he enters your chamber and finds you as skinny as a bulrush, we'll both die."

A knock sounded on the door to Jochebed's adjoining chamber. Ankhe glared at Ephah when she stood to answer it. "The amira isn't well and doesn't wish to be disturbed."

Anippe raced toward the door, glaring at her sister. "No wait, Jochebed."

She unlatched the door and swung it open. The wet nurse stood with Ephah's baby on one hip and Anippe's son on the other. The young prince lunged for his ummi, and Anippe reached out to take him. He was such a big boy these days, sitting by himself, rolling to the toy of his choice, nearly crawling.

A moment of sadness shadowed Jochebed's face but was quickly replaced by a tender smile. Was Jochebed becoming too attached? Spending too much time with the child?

"Shiphrah sent an update," Jochebed said a little too brightly. "Puah is doing well and will most likely deliver before the sun rises." She lingered, looking longingly at Anippe's son. "Would you like me to take him back so you and Ankhe can continue your talk?"

"Thank you, Jochebed, no. I'll call you when it's time for his next feeding." Anippe turned to the lazy maid. "Get out, and take care of your own child."

The girl shot a pleading glance at Ankhe, as if she might defend her, but for once, Ankhe remained silent. Jochebed gave up the second child, her empty arms making her look pitiful as she disappeared behind the closed door. Surely Miriam would return from the linen shop soon. Anippe had given her the designs to take to Mered long ago.

Anippe latched the door and held her son close, inhaling the sweet scent of lotus-scented oil Jochebed applied after his baths.

Ankhe broke the spell. "Tut will never believe he's a newborn."

"I know."

"How will we continue the deception?"

"I don't know." Anippe sang to her son, a made-up song. He giggled. She danced and swayed, delighted at his squeals.

"He'll kill us both if he finds out."

"And my life will have been a happy one, Ankhe." She stomped her foot, perched the baby on her hip, and stared at her painfully glum sister. "I haven't waited for others to give me a life. I didn't demand fortune, influence, or leisure. I have lived the life the gods gave me. Perhaps if you stopped whining about all that's wrong, you might find a way to make it right."

Anippe hurried toward the bathhouse before Ankhe could ruin what remained of their last day on earth. If Tut discovered their deceit, at least she could take today's memories with her to the underworld. Placing her precious bundle on a cushion near the canal, she let him explore his basket of trinkets—his favorite was the gourd rattle Jochebed had made.

Wrapped in her son's innocence, she hadn't heard Ankhe's approach. "Why haven't you named him?" When Anippe didn't answer, her sister pressed on. "I know why. You're afraid if you name him, Anubis will know he exists and take him away. But every child needs a name."

But what if she chose the wrong name? Anippe was still tormented by the name the Great Wife, Nefertiti, had given her—*Meryetaten-tasherit*. Why name her son now, when his future—and hers—was so uncertain?

She pulled up her knees and rested her chin there. "I want his name to hold lasting meaning, Ankhe, and I don't yet know who he is—or what he'll become." She looked again at the miracle she'd drawn out of the Nile. "I've heard Jochebed call him *Moses*. I asked her about it, and she said it meant '*draw out*' in Hebrew. For now, I'll name him Moses, but I can't give an Egyptian name yet." She looked up at Ankhe, who stood towering over her. "And that's the end of it. Understand?"

To her utter and grateful surprise, Ankhe nodded and sat beside her. "I do understand, and I think I know how we can save both Moses and ourselves from Pharaoh's wrath."

Anippe offered her a rueful grin. Ankhe was stubborn, petulant, and exhausting—but she did have good ideas. "Tell me."

The moon cast a beautiful glow on Puah's face through the single window of Mered's home. "What shall we name him?" She twisted the curls on their son's head, still damp with ben-tree oil and pomegranate wine. Shiphrah had rubbed him with salt and massaged him with the Hebrew mixture for newborn anointing.

"Should we wait?" Mered asked, refusing to meet her gaze. "Pharaoh's barque arrives in the morning."

"No." Shiphrah stilled her busy hands but didn't look up. "You will not wait to name this child. Some midwives become midwives because we can't bear our own children, but if God gave you this gift, perhaps He'll give me . . ."

Her words drowned in her emotion, and Mered left his wife's side to comfort their friend. "You and Hur are still young, Shiphrah."

She swiped at her eyes and elbowed his side, signaling the end of the sentimental moment. "If you say we're young one more time, I'll have Hur put dead snakes in your bed."

Even the exhausted new mother laughed at the genial threat. Hur had been known to play pranks on unsuspecting friends with the grain-eating rodents and vipers he'd killed at the villa.

Mered returned to Puah's side and stroked her rosy cheeks. "Our son will be called 'Jered—descendant.' As I am descended of Ezrah, and he from the tribe of Judah, so our son is a descendant of Israel."

Puah nodded and began whispering to their son. "Jered. You are Jered."

The sound of hurried footsteps stole Mered's attention, and suddenly three Ramessid guards cluttered their tiny room.

Ankhe appeared in their midst. "The amira has begun her travail prematurely. We need the midwives, Shiphrah and Puah, right away." She stared at Jered, smiling, teeth bared like a crocodile. "You may bring the newborn boy to give the amira hope through her travail."

One of the guards bristled. "We have orders to kill every male Hebrew infant."

Ankhe's anger answered quicker than Mered's fear. "Are you going to encourage the amira when she despairs in the final hours of labor, Captain?" She stabbed his chest with her finger. "Will you teach my sister to swaddle and bathe and tend Master Sebak's heir during his first days?"

The captain's face turned to stone, his lips pressed into a thin line.

"I thought not," Ankhe said. "Now escort them to the villa."

She turned and was gone, leaving the captain angry and impatient. "Get her dressed, and be quick about it," he growled.

Shiphrah was the first to gather her wits. She grabbed Mered's arm, lifting him to his feet. They stood between the guards and Puah, offering her a measure of privacy while she pulled her robe over her shoulders and swaddled their newborn son.

"I'm ready," she said in a whisper, her voice still weak. At least she'd had a few hours' rest from the birthing stool.

Mered cradled her elbow and kept his voice low. "Can you walk, or shall I carry you?"

"I can walk, but you must carry Jered while Shiphrah steadies me."

Mered reached for Jered, but the captain's cudgel came down on his forearms before he touched the babe, "You weren't summoned—only the midwives and the child."

Panicked, Mered lunged toward his son. The blow to his jaw sent Mered to the floor before he even saw it coming. Puah stifled a scream, and Shiphrah pulled her and Jered away from the scuffle.

Two guards stood beside the women, short swords drawn, while the captain stood over Mered. "Your son will swim with the crocodiles when the amira is finished with him."

Mered heard Puah's scream, saw the fist again, felt his jaw pop—and darkness took him.

15

*The midwives, however, feared God and did not
do what the king of Egypt had told them to do;
they let the boys live.*

—EXODUS 1:17

E phah peeked out the chamber door's narrow opening. "Ankhe's leading
the guards, and they've got the midwives—and a baby."

Puah's baby must have been a boy! Anippe could hardly contain her de-
light. In the midst of their despairing afternoon, Ankhe had suggested using
Puah's baby—if it was a boy—as a decoy, pretending for Tut's visit that it was
Anippe's newborn. The gods must be smiling on them tonight.

Anippe and Jochebed paced in the sitting area, too nervous to sit, while
Miriam played on a cushion with the new spindle and flax fibers Mered had
given her. He'd told her to practice spinning, promising someday—if the amira
allowed it—she could work in the linen shop. Infuriating man. What if she
didn't want Miriam to work in the linen shop? She rather liked the girl and
thought she'd make a fine handmaid—not like the one now picking her teeth
instead of reporting the guards' progress toward the door.

"Ephah, look again! Are they—" Anippe clamped her lips shut when she
heard Ankhe's voice near the threshold.

"You're dismissed. You may return to your posts."

Anippe heard heavy footsteps retreating, but a man cleared his throat.
"You will inform the amira . . . well, it's my duty . . . the king must know that
these midwives have ignored his command. We Ramessids have been killing
the Hebrew brats, not the midwives. And the midwife's newborn—he must be
disposed of."

Puah and Shiphrah slipped in through a narrow opening in the chamber door with a swaddled infant, but Ankhe remained in the corridor with the guard. Ephah left the door open a crack, while Jochebed and Anippe huddled close to hear the conversation better.

"Why does it matter who kills the babies as long as they're dead, Captain Nassor?" Ankhe's voice rose in pitch and volume. "Do you realize the amira could send you—before sunrise—to oversee the copper mines in Sinai?"

A slight pause brought Anippe's heart to her throat.

When the Ramessid captain spoke, his voice was a low growl. "I realize there's a Hebrew boy in the amira's chamber right now, and I will personally throw it in the Nile before Pharaoh's barque arrives."

Ankhe matched his threat. "I will do it myself, Captain. You are dismissed." She hurried through the door and locked it, breathing hard. She waved the crowd of women away. "Stand back. I can't breathe. Why are no lamps burning?"

Ephah hurried to trim the wicks and light a few more lamps. They'd purposely kept the chamber darkened, in case the guards followed the midwives into the sitting area—so they wouldn't see Anippe's slim form.

As the lights illumined faces, Shiphrah stood open-mouthed and gawking. "Amira, you're not pregnant." Her genuine shock proved Puah's ability to keep a secret.

"No, Shiphrah, I'm not." Casting an appreciative glance at Puah, Anippe noted her gray pallor. "Ankhe get a chair. Hurry!"

Ankhe fetched the chair from the courtyard, and Jochebed and Shiphrah eased the new mother into the chair.

As if seeing Jochebed for the first time, Shiphrah hugged her. "I've missed you in the village, my friend."

Decidedly uncomfortable, Jochebed glanced at Anippe before answering. "The amira allowed me to live in the villa with Miriam when she was taken into house service."

Miriam dropped her spindle and whorl, skipping over to join the conversation. "Mother gets to take care of—"

Jochebed clapped her hand over the girl's mouth, creating an awkward silence.

Anippe studied Shiphrah and made a pivotal decision. "I found a Hebrew boy floating in a basket on the Nile. Miriam followed him to my bathhouse, and Jochebed is his wet nurse."

Again, the midwife looked utterly bewildered. "How did a baby float in a basket without getting eaten by croc—"

"It was my baby," Jochebed said, "and I coated the basket with pitch."

Shiphrah gulped in the awkward silence and then turned disbelieving eyes on Anippe. "And you've allowed Jochebed to nurse her own son?"

Anippe squared her shoulders, refusing to let her trepidation show. "Of course. He's my son, not Jochebed's." But the niggling fear remained. Would Anippe have to kill her first slave to redeem her first son?

"Does it matter right now whose son he is?" Ankhe said, silencing her sister with a glare. "King Tut and his queen arrive tomorrow and will be told of your premature labor. They won't want to see you until after the birth because of Senpa's unpleasant memories."

Anippe noticed both midwives drop their heads, shoulders sagging, and she realized they still felt the burden of Senpa's miscarriages. She leaned forward, drawing their attention. "I witnessed only the queen's last delivery, but I assure you—as I assured my brother—you both did everything possible to save that baby. The gods are to blame. Not you."

Both women wiped their cheeks, but only Shiphrah met Anippe's gaze. "Thank you, Amira. It's not in a midwife's nature to let a baby die—or to kill one."

"I cannot change the will of a god, Shiphrah, and the son of Horus has ordered you to kill all newborn Hebrew boys." Anippe let silence emphasize her authority—lest they mistake kindness for weakness. "As Avaris's amira, even I live—or die—by Pharaoh's commands. When the Ramessid captain officially informed Ankhe of your disobedience, he put me in a corner. I can no longer say *I didn't know the midwives weren't killing the newborn boys.*"

Puah began to tremble and moan, clutching her son close and rocking.

Anippe bent before her and grabbed her arms. "Stop, Puah. Your son is safe. I need him to pose as my newborn, and you will pretend to be his wet nurse—but only during the king's visit."

The new mother continued her trembling, but the moaning ceased, and her eyes focused on a distant place. Did she hear or understand, or was she too exhausted and distraught to comprehend?

"Puah, look at me." Anippe shook her. "Look at me!" The weary woman raised her gaze to meet the amira's. "You will live in Jochebed's chamber with your son during the king's visit."

Ephah mumbled under her breath about tight quarters with Jochebed's brats and now more people in their chamber.

Anippe glared at Ankhe. "The handmaid you chose for me will move into your chamber, sister. I no longer require her service."

Ankhe's eyes narrowed. "I have no use for her either."

"Then send her back to the slave quarters. Do what you like with her. I don't care." Anippe returned her attention to Puah, softening her expression and voice. "I'll send a messenger to assure Mered you're all right but will make no mention of your son."

"But, please, Amira, he'll worry—"

"I'm sorry, Puah. Your son's life is a gift for your faithful service, but we can't tell anyone our plan to protect him—especially Mered. Not until Tut leaves. You yourself said he cannot abide deception, so I assume he would not keep our secret. When the king's barque sails away, you may return home with your son, and I'll make sure the Ramessid guards leave you in peace. Do you understand?"

With a sigh, Puah nodded and stared down at her newborn without a word.

Anippe's heart twisted, aching to hold her own son, both dreading and yearning for the morning sun. Dawn would bring Pharaoh's ship, royal attendants, and a house full of activity—but it would also bring the familiar coos of Moses's sweet voice.

"Jochebed, get Puah settled in your chamber." Anippe lifted the assistant midwife's arm, helping her stand. "Shiphrah, you must tutor me through an imaginary birth. I need to sound like Senpa sounded, labor the same amount of time, but end up with a healthy son. Then you will return home, spreading news of Master Sebak's heir."

"And what am I supposed to do?" Ankhe stood in the shadows, arms crossed over her chest.

"I don't care what you do, Ankhe, but take Ephah and her son with you."

Mered stood along the crowded path near Avaris quay, watching the king's retinue march up the hill toward the villa. His jaw throbbed, and his heart pounded, though his eyelids were heavy. After the guard's last punch, Mered had awakened to a dimly lit chamber, with Amram's kind face hovering over him. His neighbor had heard the ruckus and waited behind the dividing curtain until the guards left before coming to apply cool water and prayers to Mered's swollen face.

At dawn, a Ramessid guard had invaded Mered's home again, this one with a message. Puah would remain at the villa to care for the amira indefinitely. Delivery complications required a midwife's constant care. No mention of their newborn son, Jered. Amram prayed as Mered wept.

Trumpets had called the Hebrews to the quay moments later to welcome the king who had murdered their sons. Mered had considered staying home. He cared little about the pomp of a visiting king and cared even less about King Tut.

"Come, we can walk together." Amram had squeezed his shoulder. "I'll wake Aaron, and we'll get him a crust of bread and cheese to eat on the way."

The royal parade approached Mered and Amram, two runners with staves pressing back the curious crowd, while the king's Medjay bodyguard ordered all slaves to their knees. Ramessid soldiers lined the path to enforce the Hebrews' honor for this dishonorable king.

Musicians danced, strummed lyres, and clanged sistrums. Royal maids carried baskets of blue lotus, crushing and throwing the petals aloft, filling the air with their scent. The king's gilded palanquin fairly floated on the shoulders of eight Nubian giants, Medjays who'd undoubtedly sent enemies scampering for fear of their size alone. Tut's throne boasted figures of a lion and a sphinx as armrests, monster and myth subdued under a boy-god's power. Pharaoh sat beneath a hawk-shaped canopy, its outspread wings a supposed symbol of truth and justice.

Mered scoffed. *Where was justice for my son and Amram's? At the bottom of the Nile in a watery grave?*

King Tut passed by, never acknowledging those who knelt before him—those whose lives he'd destroyed on a whim.

When Mered thought he could stand the farce no longer, he saw the beautiful Queen Senpa, borne atop another set of Medjay shoulders. She was radiant in her waist-length braided wig woven with gold and fine jewels. Cheeks pink, dignified, lips parted in a genial smile as she acknowledged with a nod those kneeling on both sides of the path. She appeared fully recovered from her last visit to Avaris. And her gown—of course, Mered noticed—was the fine pleated linen from the palace at Gurob.

Stunning, but not as fine as the byssus woven in Avaris. The Ramessid wives of Qantir followed the lovely queen, arrayed in robes and sheaths from Avaris's shop that outshone the queen's. The husbands had paid dearly to adorn their women like royalty. Master Sebak would be pleased to return and find his uncle Pirameses's gold in the coffers.

The noblemen of Qantir paraded behind their women, most of them retired soldiers now serving as the king's officials and priests of Seth. Some carried staffs with a hawk's head, while other staffs bore the head of a jackal—Anubis, ruler of their underworld. Appropriate, considering the death and destruction rained down on Delta slaves.

The sun glinted off the Ramessids' gold collars, blinding Mered for a moment. He lifted his hand to shade his eyes. Who were the men at the end of the procession?

He recognized the stately General Horemheb.

In full dress armor, the general wore the Gold of Praise collar and a daunting expression. Behind him marched a train of filthy men chained together—necks, hands, and feet—bloodied and barely strong enough to climb the hill.

El-Shaddai, have mercy on them. Were they Hittites? More importantly, was Master Sebak providing rear guard?

Mered ached to stand above the bowing slaves, to find his master following the prisoners—but his yearning was as brief as the line of captives. Two, maybe three dozen men. No wonder General Horemheb appeared solemn. A train of captives less than a hundred long would be an embarrassment to the experienced soldier. Why had he displayed them at all?

And to Mered's own disappointment—no Master Sebak at rear guard.

The procession moved toward the villa, and slaves slowly dispersed to resume their duties. Mered returned to his workshop, still bothered by General Horemheb's appearance. There'd been no messenger announcing his arrival. Did Anippe even know her abbi Horem was here?

The royal visit was soon lost in the daily tasks of running his workshop. Accounts needed settling, and flax seed needed sowing. El-Shaddai gave them few daylight hours during these last weeks before harvest, and without Puah to go home to, perhaps he'd work through the night. Hours passed in a haze of workers' rhythmic melodies in time with the *thwack* of the weavers' shuttles. When Mered finally lifted his weary body from his stool and stretched, he felt every crack and pop.

"Quiet!" The estate foreman shouted from the doorway. Stillness descended, and Mered sensed almost a smile from the sour old rat. "Master Sebak has a son, and Avaris is host to Egypt's king and prince regent. Sing about that, you filthy slaves." He turned and disappeared into the night, and the linen shop erupted in celebration.

Though he gave no report on the amira's health, Mered felt sure she must have come through the birth safely. Perhaps the complications the guard spoke of at his home this morning were minor. Perhaps Puah wouldn't need to stay at the villa after all. Perhaps . . .

Crossing his arms to make a pillow on the desk, Mered lowered his weary head. *Perhaps Master Sebak will return to see his son.*

Struck like lightning by a thought, Mered's head popped up, eyes blinking, mind whirring. "Vizier Ay," he whispered to no one.

Vizier Ay hadn't been in King Tut's retinue. Why? Master Sebak had said the conniving vizier never left the king's side. General Horemheb's dispirited bearing flashed in his memory—and the meager offering of prisoners. Dread crawled through him like a creeping vine.

He reached for his reeds and pigment. He might as well work on inventory and designs since he couldn't sleep with a seed of fear growing in his belly.

16

Joy is gone from our hearts;
*   our dancing has turned to mourning.*
The crown has fallen from our head.
Woe to us, for we have sinned!

—LAMENTATIONS 5:15–16

Anippe hosted the first family meeting in her private courtyard. Three days had passed since the king's entourage arrived. Ankhe had stayed away, ominously silent, leaving Anippe to enjoy the quiet seclusion of Jochebed and Puah's company with Moses, Miriam, and baby Jered. Senpa was the only royal family who had tried to see her. The queen had appeared late last night—after the babies were sleeping—to suggest this morning's light meal.

Jochebed, Moses, and Miriam were safely hidden in their chamber behind a tapestry covering their adjoining door. Anippe and Puah waited with little Jered on cushions in the sitting area and were startled by a quick knock and Ankhe's abrupt entry.

Anger stirring, Anippe rose to meet her, waiting till the door closed to release her ire. "You are no longer my handmaid, so you have no right to barge in—"

"Oh, but I am your handmaid, dear sister." Ankhe offered an exaggerated bow and rose with a cold stare.

"What do you mean?" Dread coiled around Anippe's heart. "You're my son's tutor. I'll find another handmaid."

"While our brother is here, *I* am your handmaid." Her smile looked like a cobra baring its fangs.

A loud knock startled Anippe, and she jumped like a desert hare.

Ankhe inclined her head. "I'll answer your door, Amira. Why don't you and your wet nurse proceed to the courtyard and prepare to meet your guests."

Swallowing hard, Anippe turned toward the courtyard. Puah had already gathered her straw-stuffed cushion and the baby and was on her way. Heart pounding, mind spinning, Anippe tried to imagine what scheme Ankhe had engineered for her benefit at this morning's meeting.

Anippe took her place at a low-lying marble table, and Puah transferred baby Jered to the amira's arms. The surrogate wet nurse retired to a palm tree three paces away to lounge an appropriate distance from royalty. Kitchen slaves had already set the table with silver platters and goblets, a pitcher of grape juice, stewed dates, bread, and goat cheese. Simple fare elegantly presented.

King Tut entered first, Queen Senpa's hand draped on his left arm. Each had two attendants. Anippe's heart leapt at the sight of her family. Tears choked her, but she blinked them away, trying to preserve the eye paints Miriam had helped her apply that morning.

"Anippe, you look radiant." Senpa leaned down to kiss her cheek and brushed Jered's head, fighting tears of her own.

Tut smiled, but it didn't reach his eyes. "Sister. How are you feeling?"

"I'm getting stronger each da—" Anippe's words died when she saw Abbi Horem and Ankhe emerge from the shadowy chamber. Ankhe's right cheek was red with a distinct white handprint. Abbi Horem's neck was crimson, his nostrils flared with rage.

The moment he saw Anippe, though, his demeanor changed. "Habiba, you look well." His determined steps led him to her side. Lips parted in wonder, his eyes locked on the babe in her arms. "Is this my grandson?"

Anippe offered her cheek for Abbi's kiss. "Isn't he beautiful? Won't Ummi Amenia be pleased?"

"She will indeed, my treasure." He squeezed her shoulder, infusing her with love and strength.

When she glanced up at her brother and sisters, Abbi Horem's love felt like a grinding stone around her neck. Ankhe glared daggers at the general and his adopted daughter, while Tut and Senpa couldn't even look at the babe in her arms. *By the gods! Why did Tut bring Senpa back here?* Hadn't their sister suffered enough without returning her to the villa where she'd miscarried two infants? Awkward silence wrapped them in a shroud.

Ankhe sat behind Anippe's left shoulder and reached for the silver pitcher of grape juice. She made her way around the table, filling gem-studded silver goblets with shaky hands. "Will you lead the preharvest hunt in the Fayum again this year, brother?"

Anippe bowed her head, cringing at her sister's familiarity with Egypt's god on the throne. Would she never learn?

Abbi Horem rose and removed the strap securing his dagger. "A handmaid never addresses Pharaoh with such familiar—"

"Sit down, Horemheb." Tut waved his general off and squinted at his untoward sister. "You are a handmaid because you are a fool, Ankhe. If you ever address me as 'brother' again, I will feed you to the crocodiles."

Ankhe lowered her gaze, chastened but not silenced. "Oh worthy and good god, Tut—pleasing of birth, Ruler of Truth, Lord of all, who wears both crowns of Egypt." She waited for her brother's nod before continuing. "Delta crocodiles might find me less than tasty after so much Hebrew baby flesh."

Tut raised an eyebrow. "What do you know of Hebrew babies in the Nile, Ankhe?"

"I know the Ramessid captain reported to Anippe that the Hebrew midwives ignored your order, and the estate patrols are the ones throwing the slave babies to the crocodiles—oh great Pharaoh, mighty god of Two Lands."

Senpa glanced at Anippe from the corner of her eye, like a shy mare fearing the whip. Tut's gaze followed, burning a hole through the Amira of Avaris. "Is this true, Anippe? Have the Hebrew midwives ignored my order?"

Anippe's heart was in her throat. She dared not look over her shoulder at Puah. Would Tut recognize her? "I have been in my chamber all these months of my pregnancy, great son of Horus. Perhaps the Ramessid captain seeks glory stories to compare when the real soldiers return from battle." She waved his concern away with the fly trying to nibble on her cheese and dates.

"The captain spoke truth," Ankhe said. "I saw for myself this morning when I found one of our house slaves—Ephah—with a baby boy hidden in her chamber."

Anippe felt the blood drain from her face. Why would Ankhe draw attention to Ephah unless . . . *"I will do it myself, Captain,"* Ankhe had told Nassor when he threatened to throw Puah's son in the Nile. Anippe trembled at Ankhe's cold stare.

"Anippe had taken a second handmaid," Ankhe explained. "We discovered the woman had a baby boy, and I threw him in the Nile this morning. Captain Nassor sent the girl to work in dead-man's land as punishment for her disobedience. She'll work the mud pits on the plateau between Qantir and Avaris and be dead within a year."

Senpa covered a gasp. Anippe thought she might be sick.

Tut seemed utterly satisfied. "Well done, Ankhe. Perhaps there's hope for you yet."

Ankhe lifted her goblet of juice, toasting her brother's praise.

Abbi Horem reached for Anippe's hand beneath the table and gently squeezed it. Even a grizzled soldier recognized depravity when he saw it. "Queen Senpa, do you bring any news from the Gurob Palace?" he asked.

Anippe tried to regain her composure while the others spoke of parties and politics and people she cared nothing about. How could Ankhe cast an innocent child into crocodile-infested waters and send a woman—even an annoying slave—to dead-man's land? She stole a glance at her little sister and found her grinning, eyebrow arched, a look of satisfaction firmly etched on her features. What was she becoming? There seemed to be no sign of remorse or conscience.

"Unfortunately," Queen Senpa was saying, "I had no idea you'd join us here, General. I'm sure Amenia would have accompanied me if she'd known." Her gaze dropped to her goblet, watching the deep red liquid swirl during another awkward moment.

Abbi Horem cleared his throat. "I'll write a scroll for you to deliver to my wife—if you don't mind being our messenger, Queen Senpa. I'm afraid a soldier's wife grows accustomed to long absences."

"Of course, General. I'd be honored to be your messenger." Senpa turned her attention to Anippe. "Does Sebak know about his heir?" Her eyes barely brushed the baby. She hadn't truly looked at him once.

Casting a wary glance at Abbi Horem, Anippe sighed. "A Delta messenger has delivered only one message since Sebak left. I was able to send word of my pregnancy, but I'm sure Abbi will inform him about the birth of our son."

The general drew a long, slow sip from his goblet, avoiding comment on the lack of communication from Sebak. Was it so much to ask that her husband at least acknowledge she carried his child? A stab of guilt shot through her. *Even if it wasn't his son.*

"We didn't even know you were pregnant, Anippe." Queen Senpa reached out to touch the baby's cheek, the effort seeming to rob her joy. Tears twisted her expression and drained away her dignity. "The king's messenger whisked me away before I could prepare a gift for him." She covered a sob and tried to meet Anippe's gaze. "But Amenia sends her love." She buried her face in her hands, unable to speak.

Tut motioned to the queen's attendants. "Take her to our chamber." Her two maids helped her rise and led her from the courtyard. Tut's jaw muscle danced to a silent tune until Anippe's chamber door slammed shut. "Our sister still grieves the loss of our second daughter. Please forgive her rudeness."

Anippe's emotions were rising as well. Anger. Fear. Regret. "Was it rude to voice her offense to someone she loves and trusts, my god and sovereign brother? I obviously hurt Senpa when I neglected to send news of my pregnancy to Gurob."

Abbi Horem squeezed her hand again, this time not so gently. Had she spoken as foolishly as Ankhe? Perhaps, but she couldn't stomach any more of Tut's cruelty. Ay had jaded her tender, sweet brother's heart.

Tut's eyes narrowed, and she thought her fate sealed. "Your wisdom pleases me, little sister. Senpa was indeed rude, as your good god decreed, but only because of her hysteria." While Anippe was enjoying her reprieve, the king turned to Abbi Horem. "I will now voice my offense to you, General, because you are someone I have trusted since my earliest memory."

Abbi Horem humbly nodded. "I am honored, great and honorable son of Horus."

"You questioned my edict against the Hebrew male newborns the last time we met here in Avaris. Do you remember?"

"I remember." Abbi Horem met his gaze. "Perhaps Vizier Ay has proven more faithful than me, my king. These last months, we've made slow progress against the Hittites, and I could only deliver thirty-eight captives to serve in your copper mines. The rest of Mursili's army escaped north into Canaan."

Anippe pressed her lips against baby Jered's downy black hair to keep from asking about Sebak. Was he in Canaan then, or had he chased the enemy all the way back to the Hittite capital of Aleppo?

Tut's kohl-rimmed eye-of-Horus sharpened his gaze like the hawk he portrayed. "You are the most honorable man I know, Horemheb, and I have reminded Vizier Ay of that very fact. I sent him with my blessing to confer with Commander Nakhtmin and visit his daughter Mutnodjmet at the Nubian fortress. I grew weary of his constant squawking."

"My king, again I implore you to be cautious. If Ay and Nakhtmin conspire against you, they could attack from the south—"

Tut lifted his hand, silencing further comment. "I chose you as my successor, Horemheb, but I am Egypt's ruler. You will no longer treat me as a child. I know Ay's tricks, and I know your propensity to honk like a mother goose. I've become much wiser while you've been fighting Hittites."

A rueful grin from Abbi Horem loosened Anippe's grip on Jered. She hadn't realized she was squeezing him, but his growing discomfort escalated from fuss to full-throated howl.

Puah was there instantly with open arms, and Anippe offered up the hungry little treasure. "Why don't you feed him and then bring him back after our midday meal?" The midwife-turned-wet-nurse bowed and turned to go.

"Wait." Tut examined the wet nurse too closely. "Aren't you one of the midwives I ordered to kill the Hebrew baby boys?"

Puah shot a panicked glance at Anippe. "Yes, my lord."

Jered's cries had become inconsolable. Anippe leaned toward her brother and abbi. "He won't stop that awful wailing until she feeds him."

King Tut offered a begrudging nod but pinned his sister with a stare. "I want to speak with both midwives after the child eats. What were their names?"

"Puah and Shiphrah." Anippe felt her world beginning to crumble.

17

*Then the king of Egypt summoned the midwives
and asked them, "Why have you done this? Why
have you let the boys live?" The midwives
answered Pharaoh, "Hebrew women are not like
Egyptian women; they are vigorous and give
birth before the midwives arrive."*

—EXODUS 1:18–19

Mered ate his midday meal beneath the palm tree outside his linen workshop, remembering his boyhood chats with young Master Sebak. He missed his friend. If Sebak were here, he'd know how to manage the king. Sebak and General Horemheb would conceive a plan that honored their king but protected human life—or at least they'd try, as they'd done six months ago, when the edict was first handed down. Mered banged his head against his favorite tree, hoping to jostle an idea. Nothing came.

He needed to see Puah. She was his life and breath. They'd never been apart this long, and he felt like his heart had been ripped from his body—still beating, but trapped in the amira's chamber, while he lived a meaningless life at the linen shop.

"Master Mered!" Miriam came sprinting from the shop, her curls bouncing and bare feet kicking up dust. "Pharaoh found out Puah didn't kill the babies, and the big black soldiers took her to the main hall for judgment."

He stood but staggered back, her words hitting him like a blow. As reality sank in, he saw six Nubian guards exit the main entrance of the villa.

Miriam saw them too and blinked big round tears over her bottom lashes.

"They're going to get Shiphrah, too. Master Mered, you must warn Shiphrah. Save her."

Mered dragged his hand through his hair. What should he do? His heart said go to Puah, but he might actually have time to warn Shiphrah. The six Medjays turned toward the craftsmen's village. If he left now, he could beat them to Shiphrah.

He knelt down, embracing Miriam and whispering against her ear. "Run to the amira and tell her I've gone to warn Shiphrah. Have her stall the king's judgment."

She kissed his cheek. "I will." And she was off.

Mered watched her for only a moment before checking the Medjay's progress. They'd almost reached his workshop, but he could run while they marched. He may not be able to fight six Medjay warriors, but he could annoy them—which might provide enough time for Shiphrah to escape and Anippe to help Puah somehow.

Mered sprinted over the distance, kicking up dust all the way down the hill. He arrived at the corner of the first longhouse, looked back, and saw the Medjays closer than he expected. Shiphrah and Hur's rooms were at the end near the river, a few doors past Mered's. He'd never make it in time to get Shiphrah out to safety. His only hope was a diversion. He must hope Shiphrah heard the commotion, realized the danger, and fled. *El-Shaddai, make my mind and body strong to protect your faithful midwife.*

The rhythmic sound of the Medjay's marching reached him, and their leader gave hand signals, assigning each warrior one of the six mud-brick structures. *Good. They don't know where she lives.* Most of the skilled laborers were at work in the villa, or at their kilns, shops, or ovens. Those who remained in the village were old women tending children—and Shiphrah, the midwife who delivered those children.

Mered watched the chief Medjay round the corner of his building. With a deep breath and a quick prayer, the linen keeper set out to chat with a man who appeared more bent on action than words.

Anippe sat on her mattress, mirror in hand. "How could you kill a baby, Ankhe—and send Ephah to dead-man's land?"

"What else could I do? Nassor knew Ephah had a child, and I didn't send her to dead-man's land. Nassor did."

"Why did you even mention it to Tut?"

"Would you rather our brother heard of the midwives' disobedience from Nassor?"

Anippe wiped the last remnants of kohl from her eyes. She'd cried most of it off after Tut and Abbi Horem left. "I suppose it would have been worse coming from Nassor, but did you see Tut's face? He knows something isn't right. Do you think he suspects the baby isn't mine? He's a god, you know." She laid the mirror aside and fell back on her bed. "Oh, why did we think we could deceive him?"

"He's no more a god than you or I. He's a spoiled boy, manipulating those who taught him to manipulate." Ankhe continued her embroidery, completely unconcerned by her heresy and treason.

"You will be crocodile food if anyone hears you."

A frantic, pecking knock on their door startled Ankhe. Perhaps she was more concerned than she appeared.

Anippe lifted an eyebrow. "Maybe it's your executioner."

Ankhe rolled her eyes, put down her sewing, and stomped toward the door.

Miriam scooted past her and sprinted across the room into Anippe's arms. "Mered has gone to the village to warn Shiphrah. He says you must stall King Tut's judgment of Puah."

Anippe couldn't move. She stared at the sobbing little girl and wished she could comfort her. But stall King Tut's judgment? Was she mad? "Little one, Pharaoh is a god, and a god cannot repeal his law once it is spoken. His law will stand, and I can do nothing to change it."

"Tut isn't god. El-Shaddai is the one true God." Miriam's stormy expression stirred Anippe's anger.

"Well then, pray to your one true god to save the midwives—and us— because if Puah and Shiphrah tell the whole truth, we'll all die." The moment the words were spilled, Anippe regretted them. Fear replaced Miriam's anger and broke Anippe's heart.

Ankhe wrenched the child's arm and dragged her toward the door. "Yes, pray to the Hebrew god I hear so much about. Let him deliver the midwives."

"Release her." Anippe spoke in barely a whisper, but Ankhe heard and released the girl.

Miriam fled back to Anippe, this time clutching her feet. "Thank you. Thank you, Amira."

"Don't thank me, Miriam. I'll do what I can, but right now you must tell Jochebed to hide with Moses and baby Jered in my private bathhouse. You stay with them. It's the last place Pharaoh will search for a Hebrew baby boy."

King Tut sat on the gilded throne from his palanquin, transferred to Avaris's main hall as a makeshift throne room. Horemheb sat at his left, Senpa on his right. Anippe had been standing at the entrance, awaiting Tut's invitation to enter, for what seemed like hours. He refused to acknowledge her until Shiphrah was dragged in, her knees bloodied because of the Medjay's long and hurried strides.

Anippe kept her eyes focused on the villa's garden, remembering her wedding feast, Sebak's touch, and Amenia's kindness. Only good thoughts should accompany her to the underworld. Surely that was where she'd witness today's sunset—from the judgment halls of Ma'at, where Anubis would weigh her heart on his scales of justice. There was little doubt which way the scales would tip.

"You may enter, Amira of Avaris." Tut's voice boomed in the modest villa only half the size of the Memphis Palace.

Desperation set Anippe's feet in motion. Invitation or no, she must speak on behalf of the two women who'd become more than her slaves. "Please hear me, Oh mighty son of Horus."

But before she could fall at the king's feet, Abbi Horem rushed to gather her under his protective arm, forcing her to stand. "Anippe has obviously overtaxed herself—only days after bearing her son. I'm sure you've discerned the undeniable ma'at resting on your sister—her newborn son proof of the gods' pleasure. May I escort her to my chair, mighty Pharaoh, so she may rest while witnessing your mercy toward her midwives?"

Silence. Anippe's legs trembled beneath her heavy linen robe.

"Your daughter may sit at my left, but I have yet to determine if the midwives deserve mercy."

"Thank you, good and mighty king." Abbi Horem guided her—fairly lifted her—to the chair and stood behind her, in line with the king's Medjays.

Puah and Shiphrah stood before the king between their escorts, hands bound.

"Come." Tut's repeated invitation surprised Anippe, and she wondered who else would fall under her brother's judgment this day.

She covered a gasp when she saw Mered dragged in, face bruised, lip bleeding.

Tut glared. "Control your emotions, sister."

She placed both hands in her lap, sat straighter, and breathed evenly. Anippe carved her features into stone. "Forgive me. It won't happen again." She raised her chin and blinked back tears.

The guards nudged Puah and Shiphrah to their knees, and Tut began his inquisition. "My Nubians have questioned the Ramessid guards on both the Qantir and Avaris estates and discovered it was the guards who cast over one hundred male babies into the Nile during the past year." His eyes narrowed as he studied the two midwives. "Was my command unclear? Why did you let the boys live?"

Shiphrah raised her head. "Hebrew women are not like Egyptian women; they are vigorous and give birth before the midwives arrive."

Tut's brow knit together. He signaled the guard nearest Shiphrah, who landed the shaft of his spear against her head. The midwife tumbled forward, but the guard planted her back on her knees so the king could question her further. "Are you saying Egyptian women are inferior?"

"No, my king." She blinked her eyes oddly—tightly closed and then opened wide. Had the blow addled her? "I'm simply stating a fact. Puah birthed a child on the day your sister labored." Shiphrah nodded at Anippe. "Judge for yourself. A slave's body must heal more quickly or die. So it is with our laboring women."

Anippe wanted to stand and applaud, but she remained stone still as King Tut considered Shiphrah's well-phrased remarks.

After a span of several heartbeats, the king peered behind the Medjay guards. "And who is the linen-clad ruffian, whose face appears to have met my Medjay's fists or cudgel?"

The Nubian on Puah's right bowed slightly. "This is the husband of one of the midwives. He, uh, interfered with my search."

Abbi Horem chuckled, and a slow grin curved Tut's lips. He glanced over his shoulder, eyebrows raised. "Must I remind you to control your emotions, General?"

"Forgive me, my king. No, I, uh . . ." His humor faded when the king's smile dimmed.

Tut leaned on his armrest and squeezed the bridge of his nose. He seemed as tired of this mess as the rest of them.

They waited—everyone—while Anippe's sixteen-year-old brother decided the fate of hundreds of Hebrews—present and future. Ankhe was right. Tut was no god, but he was the king.

"I will amend my decree. Not just the midwives, but any of my people who witness a male Hebrew's birth must throw the baby immediately into the Nile. However, every newborn girl shall live."

Puah and Shiphrah bowed their heads, shoulders shaking in silent sobs. Mered dropped to his knees, cradling both women. The Medjays made no effort to stop him.

Anippe spoke evenly, not loud enough to proclaim, but not quiet enough to be hidden. "Do I understand correctly that the mighty ruler of Two Lands has added further wisdom to his command by applying this edict to only Hebrew baby boys immediately after their birth? If anyone witnesses the birth of a Hebrew boy, they are at that moment to cast the child into the arms of our Nile god, Hapi?"

Tut stared straight ahead, gaze fixed and empty. "Only feed the Nile god, Hapi, a freshly born Hebrew boy. That is my command."

Puah and Shiphrah looked up, faces tear-streaked but eyes hopeful. Wisely, they remained silent. Anippe scanned the room, not letting her gaze linger on her Hebrew friends, but feeling a joy and hope that she hadn't felt in almost a year.

"Queen Senpa and I leave in the morning." Tut's voice echoed in the small space. "My wife cannot sleep or eat because of her sadness, and I . . ." He leaned toward Anippe, grabbing her wrist and whispering for only her ears. "And I will not enforce a law I know is wrong but cannot change—because I am the god who decreed it. My mind is clearer without Ay's prattling, but I cannot appear weak by changing laws I made when my pain shouted louder than reason."

Anippe placed her hand over her brother's and kept her voice as quiet as his. "Your decree stipulates newborns. You have done well, wise and mighty ruler of our Two Lands." She held her breath—and his gaze.

He cupped her cheeks, the hint of a smile on his lips before he kissed her forehead. "You are tenacious, my sister. Our ummi Kiya would be proud." Resuming his stately air, he addressed the guards. "Release the midwives."

Anippe didn't dare glance at Abbi Horem, but surely he was pleased. Tut had maintained his authority, but Hebrew infants were safer now. Vigilant Ramessids might still barge in on a Hebrew birth and snatch a newborn son from his mother's arms, but at least the chances of Avaris living peacefully would improve.

Senpa leaned forward to peek around her husband. "We're going to Gurob when we leave here, Anippe. Come with us. Tut and Horemheb will be hunting, and Amenia would love to see you"— her smile quivered a bit—"and her grandson."

Anippe ached to see Ummi, but how could she take Jered and Puah, when Moses was her real son? She might fool Tut, Abbi, and Senpa with an alternate baby today, but Ummi Amenia would inspect him from head to toe. She'd know if Anippe switched children.

"I wish I could, but I'm still quite weak from the birth." Trying to appease Senpa's apparent disappointment, she said, "The midwife was right. We Egyptian women are weak as lambs when it comes to childbearing."

Lighthearted banter eased the tension that had bound the royal guests since they arrived. Anippe laughed with them but felt like an observer, an outsider. It was good to be with family, but she realized that at some point Avaris had become her home. While listening and nodding, she cast a discreet glance at her surroundings and released a contented sigh. This was where she would raise her son and wait for Sebak's return.

"Anippe, my treasure." Abbi knelt before her, his touch on her cheek an awakening. "Are you dreaming of your husband?"

Heat filled her face, and she ducked her head. "How did you know?"

"Because I see that look on Amenia's face each time I come home from battle." He tipped her chin up. "So you're pleased with the husband I chose for you?"

She wrapped her arms around his wide neck. "He's wonderful Abbi, and I miss him terribly." Sitting back on her chair, she hesitated. "Can you tell me where he is or when he'll return home?"

"No, daughter. I can tell you only that he and his uncle Pirameses are the bravest men in my army. They are the best men I know."

"And you are the best man I know." She hugged him again and was struck by a thought. "Abbi."

His face clouded. "What? Are you in pain?"

"No." She cupped his cheek, struck anew by his care for her. "I've just decided what I'll name my son."

Tut leaned close. "I wondered if you'd wait until he was weaned or if you'd tempt the gods and name him before his three years."

"He is strong and a fighter—like his Jad Horemheb." Anippe winked at her abbi. "Which is why his name will be Horemheb."

Abbi Horem's eyes misted. He swiped a callused hand down his face and fairly jumped to his feet, clearing his throat. "If the name suits him. It's a fine name, you know."

The siblings laughed at the elder's awkwardness.

"It is indeed a fine name, General," Tut said with a grin.

Anippe stood and took his hand. "Tell Ummi Amenia, when you see her in Gurob, that now she'll have two Horemhebs to love."

PART 2

Why should I fear when evil days come,
    when wicked deceivers surround me—
those who trust in their wealth
    and boast of their great riches? . . .
People, despite their wealth, do not endure;
    they are like the beasts that perish.

—PSALM 49:5–6,12

18

Then the Lord said to [Abram], "Know for certain
that for four hundred years your descendants will
be strangers in a country not their own and that
they will be enslaved and mistreated there."

—GENESIS 15:13

THREE YEARS LATER

Windstorms were common during harvest season, but that morning's storm had started early and pounded Avaris without reprieve. Puah had stuffed baskets and sackcloth in their single window to block the dust, and Amram and Mered tipped their table on its edge against the curtained doorway. Mered spent his morning chasing his two-year-old daughter, Ednah, while Amram took breakfast duty, supervising seven-year-old Aaron and four-year-old Jered. Puah ground grain for the day's supply of bread, and all of them prayed the winds would be wild enough to postpone the day's labor but gentle enough to avoid damage to crops and buildings.

When the field foreman arrived, commanding little Aaron to the harvest, Amram and Mered knew they must go to their workshops as well. Amram walked quickly toward the mud-brick shelter of Avaris's metal and gem shop on the south side of the villa. Mered's linen workshop, with its thatched walls, let in gentle breezes in the hot late days of Shemut, but in these early days of harvest season, both workers and cloth would suffer.

He trudged through the blowing dust and sand, a long strip of byssus linen around his head to protect him from the gust-driven debris. When he stepped across the shop's threshold, he unwound the headpiece and gingerly

shook out the dust and sand on the tiles at his feet. The normal rhythmic humming of workers was absent, and he heard only the angry fluttering of thatched
walls all around frightened Hebrew slaves. They sat sullenly at their tasks,
glancing over their shoulders at walls that felt woefully unstable against such
heavy winds.

"Why are these slaves working in this?" The amira stood at the doorway
nearest the villa, seemingly unwilling to enter the wind-battered shop. "It isn't
safe . . . can't expect . . ." Her words were muted by sudden increased gusts, and
her expression changed to sheer terror. "Everyone into the villa. Now!" She
beckoned them all to the door where she stood, then directed them down the
path toward the garden. "Bring your supplies. You'll work in the main hall
today. Hurry!"

After another strong gust, the hesitant slaves scooped up what their arms
could carry and hurried past their amira toward the spacious interior of a villa
they'd never entered.

Mered grabbed a basket and threw several scrolls, his reeds and pigment,
and a few of Anippe's designs in it. Since the birth of little *Mehy*—the nickname she'd chosen for her little Horemheb—her designs had increased both in
quantity and quality. Royalty in Egypt and abroad wore the amira's designs on
Avaris's finest linen robes. The weavers had come to appreciate her artistry and
actually preferred her designs to Mered's.

He noticed the weavers hadn't budged. They remained standing at their
vertical looms, lost in the rhythm of their craft.

"You heard the amira. Into the main hall! I'll lose my most skilled workers
if this roof tumbles down on your heads."

"What about the looms?" one of them shouted over his shoulder, never
ceasing his work. "We can't carry them. They're already strung and way too
heavy."

The other nine weavers nodded in agreement. Each loom was as tall as a
man and as wide as three. Avaris's linen was only as good as the men and looms
working in concert.

Anippe appeared at Mered's side. "Two of you stay. The other eight come to the main hall and meet with me about future designs." She turned her attention to Mered. "When this windstorm passes, we'll talk about getting real walls—or at least better supports—built for this workshop. If we're going to make Egypt's best linen, we must have Egypt's best workshop."

The weavers decided among themselves which two would remain, and the others joined the mass exodus from the shop.

Mered stood beside his amira, watching proudly. "Thank you."

"Thank you, Mered. You and your family have become quite dear to me. When Sebak comes home—" Her voice broke. She paused, cleared her throat, and lifted her chin. "When Master Sebak returns, I will have only good things to report of your work here."

She was trying so hard to be grown up and brave. Three years and no word from her husband. The war with the Hittites still raged, but they'd had no news from the Delta messenger for two years now. Even Anippe's inquiries sent to King Tut himself had been left unanswered.

"I'm sure he'll return home soon, Amira. Surely the war won't last much longer."

"I hope you're right, Mered. If I didn't have Mehy and Miriam, I don't know what I'd do."

He thought it odd that she'd speak of her son and a slave girl with equal affection but didn't want to seem coarse by asking. From the corner of his eye, he noticed the amira's glistening eyes and knew more than a windstorm was raging.

"Is there anything I can do to help you, Amira?"

She chuckled, then dabbed her painted eyes with a neatly folded cloth. "No. I suppose you'll think this is good news. I'm returning Jochebed to the craftsmen's village tonight."

Mered clapped his hands, the sound muted by the wind. "I'm indeed happy about it. If Jochebed and Miriam are returning to the village, does that mean I can train Miriam for my linen shop?"

"I said Jochebed is returning. Not Miriam." Turning to meet his gaze, Anippe's eyes grew hard, as if leveling a challenge. "Miriam will remain in the chamber adjoining mine as my handmaid. I allowed her mother to serve as a house slave while the girl was young, but Miriam has seen nine inundations. She's old enough to serve on her own."

"Of course, Amira." Mered bowed. "You've been more than gracious."

Anippe walked away without a backward glance, the storm outside dwarfed by the storm in her eyes.

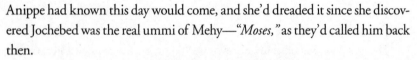

Anippe had known this day would come, and she'd dreaded it since she discovered Jochebed was the real ummi of Mehy—*"Moses,"* as they'd called him back then.

She watched her precious boy play with his acacia-wood blocks in the sitting area at the end of a long day. Tapestries still hung between the courtyard pillars, keeping as much dust and sand out of the chamber as possible. The winds died with the setting sun. Hopefully they were over for the season so harvest could start in earnest.

Miriam appeared from the shadows with a small flask of scented oil. "Would you like me to massage your face and head, Amira?" She'd been especially quiet this evening. No doubt missing Jochebed.

"Yes. Please."

Anippe's heart twisted as the girl removed her wig and helped her recline on the embroidered couch. Closing her eyes, Anippe's mind began to spin. Could she have treated Jochebed better? Done more for the woman who'd given up her son so Anippe could be an ummi, an amira, a true wife to Sebak?

Though children were usually weaned at three years, she'd allowed Jochebed to nourish him six extra months, and she'd even let her continue to call him *Moses*—when no one heard. To everyone else, her son was *Mehy*—a nickname he'd stumbled on while trying to say his given name, Horemheb.

As Miriam massaged her temples, Anippe replayed their nightly routine in her mind. Miriam often did as she was doing now, but Jochebed held Mehy, twirling his black curls around her finger. Nursing him, singing a Hebrew lullaby, speaking of the Hebrew god. Now her son played alone.

Where was Ankhe?

Anippe fairly leapt off her couch, startling both Miriam and Mehy. Grabbing the striker, she banged the Hathor chime—again and again and again. Where was her lazy sister?

Mehy began to cry, and Anippe swept him into her arms, pressing whispered comfort against his ear. "Shh, Ummi just wants Ankhe to come see you and play with you, habibi. You deserve to be treated like the prince of Egypt that you are."

She bounced and cuddled, coaxed and cajoled, while Miriam sat quietly on the couch, watching.

Anippe lifted the single prince's braid on her son's head. As testimony of his weaning and part of the sacrifice to the Ramessid patron god, Seth, the priests had shaved his lovely black curls. He wore the braided princely sidelock, a sign of royalty, and proof of the success of Anippe's well-played deception. But her beautiful boy would trade Ankhe's indifference for Jochebed's love any day.

Her sister spent barely an hour a day with her charge—and that at Anippe's strict requirement. *Why did I agree to let Ankhe tutor him?* Her sister had become a stranger.

Sequestered in her private chamber, Ankhe spent her days alone. Though only across the hallway, she refused to join Anippe at the bathhouse and sulked during the hour she was required to care for Mehy. When Jochebed and Miriam tried to engage her in conversation, she treated them worse than house slaves. It was as if Ankhe was drowning in hate, but Anippe couldn't save her.

"It's done." Ankhe stormed into the chamber and slammed the chamber door behind her. She walked past Anippe and Mehy without a glance, shoving Miriam aside and plopping onto the couch. "I ordered Nassor to escort Jochebed to the slave village."

"At least you didn't make her walk alone in the dark." Anippe was more concerned with Mehy's neglect than Jochebed's return home at the moment. She lowered herself and her son onto a cushion and reached for the goose-shaped bowl of kohl on the table beside them. Using the alabaster applicator, she placed three black circles on the pudgy back of Mehy's hand. "This dot is

Mehy. This one is Ummi. And this one is Re—the great sun god. We are always together—we three. Nothing can separate us."

He picked at the marks with his little finger, and then turned sparkling eyes on her. "Oohh."

Ankhe rolled her eyes. "He doesn't understand what you're saying. He hasn't even celebrated four inundations yet."

"Mehy, tell Ankhe you're a very smart boy, and you can learn."

"I wurn." He threw his hands in the air, and Anippe tickled his ribs, showering his neck with kisses.

Then, gathering his hand in her own, she reviewed. "Tell Ummi about these dots. Who is this one?"

"Mehy."

"And this one?" Her bright little boy recited each dot correctly, and Anippe's heart swelled. "Your tutor, Ankhe, will apply these three circles to your hand every day to remind you that Ummi Anippe and the great god Re will always be with you." She pinned Ankhe with a glare. "Won't you, Teacher Ankhe?"

Seeming bored, Ankhe sighed and offered a noncommittal shrug.

Anippe's frustration rose. "So, sister. What lessons have you planned for my son tomorrow?"

Ankhe's casual manner fled like a hippo backed into a crocodile. "What do you mean 'lessons'? He doesn't even say all his words properly. How can I teach him anything?"

Anippe's rage burned hot and quick. "Take care, sister. I'm giving you one chance—one—to tutor a Ramessid heir. Teach him well, and Sebak will match you with a Ramessid when the war ends. Teach Mehy poorly, and Sebak will pay you with his strap."

Genuine fear lifted Ankhe off the couch and opened her arms to her nephew. "Well, little Mehy. Shall we go to the garden and talk about frogs and flowers?"

"But it's dark." Miriam's practical statement raised Ankhe's ire.

"Shut up, little brat. I've already told you what would happen to you if you got in my way."

Miriam flinched, ready for Ankhe to strike her.

Anippe stepped between them. "Stop it, Ankhe. How dare you threaten my handmaid?"

Tears welled in Ankhe's eyes. "Of course, you defend your precious Miriam. You've chosen her over me since the day she followed that cursed basket into your private canal."

"That's not true—"

"It is true, and I'm sick of it. You'll give me the respect I deserve, Anippe, or—"

"Or what, Ankhe? Or you'll tell Tut and Abbi Horem about Mehy? You wouldn't dare. You've kept the secret too long, sister. You'd lose your head with me now."

Ankhe's expression grew suddenly calm and eerily composed. "You will show me respect, or every one of your treasured Hebrews will live their last days in dead-man's land."

A cold chill crept up Anippe's spine, and she heard Miriam's whimper as in a dream. She turned to see the girl's face hidden in her hands and turned back to face Ankhe.

"What did you do?" Her sister's savage smile fueled Anippe's fear. "What did you do, Ankhe?"

"I did what needed to be done. Puah and Shiphrah know about Mehy, but they've proven their discretion. Jochebed has no incentive to keep our secret, and she might even entertain the hope of getting her son back someday. I told Nassor she had displeased the amira and suggested she be sent to dead-man's land."

Anippe began to tremble, her breathing labored. Sweet, gentle Jochebed in the mud pits on the plateau? Her knees felt weak, and she feared she might drop Mehy. Sinking to the floor, she looked up and found Miriam still whimpering softly, Ankhe standing over her like a victor.

"Shut up, and get out," Ankhe said to the girl. "The amira has no further need of you."

"No, wait." Anippe reached out for Miriam's arm as the girl ran past. "I do need you." The girl's big doe eyes met her gaze, and seeing the pain in those eyes, Anippe regained her wits. "I need you to watch Mehy while Ankhe and I retrieve your mother. There's been a terrible mistake. A mistake, that's all. She'll be back in the craftsmen's village tonight—with your father and little brother."

Miriam nodded and scooped Mehy into her arms. Sensing her need, he laid his head on her shoulder and hugged her tight.

"You'll regret this, Anippe." Ankhe shook her head, panic beginning to rise. "Jochebed will tell the whole village. Besides, we can't go to the plateau after dark. Animals begin prowling, and I don't mean only hyenas and jackals. Ramessid guards on night duty are unpredictable."

Anippe grabbed Ankhe's arm, shoving her toward the door.

"Listen to me, Anippe. We can't go."

Anippe leaned around her to open the chamber door. Nassor had returned and stood at strict attention with three other Ramessid guards.

"You four will escort my sister and me to dead-man's land," Anippe ordered. "Ankhe mistakenly sent one of our skilled workers there, and she wants to offer her apology in person."

19

So they put slave masters over them to oppress them with forced labor.

—Exodus 1:11

Mered placed the last papyrus scroll into its basket under his desk and scanned the still-mussed but somewhat-settled linen shop. Most of the workers had cleared out of the villa's main hall and returned to the shop with all their supplies. They'd begin the real cleanup in the morning, sweeping and washing the linen cloth, thread, and fibers with natron to reduce the lingering dingy effects of the storm.

"All those going to the skilled camp, let's go," he called. "It's almost dark."

The group gathered at the door, the frontline and stragglers assembling sticks and torches. Mered grabbed a torch and lit it from one of the others in the back line.

With his first step outside the door, he noticed a small knot of Ramessid soldiers and . . . the amira? Her sister Ankhe was with them, looking . . . rumpled. Something was most certainly wrong. They were all marching with purpose toward the plateau . . .

Without permission, Mered's legs carried him toward the amira's small retinue, his mind spitting threats as the distance between them lessened. *The Ramessid guards will beat you on sight. The amira will leave you in dead-man's land.*

But Mered's legs and his thoughts didn't seem to agree, and all too quickly he was face to face with a Ramessid's sword.

"Get back to your shop, linen keeper."

"Actually, I was on my way home when I saw you escorting the amira—

umph." The hilt of the sword landed in his belly, doubling him over, and he dropped the torch.

"Stop, Nassor!" Anippe shoved the guard aside. "Mered, are you hurt?"

A strange question. Apparently, she'd never been struck by a sword hilt. He knew better than to speak again. This captain was known for his cruelty.

"We must hurry, Amira," the guard said, nudging her away from Mered. "We have no time for an arrogant slave who doesn't know his place. I'll feel Master Sebak's strap if he returns to find you've been injured on a silly jaunt to dead-man's land." Moonlight glistened on tears welling in Anippe's eyes, and the Ramessid's harsh bearing softened. "Please, Amira. Don't cry. I'm sorry I was gruff."

"Mered might be able to help us find Jochebed on the plateau."

"Jochebed?" Mered winced at the thought of his friend on the plateau.

The Ramessid glared at him, but Anippe placed a hand on his shoulder. "Ankhe sent her to the unskilled village and is about to apologize in person."

A single look at the wicked sister, arms crossed and sandal tapping the dust, told Mered the apology would not be heartfelt.

"I know where some of my unskilled linen workers live in the long houses up there," he said. "They should be able to help us locate a new arrival."

The angry captain grabbed his arm and shoved him ahead—without letting him retrieve his torch. Mered hoped they wouldn't have to search long. Without fire, they'd be at the mercy of predators.

After trekking across the land bridges between the canals of the Delta marshlands, they began climbing the dividing plateau between Avaris and Qantir. Mered had only visited the nightmarish netherworld of mud and grain once, years ago, on a hurried delivery of robes to Qantir. He'd hoped never to witness this level of Hebrew misery again.

When Anippe reached the top of the plateau, she grabbed her knees, panting. Was it the climb that stole her breath or the inhumanity stretching before her? By the light of a full moon and clear sky, men yoked together with papyrus rope cut endless rows of ripened grain. Women stumbled under the weight of full baskets on their heads to dump their loads on a cart only to return and fill their baskets again. Children gleaned in the fields, their small hands cut and bleeding as they probed the heads of grain for every morsel. In mud pits beyond the fields, faint shadows showed bent slaves working under the looming shadows of their taskmasters.

Nassor shouted at the Ramessid in charge, who lounged on an elevated chair between the fields and mud pits, picking his teeth with his dagger. "Overseer, we're looking for a woman."

"We're all looking for a woman, eh soldier?" The overseer slapped his knee, laughing like a hyena. "Pick one. Any one. Just be sure you send her back to the field or pit when you're finished with her."

Mered tried to lead Anippe away. "Please, Amira, let's go look at the long houses. Perhaps it won't be so bad there."

But she stood like a granite pillar, hands covering her mouth, tears streaming down her cheeks. "I didn't know, Mered. I didn't know." She flinched each time a whip snapped and wept in the purple shades of night.

Mered gently gripped her arm. "Come, let's check the long houses. Maybe Jochebed is settling into a new home." It was a desperate attempt at comfort, but he didn't know what else to do.

He looked to Ankhe for help but found her mesmerized by the sights—and smiling. Mered's stomach lurched. She seemed entertained by the suffering, gratified by the ruthlessness.

"This is the Amira of Avaris," Nassor said, "and she has come to retrieve a Hebrew woman named Jochebed who I delivered to the plateau at dusk."

"So you're in trouble, are you, Captain?" the overseer sneered.

"Where are your new arrivals?" Nassor's tone left no room for a chat.

"Some in the fields. Some in the mud pits. There's a guard at each quadrant that can help start the search. You might find her by morning." The foul man poked his dagger at his teeth again and leaned forward, inspecting the amira and her sister. "So you're the amira. You don't look as testy as the one at Qantir."

"Wait here," Nassor growled and stalked away.

Mered reached for both the amira and her sister to draw them close, but Ankhe yanked her arm from his grasp. "Don't touch me, Hebrew."

"Forgive me." Mered bowed his head and backed away to join Anippe.

An eerie hum rose among the guards and slaves. "Are you Jochebed?" First one guard, then another. "Jochebed! Jochebed!" The name spread down the rows and through mud pits. "Have you seen a woman called Jochebed?" Whips snapped, and slaves cried out. The slave masters moved down the rows, growling, threatening, beating, terrifying.

"I didn't know. I didn't know it was like this," Anippe whispered, unable to look away from the inhumanity before her. "How do they do it, Mered? How do they keep breathing? Keep living day after day?"

Mered tried to imagine seeing his people through an Egyptian's eyes. His amira was trembling, repulsed but oddly inspired. "The Hebrews have lived in bondage for hundreds of years, but we endure it because El-Shaddai will one day give us land of our own."

Ankhe turned slowly, a sly grin shadowed by the moon. "So you're planning an uprising, linen keeper? Maybe to reconquer the land your Hyksos ancestors lost?"

"That's not what he said, Ankhe." Anippe stepped between them. "You are not to repeat what Mered said to anyone." Then, turning on Mered, her voice became low and urgent. "Don't ever speak of freedom again. It's treason to dream of your own land."

"The Israelites don't dream of Egypt, Amira. Our God has promised us another land—in Canaan."

Ankhe laughed—a cold, harsh sound—but Mered watched his words tumble and churn in Anippe's eyes. Finally, pity washed over her expression. "An ancient promise isn't enough to sustain your people, Mered. Look at them."

He followed her gaze and knew she was right. Most of his fellow Hebrews had given up on Yahweh's promise generations ago. "Perhaps it is simply love, Amira. Like you and me, those slaves love someone—and it gives them hope."

She smiled a little then and nodded. "I can believe that. Loving Sebak and Mehy gives me hope—and a reason to design linen robes, to maintain Avar—"

"You're ridiculous—both of you." Ankhe's eyes blazed. "These slaves don't live because of some forgotten promise or empty emotion. They live because they can't die—no matter how much they wish it."

Mered was as startled by the girl's declaration as her sister. The passion behind her words clearly erupted from a place deep within. Ankhe wasn't just commenting on the slaves.

Before either could probe her deeper meaning, Ankhe stomped away toward a barley field, where a knot of women waited to empty their baskets into a cart.

Anippe squinted in that direction. "Mered, I think . . . yes, it's Jochebed over there."

Ankhe's fine white linen fairly glowed amid the filthy rough-spun cloth of slaves and guards. She looked like a goddess floating across the field—until she knocked Jochebed's basket from her arms and dragged the poor woman by the collar toward the overseer.

Standing at the base of his elevated chair, Ankhe shoved Jochebed to her knees and shouted at the overseer. "This is Jochebed, you lazy ox. Do you know what Amira Anippe does with lazy oxen that will not work? She cuts them into pieces and serves them to her slaves for their evening meal."

The overseer sat utterly still. Whether shocked or intimidated by this girl's threats, Mered couldn't decide. He leaned close to whisper to the amira. "Have you ever served roasted ox to the house slaves?"

"Never, but I think Ankhe has the man's attention." Anippe raised her voice in the dark silence. "Captain Nassor. Show yourself."

Nassor's large form hurried toward them from where he'd been searching in one of the fields. "I'm here, Amira. How may I serve you?" Breathless, he bent to one knee.

"You will choose a man from among the field captains to replace the overseer. Make sure he leaves at dawn—to join the Ramessids at the Sinai copper mines. He's spent his last day on my estate."

"It will be my pleasure, Amira." Nassor marched toward the overseer's chair, passing Ankhe and Jochebed on his way.

Ankhe was speaking quietly but adamantly to Jochebed, whose head was bowed. When the two women joined Mered and Anippe, Jochebed fell at the amira's feet, weeping but silent.

Anippe braced her shoulders and helped her stand. "Are you all right, Jochebed? Did they hurt you?"

"All is well, Amira. No harm done." Her lips quivered as she spoke, her eyes darting to Ankhe as if checking for approval.

Mered knew his friend. Jochebed was terrified. Ankhe had threatened her somehow.

"You see?" Ankhe said to her sister. "No harm done. And because of this little misunderstanding, you rid Avaris of a lazy overseer. The gods smiled on this night, Anippe." The young woman's cheery disposition laid bare her scheming.

But the amira wasn't distracted by Ankhe's good deed. With her jaw set like Hittite iron, she glared at her sister. "You owe Jochebed an apology, Ankhe."

"I will never apologize to a slave."

Mered watched the sisters' silent war. A thousand moments passed between them, their expressions reflecting both yearning and pain. The two women couldn't be more different, yet they seemed to share a bond as strong as life itself. Or was that bond a shackle?

A single tear crept over Anippe's bottom lash. "You may think Hebrews live only because they cannot die, but Jochebed lives for the people who love her—and you almost took her away from them. You will apologize, Ankhe, or you will join the overseer in the copper mines."

20

In his arrogance the wicked man hunts down the weak,
who are caught in the schemes he devises.

—PSALM 10:2

A quiet knock sounded on Anippe's door, and Mehy looked up from where he and Miriam were playing with his wooden blocks on the goatskin rug.

"Ankhe?" he asked. "Is it Ankhe?"

As if summoned by her wide-eyed pupil, Ankhe entered, Captain Nassor a looming shadow behind her.

"Good morning, Amira." Nassor bowed and winked at Mehy. "I'm delivering Master Mehy's tutor as scheduled. Would you like to choose which guard accompanies the young master and his tutor for their lessons today?"

Ankhe joined Miriam and Mehy on the rug and began playing quietly with them. Anippe glanced at the trio, marveling at her sister's changed behavior. Only two weeks had passed since she'd threatened Ankhe and forced her muttered apology to Jochebed. Watching her now with Mehy, Anippe nearly wept. How could she have threatened to send Ankhe to the copper mines? She hardly recognized the gentle young woman before her. Dressed in a new robe and pleated sheath, Ankhe's eyes were painted with a dazzling malachite and kohl design that rivaled Anippe's own.

"Amira?" A slight touch on her arm awakened her to Nassor's troubled expression. "Has something upset you?"

Anippe realized she was crying and dabbed her eyes with the linen cloth she kept tucked in her belt. "No, Nassor. I'm fine."

"You need only give me a name, and I'll deal quickly with whatever is troubling—"

"No, really." She leaned close and whispered, "I'm just so relieved that Ankhe and Mehy are enjoying each other. My son can hardly wait to see his auntie each day." How could a soldier understand what a child's love could mean to Ankhe? Her sister had never shown love for anyone. Anippe had often wondered if Ankhe was capable of the emotion.

"I'd be happy to accompany Master Mehy during his lessons today." Nassor lowered his voice and smiled at her son. "He's a fine boy."

Ankhe must have thought his approval was meant for her and cast a shy grin over her shoulder, lifting an eyebrow at the Ramessid.

Was Ankhe flirting? Had Nassor taken an interest in her? Anippe shot a glance at the captain but found him waiting on her answer.

"I can summon their usual guard if you'd rather." He seemed totally oblivious to the playful pout on Ankhe's lips.

Anippe looked back at her sister, whose hopeful expression begged for Nassor's attention. He was undoubtedly the reason for Ankhe's paints and pleasantness. "Please wait outside while I speak with Ankhe," Anippe said. "I'll call for you when I've made my decision."

"As you wish, Amira." He bowed and was gone without a second glance at Ankhe. Either he was good at hiding his interest, or Ankhe was headed for heartbreak.

The door clicked shut behind him, and Ankhe was on her feet and growling. "You must let Nassor stay with Mehy and me today. There's no reason to leave him lingering at your chamber door when Mehy and I could benefit from his protection."

"His protection? Is that all you hope to gain from the captain, Ankhe?" Anippe's teasing fell flat.

Ankhe's amiability fled, swallowed up by her familiar defenses. Anger. Bitterness. Indifference. "I'm sure I'll gain nothing. You always make sure of that."

"That's not true, Ankhe. It's not my fault that you refuse to—"

"That I refuse to beg for favor from arrogant men who hate me?"

Anippe shook her head. It was always the same story with Ankhe. She was always the victim. Never at fault. "Do you think Nassor can make you happy, Ankhe?"

"Well, he can't make me any more miserable than I am as your handmaid or Mehy's tutor."

Anippe felt as if she'd been slapped. How could anyone be miserable in the presence of her son? He was light and joy and life—but it was normal for Ankhe to want a son of her own. Her heart softened, seeing her defiant sister as a lonely young woman in need of a man to love her.

"All right, Ankhe. I'll talk to Nassor today, find out if he's worthy of the king's sister. If I approve, I'll write to Tut and ask him to make the match. But I must also be convinced you truly love Nassor before I give my approval. I won't have you wreaking havoc as wife of my villa captain."

Ankhe's eyes filled with tears. "I've always been worthless to you and Tut. I won't expect Mered to design a wedding dress yet." She turned and marched toward the bathhouse, calling to Mehy over her shoulder. "Come, little one. We're already late for your lesson."

Anippe watched her go, heart twisting. She wanted Ankhe to be happy, to be loved. But could Ankhe receive it? Would she?

Miriam tugged on Anippe's robe, bringing her back to the moment. "Do you want me to stay with Mehy and Ankhe today, Amira?" Her message was clear. She feared for Mehy when Ankhe was angry. This slave girl knew better than most how dangerous Ankhe could be.

"No, Miriam. I'll send a chamber guard down to watch over Mehy."

Anippe opened her door and motioned for Nassor.

"Yes, Amira?"

"I'd like you to escort me to the linen shop, but I want your best man, the most trustworthy Ramessid on the estate, to watch over my sister and son today."

"As you wish, Amira." He bowed and left, returning quickly with an older guard about the same age as Abbi Horem. Had Nassor chosen the best Ramessid to guard her son—or a soldier who wouldn't steal Ankhe's heart? She hoped to learn the answer by asking Nassor to introduce the new chaperone.

"Master Mehy, this is my friend, Akil," Nassor said, approaching Ankhe and Mehy near the bathhouse. "He'll take good care of you and Ankhe today." Nassor gave no indication of his feelings, but he nodded and smiled at Ankhe before turning to go. Ankhe beamed, seeming pleased that if Nassor wasn't staying, at least Anippe would pursue Ankhe's match.

Her sister was smitten. Perhaps she could even learn to love.

After returning to Anippe's rooms, Nassor opened the chamber door and allowed little Miriam to go first. The girl's bouncing curls and sweet songs led him and Anippe up the main corridor. Thankfully, Miriam was distracted and wouldn't care about the adult conversation Anippe needed to broach with her captain.

"Nassor," Anippe began haltingly, "you've been my chamber guard since Master Sebak and I married, and you never seem to go home." She chuckled, feeling awkward. "Isn't there a wife who misses you? Children? A dog or cat?"

His lips curved into a tentative smile. "No, Amira. I live in the soldiers' barracks and take short naps in the villa's servant quarters."

No wife or home. This could be good. If Tut offered him a home as part of Ankhe's dowry, Nassor's circumstances would improve considerably.

"I see. You must get lonely."

When he didn't answer, Anippe glanced up at the big man beside her and found his smile replaced with a grim expression. "Master Sebak trusts me to protect you, Amira. I couldn't . . . I would never betray his trust by inappropriate—"

"Oh no. I didn't mean . . ." Anippe pressed her palms against her cheeks, feeling the heat. Shaking her head, she tried to explain without giving away Ankhe's secret. "I heard one of the servant girls talking. She seemed quite taken with you, and I just wondered if . . ."

He sighed, and his grin returned. "Don't worry, Amira. I'm not like other Ramessids. I'd rather bed a jackal than a Hebrew."

His comment, meant to reassure, broke Anippe's heart. How could a man who seemed so kind and gentle harbor such hatred for another human being? She felt the blood drain from her face, remembering the way Nassor had shoved his sword hilt in Mered's belly the night he'd offered to help find Jochebed.

Turning away, she pretended to peruse the garden as they walked the sandstone path to the linen shop in silence. Nassor's comments might not have bothered Ankhe, but how could Anippe allow such a coarse man to marry her sister?

"Good morning, Amira." Mered greeted her, carrying a scroll with a half-finished design on it. "I've been working on this all morning, but I can't envision the angle of the palm branches."

Captain Nassor stood behind her, waiting. The amira seemed distracted, perhaps even upset. She said, "Thank you, Nassor. That will be all." After a curt nod, the captain walked away, and Anippe heaved a sigh.

"Is everything all right this morning, Amira?" Mered kept an eye on Anippe but also glanced around for Miriam. The little girl was a walking banner, her activity revealing the mood of the amira's chamber each morning. If trouble plagued the amira's world, Miriam stayed near, attentive and sensitive to her needs. If the morning had progressed smoothly, Miriam flitted from station to station in the linen shop, chatting and entertaining Mered's workers.

"All is well, Mered. I'm a little tired, that's all." The amira reached for the design scroll. "Let's look at this partial palm tree."

Mered listened to her ideas, watching her creativity bloom as her countenance brightened. Whatever had worried her on her arrival was lost in the world of linen. She set aside the scroll, content with her planned design.

"Miriam is learning quickly." Anippe nodded toward the girl, who flitted between workers like a bee gathering pollen. "She doesn't miss Jochebed as much when she's here with the other Hebrews."

Mered was struck by his amira's compassion. What other master would care about the feelings of a little slave girl? Jochebed had returned safely to Amram and Aaron two weeks ago, but she and Puah shared many tears over Miriam's absence. Puah kept Jochebed busy at home, spoiling their son Jered and helping with daughter Ednah. Their home felt more complete with Jochebed there. If only Miriam could return to them someday.

"I think the others enjoy having Miriam here as much as she enjoys learning." Anippe giggled as she watched one of the bead workers sewing beads into the little girl's hair.

Mered sighed. "Our busy little bee should be visiting every station, not lingering too long at any one." He crossed his arms and tried to scowl.

Miriam had learned to wait near the men hackling flax fibers with sharp-toothed combs and then rush their finished product to the women twisting fibers into long *roves*. She sometimes helped wind roves around pottery pieces, filling baskets to the rim, and then she'd lug the baskets to spinners, who used spindle and whorl to create various weighted threads. Finally, the cheerful little bee buzzed huge spools of thread to the men at the massive vertical looms to be woven into the heart and soul of Egyptian commerce. The Avaris estate symbol would only be woven into byssus linen—fabric so sheer and white, even the clouds grew envious.

"She must learn to listen more than she talks. I won't have her disturb my workers." Mered lifted an eyebrow and left his stool.

He found Miriam chatting with his best rover and guided her away. Kneeling before her, he schooled his features and met her big brown eyes. "Good rovers are essential to linen making. You must watch quietly to learn the skill, not distract them with stories about flowers and butterflies." He walked away, hiding a grin, and returned to his desk.

Anippe raised a brow. "That was supposed to be firm?"

"Well, I didn't jab her with a cudgel, if that's what you mean." His teasing robbed the amira's good humor. "I'm sorry, Amira. I didn't mean to . . ."

Anippe studied her hands, rubbing at a stray mark of pigment from the design. "Nassor is a good man. He doesn't know you, Mered. I'm sure if he'd known you were trying to help find Jochebed—"

Worried by his amira's sudden silence, Mered followed her gaze and saw a dirty, weary Medjay running toward them.

The Nubian fell at Anippe's feet. "Forgive me, Amira, but you must come quickly to the Gurob Palace. Our great King Tut, mighty son of Horus, has met with an unfortunate accident and commands your immediate presence."

"What happened? How seriously is he injured? What kind of accident?"

The Medjay lifted his gaze. "The axle of his chariot snapped while he was pursuing a lion in the annual Fayum hunt. The bone in his leg broke through the skin, and now his body rages with fever."

Anippe's sorrow transformed to suspicion, then to fury. "How can an axle just snap?"

"We must leave within the hour, Amira. I will accompany you to the Gurob Palace, and we will both find the answers we seek." He held her gaze, communicating more with his silence than with his words.

Anippe bolted from the shop without a word, not even a tear. Mered could barely breathe at the implications of the Medjay's report.

The warrior stood, towering over the linen keeper. "Your face healed without scars." He nodded and turned to leave, but Mered stopped him.

"Wait, please." Looking more closely, Mered recognized him as the guard who'd beaten him before arresting Shiphrah. "Please, you should eat before you begin your return journey to Gurob." Mered stood, motioning the Nubian to follow toward his favorite palm tree. "You can share my midday meal."

"Why offer food to a man who beat you?" He offered a wry grin. "Is it poisoned?"

"Maybe if I'd known you were coming." Mered grabbed the basket of bread and gold beer Puah had packed that morning and walked toward the north door.

The Nubian followed, still cautious. Outside he inhaled deeply, seeming to enjoy the view of the Avaris quay. When he reached the palm tree, he folded his legs beneath him, and rested his back against the tall, jagged trunk— keeping his spear nearby.

Mered opened the basket and offered the whole portion of bread and beer Puah had packed. "May I ask your name?"

The Medjay looked at the proffered food and then back at the quay. "No."

"No, I can't ask, or—"

"No, I don't want all your food. My name is Mandai."

Mered shoved the bread at him again. "Mandai, take the food. It sounds like your long journey is only half over. You'll have another two days on the Nile to return to Gurob."

"Three days because it's against the tide—longer if the amira insists on stopping at night." Mandai accepted the bread and beer with a gracious nod and ate ravenously.

"What do you mean if the amira insists? If Anippe doesn't insist, Ankhe most certainly will. It's suicide to travel on the Nile after dark."

The Medjay paused between bites. "My orders were to bring Anippe. King Tut mentioned nothing of the other sister."

Mered shook his head, suddenly feeling deep sympathy for the unsuspecting warrior.

Mandai noticed and paused chewing again. "Out with it, Hebrew."

"Ankhe is a warrior like you've never seen before. You should prepare for a battle."

Mandai grinned and took a final swig of beer. "You keep making linen, and let me get the amira to Gurob safely to comfort her brother." His hunger now satisfied, curiosity piqued. "Why do you help a soldier of the king who beat your face and arrested your friend?"

"Because you serve the king as I serve my amira. They are human, like you and me, and each of us must answer before El-Shaddai for our sins."

"This El-Shaddai—he is your Hebrew god?"

"He is the one true God."

Mandai turned his gaze on the quay and was quiet for many heartbeats. "You should tell your one god to help me find the man who partially sawed through King Tut's axle. Pharaoh's accident was no accident." The Medjay turned raging eyes on the linen keeper. "And if you tell anyone I said so, you will meet your god very soon."

21

Be still before the Lord and wait patiently for him;
do not fret when people succeed in their ways,
when they carry out their wicked schemes.

—PSALM 37:7

Anippe saw the Gurob quay as the sun was setting and nudged Ankhe off her shoulder. "Wake up, sister."

Their small papyrus skiff had left Avaris two days ago after midday. When Ankhe heard Tut had summoned only Anippe, she tied herself to the skiff, daring Mandai to—as she put it—*"touch the king's sister and die."* They'd needed a second oarsman when Ankhe insisted on coming, so Anippe asked Nassor. Ankhe was thrilled.

"Did you bring a mirror?" Ankhe tried to neaten the smudged kohl around her eyes.

"No, I didn't bring anything except food for our journey." Anippe bit her tongue to keep silent. Could anyone be that self-absorbed? "Go find Ummi Amenia or Senpa. They'll have a cursed mirror, and you can tell them we're here. I'm going to see Tut."

The skiff slid onto the sandy bank, and Anippe sprang to her feet before Ankhe could whine.

"Let me help you." Nassor offered his hand, but Ankhe grabbed her shoulder, almost toppling them both into the river.

"Don't forget, Anippe. Don't forget to ask Tut . . ." Ankhe cast a shy glance at Nassor and lowered her voice. "Please, Anippe. I'm begging you." No threats. No tricks. Ankhe's pleading seemed utterly guileless in that moment—and Anippe would do anything she could to make her sister happy.

But where was Ankhe's concern for Tut? She hadn't asked about Tut's condition once except to inquire if he was strong enough to write. Mandai had looked at her as if she'd lost her mind, but Anippe knew Ankhe needed their brother's written marriage match if he couldn't make the match in person.

Mandai jumped to the bank and gripped Anippe's elbow, fairly pulling her from the skiff. "Hurry, Amira. I hope we've arrived in time."

Anippe could only nod her agreement—and her gratitude. Mandai and Nassor had rowed against the tide for two days and nights, stopping only to relieve themselves and swat an occasional crocodile. How could she repay their kindness?

She was panting by the time they entered the king's residence. Anippe had never been invited into the House of Adoration, Tut's inner sanctum, the room he shared only with Senpa. But Mandai escorted her past every guard in the palace, returning their salutes and hardening his stare.

"These are Vizier Ay's men." He spoke in a whisper, his focus and gait unchanged.

Anippe's heart skipped at the mention of Abbi Horem's fiercest enemy. The handsome governor hadn't come to Avaris with the other royals when Anippe had feigned Mehy's birth—and Tut had regained his wits in Ay's absence. Why was Ay back in the king's favor—or was he?

They arrived at ebony double doors inlaid with lapis and ivory and trimmed in gold. Mandai spoke to the two Medjay guards in their native tongue, raising his voice when they obviously refused Anippe entry. One of the guards disappeared into the chamber, returned quickly, and then bowed low as he opened the door for the king's sister.

Anippe nearly retched at the stench. A serving maid quickly handed her a sachet of crushed lotus petals to hold over her nose. Tut lay in his bed, his left leg wrapped to twice its normal size and elevated on pillows. Vizier Ay sat in a gilded chair on the other side of the bed, writing with reeds and pigment. Four Medjays and three priests of Amun-Re surrounded Tut, while a physician and two handmaids busied themselves in the chamber.

The vizier stood when she entered, offering a cursory bow. His dove-gray eyes roamed the length of her, and Anippe wished she'd worn rough spun instead of byssus linen. "Your brother will be happy to see you when he wakes—if he wakes."

Anointing oil glistened on her brother's head and face, beading on his fevered brow. Without the kohl-black eye of Horus extending from brow to temple, he looked like a little boy.

Overcome with anguish, Anippe leaned down to hug him—but halted suddenly and turned to the physician. "Will I hurt him if I touch him?"

He looked to Ay for the answer. Anippe wanted to scream. *Why ask him? Has he learned a priest's magic arts while I've been in Avaris?*

Still raging inwardly, she felt a hand on her shoulder.

"Amira, sit in this chair." Mandai had placed it near the bed. Again, his kindness overwhelmed her.

"Thank you." She gratefully complied and lifted Tut's hand, leveling a malicious glare at the vizier. "How long since he last woke? Have you summoned Abbi Horem?"

"He opened his eyes yesterday but was barely coherent. I summoned you when the infection began a few days ago. Surely you sent messengers to the general." A sinister smile creased his light-brown face, extending his beaklike nose over his top lip.

"Why would I send a message to the prince regent? That's your job, Vizier."

Ay leapt to his feet, leaning over the bed, grinding out his words. "My job is to protect Egypt from children and fools who would idly watch it dwindle or lose it to savages."

His gaze held her, daring her to look away. Anippe's heart pounded at his veiled confession. Tut was the child and Abbi Horem the fool, and Ay was obviously determined to have Egypt's throne. How could she fight him alone?

She felt a slight squeeze of her hand and looked down at her brother.

"Out." Tut's voice was barely a croak, a whisper pushed through dry, cracked lips. A handmaid rushed to him and pressed a wet cloth against his mouth. He received the moisture before trying to speak again. "Everyone out—except Anippe." He opened his eyes—barely two slits—but they closed in relief at the sight of his Medjay. "Mandai, you stay too."

Ay's aggression turned to feigned loyalty. "I had no idea you were awake, lord of all, good god who wears Egypt's crowns. I would be happy to remain—"

"Get out."

As the vizier moved toward the door, he turned his polite banter on Anippe. "Don't stay too long. The king is extremely weak—as you can see. I'd be honored if you'd join me for a private meal in my chamber tomorrow evening, Amira Anippe."

He offered a curt bow, and a trail of Nubians, priests, maids, and the physician followed him out.

The chamber grew quiet, and Tut appeared to be sleeping again. Anippe abandoned her chair, rattled by the invitation, but sat beside her brother on his mattress. Tut winced at the movement.

"Oh, I'm sorry. I'll go back—"

"No, stay with me." He clutched her arm, his grip stronger than expected, and a tear slid from the corner of his eye. "I finally have someone in the room not trying to kill me."

Grieving for all they'd lost, Anippe laid her head on her brother's bandaged chest and listened to his heartbeat. "How can I help you?"

"Horemheb was right. Ay will take Egypt from me if I don't die first. Mandai, did you tell her about the axle?"

"No, my king."

"The axle was sawed halfway through. My accident was no accident. I know Ay ordered it."

Anippe's head sprang off Tut's chest. "So there's proof? You can have him arrested?"

Mandai stepped forward, leaning over the king. "I will lead my Medjays against the vizier. We are your loyal servants, my king, and will hunt and kill Ay like the jackal he is."

"There is no proof. Ay is shielded by some of my own bodyguard. Even if you could find proof and enough loyal noblemen to stand with me, I can't return to Memphis to judge him." He paused, taking several breaths, his pain evident. "Our homeland troops are loyal to Ay, and Commander Nakhtmin rules the Nubian army through brutal threats on their families." Tut grasped Anippe's hand. "I'm dying, Anippe, and Ay will take the throne if Horemheb is not here when . . ." His words trailed off, his strength spent.

Anippe finished for him. "The next pharaoh must be present to receive the embodiment of Horus."

"I didn't realize Ay hadn't summoned Horemheb . . . but why would he? Why didn't I listen to Horemheb?" Tut turned away, regret clinging to him like the sweat-soaked bed sheets.

Anippe's thoughts began to whir. "Don't give up, brother. Ay thinks he's won the battle—but he's foolishly declared war against Horemheb and his daughter." She rose from her chair and kissed the cheek of a god. "I love you, King Tut. Rest and let Lady Isis, goddess of healing, do her work while your sister prepares a feast for our enemy he'll not soon forget."

❧

Anippe peeked through the curtained doorway of Gurob's banquet hall, counting the guests of the banquet she'd arranged to trap her enemy. Rather than accept yesterday's invitation to dine in his chamber, Anippe had arranged a banquet—in Vizier Ay's honor—to show gratitude for his devotion during Tut's convalescence. The arrogant governor had invited even more guests.

Why hadn't Ummi Amenia arrived yet? She'd been as anxious as Anippe to see their enemy exposed when they'd shared their midday meal earlier. Senpa had joined them, and Ankhe, of course, had been furious that Anippe had neglected to secure a written document of Tut's order for her to marry Nassor.

Even now, Ankhe chatted with others at the women's head table as if their brother were not dying in his chamber. Beside her sat Ummi Amenia's empty cushion, and on the other side Senpa, withdrawn and mournful. The Gurob Harem wives filled ten tables in the hall, their chatter growing restless. They shouted rude comments from one table to another about Anippe's absence. The women of Gurob had never been short of opinions.

Across the aisle, Vizier Ay lounged at a table with twelve other noblemen, laughing, drinking, and grabbing at dancing girls. Musicians played, acrobats

tumbled, and the barely clad dancers kept the men entertained while Anippe
kept watch for Ummi Amenia.

What could be keeping her?

Mandai and Nassor stood guard behind Ankhe, impatiently awaiting
Anippe's arrival. They examined every guest and servant like hawks watching
for mice in a field. Anippe captured Mandai's attention and summoned him
silently. The Medjay's speed and stealth were as useful in a raucous banquet
room as on a battlefield.

Moments later, he slipped behind the curtain with her. "What is it?
Trouble?"

"I don't know. Ummi Amenia should have been here by now. Go check
her chamber while I begin the banquet."

With a nod, he was gone.

Anippe emerged from the curtain and bowed to the chief anointer, who
affixed a waxy cone of scented oil to her wig. Like the cones worn by the other
guests, her carved ornament would melt away by night's end, dripping its sweet
scent into and through her wig—much like the melting of Ay's dreams of
Egypt's throne. Anippe would expose his treachery among witnesses tonight.

The thought brought a smile to her face as she strolled up the center aisle.
She nodded greetings to lifelong friends and settled on the vacant cushion beside Queen Senpa, bowing politely to the vizier across the aisle. "Thank you for
indulging my need to reunite with the women of Gurob, Vizier. I haven't seen
them since my marriage three years ago, and I know Tut will be pleased when
I bring him tidings of our celebration."

The vizier wiped sweat from his brow and, though answering her greeting,
addressed the men at his table. "I would think the king's sister would be grieving his serious injuries, not celebrating his imminent death." His booming
voice captured the attention of every guest.

Anippe's heart fluttered; this was the time. She searched the doorway—
Mandai hadn't returned with word of Amenia, but she couldn't wait. Servants
were streaming in from the kitchen, platters laden with roast goose, gazelle, and
wild boar—a happy distraction for the guests when the conversation became
heated.

"I learned from King Tut that his so-called accident was instead an at-tempt on his life," she said. As one, the audience gasped, leaving the room sti-fling. "What do you know about it, Vizier?"

"I was given the same information by the king's bodyguard—but I don't think we should discuss it here." He lifted an eyebrow, challenging her with an arrogant smirk.

"In front of Pharaoh's noblemen is the perfect place to expose a crime. Don't you agree?" She directed the question to their audience, who ardently approved, shouting and pounding the marble tables. Quieter, she said to Ay alone, "I've got you, jackal-headed cobra."

He answered as quietly. "You've fallen into your own trap." Lifting his voice over the din, he shouted to his Nubians guarding the side doors. "Bring in the prisoner."

The doors opened slowly. Two Medjays entered, one small woman be-tween them.

"Amenia?" Anippe jumped from her cushion and sprinted toward the lone prisoner. Her legs couldn't keep up, and she fell at her ummi's feet, clutching her shackled ankles, sobbing.

"Will you kiss the feet of the woman who tried to kill your brother?" The vizier's voice resounded like a trumpet in the sudden silence.

"Get up, my daughter. Get up." Amenia's voice was as strong and compas-sionate as it had been the first time Anippe heard it. "You are sister of the King, daughter of Horemheb, Amira of Avaris—you do not grovel at a prisoner's feet."

But Anippe would grovel at anyone's feet if she could save Ummi Amenia.

Pressing the hem of Amenia's robe to her eyes, she dried her tears, leaving streaks of kohl on the pure white linen. She stood to face the one man she hated enough to kill. "Vizier Ay, you know Amira Amenia would never harm King Tut." She returned to the head table but this time knelt opposite the vizier in a supplicant's position. "General Horemheb loves the king as his own son—as does Amira Amenia."

"My spies intercepted secret papyri passed between Amenia and Horem-heb, in which Amenia informed the general of delicate matters concerning Egypt's government."

"You mean Amira Amenia informed her husband, General Horemheb, the prince regent, that you conspired with Commander Nakhtmin to steal King Tut's throne?" Anippe retorted.

The gallery hummed—ample grain for Gurob's gossip mill.

Ay smiled. "The general has been singing that dirge for years, my dear, and King Tut himself agreed it was foolishness. Please, if you have any proof that I've conspired against our god and king, present it now."

Anippe stood trembling with rage—speechless and alone. She'd sent Mandai to look for Amenia, but even he had no proof Tut's axle had been sawed. She stared longingly at Amenia, helpless to save the woman who'd saved her.

"Ummi!" Anippe ran toward her, but two Medjays grabbed her arms with iron hands.

Ay's singsong voice rose above Anippe's cries. "We must all remember that Princess Anippe has endured a long journey from Avaris and arrived to see her dear brother, the divine god Tut, nearing his eternal home. And then to realize her adoptive parents were likely responsible for the king's death . . . Well, friends, her despair proves she knew nothing of Horemheb and Amenia's plot to kill Tut."

The audience hummed its approval of Ay's hypocrisy, and Anippe saw pity on their faces. She growled, lunging at the vizier. "No! You're a liar!"

He waved his hand at the Medjays. "Take her back to her chamber. I'll speak with her in the morning after she's had more rest."

The Medjays began dragging her up the aisle. Nassor's guttural cry and heavy footsteps came from behind, and the Medjays dropped her. In an instant, a few well-placed Medjay blows stopped the Ramessid cold and left him moaning in a heap.

Anippe closed her eyes, unable to bear her hopelessness. The warriors grabbed her arms again, their fingers biting into flesh. She cried out, and to her surprise, they released her.

When she opened her eyes, Mandai stood blocking the center aisle, strong and immovable as the dark stones of Coptos.

"I do not wish to kill you, brothers," he said, "but King Tut has charged me to protect Amira Anippe."

Her captors backed away. Nassor stood, shaky but able, and helped Anippe to her feet. Head held high, Mandai led her from the room, Nassor serving as rear guard.

Anippe didn't speak until she was sure they weren't being watched or followed. "I'm not going back to my room, and I'm not meeting that reptile tomorrow morning."

Mandai kept watch all the way through the pillared corridor between the harem and the king's private residence. "I'm sorry to disagree, Amira, but for now, you are going back to your chamber—to gather food and wait for me. Nassor will stay with you until Ankhe returns from the banquet." They arrived at the northern-most corner of the harem. "By that time, I will find a way to rescue Amenia, and I'll bring her back to the skiff before the moon rises full."

"Tonight? Do you think you can save Amenia and get to the skiff tonight?" Breathless, Anippe dared to hope.

"That is my plan." Mandai glanced over her head at Nassor. "If I'm not back by the moon's zenith, take both the king's sisters and leave without me. Ay will kill them if they're still at Gurob in the morning."

Anippe lay in her bed, listening to the familiar sounds of the Fayum. The sheer netting around her bed kept mosquitoes from feasting on her, while lions roared and owls screeched. The whole earth was restless when evil prowled—and Ay was evil. More than she had imagined.

Would she ever see Tut or Senpa or her ummi again? She'd said her good-bye to her brother, but Ummi . . . And what would happen to Senpa? Tears streamed from the corners of Anippe's eyes as she lay deathly still on the turquoise neck rest.

"Anippe, are you awake?" Ankhe's whisper sounded gravelly.

Anippe swallowed her tears and forced calm. "No. Sound asleep."

"Do you think we should leave without Mandai? I can see the moon, and it's almost—"

"We'll leave when Mandai returns with Ummi Amenia."

Silence. Ankhe was dealing with her own disappointment. Anippe hadn't spoken to Tut about Ankhe's marriage. There would be no wedding now.

"After you left the banquet, Vizier Ay passed judgment on Amenia. *Treason*, Anippe. Do you really think one Nubian warrior can rescue her?"

Anippe's tears flowed freely in the darkness. She need not answer a question void of hope.

"And you should have seen the way the vizier fawned over Senpa. He poured her wine, fed her grapes. I think he would have wiped her nose if she had sneezed."

"Ankhe, enough."

"I was just—"

"You were just prattling on about a man who's trying to kill our brother, Amenia, and us—and who might marry Senpa to secure the throne."

Their chamber door burst open. Nassor grabbed both women, wrenching them to their feet. "Out the courtyard gate."

Anippe ran, glancing over her shoulder. She saw Mandai behind them, but he was alone. "Where's Ummi?"

Nassor still ran, forcing both women to keep up.

"Where's Ummi Amenia?" Anippe cried, bare feet kicking up sand and small rocks as they neared the quay.

"Get in the boat." Nassor shoved both sisters into the waiting skiff, and Mandai hurried aboard, clutching his bloody abdomen. Three Medjays crested the hill above the quay, swords drawn.

"You can't row, Mandai." Anippe grabbed one short oar and shoved it into the sandy shallows, helping Nassor push them off shore. The Ramessid knelt with the second oar to steer them.

No one looked back as Nassor and Anippe paddled like mad. When they were safely on their way in the canal, Anippe glanced over her shoulder and saw their pursuers kick the sand in frustration. Not even Medjays braved the Nile without a boat at night.

Mandai lay against the side of their skiff, checking the long gash in his side. "No trumpets sounding. This is good." He reached over and tore Ankhe's linen robe.

"Stop. What are you doing?"

Mandai drew his dagger, and Ankhe grew quiet. "I need a portion of your robe for a bandage. Keep still or my blade may slip."

Anippe kept checking behind them. Mandai was right—no trumpets meant no pursuing soldiers on the Nile's moonlit waters. She watched him tend his wound and imagined the worst, but she needed to hear it. "Mandai, what happened?"

He wrapped his belly in silence, wincing only when he drew the strip of Ankhe's robe into a tight knot. Crimson seeped through the fine linen, but his bleeding slowed considerably. Moonlight revealed the Medjay's sadness. "By the time I discovered where they'd hidden Amira Amenia . . ." He shook his head and grew silent again.

"Please, Mandai. I need to know."

Head bowed, he whispered, "She was begging Ay's guards to kill her."

Anippe covered her mouth in horror.

Mandai reached for her loose oar before it toppled into oblivion. "I knew your ummi couldn't survive this journey, so I ran away—but one of my own men turned his sword on me."

"Thank you for trying, my friend." Anippe buried her face in her hands, releasing the waves of grief that had built since she'd heard of Tut's injury.

By the gods! Ay will pay for what he's done.

The steady rhythm of splashing oars lulled her into a dazed despair. Faded memories resurfaced—spinning flax with Amenia and Senpa, Tut playing with wooden soldiers. Would she really see them in the afterlife? Were the legends of the gods truth or lies?

"Amira, you should rest." Nassor switched the oar to his left side, while Mandai switched to his right. The Medjay's bandage was completely saturated with blood.

"I can't sleep. Give me your oar, Mandai." Anippe didn't wait for his protest. She took the oar, and Ankhe eased the warrior back against her.

Their journey would be slower, but at least they'd escaped to get word to Abbi Horem. They would burrow into the safety of the Delta and Ramessid military strongholds. Abbi would know what to do—and maybe Sebak would finally come home to her.

Her arms and back burned with every stroke of the oar, but the memory of her husband's embrace made her strong.

22

For the sake of my family and friends,
I will say, "Peace be within you."

—PSALM 122:8

Mered laughed so hard his sides ached as he watched his children and Mehy play with Miriam in their single room at dawn. When Anippe had asked Mered if he and Puah would tend the young prince while she and Ankhe traveled to Gurob, he'd felt honored. Watching Miriam bask in her family's presence was an added blessing.

The only tarnish on this joyous morning were Mandai's cryptic words, which still echoed in Mered's memory. *Pharaoh's accident was no accident.* What had the amira discovered when she arrived at Gurob?

Amram shoved aside their adjoining curtain. "Sounds like we're missing the fun." Young Aaron darted around his father to join the three little ones in a crawling chase around the low-lying table. Miriam played shepherdess, herding them in the same direction.

Mered waved his old friend over to his safe corner. "Amram, come over here before you're trampled by the stampede."

Amram tucked his feet under him and sat in amiable silence. Two proud fathers, enjoying lively households before the day's work began. Puah and Jochebed continued their work near the cook fire, partly cooking, partly protecting little fingers and toes from the flames.

"Stay on those knees," Puah scolded when Jered pushed to his feet to run. "You may chase all you like—as long as you chase on your knees."

Brilliant. Mothers were creative geniuses when keeping children safe at play.

"Gruel is ready." Jochebed placed seven clay bowls on the table, each filled with steaming porridge. Their families had begun eating together while Jochebed served in the villa and Puah cooked for Amram and Aaron. They'd grown used to the company, and Jochebed gladly helped when she returned. Family of the heart was as thick as blood.

The sound of shuffling feet outside warned Mered of an intruder before the doorway curtain stirred.

"Mered, we need Puah at the quay."

"Ankhe?" Mered was on his feet in an instant, the children cowering at their mothers' skirts. "Why? What happ—"

"Mandai is hurt. They're waiting at the quay." She looked for Miriam and motioned toward Mehy. "Take him to Anippe's chamber. Now."

Mered cast a quick glance at Puah, who was already gathering healing herbs in a basket. He couldn't wait any longer. "I'll run ahead and see if I can help."

"I'm going too," Ankhe said. "Puah knows the way to the quay."

Mered followed Ankhe out the door and up the hill toward the villa. He'd never seen the girl genuinely rattled, but fear made her run like a desert hare. He could barely keep up.

"Ankhe, what happened?"

"Vizier Ay tried to kill Tut. He accused Amenia of treason." She gulped for breath at the top of the hill and pointed toward the quay and their small skiff. "Mandai was injured trying to save her. We barely escaped. We drifted with the current at night, and Anippe and I helped Nassor paddle during the day."

Mered ran down the hill, where Anippe and Nassor hovered over Mandai, who leaned against the side of the boat with a blood-stained bandage wrapped around his abdomen.

Nassor bent to one knee and greeted Mered with a burning stare, but the Medjay smiled at his approach. "Linen keeper, your prayers worked. Your one god proved beyond doubt who sawed the axle."

Mered bent over, gulping air, his side aching from the run. "Perhaps you should have . . . been more specific . . . about my prayer. I didn't know you planned to fight the saw."

"Mered, thank you for coming." Anippe was pale and trembling. Without her face paints, she looked like a little girl. "Help Nassor carry Mandai to the villa."

"Of course, Amira. Which chamber?"

"Put him in Miriam's chamber. She and Mehy can sleep in my sitting area." Tears spilled over her bottom lashes. She turned to Nassor. "Who can we trust to send word to Abbi Horem?"

Nassor tilted his head, gentle compassion from a rough-spun cloth. "Don't worry, Amira. You're safe now. Every Ramessid in the Delta is loyal to General Horemheb. We protect our own—and you are Master Sebak's own."

Her composure crumbled with Nassor's tender promise. Ankhe promptly cradled her sister's shoulders and turned toward the villa. "The men can wait for Puah at the quay. You need to rest."

Confused—and more terrified because of Ankhe's kindness—Mered looked to Nassor for an explanation. "What happened at Gurob?"

"A slave has no need to know."

Mandai raised a brow, glancing from the Ramessid to the Hebrew and back. "I see you two have met." He reached for Nassor's shoulder and waited for the captain to meet his gaze. "This linen keeper can be annoying, it's true, but he is a good man and the amira trusts him. You would be wise to trust him too."

Not the most glowing recommendation Mered could've hoped for, but the Medjay's words seemed to soften Nassor's hard stare. With a deep sigh, he sat down and shoved off his wig, wiping perspiration from his bald head and face. He rested his arms on his knees and waited for Mered to sit.

For Nassor, it was as cordial as he could be to a Hebrew slave. Mered felt privileged and sat.

"We arrived at Gurob at sunset on the third day," Nassor began, "and the amira spoke with King Tut briefly—enough to confirm Ay's guilt in the so-called hunting accident. But he had no proof. At a banquet that night, Vizier Ay accused General Horemheb's wife of treason." Nassor turned to Mandai, indicating the rest of their story was his to tell.

"Amira Amenia is most certainly dead by now—probably King Tut as well. I must leave tonight to warn General Horemheb of Ay's treachery." Mandai tried to stand, and both Mered and Nassor tried to help him. The Medjay stumbled, and Mered caught his chest, barely missing the gash on his belly. The warrior cried out.

Mered looked over his shoulder, wondering what was keeping Puah. She should have been here by now.

"You're not going anywhere tonight, Medjay." Nassor's commanding voice allowed no argument. "Help me lift him, Hebrew. Your wife can find her patient at the villa."

The two men braced the injured warrior and began walking uphill.

Nassor looked toward the plateau separating Avaris from Qantir. "We must alert the Ramessids on both estates and then spread the word to all Delta fortresses. Ay will attack Avaris first, then other estates, and leave the fortresses until last."

"Attack Avaris?" Mered's heart leapt to his throat. "We're an estate full of unarmed slaves and a few guards. Why would he attack us?"

"If the vizier can seize estates, he gains wealth and resources while crushing Ramessid morale. As I told the amira, every Ramessid is loyal to Horemheb, but if Ramessid families are butchered before Horemheb returns with his army, Ay has won the war before the battles really begin."

Mandai winced. "Stop, please." He removed his arms from their shoulders and braced his hands on his knees. "Nassor is right. I won't be well enough to travel on the river tomorrow, but the Delta estates and fortresses must be warned immediately." He stood and gripped Nassor's shoulder. "You must alert the Delta, while I warn General Horemheb. The last report sent to King Tut said Horemheb's army was deep in Hittite territory on their way to Kadesh. I'll travel with the next merchant caravan that leaves Avaris and find a ship headed to Byblos. By then, my wound will have healed, and I can cut across the mountains to find the general."

Mered began shaking his head before Mandai finished speaking. "No merchant will allow a Medjay warrior—an injured Medjay warrior—to join his caravan or board his ship. Traders are suspicious by nature, my friend. You need someone who looks like a trader and thinks like a merchant to win their trust and get you on their ship."

Nassor and Mandai glanced at each other and then back at Mered with conspiratorial grins.

Mered realized he'd sealed his own fate. "Oh, no. I can't go. Who will run the linen shop?" Even as he spoke, he knew Anippe could do it. She knew every process and could write better than he.

"You do look like a merchant, linen keeper." Nassor squeezed his shoulder.

"But I—"

"It's not a request." Nassor's good humor was gone. "The Medjay said you were a good man who could be trusted. I'm a Ramessid guard allowing a Hebrew slave to leave Master Sebak's estate. Can I trust you to do this?"

Mered swallowed hard. The thought of escape hadn't occurred to him. "Of course, you can—" A sudden realization stole his breath. "A Phoenician merchant is scheduled to pick up his order of linen tomorrow. He always travels with a large caravan."

Mered saw the same wonder he felt dawn on the faces of his comrades. *Is it more than coincidence, El-Shaddai? Is it Your will that I go with Mandai?*

"It's settled then." The Medjay gathered his human crutches and resumed their trek up the hill. "Nassor will warn Delta estates and fortresses and return to Avaris to keep our guards on alert. Mered and I will leave—"

"Tomorrow," Mered said with a wry grin.

Mandai chuckled. "Perhaps this one god of yours is worth praying to after all, linen keeper. Can he bring a physician to Avaris to tend my wound?"

"He probably could, but I think He's provided Hebrew midwives for the task instead." Mered nodded toward two women approaching from the craftsmen's village. "Puah must have called for reinforcements. It appears she brought your old friend to help, Mandai. Remember Shiphrah—the midwife you arrested?"

Fear washed over the Medjay's face, drawing a full belly laugh from Nassor.

23

*When the child grew older, she took him to Pharaoh's
daughter and he became her son. She named him
Moses, saying, "I drew him out of the water."*

—Exodus 2:10

Anippe held Mehy close, inhaling the comforting scent of a sweaty, happy, healthy little boy. His head hadn't been shaved during his few days in the craftsmen's camp, so fine fuzz grew around his princely lock. Anippe brushed her cheek against the soft growth. Her boy was rumpled and joyful. Balm to her soul.

Miriam had been waiting in their private chamber when Anippe and Ankhe stumbled in from the quay. Anippe had nearly collapsed with relief at the sight of her son. Ankhe turned on her heel and retreated to her private chamber. Anippe didn't have the strength to beg her to stay. Perhaps Ankhe needed time to grieve alone.

"Please, Amira, come sit on your couch." Miriam had poured a bowl of cool water and washed Anippe's travel-weary form, ministering to her body and soul.

The chamber was quiet now—except for Miriam's lovely Hebrew tune. She sat spinning flax fibers at Anippe's feet, while Anippe rocked her sleepy boy on the embroidered couch.

"Amira, shall I take Moses for a nap at the bathhouse?"

Anippe looked down to see if he was sleeping. His lids were heavy, but he was still awake—just quietly resting on her chest. Her heart melted and tears came. "No, Miriam. I need to have him close."

In the stillness of that moment, Anippe could almost forget they could soon be fighting for their lives. She must prepare her handmaid for the possibilities. "Miriam?"

The girl looked up, innocence framed between shocking brown curls. "Yes, Amira?"

Anippe swallowed her rising panic. "You must never let anyone hear you call him Moses. Do you understand?"

"I understand. My mother warned me of the same thing before we stayed in the Hebrew village. We never called him Moses in front of father or Mered."

Anippe's heart twisted at the thought. Mehy had lived in the same rooms with his real father, and the man didn't even know it. She shook her head to regain focus. "That's very good, Miriam. Now, do you know what to do if we're ever in danger—for instance, if an enemy ship docked at the Avaris quay? Do you know how to call for help?"

Miriam blinked several times, her expression unchanged. "No, Amira. I don't think I do."

"If it ever happens, you should take Prince Mehy and run across deadman's land to the Qantir estate." Anippe resumed rocking her son, holding him tighter as she spoke. "If a guard tries to stop you, tell them who Mehy is—Master Sebak's heir. They'll let you pass."

"All right." Without further comment, Miriam resumed her spinning and humming. Anippe breathed deeply, trying to slow her heartbeat to its normal rhythm. The tune Miriam sang was haunting but lovely, and Anippe closed her eyes and let the music sooth her soul. Her rocking slowed.

A knock on the door startled them both.

Miriam jumped up to answer it, peeked to see who was there, and then opened the door. The three men Anippe had left at the quay walked in.

"Mandai, you're supposed to be in the next chamber, resting." But their expressions told her rest was out of the question. "Miriam, perhaps you should take Mehy to the bathhouse now, while I talk with Mered, Mandai, and Nassor."

Mehy clung to Anippe's neck when Miriam tried to take him. His cries tugged at Anippe's heartstrings and unleashed a new wave of tears from her eyes.

"I'm sorry," she said to her visitors. "I can't seem to stop crying since I returned to Avaris."

Mered patted Mehy's back as Miriam carried the boy toward the bathhouse. "It sounds as if you were quite brave, Amira. You're entitled to tears."

Anippe sniffed and looked up as she tried to regain control, then she steadied herself with a deep breath. "All right, what is it?"

Mandai took a step forward, spokesman for the group. "We have a plan to protect you and Mehy here at Avaris, as well as the other estates and fortresses in the Delta."

"But what about Abbi Horem? He must be told—"

Mandai silenced her with an upraised hand. "Yes, Amira. We have that arranged too." He paused, swallowing hard, and exchanged a glance with Nassor.

Anippe's anxiety soared. When had this Medjay ever been nervous? "So tell me."

Nassor was the brave one. "I leave immediately to alert Qantir and other Ramessids in the Delta. Mandai knows the whereabouts of the general and his army, but because of his injury, he'll travel by ship with a merchant's caravan."

"That's where my help is needed." Mered knelt before her, drawing her attention. "There's a trader scheduled to pick up his order of royal robes, sheets, curtains, and other items tomorrow. Since he trusts me, I'll ask to travel with his caravan for certain business I must conduct in Phoenicia. Mandai will act as my personal guard."

"What? No. You can't all three leave me." Anippe sounded like a spoiled child, but she didn't care. "What if Ay attacks while the only three men I trust are tramping across the Delta—and into Phoenicia?

Mandai knelt beside Mered. "Nassor will return after he's alerted the Delta estates and fortresses."

Nassor joined them on his knees. "I'll alert the Sile fortress first and ask if they've received any word from the general. It's the last Delta fortress on Egypt's eastern border, and if General Horemheb has gotten wind of Ay's treachery and started his return, he would stage his defense from Sile." His tone softened, showing the compassion she knew lay hidden within him. "I'll enlist the help of Sile guards to help me spread the word, which will bring me back to Avaris sooner."

Anippe could only nod. She turned away, overcome with emotion, and her three friends rose from their knees and turned to go. Shoulders slumped, they looked defeated. She couldn't let them go feeling as if they'd betrayed her when they were among the bravest men she knew.

"Thank you." The words tumbled out on a sob.

Each one turned, offered a smile, a bow, and a gaze that promised, *I will see you again.*

Mered had returned home after the difficult meeting with Anippe and encountered an even more difficult meeting with his wife.

"Why must you go, Mered?" she said through tears. "You're not a soldier. You're not even a real merchant. You've never even bartered in a city market."

He tried reason, explanation, even bribery. All failed.

"I will come back to you, Puah." He leaned in for a kiss, but she shoved him away. Wounded, he held his temper but knew he needed to leave before he said something he'd regret. "I'm going to the shop so I can brief the amira on upcoming orders and daily tasks. I'll probably be late tonight."

As he moved the curtain aside to leave, a clay lamp shattered on the wall beside his head.

"Tell the amira I said hello," Puah snapped.

He'd never seen her so angry—or so frightened.

His fear matched hers, though he'd never tell her. *El-Shaddai, guard my wife and child while I'm away. Bring me back to them—safely and soon.*

He trudged toward the workshop, heart heavy in the midday heat. As he topped the hill, he caught a glimpse of the villa's main entrance, where Mandai and Nassor were gathered. The Medjay looked refreshed, a fresh linen robe covering his new bandage.

Mered lifted his hand in greeting, and Mandai waved him down to join them. Nassor didn't sneer or threaten him with a cudgel. It was progress.

Mandai's wide smile greeted him. "See the bandage under this linen robe?" He pointed to the neatly tied wrap beneath the sheer byssus. "I told your wife about our mission, and she was so angry, I asked the other midwife to dress my wound."

Mered's eyebrows peaked. "You thought Shiphrah—the midwife you arrested—was the safer option to dress your wounds?"

Nassor's booming laughter echoed down the hillside. "You were doomed, my friend, no matter which woman tended you."

Mandai ducked his head, becoming serious. "Those women were very kind to me, Mered. You've all been very kind."

They stood in weighty silence until Nassor spoke. "I warned Avaris's estate foreman of possible attack and then apprised the guards on the plateau of the situation. I've just returned from Qantir. Their estate foreman has placed more guards on the lookout for Ay's war ships."

"You've accomplished much in a morning." Mered smiled at the coarse but efficient Ramessid.

"I meant it when I promised the amira I'd get back as soon as possible. I'm leaving now for Sile."

Mandai gathered Mered under his arm. "We'll walk you down to the quay."

"Wait," a female voice called from behind them. Anippe appeared, Miriam and Mehy in tow. "We'll come with you."

As the spontaneous farewell group started toward the quay, Miriam pointed to a sailing mast in the distance. "Is that the king's barque?"

The question, like a hammer to Mered's chest, stopped him where he stood. All four adults shielded their eyes from the harvest sun, trying to distinguish the ship through the waves of heat. Was that one sail—or three?

"You should go with Miriam and Mehy, Amira." Mandai drew his sword. "It is not the king's barque only. I see the sails of two troop ships accompanying it. These men did not come to talk."

This was her chance to run. It made sense to hide at Qantir until the fighting was over—perhaps escape on a ship, north to the Great Sea. But she was Horemheb's daughter.

"An army knows how to fight. A woman knows how to talk. Abbi Horem always said surprise is the best weapon when you're outnumbered. They expect your sword, Mandai. They don't expect my words." She pressed against his hand, pointing the weapon at the ground.

Reluctantly, he sheathed his sword.

Anippe began the march with her troops: a Medjay, a Ramessid, and a linen keeper. They arrived at the quay before the king's barque docked. Since it was early harvest season, the Nile's level was high enough to sail but low enough to give Anippe a chance to prepare her thoughts. The amira and her men waited on shore, twenty paces from the dock, watching the ships arrive and the first gangway thump onto sand.

One nobleman and six soldiers mounted the plank, but Anippe halted them with her first words. "Any representative of the traitorous Vizier Ay is not welcome on this estate. Ay killed my brother, our good god King Tut, and he falsely accused and unjustly murdered the beloved Amira Amenia, wife of General Horemheb."

Oarsmen, soldiers, and slaves exchanged nervous chatter, the effect Anippe had intended. Let them wonder at her side of the story.

The pompous nobleman, spokesman for Ay, opened and closed his mouth—repeatedly—seeming incapable of sound. He resembled a fish out of water rather than a herald.

Gaining her first victory, she continued. "In moments, the hills behind me will fill with Ramessid guards. Debark and die."

Her final threat seemed to awaken the gaping fish. "Let me clarify our intentions, Amira. I am indeed here on Vizier Ay's orders—but to implore you to return for the sake of Queen Senpa. The troop ships you see behind me were Vizier Ay's attempt to ensure my safety. He anticipated your hostility, but wanted me to assure you again that our king's fatal accident has been avenged—indeed, the woman you mentioned died on the very day the king himself journeyed beyond the horizon. Unfortunately, you left without a farewell to Queen Senpa, and now your sister grieves alone, feeling betrayed."

Anippe covered her mouth, silencing the cry that clawed at her throat.

"Vizier Ay sent the king's barque and this military escort to bring you, Princess Ankhe, and your son safely back to comfort Queen Senpa and attend King Tut's burial celebration."

Mandai furtively grabbed her arm, whispering, "It's a trap, Amira. The three of you and Queen Senpa are the only royal blood left to legitimize his right to the throne. We don't know what he's done with the queen."

The old fish took a step toward shore. Nassor drew his sword, but the nobleman's guards drew their weapons masterfully. "Please, Amira Anippe. Vizier Ay has sent me to avoid bloodshed. Even the queen realizes she can use this tragedy for the good of Egypt. She plans to marry the Hittite prince Zannanza. Their union will join Egypt and Hatti as one nation—mending her broken heart and the rift between our nations."

"It's not true! Senpa would never join Egypt with Hatti." Anippe began trembling. "It's another scheme that stinks of Vizier Ay. How can you be so cruel?"

"I am no crueler than a sister who refuses to comfort her family or attend her brother's crossing over. Come, Amira. Come with us." Was it his feigned innocence that sickened her or the kernel of guilt his ruse exposed? "King Tut's body is being reverently prepared for his journey beyond the horizon. He'll be carried on the sacred barque to the Valley of the Kings and his heart presented to Anubis at the end of seventy days' grieving. Surely you will attend the succession, when the new pharaoh receives the incarnation of Horus."

New pharaoh. The words were like a trumpet, clearing her clouds of grief, fear, and guilt. "I will attend the ceremony for the true successor when my abbi Horemheb arrives. He is prince regent. He is the divinely chosen son of Horus, and he will cut out your heart and offer it to Seth if you do not leave my estate immediately."

The nobleman chuckled. Then laughed. Then grew hysterical, drawing his whole crew and two troop ships into raucous amusement.

And she couldn't stop them.

If they came ashore to take her by force, the Ramessids would fight valiantly—and lose. Had the gods given Mehy to her only to watch him die by her enemy's sword? She bowed her head and waited for their laughing to stop. And it did—suddenly.

Anippe glanced at the nobleman and then followed his gaze to the plateau behind her. It was the most beautiful sight she'd ever seen. The high flat plain separating Avaris and Qantir was filled with men—all toting glimmering shields or swords or daggers. The sun glinted gloriously off every piece of metal atop that high ground, making the gathered slaves and guards into a valiant army. Miriam had somehow rallied help from the Ramessids of Qantir.

Feeling her courage surge, Anippe ventured a few half truths to challenge the nobleman. "Warn your vizier that the Delta estates have armed their Hebrew slaves, matching his army in number and valor. We've already sent word to General Horemheb, and Ramessids have cut off the vizier's trade routes and communication through Egypt's eastern border and the Great Sea. Tell Vizier Ay his communication with the Hittites is over. I'm sure Senpa's marriage proposal was never her idea."

The old fish grinned. "The messenger was already sent to the Hittites six weeks ago."

Anippe could barely breathe. *Already sent. Already sent. Already sent.* Were they too late? If Ay's plan succeeded, Egypt would become one of the Hittite empire's vassal nations, robbed of independence, wealth, and their best soldiers. No doubt, Ay would become Egypt's token pharaoh under Hatti's iron thumb. Abbi Horem would be hunted like a criminal, and those loyal to him would be arrested, their lands seized.

The nobleman ordered his guards back to the ship, and glistening black bodies pulled up the gangplank. They cast off immediately against the low tide, the pilot droning at the oarsmen, "Out, in, *pull,* out, in, *pull . . .*"

Anippe stood like a statue until all three vessels were out of sight—and then collapsed into a heap, crying, trembling, babbling. Her three champions hovered near, trying to lift her, console her, help her.

"Go away. Let me be."

Gentle arms scooped her up. She curled into a ball, her conveyance unknown, unimportant. All was lost.

She awoke shortly before dusk in her bedchamber. Alone.

24

Start children off on the way they should go,
and even when they are old they will not turn from it.

—Proverbs 22:6

Anippe felt as if she'd been holding her breath for two weeks—since Nasor, Mered, and Mandai had left. The sounds of the linen shop soothed her most days, but not today. The amira of neighboring Qantir had requested a visit, and she'd arrive for the midday meal. It would be Anippe's first meeting with Sitre alone, their first encounter since Anippe and Sebak's wedding.

Why now? The question haunted her.

Fairly leaping from her stool, Anippe left her desk covered in figures and designs and went to find Miriam. The girl could be anywhere. Having proven skillful in roving, spinning, and beadwork, Miriam moved from station to station, helping wherever she was needed.

Anippe found her chatting with the rovers. One knee tucked and the other leg splayed, Miriam rolled the dried flax fibers on her thigh, drafting fibers into thread and winding the thread onto broken shards of pottery.

"Miriam, please find Ankhe and Mehy and send them to my chamber. I'll meet them there in a few moments." Anippe needed to hold her son to steady her shaky thoughts.

The girl immediately set aside her project and bade the women farewell. Anippe approved their work before leaving and assured them of her appreciation. These were good people, hard workers. Mered's linen shop could run itself. With the improvements made to the structure of the building, the workers seemed even more eager to please him—and their amira.

Anippe hurried through the garden, past the main hall, and down the long corridor toward the residence chambers. She'd barely caught a whiff of the lotus blossoms, but perhaps the garden would be a nice place to host the meal with Sitre.

Why did the amira of Qantir suddenly feel the need to be chummy?

Sebak had warned Anippe at their wedding to stay away from the other amira. He'd said both his uncle Pirameses and Sitre might try to steal Avaris if Sebak died in battle. Did Sitre know something about the war? Was that why she was coming today? Had something happened to Sebak?

"You're being ridiculous," Anippe whispered to no one. The words echoed in the empty hallway as she approached the chamber of suites in the master's wing. The four Ramessids snapped to attention when they saw her. She was still disappointed every time Nassor wasn't guarding her door. She prayed to the gods he'd return from Sile fortress soon.

A nameless Ramessid opened her chamber door without a word. Anippe walked in without a nod.

"Ummi!" Mehy ran from the courtyard, through the sitting room, and captured her around the waist—making life worth living.

Miriam followed closely behind. "He's been anxious for you to walk through that door."

"There's my big Ramessid prince." Anippe swept him into her arms, snuggled him close and twirled him around to the sounds of giggles and squeals. Yes, this was what she needed.

"He did it again." Ankhe's sour voice came from the courtyard, spoiling the moment. "He told the chamber guard his name was Moses."

Anippe closed her eyes and ceased her twirling but didn't release her grip on Mehy. Ankhe had retreated into her impenetrable shell after their return from Gurob. Keeping to her chamber, she emerged only when the chamber guard accompanied her to Mehy's lessons.

"You've got to punish him, Anippe. We can't just keep reassigning chamber guards to dead-man's land. He needs to keep his mouth shut."

"Enough, Ankhe." Anippe silenced her with a glare.

Mehy whimpered and curled his arms to his chest, trying to distance himself from the angry ummi who held him.

"It's all right, my big boy. Ummi is cross but not with you. Forgive me for shouting." Anippe looked at his pudgy hands. Both were immaculate—no dots. Fire shot through her again, but this time she controlled her temper. Trembling with rage, she set her son on his feet and nudged him toward Miriam. "Take Mehy to the bathhouse until I call for you."

"Yes, Amira." The girl's eyes went wide with fear. Perceptive child.

Ankhe strolled into the sitting area, too arrogant—or stupid—to be afraid. "I don't know why you're yelling at me. It's your son that needs to keep his Hebrew name—"

Anippe slapped her into silence.

Ankhe covered her cheek, shock turning to fury. "How dare you—" She tried to slap Anippe, but the Amira of Avaris caught her wrist—and then caught her other wrist.

"I know you're angry and hurt, Ankhe, but I'm grieving too. We both lost a brother, but my ummi was innocent. Amenia was tortured and killed."

"It's true, and I'm sorry, but Amenia and Tut were our past, Anippe. Nassor was my future—my only future." Ankhe's lips trembled, her eyes glistening. When Anippe let go of her wrists, she turned away, wiping her cheeks.

Anippe released a long, slow breath. Was she the one being selfish now? Ankhe had no one but her and Mehy. Another deep breath, and she placed both hands on her sister's shoulders. "I'm sorry I hit you."

Ankhe shrugged her away, still resistant to touch.

"You've always been smarter than me, Ankhe. It's one of the reasons I allowed you to become Mehy's tutor."

Ankhe whirled on her. "You allowed me to be his teacher so I'd keep your secret." Her eyes sparked with the familiar anger.

"In the beginning, it's true, but you've become quite good at it. Mehy looks forward to his lessons with you. He can't wait to see you each day."

The compliment seemed to soften Ankhe's tone. "I love Mehy, but I don't want to be his tutor for the rest of my life. I want a husband, Anippe, and children of my own. Surely, you can understand that."

"I do understand, but now your match must be determined by Sebak since you're a servant in his household."

"I know." Ankhe turned away again, wrapping her arms around herself. "I know."

Anippe walked across the sitting area to retrieve the goose-shaped box of kohl. She was waiting when Ankhe's curiosity got the better of her and she turned around. "Mehy is to have three black dots on his hand every day to remind him of my love and Amun-Re's protection. It is the one thing I require as a part of your lessons. Everything else you may decide, but choose wisely what you teach my Ramessid heir. When Sebak returns, your progress will determine his willingness to match you with Nassor."

Tears welled in Ankhe's eyes as she nodded. Anippe knew better than to hug her, so a pat on the shoulder must suffice to show her love. "Your future is with me, Ankhe. You are sister of Anippe, who is Amira of Avaris, wife of Sebak, daughter of Horemheb."

Walking toward the courtyard, Anippe called for Miriam. "Bring Mehy back for a quick lesson." Then she spoke softly to Ankhe. "I don't need to punish my son to teach him not to use the name Moses."

Mehy followed Miriam toward the courtyard, his route far more circuitous. He chased a gecko, a butterfly, and a frog, and finally meandered to where the three females waited at the low-lying table in the palm shade.

Anippe pulled him into her lap and transferred the wiggling gecko to Miriam's care. "What is your name, habibi?"

His dark brow furrowed. "Which one?"

She smoothed the little creases from his forehead, realizing she should have explained this much sooner. "Did you know your ummi has two names like you do?"

Wonder lit his sparkling brown eyes. "Who are you, Ummi?"

"I am Anippe, but I was once called Meryetaten-tasherit."

"I like Anippe better."

She chuckled and hugged him close. "Me too, and I don't talk about my secret name, Meryetaten-tasherit, with other people because—well, because it's a secret name."

Pondering, he fell silent, his brow wrinkling again, this time into deeper lines. "Why must your *Mariasniten-kanusit* name be secret?"

She choked back a giggle and thanked the gods he'd asked the question. Widening her eyes, looking right and left, she lowered her voice to a conspiratorial whisper. "Because even Amun-Re has a secret name."

"He does? What is it?"

Ankhe sighed and rolled her eyes. "It's a secret. That's the point."

Anippe shot a warning glare, cowing her belligerent sister. "We can't know Amun-Re's secret name because it will drain away his power. The more people who know our secret names, the less power we have." She lifted her arm, exposing her muscle. "See how strong your ummi is? That's because I don't tell people my secret name."

Mehy's immediate pout told her she'd bungled the lesson.

"What? What's wrong?"

"You and Ankhe and Miriam already know my secret name. And Jochebed. And those three guards I told."

"But we're the only ones, right?" She lifted his arm and felt his little muscle. "I think you could grow a big strong arm—if you don't tell anyone else your secret name."

"Okay, Ummi." He nestled against her. "Does anyone know Amun-Re's secret name?"

"Yes, habibi. Do you want to hear the story?"

He nodded and yawned. She'd have to keep him awake. He didn't have time for a nap before Qantir's amira arrived.

"The Lady Isis became vexed that the sun god Re still ruled all the gods—though he'd grown old and tired. But no one could defeat him because they didn't know his secret name. One day Re spit on the ground, and Isis stirred his spit with Egypt's black dirt and made a worm. When the noble Re walked in his splendor, as he did each day with the pharaohs and other gods, the black worm stung him—" Anippe jumped and tickled Mehy's belly until he dissolved into giggles and squeals.

"Go on, Ummi. Tell the rest."

"The great god Re opened his mouth but could not speak. His limbs burned, and his jawbones chattered. The worm's poison worked its way through him. His companions—Hathor, Nun, Seth, and the great gods—could not help. Finally, Isis drew near. 'Tell me your secret name, divine father.' And when he could no longer stand the torment, Re divulged the name, giving Lady Isis power over life, health, magic, and motherhood."

"So what is Re's secret name, Ummi?" His eyes, full of wonder, gazed at her as if she herself were the great goddess Isis, knowing every answer of life.

She hugged him and whispered, "Every ummi knows Re's secret name, my son—but only you, me, and Miriam must know your secret name. Do you understand? You will lose all your power if anyone discovers the name *Moses*."

Anippe waited for Qantir's amira in the garden, alerted by her guards that Sitre had sailed around the bend of their estates by skiff rather than cross dead-man's plateau for her visit. Anippe wondered if the famously cruel amira had ever experienced the inhumanity of the plateau's mud pits and fields.

Hearing sandals clicking on tiles, Anippe's heart raced.

Ankhe leaned over and whispered, "Stop fidgeting with your jeweled belt."

Perhaps it wasn't a good idea to include Ankhe and Mehy in the meeting, but she thought her son might provide a welcome distraction if the conversation turned awkward. Miriam brought a pitcher of honeyed wine with a tray of fruit and cheese for refreshment.

Pirameses's wife, Sitre, appeared in the arched doorway, her shape as finely sculpted as an alabaster pitcher, and—according to Gurob gossip—her heart made of the same cold stone.

Anippe stood to greet her, surprised when a little boy toddled around the corner, handmaid chasing him.

"I told you to tend him," Sitre barked at the maid, halting both her and the boy where they stood. The Qantir amira returned a practiced smile to Anippe. "Forgive our disruptive entrance."

The little boy, perhaps a year old, peered out from beneath thick, dark eyebrows—almost a single line shading his deep brown eyes. He reminded Anippe of Sebak. The boy had already spotted Mehy. His expression brightened at the sight of another little one.

Anippe extended her hand, calling Mehy closer, and tried to assuage Sitre's discomfort. "I'm glad you brought your maid's son. Mehy will enjoy a playma—"

"This is my son, and his name is Sety."

Speechless, Anippe gripped Mehy's hand tighter. How could Sitre have a son so young, when their Ramessid husbands had been at war for nearly four years?

Miriam dislodged Mehy's hand from her grasp and took the boys and the handmaid to a shaded corner of the garden.

Mouth suddenly desert-dry, Anippe croaked, "Would you like a glass of wine, Sitre?"

As Anippe returned to the table and cushions, she nodded at Ankhe, hoping her sister would simply pour the wine and not choose to display her independence. Ankhe poured three goblets full.

Sitre lifted her cup as if to toast. "Vizier Ay's henchmen should be glad they stopped at Avaris and not Qantir. I would have let Ramessid soldiers do the talking." She sipped slowly, watching Anippe over the rim of her cup.

"I'm sure others would have handled the situation better than I." Anippe picked up her goblet, sipped the nectar politely, and returned it to rest.

"Well, I have been a Ramessid a bit longer than you, so I suppose I've grown accustomed to their military minds." Sitre appeared to be the same age as Anippe—perhaps a few months older. How much longer could she have been a Ramessid? By all accounts Pirameses had stayed in Qantir after their wedding less time than Sebak had remained in Avaris.

Growing tired of the game, Anippe asked the question she couldn't get out of her head. "How old is your new little Ramessid? Sety, is it?"

Sitre set aside her wine and gazed at the handmaids and boys at the opposite end of the garden. "He's over a year old, and I've only recently gotten my figure back." She picked up the wine again and sighed, returning her attention to Anippe. "Babies are tiresome, aren't they? Crying, vomiting, messy little creatures. Aren't you grateful for nursemaids and tutors?" She chuckled, assuming they were bonded in maternal understanding.

But Anippe sat utterly stunned. "What will Pirameses do when he finds out?" Sebak had hinted at his uncle's ruthlessness in battle. What would he do when he returned to find his wife had born another man's child?

"Pirameses knows the nursemaid cares for Sety and expects the child to have tutors—at least until he goes to the Memphis School of the Kap." She studied Anippe's expression, and understanding dawned. Sitre's eyes widened, and she cackled so loud, the doves scattered from the acacias. "Oh, you thought Sety was the son of another lover?"

Anippe felt her cheeks grow warm. "Our husbands haven't been home in almost four years. How can he be—"

"Your husband hasn't been home in four years, Anippe." No more laughter—only Sitre's stone-cold stare.

Anippe felt as if the ground shifted beneath her feet. "What do you mean?" She hated herself for asking, but she had to know. "Pirameses came home to you? When?"

Sitre downed the last of her wine. The triumph so evident moments ago drained away with the dregs. "Sety's a year old. You figure it out."

Pain, greater than any Anippe had known, twisted inside her chest. Why had Pirameses found a way to visit his wife but Sebak hadn't? *He doesn't love me.* It was the only answer that made sense. Was anyone left on earth to love her? Abbi Horem, perhaps—but would he return in time?

Sitre stared at Anippe while Ankhe refilled her cup. "The last merchant I slept with said the Egyptian army had advanced to Kadesh and ruined his business in Palestine. Lucky for me. He gave me a lovely Persian vase."

Anippe schooled her features and felt a pang of pity. Had Sitre expected shock? Horror? Anippe had grown up with hundreds of bored and lonely noblemen's wives at Gurob, and their stories were the same. "If you sleep with so many merchants, how are you sure Sety is the son of Pirameses?"

"Look at that heavy brow, Anippe. All Ramessid men have it. Haven't you noticed?"

Anippe thought of Mehy's light brown eyes and thin brows. The sun was suddenly too warm—the company too cold. "Thank you for coming, Sitre, but I'm not feeling well. Please excuse me. I must go lie down."

25

The valiant lie plundered,
they sleep their last sleep;
not one of the warriors
can lift his hands.

—PSALM 76:5

EAST OF BYBLOS, NEAR KADESH

Mered had never been so miserable in his life.

He and Mandai had traveled for sixteen days. Skiffs, camels, and then a trader's ship on rough waves in the Great Sea that made Mered wish for Sheol. They'd purchased supplies with the goods they sold in Byblos and begun their trek across the mountains. The gash in Mandai's side had healed adequately, enough that Mered could barely keep up. They'd both purchased heavier robes to brave the colder nights in the mountains since they didn't dare light a fire and draw attention to themselves.

"Please, Mandai." Breathless and aching, Mered eyed the steep rise above him and leaned against a rock face. "I can't go any farther. I need to stop for the night."

The Medjay continued climbing as if he hadn't heard. Mered knew him well enough by now—he'd come back when Mered didn't follow.

From this vantage in the mountains of Amurru, Mered gazed south into Canaan—the very ground El-Shaddai had promised to Abraham with an oath. Mered's grandfather had described it during family mealtimes. *El-Shaddai will one day deliver us from Egypt, and we'll walk on the rich, fertile soil of God's promise. Soon. Soon.*

His grandfather had died twenty years ago and had never walked anywhere but the dusty paths of Avaris. Hadn't El-Shaddai said four hundred years of slavery? How many years had it been? Hadn't anyone counted?

Mered checked the shepherd's trail ahead. Mandai hadn't returned for him yet, but he would. The Medjay was stubborn but resourceful. He knew to follow mountain trails, avoiding trade routes in the Jezreel and Hula valleys, since the heaviest fighting occurred on open plains. The Egyptian army had been fighting toward Kadesh for months, pushing back the Hittite rebels, gaining back hard-fought ground.

"How much farther tonight, Mandai?" Mered shouted, but he heard no answer. The Medjay had been in a foul humor since Mered insisted on using the warrior's linen robe to wrap his blistered feet. He still had his leopard-skin loincloth. Wasn't that what Medjays were supposed to wear?

Prodded by his friend's stubborn silence, Mered pushed back to his feet and set his hand on a secure outcrop, ready to climb the small rise. "Wait for me, I'm—"

"I assure you"—a large, dirty soldier extended his hand from a boulder higher up—"your Medjay is waiting for you with my men."

Both terrified and thrilled to see an Egyptian soldier, Mered accepted the proffered hand. "I notice the emblem of Seth on your armor and assume you're a Ramessid." Polite conversation while being rescued seemed appropriate.

The hulking officer hauled him up the rise effortlessly and then wrenched Mered's arm behind his back. "And I see by the linen under that woolen cloak that you're pretending to be Egyptian—but your Hebrew accent says you and your Medjay are slaves on the run."

Trying to think beyond the pain in his twisted arm, Mered gasped, "Good guess, but wrong."

The soldier pressed harder.

"We have a message for General Horemheb."

"Prove it."

"The Medjay and I came from Avaris and Qantir—we also carry messages for Sebak and Pirameses from their wives. Surely if you're a Ramessid, you know my Master Sebak. I am Mered, his chief linen keeper."

The officer released Mered's arm and examined him face to face. "Why would anyone send a linen keeper with a message?"

Mered glanced beyond the officer's shoulder and saw Mandai lying face down. "What did you do to him?" Without waiting for an answer, Mered hurried to help his friend. Rolling him over, he noting a bleeding gash on his head.

"He wasn't as cooperative. He'll awaken shortly—with a headache." The officer motioned two of his five soldiers to close ranks around Mered, their odor as imposing as their spears. "Why should we believe your story, linen keeper?"

Mered squared his shoulders and set his jaw, giving his best impression of bravery, then assumed by their smirks that he had failed. "Because if you don't take me to General Horemheb, the Egypt you once knew will be gone when you return."

Their smirks faded. After only a moment's pause, the Ramessid jerked his head toward his new prisoners. "Bring them both. If the Hebrew is lying, Commander Sebak will do worse than I could ever stomach."

One of the guards secured Mandai's wrists with leather straps, while another emptied his waterskin on his head, rousing him. The Medjay sprang to his feet and leveled a guard with a kick to his throat before the others could pin him back to the ground.

"Please, wait." Mered moved between the guards and his friend. "This Medjay was King Tut's personal bodyguard. If you harm him further, the general will send you to the copper mines before dawn."

Anippe had effectively used that punishment with the overseer on the Avaris plateau. Mered had no idea if General Horemheb would defend the man who'd served King Tut, saved his daughter, and tried to rescue his wife, but Mandai deserved better than a gang killing by desert lackeys.

The Ramessid officer shoved his men to get them marching and helped the Medjay stand. "No more kicking."

Mandai scowled but didn't argue.

Relieved, Mered felt a sense of anticipation stir. They'd actually completed their mission. He, a linen keeper, a successful military messenger. "How far to your camp?"

"A half day's walk."

Mered grimaced. "But it's nearly dusk."

No one answered.

He wasn't sure his feet could stand the journey. "Perhaps we should stop for the night."

Silence.

"Will we encounter Hittites on the way?"

The officer heaved a sigh. "Doubtful. We've retaken the fortress at Kadesh on the Orontes River. It's clear from here to there." He glared at Mered as if daring him to speak again and then turned his back. Evidently not much for conversation.

They walked another few paces, and Mered's stomach growled. Surely someone else was hungry too. "We brought food."

Everyone kept marching.

"We have enough for everyone. Don't you think, Mandai? I think our rations are—"

The guard shoved his dagger hilt into Mered's gut, doubling the linen keeper over, and then asked Mandai, "Did he talk this much all the way from Egypt?"

The Medjay offered a slow, single nod.

"I would have killed him," the guard grumbled.

Mered refrained from more comments.

Their journey passed in a blur, the pain in Mered's feet forcing him to lean heavily on Mandai. At some point the terrain changed from mountainous to a lush river valley, shrouded in darkness.

Mered noted small fires in front of primitive tents and a watchtower in the distance. "Is that where we're headed?"

The officer ignored him, seeming intent on their destination.

They passed a mound of smoking, foul-smelling ash. Mered covered his nose and mouth with his head covering.

"Turn away." Mandai marched, eyes forward, nothing covering his nose to abate the stench. "Don't stare at the dead."

Only then did Mered glimpse human bones at the edge of the pile, and he realized they were walking through what had been a battlefield days before.

A full moon illuminated their gruesome surroundings. The ground beneath their feet was saturated with blood—as was the linen wrapped around Mered's feet. Wounded men and horses lay near their tents, exhausted, while filthy women hurried from one demanding patient to the next. Closer to the watchtower, men celebrated with full wineskins and bloodied swords.

"How long ago did General Horemheb take Kadesh?" Mered spoke in a whisper.

The Ramessid officer slowed, coming alongside Mered and Mandai. "I only tell you this because you are surely trustworthy if you are who you claim to be—and if you are lying, you will be dead."

Mered found no comfort in his reasoning but was happy to get some answers.

"We took the Kadesh fortress last week, and—as you can see—we're still cleaning up. But the general sent Commanders Sebak and Pirameses on another mission a few days ago." He sighed, taking inventory of their surroundings. "It appears they've returned victorious—but with considerable losses. If you have a god, you should pray your master receives you in good temper."

Mered exchanged a wary glance with Mandai, feeling at once elated and sickened by their surroundings. He'd never been on a battlefield before, never realized that even victors endured significant losses. He'd never conceived it possible that human bodies could be a pile of refuse needing disposal. Life in Avaris flowed with the waters of the Nile, as colorless as the natron-bleached linen he produced in his shop. Respect for his master grew as they approached the three-story, hive-shaped tower. *How does Sebak live in both worlds so seamlessly?*

The Ramessid officer halted and pounded on the wooden door of the tower with the hilt of his dagger. "Squad four, returning with prisoners."

A metal latch clanked, and a small peep door opened. A set of dark eyes squinted beneath a bushy black brow. "Why take prisoners? If they're Hittites, kill them. If they're escaping slaves, kill them. If they're—"

Mered's captor bashed his dagger against the door. "They say they have a message for the general and commanders Sebak and Pirameses. Do you want to withhold a message from any of the three?"

The peep door slammed shut, the cedar door opened, and the bushy-browed fellow sneered. "General Horemheb is at the top with Sebak and Pirameses, but the commanders returned only moments ago. Careful, they're still in battle frenzy."

Mered saw only two windows in the rough-cut limestone structure and no other entry. The watchtower had three stories, a simple design, with each upper level smaller than the one below. The Ramessid officer led them to the central ladder on the first floor to access the next story. Mered followed him, then the Medjay, and then a second guard. As the officer mounted the ladder for the third story, the sound of raised voices grew louder—and one angry voice was terrifyingly familiar.

"Yes, we regained Amurru, but at what cost?" Sebak shouted. "If we press the Hittites toward Ugarit, they could flee by ship or farther north, taking us farther from our already exhausted supply lines!" Something pounded a wooden table above them.

The Ramessid officer leaned down to whisper before lifting his head above the third-story floor. "You'd better be who you say you are, or we're both dead men." He grabbed Mered's collar and dragged him up the ladder's last two rungs. "Excuse me, sirs, but we're reporting two prisoners who say they have a message." His words tumbled out, and he held Mered in front of him like a shield.

Mered had only a moment to see fury turn to fear on Master Sebak's face before he charged Mered like a bull. Two giant paces, and he'd grasped Mered's cloak, snatching him from the Ramessid's grasp.

Mandai leapt from the ladder, taking everyone by surprise.

The Medjay grabbed Sebak and his dagger in one swift motion, somehow pinning his arms back and holding the blade at Sebak's jugular. "Commander,

I mean you no harm, but you will regret hurting your linen keeper if someone doesn't stop you."

Sebak panted, his eyes wild. Mered barely had time to think before Pirameses seized him from behind and held a dagger at his throat. "It seems we should negotiate, Medjay."

General Horemheb approached Mered, calm as the Nile's lowest tide. "You're that linen keeper from Avaris, aren't you?"

Mered couldn't answer, couldn't blink. He felt the flint blade biting into his neck.

The general paced in front of the wooden table, hands clasped behind his back. "Well, I know Sebak as well as I could know a son. He fears you've come with bad news about Anippe or his son. Simply tell him his wife and son are safe, linen keeper."

Warm blood trickled down Mered's neck. "Anippe and Mehy are well . . . but King Tut is dead."

Horemheb's control faltered slightly. He nodded at Pirameses, who released Mered, and then turned to Sebak. "Are you satisfied?"

Something frightening still danced in Sebak's eyes, but he whispered, "Yes."

The general ordered the Medjay to release him. Mandai withdrew his blade and jumped clear of the commander's reach. Mered thought it odd—until he saw Sebak's reaction. His master's fury turned on the fortress wall, Sebak screamed and pounded until his fists were bloody. Then he fell against it, resting his head against his arm, exhausted.

The general cleared his throat, nudging Mered to gain his attention. "Tell me everything."

Mered stood frozen, unable to focus. He kept glancing back at Sebak to be sure he wouldn't attack again. For the first time, he was afraid of his master—his size, his fury, his violence.

Mandai stepped forward and bowed to the general. "Vizier Ay sabotaged Pharaoh's chariot during the Fayum hunt, and King Tut died from his injuries. General Horemheb, I'm deeply sorry to inform you that the vizier publicly accused your wife of planning the treachery and . . ."

The Medjay stumbled over the awful truth, and Mered knew he must intercede. "Mandai attempted to save your wife from Ay's traitorous Medjays, but he arrived too late. He was severely injured in the fight but rescued Anippe and Ankhe before they were harmed."

Horemheb's shock was quickly displaced by sorrow. He sniffed back emotion, staring at the ceiling. "I will destroy Ay. How long before Tut's burial, before Ay steals the incarnation and the throne? Could we make it back to the Valley of the Kings if we—"

Horemheb stopped when he noticed Mered shaking his head. "You could make it back for the burial, but Vizier Ay has already set a plan into motion that makes your succession impossible." Mered took a deep breath, feeling like a cat surrounded by tethered dogs. "Ay sent a messenger to the Hittite prince, proposing he marry Queen Senpa to unite Egypt with Hatti."

He braced himself, waiting for someone to slice his throat for reporting the news.

Instead—silent disbelief. Egypt's three top soldiers exchanged glances, eyes sharp, jaws clenched.

Horemheb spoke with icy calm. "Sebak, Pirameses. You two are the best. First initiative, intercept Ay's messenger. If we're too late—may the gods forbid it—you must kill the Hittite prince and his escort before they reach Egypt for the wedding." Both commanders nodded, and Horemheb gazed from beneath his bristly gray brows. "How many men do you need?"

Pirameses answered, checking each assertion for Sebak's approval. "We'll be more effective with fewer men—ten at most. Sebak will take five along the sea, and I'll take five through the mountains. We'll meet at the Hittite capital, Aleppo. If neither of us intercepts Ay's messenger on our way, it means we must kill the bridegroom prince and his escort on our way back to the Delta."

Mered's heart was in his throat. How could they suddenly be calm? They spoke of murder and missions like he spoke of flax and linen. This world of war was insanity, and though he had wanted to help, he was grateful to know nothing of this life.

General Horemheb massaged the back of his neck. "I'll leave enough troops in Kadesh to maintain what we've gained in this campaign. We'll break camp for the Sile fortress at dawn. I hope we have enough supplies for the journey."

Mered's heart skipped a beat. Finally, something he could help with. "Isn't Damascus a day's journey south? If you can spare a few soldiers and wagons to guide me, Mandai and I can gather supplies and rejoin your troops on the way to the Delta."

The general's forehead wrinkled, giving his short black wig a bounce. "That would greatly relieve my supply-line troubles. You've just joined the army, linen keeper. We'll rest tonight and proceed with our duties at dawn."

Mered couldn't move, couldn't speak. *Joined the army?*

Master Sebak grabbed his arm and Mandai's. "Both of you come with me." He shoved them toward the ladder and the hole in the floor. Sebak was calmer but still ill mannered.

One step onto the ladder's rung, and Mered cried out, earning him heated gazes from every soldier. "I'm sorry, but my feet hurt."

General Horemheb grinned. "You'd better toughen him up by dawn, Sebak. He's a soldier now."

Mered climbed down, biting his lip against the pain until he tasted blood. Sebak led him and Mandai out of the fortress to a nearby copse of trees and a two-room tent near the river, guarded by four Ramessid soldiers. Nodding to the guards, Sebak ducked his head and marched inside, Mered and Mandai close behind.

"Are you hungry?" he asked abruptly, shoving a half-eaten loaf of bread at them.

The visitors sat on woven reed mats and ate in silence while Sebak paced. Like a caged beast, he walked the length of both rooms and back again, removing his weaponry and pieces of armor as his expression twisted in unspoken conflict. The spear went first, then a blood-stained cudgel and throwing stick. He hung his bow and quiver of arrows on the center tent pole, and then stood over Mered, silently staring down at him.

Mered rose, still chewing his last bite of bread. "May I assist you, master?"

Sebak lifted his right arm, revealing the laces of his bronze-plated breast piece. Mered fumbled to untie them.

"Why did you come? And—by the gods, Mered—why did you offer to go to Damascus?" Sebak shoved Mered aside and loosened the laces himself. Then he pulled off the breast piece and threw it across the tent, turning his back to his visitors.

Mandai stood. Mered sensed his protectiveness and was grateful. "We needed to gain passage on a merchant's ship, and Mandai knew how to find you. Besides, I knew you and General Horemheb would trust the message from my lips." He stepped nearer to Sebak. "Anippe has learned to run the linen shop. I hadn't intended to volunteer as the general's supply chief, but the workshop at Avaris will endure."

"I don't care about linen. I needed you to protect my wife!"

Mandai stepped between them, but Mered nudged him aside, fear subsiding at his master's transparency. "Your wife is well protected. We left her in the care of an honorable Ramessid."

Sebak's eyes went cold. "If he touches her, I'll kill them both while you watch—and then I'll slaughter Puah and everyone you care about. A woman cannot live without her husband for so long and remain faithful. Look at Sitre. She'd be dead if she were my wife."

Mered gulped for air and felt the ground swim beneath him. Who was this man? What had happened to the Sebak he knew? "Anippe loves you. She yearns for your return and wants no other man."

The commander waved him away as if he were a fly on a horse's rump.

Mered grabbed his muscled arm. "No, you will listen to me."

Sebak drew back to strike his friend but stopped before the blow. He suddenly looked like a little boy, terrified of a bad dream, and Mered's heart broke.

Avaris's Chief Keeper of Linen voiced the forbidden question. "Why have you not come home to your wife—even for a short visit?"

The commander stared at Mered long and hard, and then began trembling. He looked down at his hands and rubbed at the dried blood still clinging from battle. "I can't live in both worlds, Mered." He rubbed harder, frantic now. "It took months after I left Anippe to sear my conscience—to take out a man's eyes without remorse, to do what no other commander will do to get information we need to conquer our enemy. *I am Seth reborn.* I am darkness and chaos." He grabbed his linen keeper by the throat, lifting him from the ground. "Shall I come home to visit my wife and son? Should they know Seth reborn?"

Mered slapped at Sebak's forearm, but it was Mandai who stomped the commander's foot and kneed his gut to break his hold. Sebak landed a blow against Mandai's jaw, and the Medjay fell hard, unmoving. Sebak shook with fury, and Mered waited for a fist to end him.

But Sebak leaned close, grinding out the vow. "I will return to my wife and son when I can be the man they deserve—but not before."

He marched from the tent, leaving Mered panting.

26

In their hearts humans plan their course,
but the Lord establishes their steps.

—PROVERBS 16:9

Anippe eased into the cool waters of the Nile that had risen to her bathhouse, enjoying the solitude of midday while Ankhe worked with Mehy in the garden on his first hieroglyphs.

The inundation had been rich this year, bringing its fertile black deposits from the southern lands beyond Nubia. Raging in its early northward journey, it calmed to glorious rushing waters in the Delta's marshland. Avaris would sow their crops within days.

Or will we? She gazed beyond her privacy wall to the quay and wondered if Ay would attack now that his ships could easily sail into the Delta's swollen branches of the Nile. The Ramessids had posted guards where the Nile split into seven channels—north of Memphis—each a separate path to fearful estates and Ramessid fortresses on alert. Would Abbi Horem's troops arrive in time?

Would her husband ever return to her? Perhaps he'd taken another woman in the camp. She'd heard some soldiers did—some even had families with their "war wives." Anippe dipped her head beneath the water so no one could see her cry.

When she emerged, Mehy ran down the slope toward the bathhouse, waving a papyrus toy boat. "Ummi! Ummi! Look what Ankhe made for me today."

Ankhe followed him, Nassor not far behind.

The Ramessid captain had returned six months ago from Sile, reporting no news from Egypt's army in Palestine. Anippe knew he was lying as all men did when speaking of war, but Nassor's return had settled Ankhe—a welcome relief amid greater tensions. Though he still seemed oblivious to Ankhe's affection, his presence seemed enough to satisfy her for now.

"It's a boat. Do you like it?" Mehy rushed into the water to show her his treasure. "I'm going to find a baby pigeon and put it in the boat to sail across the Nile."

Anippe redirected him toward shore and knelt down beside her growing boy. He was four inundations old now by public reckoning—nearly five, truth be told.

"Why would you sail a baby pigeon across the Nile in a boat, Mehy? Won't the ummi bird miss her little chick?"

"Perhaps, but Ankhe says maybe a jackal will find the baby bird and raise it as its own."

Ankhe arrived with a smirk on her face. "Doesn't that sound like a story for the gods, Anippe? A simple pigeon found in the Nile, raised by a jackal."

Anippe's heart skipped, but she struggled for calm in Nassor's presence. "Perhaps Nassor could make you a wooden sword today." She raised an eyebrow at her faithful captain, who nodded his consent. "It's time you learned how to protect your ummi, young man." Mehy dropped the boat and was already skipping away with Nassor when Anippe grabbed Ankhe's arm. "How dare you!"

"I'm simply preparing him for the truth when it comes out—and it will come out, Anippe. How do you expect to keep this secret when your husband and the general return? Mehy looks nothing like Sebak. His skin is olive, not deep brown; his hair brown, not black. And he doesn't have the Ramessid brow."

"He has our complexion, the coloring of Ummi Kiya—the Mitanni princess."

Ankhe laughed. "Surely you're joking."

Anippe stepped closer, growling. "I'm deathly serious."

"Amira." Nassor's voice startled her.

She turned toward the villa. "Mered?"

He stood on the tiled path between her chamber and the bathhouse, looking worn and weary.

But alive.

Abandoning decorum, she ran to greet him and threw her arms around his neck, sobbing.

Even Nassor offered him a smile. "Welcome home, Hebrew. Where's Mandai?"

Anippe released him, suddenly frightened. "Yes, where's Mandai?"

"He's safe, guarding General Horemheb." Mered tilted his head, compassion in his gaze. "Your abbi Horem sends his love, Amira."

No mention of her husband. Perhaps Sebak had given up feigning love for his wife at home.

Mehy peered around Nassor's leg, and Mered leaned over, offering a smile. "Greetings, Master Mehy."

"I remember you," the boy said, beaming. "You're Jered's abbi. I stayed at your house in the slave village." He hugged Mered's knees.

"I remember you too. Have you seen Jered and Ednah lately? Or Puah?"

"No. I've been busy learning."

"I see. Well, learning is very important because someday you'll be master of Avaris."

Mered's words struck Anippe like a blow. *"Master of Avaris."*

When Mered met her gaze again, she knew before he spoke. "I have news that I'd like to share without Mehy hearing." He glanced at Nassor. "But you should stay."

Anippe whispered around the emotion lodged in her throat. "Ankhe, take Mehy into the villa."

"Please, Ummi. I want to talk to Mered too."

"Mehy, go!" Anippe shoved him toward her sister, his wounded expression inconsequential in light of Mered's glistening eyes.

Ankhe hurried the boy toward the villa, glancing over her shoulder with each step. Mered's chin began to quiver, his cheeks quaking. Before he spoke a word, Anippe's knees gave way. Mered caught her before she fell and then produced a papyrus scroll tucked in a fold of his robe.

She stared at the papyrus and then into the eyes of the friend she trusted. "You tell me."

He lowered her to the ground, and Nassor sat with them. Mered cleared his throat and met her gaze. "Master Sebak and five other men were ordered to kill the Hittite prince before he reached Egypt to marry Queen Senpa. Sebak's troops intercepted the prince, who was escorted by fifty men. They killed Prince Zannanza, but"—Mered's voice broke—"Master Sebak was killed as they made their escape." He reached for her hand. "He loved you, Amira."

Sobbing, she shook her head. "No, Mered. If he loved me, he would have come home. Even Pirameses came home to visit a wife who cares nothing for him."

"He was protecting you, Amira." Mered dropped his head, shaking it as if fighting his own thoughts. When he looked up again, tears stained his cheeks. "You wouldn't have known the man he'd become. Have no doubt that your husband loved you with his last breath."

Anippe closed her eyes, not sure if Mered's words made Sebak's death easier or harder. But the reality was all too clear. Sebak was gone forever.

When she opened her eyes, she saw Ankhe staring anxiously from the courtyard while Mehy chased a butterfly. When the sisters' eyes met, Anippe offered silent regret—Sebak wouldn't return to make Ankhe's marriage match. Ankhe's features hardened, and she stormed into the chamber. Ankhe's first response was always anger—Anippe's was fear.

Her son abandoned his butterfly chase and began tapping a stick on clay tiles to a silent beat. Happy and carefree, Mehy had never known his abbi. How could he grieve? But who would teach her son honor, courage, and integrity? Anippe turned to the two men before her. Nassor could teach him to be a Ramessid, but he couldn't teach Mehy to be a man.

She squeezed Mered's hand, the man who'd known her husband best. "At least you're home now, my friend. You can return to your family and the workshop."

"No, Amira." Mered shook off her hand and wiped his face. "General Horemheb requires my presence as his supply officer."

"But I need you here." Fear rose to panic. "Sebak warned me that Pirameses might try to take Avaris from me if something ever happened to him."

Nassor reached for her hand. "The general wouldn't let that happen, Amira." His eyes flashed with knowing. "You're safe under my care."

A cold shiver worked up her spine, and she pulled her hand away. "What aren't you telling me, Nassor? Did you know about Sebak's death?"

"No, Amira, I didn't know about the master's death; however, I received a message from *Pharaoh* Horemheb yesterday that I was now estate foreman of Avaris. I'm sure Pirameses wouldn't interfere with an estate over which Pharaoh himself has taken charge."

"Pharaoh himself has taken charge." The words stung with betrayal.

Anippe's fear settled into simmering fury. "My abbi has taken both my linen keeper and my estate from me, then? Is that it?"

Nassor shrugged. "Who are we to question the mind of a god, Amira?"

Anippe wanted to scream, *"He is no god!"* If Tut had been a god, why hadn't he healed himself? If Abbi was a god, why couldn't he kill Ay?

She looked at Mered, who sat studying his hands. "Where is the army? Is Abbi at least bringing them back to the Delta to protect us?"

"I am to report to the Sile fortress tomorrow."

Anippe felt as if he'd slapped her. "Sile? Abbi Horem is within a day's journey, and he didn't come here himself?"

Nassor brushed her arm. "He is deeply engaged with his campaign against Vizier Ay. A man at war cannot pause to visit a woman."

Anippe swiped at her tears but couldn't keep her cheeks dry. "War is no excuse." She turned to Mered, temper rising. "War shouldn't drive Sebak away from his wife. War shouldn't keep Abbi Horem from seeing those he loves."

"Your abbi offers no excuses for his actions, Amira." Mered's features hardened. "Pharaoh Horemheb answers to no one."

The deep lines on Mered's features revealed more than physical exhaustion. Six months as Abbi Horem's supply chief had aged him, changed him. He was a man in need of home.

"Go home to Puah and your children, my friend, but come to the villa to say good-bye before you leave in the morning."

"Thank you, Amira."

The two men helped her to her feet, and Nassor cradled her elbow, offering support as she walked on shaky legs toward her private chamber. Ankhe appeared at the door and looked first at Anippe—and then at Nassor's hand so tenderly placed. Ankhe's face reddened, and she fled the chamber, slamming the door behind her.

Nassor and Mered exchanged a shrug, but Anippe knew too well the suspicions now brewing in her sister's mind. Ankhe had opened her heart to only one man, and he was standing at Anippe's side. She had no interest in Nassor, but would Ankhe believe her? Had her sister already realized that Sebak's death meant the death of her marriage match?

27

Though I cry, "Violence!" I get no response;
though I call for help, there is no justice.

—JOB 19:7

THREE YEARS LATER
SILE FORTRESS, DELTA, EGYPT

Mered watched the buzzing courtyard of Sile fortress from his perch in the *barbican*—the north defensive tower—where he and twelve other slaves had taken refuge during Ay's surprise attack. Three days ago, Ay's son-in-law, Commander Nakhtmin, successfully breached the Ramessid fortress north of Memphis and sailed his troops through all seven branches of the Nile into the Delta marshlands—at least that was what Ay boasted through his messenger when his troops surrounded Sile.

Commander Nakhtmin had brought Nubian soldiers to feast on his grandest victory, Medjays from Cush he'd trained himself. Nakhtmin's army advanced toward Sile by land and ship, halted abruptly by a flood-swollen moat teeming with lively crocodiles.

Only one gate opened to Horemheb's inner sanctum. The high walls of Sile were fortified three layers thick with sand and stone and Hebrew mud brick. After two days of Nakhtmin's useless arrows, rocks, and spears, the commander sent a whole battalion of Medjays into the crocodile-infested moat. Perhaps he planned to march across their floating corpses and tear Sile's gate from its Hittite-iron hinges.

The gate held, and Nubians didn't float.

Mered served General Horemheb roast goose with leeks and onions for his evening meal that night—last night. The general complimented his supply chief on his resourcefulness and guaranteed Mered a place in his administration "when this ugly business is over." Mered just wanted to go home.

Before dawn, Horemheb rallied silent Ramessid troops, with Commander Pirameses leading the army inside the fort, while guards lowered Mandai down the northern side of the wall into a skiff waiting among the crocodiles. He was pulled safely to shore by Nubian soldiers, compatriots who would soon exact their revenge on Ay and his wicked commander, Nakhtmin.

Weary of Nakhtmin's abusive treatment of their wives and children, the Nubian army was eager to mete out vengeance. Mandai had worked three years to build secret alliances with his Nubian brethren in the south, and they'd pledged allegiance to Pharaoh Horemheb—the god Mandai served.

At dawn, Ay initiated another attack. More arrows, spears, and Nubians slaughtered by crocodiles—and then Sile's gate opened wide. Commander Nakhtmin led the advance. Even the arrogant Vizier Ay rushed toward the moat banks to watch what would surely be his final victory.

Mered would never forget the violence of this day, watching from the barbican as every soldier—Nubian and Ramessid—turned their rage on two men. But General Horemheb had forbidden them to kill Ay or Nakhtmin. So the troops in their battle fury turned on the crocodiles—and each other.

Senseless. Meaningless. Dead Ramessids and Nubians littered the land, their blood turning the Nile red. And Horemheb called it victory.

The courtyard of Sile fortress hummed below with weary, wounded, yet "victorious" Nubian and Ramessid soldiers. General Horemheb had outsmarted and undone his enemy and seized Egypt's throne—at great price.

Mandai stood at Horemheb's right shoulder, cut and bruised, but his bearing as regal as any king. The soon-to-be-deified king sat on a limestone throne, tapping his fingers, waiting for a signal that his captives were ready to be presented. Finally, Pirameses swung open the prison's wooden gate and shoved two bloodied figures through the sea of battered soldiers. The prisoners were spit on, shoved, and bludgeoned.

"Enough!" Horemheb shouted, silencing the crowd. Pirameses enlisted help to drag the prisoners before their new king.

Mered and twelve other slaves huddled around the barbican window, peering down on a proceeding they need not hear to understand. Ay and Nakhtmin faced death. The only question was how. Beheaded? Flayed? Diced?

Horemheb spoke calmly, too calmly for slaves in a three-story barbican to hear. Ay began to wail, his wiry form doubled over, groveling at the feet of a man with no heart. Commander Nakhtmin rested on his knees, head bowed. Evidently, the commander expected the sentence Horemheb had pronounced.

"We leave for Avaris tomorrow!" Horemheb shouted, lifting his hand in triumph, and the courtyard of soldiers cheered.

Mered's heart skipped a beat when Pirameses reached for the prisoners and dragged them away. No execution? Why weren't they killed? A terrible dread crept up his spine, made worse by Mandai's slumped shoulders and distant stare.

Mered knew his friend and sensed his disapproval. If Mandai was disturbed by Horemheb's ruling, the fate of Ay and Nakhtmin must be horrible indeed.

AVARIS ESTATE, DELTA

Anippe sat beneath the shady palm tree outside the linen shop, sharing her midday break with Puah. Miriam tended Ednah, Puah's little girl, while Jered and Mehy fought an imaginary war with wooden swords. The midwife had become a good friend, bringing her son Jered to play with Mehy after the young master completed his morning lessons with Ankhe. Perhaps history was repeating itself. Mered had often told Anippe that he sat beneath this tree to comfort young Master Sebak after the death of his abbi—and now Mered's son played with the heir of Avaris under the same tree after Sebak died.

No matter that Mehy wasn't really Sebak's son—or did it matter? Had the gods punished her for her deception?

Mehy and Jered thwacked their wood-and-papyrus swords, blocking blow for blow. Jered was smaller but quicker, and Mehy's sword was heavier to wield.

"Take that, Ramessid." Jered poked at the same time Mehy dodged, and Mehy brought his sword down on the young Hebrew's arm.

"Ouch!" Jered ran to Puah, who set aside her bread to inspect her son's war wound.

Anippe gave her most disapproving frown to her little victor. "Mehy, you mustn't play so rough. Apologize to Jered."

"Ramessids don't apologize for winning a battle." At nearly eight, Mehy's logic was faultless.

Puah tugged on Anippe's sheath, giggling. "He has a point, Amira." Then she turned to her son. "When an enemy—even a playtime enemy—bests you, you must bow and congratulate him. It is the honorable way to lose."

"There is no honor in losing, Mother." Jered's tears perched like gemstones on his cheeks.

Anippe covered a grin and whispered, "He has a point, Puah." She lifted her voice to include both boys. "Come sit with us on the mat. We'll teach you to play Hounds and Jackals."

She turned to find Puah gathering her bowls into her basket. "Amira, we can't stay any longer. Jered must join the other children in the villa. Shiphrah's husband, Hur, is ratting and plugging snake holes today." Puah waved Miriam up the hill. "Bring Ednah. We must go."

Anippe had noticed Hebrew children wandering about the villa and had shuddered at the thought. The inundation chased rats and snakes out of their nests near the banks and into the villa and granaries.

Mehy sidled close, staring wide eyed at his friend. "Has anyone ever been bitten?"

"Not often, Master Mehy." Puah's eyes were kind, her voice gentle. "Hur is very good at his job. He trains the little ones to distract the snakes while he snares them, and he gives the children large bundles of rags to press into the rat holes. Their arms are small enough to fit inside, protected by the rags."

Anippe shivered. "Why must Jered help? There are plenty of other Hebrew children."

Puah knelt, her features as stern as Anippe had ever seen. "Jered helps because he is a slave and a child of slaves. We do what we must—as our ancestors did."

Puah's words were harsh but true—as was her life. Anippe averted her gaze, ashamed to have offered favoritism to a woman of such character. An idea struck her in the awkward silence. "Puah, I could hire one of the snake charmers that travel the Nile this time of year. The Gurob Palace used their services because the Nubians worshiped snakes and refused to kill them."

"No, Amira, please. Hur's talent for ratting is considered skilled labor. As long as both he and Shiphrah are skilled workers, they're assured a place in the craftsmen's village."

"I can speak with Nassor and make sure Hur and Shiphrah stay—"

"No, Amira." Anger flashed in Puah's eyes, but she regained her composure before continuing. "Jered and I can't stay with you any longer. I'm your friend but also your slave. We can blur the lines between us, but we can't erase them. A slave and her son can provide entertainment while the amira lounges for a meal, but if I linger too long, Hebrews will resent me and Egyptians will mock you."

Without being dismissed, Puah gathered her children and hurried toward the craftsmen's village.

Mehy snuggled close to Anippe and turned his tear-filled eyes upward. "Did they leave because I hurt Jered? I didn't mean to, Ummi. I'll apologize. Ramessids apologize to their friends."

She hugged him close. "No, Mehy. Puah and Jered left because they're good friends who love us. You can apologize when you see Jered tomorrow." She lifted his hand, pointing to the three dots. "The great god Re will give us both wisdom to deal with our friends wisely." She kissed the top of his smooth head and tugged his princely lock.

Movement downhill by the quay stole her attention. A lone figure trudged uphill, and she shielded her eyes from the sun's glare.

"Mered." His name slipped out on a whisper.

"Mered!" Her son turned and shouted, running toward the linen keeper.

Anippe saw Puah, halfway to the craftsmen's village, turn at the commotion and stop. Hands to her face, she stilled and then scooped Ednah into her arms and ran back toward her husband. Jered ran after them and hugged his parents' legs. Mehy joined the family circle.

"Mehy, come back. Let them have this time." Anippe turned away to hide the gaping void in her heart. *Oh, how I wish Sebak could return to hold me in his arms.* Mehy grabbed her waist, and she fell to her knees, rocking him. He would be her only reminder of Sebak's love—though even Mehy was an illusion. Had anyone truly been hers, or had the gods cheated her completely?

"Hello, Amira." Startled by the familiar male voice, she released Mehy and stood. Mered smiled broadly, Puah and Jered tucked under each arm. "Are you well?"

She bowed her head, unable to answer.

"Come, Mehy," Puah gently coaxed. "Your ummi and Mered must speak of workshop business."

Mehy's warmth left her side, and Anippe shivered in the midday heat.

Mered sat on the ground, seeming too weary to stand. "I have a beautiful family, don't I?"

Anippe chuckled. "You do indeed."

Mered's eyes shone with pride, but the light faded quickly, as did his smile. "I've been sent ahead of Pharaoh Horemheb's procession. They'll arrive in five days—allowing time for Ay's daughter, Mutnodjmet, to be brought to Avaris from the Gurob Harem."

"Mutno?" Anippe knelt beside him. "Why would Vizier Ay's daughter come to Avaris?"

Mered looked like an old man. Deep lines were etched around his eyes, and his mouth was drawn down in uncharacteristic gloom. "Your abbi Horemheb plans to marry Mutnodjmet—after he kills Ay and her husband, Nakhtmin, before her eyes."

"That's not funny, Mered." Anippe sat beside him but kept her distance. "Your humor has grown dark since you've been with the army."

His expression was chiseled stone. "Nothing has been funny for three years, Amira."

Angry now, she glared at him. "My abbi Horem wouldn't marry Mutno, and he certainly wouldn't stoop to the level of torture you describe—"

"Perhaps your abbi Horem wouldn't." His voice lowered in disgust. "But I assure you, Pharaoh Horemheb will most certainly do as he promised—and more." Mered held her gaze, unflinching and cold.

Swallowing her anger, she reminded herself of all Mered had endured and dismissed his outrageous claims. After leaving to deliver a message, he'd been caught in the snare of master schemers. "I'm sorry, Mered. This war has ruined many lives."

He seemed to soften—perhaps remembering the atrocities she'd seen in her royal life. "As Horemheb's deputy, it's my duty to make arrangements for the feast."

"A feast?" Anippe grimaced. "You see? Why would Abbi Horem order a feast if he planned to murder prisoners?"

Mered's shoulders slumped, and he offered her a weary smile. "Amira, I have one request."

"Name it."

"May I spend one night with my wife before I move to the villa?"

"Move to the villa? Why would you move to the villa? You're a linen keeper. You live in the craftsm—"

"I am Pharaoh Horemheb's new deputy. As his chief aid, I must tend the details of his succession, and then I'll live at the Memphis Palace."

Anippe covered a gasp. "Mered, no. I won't allow it. You're my linen keeper, and that's the end of it."

His features hardened again. "No one says no to Pharaoh Horemheb, Amira. I beg you—don't risk your life for me."

"Horemheb can't have you!" Puah slammed the bread dough into the kneading trough and shoved both fists into it. "Let him choose another chief aid. Surely someone else in Egypt knows how to export papyrus and import wine."

Mered sat on their reed sleeping mat, watching his wife. She perched on her knees over a mound of leavened dough, rhythmically kneading and turning, swaying back and forth. His pulse quickened, and his desire stirred. "Did you say something?"

She continued her rant, but he couldn't concentrate, couldn't take his eyes off the beautiful woman he'd married years ago.

He interrupted, "Where's Ednah?"

"Shiphrah took her for the afternoon so I could catch up on household chores. She and Hur still haven't been able to conceive—"

"Where's Jered?"

Wiping sweat from her forehead, Puah left floury traces above her left eyebrow and sat back on her heels. "Hur came shortly before you returned from the linen shop and gathered all the little ones. Jered will be ratting at the villa until sunset." She resumed her task, the slow, methodical *knead, turn, fold*. "He said five villa cats died, and he's late plugging rat holes in the granary this year, so the cobras may have already made nests in the villa and laid eggs."

Mered thought of their seven-year-old son meeting a rat or cobra and shivered, but every Hebrew child was needed for the task.

"Puah." He left the sleeping mat and crouched behind her.

"Perhaps if you ask Anippe to intercede on your behalf, you won't have to go to Memphis. Or maybe—"

He nudged aside her head covering and kissed the back of her neck.

Her breath caught, interrupting her for only a moment. "Why is Horemheb wasting time in Avaris with a feast? Not that I'm anxious to lose you, but perhaps El-Shaddai will use this time to intervene and make a way for you to stay here, and—"

Mered tipped her chin up to meet his gaze. "I've missed you, wife." He silenced her with a kiss. Her body relaxed into his embrace, and her emotional defenses came tumbling down.

Weeping, she wrapped her arms around his neck, and he kissed the tears from her cheeks. "I can't let you go again."

He lifted her into his arms, and she clung like a wet robe to his body. Laying her on their sleeping mat, he nestled close and pulled her into the bend of his form. "El-Shaddai is our dwelling place, my love. We will dwell in Him together and endure whatever comes."

28

The words of their mouths are wicked and deceitful;
they fail to act wisely or do good.

—Psalm 36:3

Anippe waited in her chamber, heart racing. Why was she so nervous to welcome Abbi Horem—the man who deemed her his treasure, the one who'd protected her since she was a child? But his expression had been so distant, so impersonal, when his royal procession disembarked at Avaris's quay yesterday. Had she offended him? Somehow disappointed him?

Fear bound her chest. Had he somehow discovered the deception of Mehy's birth?

A loud knock nearly sent her running. Nassor pushed open the door slightly, asking permission to enter. Permission granted, he slipped through and nodded his morning greeting. "Do you want me to attend during Pharaoh's visit? Or should I wait outside your chamber door?" He searched her eyes as if he could read the troubled ka behind them. Perhaps he could.

Nassor had become her champion among the Ramessids while Sebak and Mered were gone. Their friendship, like Nassor himself, wasn't dazzling or bejeweled, but rather simple and sturdy. As she did under her favorite palm tree near the linen shop, she rested in the shade of Nassor's protection. It was all she needed of a man. She had Mehy, but Ankhe had no one.

"I'd rather you go check on Ankhe. Since Mered's news of Abbi's return, she tutors Mehy and then hides in her chamber. I think she's avoiding me."

His expression clouded. "Your sister doesn't want to see me, Amira." He focused on a distant spot on her chamber wall, jaw muscle dancing.

"Would you care to explain why, Captain?"

"Perhaps Ankhe should be the one to inform you of the . . . misunderstanding." He glanced at Anippe and then turned back to the wall, nervous as a bird in a fowler's snare.

Anippe's cheeks warmed. Surely Ankhe hadn't chosen the day of Horemheb's visit to spew a jealous tirade at Nassor. She'd been quiet and shy in his presence for three years. "Tell me, Nassor."

"Your sister had imagined that she and I would someday marry." His nervous laughter and dazed expression confirmed his utter astonishment. "How could she think it? I've barely talked to her except while supervising her lessons with Master Mehy. She's lovely, but I have nothing to offer a wife."

"Ankhe needs only to be loved, Nassor." The words were out before Anippe could restrain them.

They hit her captain like a blow. "I'm afraid I love another," he said, reaching for her hand. The longing in his eyes startled and terrified her.

"No, you can't. You mustn't." Anippe broke from his grasp and turned away, wrapping her arms around her waist. "Nassor, you may wait outside the door. Please announce Pharaoh Horemheb with a knock before you admit him to my chamber."

What else could she say? She could never love Nassor. He was Ankhe's or no one's.

She tried to steady her breathing, waiting in the lingering silence for the captain's retreating footsteps. Finally, she heard shuffling and the quiet *click* of the door closing. Releasing the breath she'd been holding, Anippe collapsed onto her couch, heart pounding wildly.

How could she have been so blind? Poor Ankhe. She'd tried to tell Anippe that Nassor wanted more, but Anippe refused to listen, wouldn't believe it. How could she face her sister—and Nassor—every day with this constant tension?

A knock put an end to her questions. She must greet her abbi—the man soon to become a god. Perhaps a god could untangle her jumbled world.

Miriam appeared at her side, having returned from alerting the kitchen slaves to re-create the sentimental meal she and her abbi had shared on King Tut's barque on their way to Avaris all those years ago. *"Tear, dip, chew!"*

They'd laughed and eaten their bread and stewed dates. The sweet memory calmed her as Egypt's soon-to-be king entered her chamber.

Horemheb wore a long linen shenti cinched by a jeweled gold belt at the waist, his torso covered by a byssus linen overshirt. His Gold of Praise collar remained his only adornment until the incarnation of Horus indwelled him at the coronation in Thebes. Once a god, he would wear the robes and crowns of Egypt's Two Lands, carry the crook and flail, and be the representation of the many gods on earth.

"Greetings, my most honored Abbi Horem, victorious general, and imminent king of Egypt's Two Lands. I am delighted to bask in your presence and anxious to hear of your conquests." She bowed deeply, waiting to be embraced.

"You may rise." He walked past her toward the courtyard, followed by Mandai and another Medjay.

Feeling as if she'd been slapped, Anippe caught her breath and glimpsed Nassor's wounded expression as he disappeared behind her chamber door.

Regret battled with angst as Anippe hurried to catch up with her guests. "Please be seated, and your Medjays may sit on the cushions." Anippe pointed Miriam toward the brightly colored pillows stacked nearby, and the girl immediately placed them on the tiles for the soldiers.

"My men stand." Abbi lowered his bulk into a wooden chair, his expression as empty as the table.

Anippe nodded at Miriam, the signal to serve their meal. "I hope you haven't eaten. We'll have bread and stewed dates like we shared on our journey from Gurob before my marriage feast—"

"I've already broken my fast, Anippe. There's no time for such nonsense."

Miriam stopped three paces behind him. Anippe shooed her away, while Abbi continued with his agenda.

"Mehy is to be educated at the School of the Kap in Memphis with other noblemen's sons," he announced. "He'll leave with me at the end of the week. Mered will arrange it."

Anippe's heart leapt to her throat. "No." Respectful but firm, she lifted her chin and waited for the storm.

Abbi Horem's face flushed, but he remained equally calm. "Leave us. All of you." The Medjays took Miriam and exited. Abbi's expression remained fixed on a distant nothing. "You will never again contradict or disobey me with others present." He slammed his fist onto the ebony table. "Is that clear?"

Anippe jumped but remained composed. "Why are you angry with me?"

"Because you defied me!" He shoved the table with his foot, sending it sailing across the tiles.

She squeezed her eyes shut, refusing to be cowed by his fury, and then opened them with renewed calm. "I'm sorry, but it's more than my refusal of Mehy's schooling. You've been angry since you stepped foot on this estate." She held his gaze without flinching. "I ask again, why are you angry with me?"

They stared at each other, neither blinking.

And then her defenses began to crumble, an inner trembling becoming visible. *By the gods, why can't I be strong in Abbi's presence?*

"I'm not angry with you." He bolted from his chair as if fleeing from Anubis himself and walked down the tiled path toward her bathhouse.

Anippe blinked back tears, knowing he wouldn't respond if she became emotional. Smoothing her linen robe, she breathed deeply and pursued the soon-to-be king.

He stood at the shoreline not far from where she'd found Mehy in the Hebrew basket. Her heart nearly failed. Did he know? Had Ankhe told him?

Abbi walked into the water and brushed his hand over the reeds, seeming almost wistful. "It's my fault, Anippe. Tut, Amenia, and Sebak are dead, Senpa married to Ay, and Egypt in chaos—all because I let Ay outmaneuver me." He looked at her, worn, weak, and weary. "I won the war—but at too great a cost. I've failed so many people. I failed you, my treasure."

She fell into his arms, years of forbidden tears flowing—and he didn't push her away. He rubbed her back, one strong hand nearly covering the span between her shoulder blades. This was the abbi she knew. This man would never take Mered from Avaris or sentence Ankhe to a life of loneliness.

Anippe's mind began to spin with possibilities, and her tears dried. "You are the best man I know, Abbi, and the deaths of our loved ones aren't your fault. Is a cobra at fault when it eats a rat? Or a cat when it eats them both? War steals lives, Abbi, but the war is over. Can't we live again?"

He grasped her arms and held her at arm's length, a glimmer of hope in his gaze. "Do I detect a plan?"

She chuckled and twisted away, spying a nearby cloth to wipe the smeared kohl from her face. "I would not be Horemheb's daughter if I did not negotiate for a favorable outcome."

Abbi came alongside her, wrapping his arm around her shoulder. "And you are my daughter, Anippe." He kissed her head as they ambled back to the courtyard and the broken ebony table. Abbi sheepishly pointed at his destruction. "I'll have Mered send a replacement when we've settled into the Memphis Palace."

"Let's talk about Mered for a moment." Anippe wished Miriam had brought the stewed dates. Now would be a good time to distract Abbi Horem with food. "When you stole my linen keeper to make him your supply chief—"

"I didn't steal—"

Anippe lifted her hand, halting his protest. "Let me finish. In Mered's absence, I've maintained the workshop despite Ay's attempts to bolster Gurob Harem's linen trade by blocking our access to southern merchants from Arabia and Cush. I, in turn, blocked all Gurob's access to northern trade routes through the Delta and from the Great Sea."

Abbi clapped his hands. "That's my little warrior."

She nodded, acknowledging his praise. "So while the production at Gurob's workshop shrank, struggling to import goods and export their linen, our Avaris workshop has grown to twice Gurob's size—so my merchant spies tell me."

Abbi reached for her hand. "I'm proud of you, my treasure."

Anippe let his goodwill simmer like a well-seasoned stew. She planned to ask for three favors in hopes of securing two. First, the decoy. "I've been able to concentrate fully on the linen shop because Ankhe has been a remarkable teacher for your grandson—"

"I'll not have—"

She lifted her hand to silence him again. "We must reward her faithfulness by honoring Sebak's promise to match her with a Ramessid soldier now that the war is over." It wasn't the whole truth, but what did it matter? Anippe was confident Abbi Horem would refuse.

"Ankhe is not now and has never been my concern."

"But she is mine, Abbi."

"Then do what you like with her."

Ah yes. The answer she'd hoped for. "My decision is that she remains Mehy's tutor while he attends the School of the Kap in Memphis."

Abbi Horem's eyes narrowed to slits, the goodwill she'd amassed draining away. "You would send a woman to teach your son at a noblemen's school?"

"I would send King Tut's sister, who was educated by the king's personal tutors, to instruct Pharaoh Horemheb's grandson at the Kap." She wanted to elaborate, to list every good and logical reason, but instead sat in quiet confidence despite the churning she felt inside.

Abbi Horem's gaze unnerved her, but to falter would imply weakness and might leave Mehy unattended in Memphis—without Ankhe to inform Anippe about his daily life and care. And if Ankhe could prove herself to Abbi Horem as a valuable tutor, perhaps he would match her with another tutor—or Nassor, if he agreed in time.

"Are you so intent on coddling your son that you'll provide Mehy with a nursemaid till he graduates from the Kap? Will you become his military trainer at Sile when he turns twelve?" Abbi Horem's voice rose with each word.

Sensing his frustration, she lightened her tone. "Thank you for offering, but no. I can't hold on to my son forever, you know." His expression lightened— almost a grin—and she knew it was time to press her final request. "I'll be too busy at the Gurob Harem—reviving their linen business." It was her perfect escape from Nassor's misplaced affection.

"Oh, I see," he chuckled. "And who will oversee Avaris linen production while Gurob benefits from your expertise?"

She left her chair, knelt beside him, and placed her forehead against his hand. "Mered has a wife and children here in Avaris, Abbi. Please don't take him away from them."

He yanked his hand from her grasp. "He is a slave, Anippe. Property. He performs a service, a duty, a task—and he's quite good at getting what I need when I need it."

Anippe lifted her head but remained on her knees. "Why not employ Tut's Keeper of the Treasury?"

"Because he also served Ay, my enemy. How can I trust him?"

"Use his knowledge of Ay's activities to serve your purpose. Demand that he defile the tomb he builds for Ay. Wipe away every trace of Nakhtmin's military victories. No one knows Egypt better than the man who built King Tut's thriving kingdom and raided temples for despicable Ay. Use him like a pet crocodile."

Abbi's bushy eyebrows drew together, but he didn't argue, a hopeful sign that gave her courage to continue.

"The man who served Tut—and Ay—can keep records, plan ceremonies, and organize the nation, but he can't love Mered's wife and child. And Mered can't hunt political jackals in Memphis, Karnak, and Thebes when he's never sailed south of the Delta."

Leaning back in his chair, Abbi tilted his head, examining her closely. "You've changed, my treasure."

"As have you, Abbi."

Continued silence left her time to lift his hand to her lips, and he returned her smile. "Don't think I'm fooled by your scheming, but I will agree to your requests. Ankhe will tutor Mehy. You will oversee the linen shop at Gurob, and Mered will remain in Avaris."

She bowed her head, hiding her satisfaction. "Thank you, Abbi."

"But you must agree to my wishes." His words stirred her dread and drew her gaze. "You will befriend my new wife, Mutnodjmet, at the Gurob Harem and keep me apprised of her activity."

Anippe's stomach knotted. "Your new wife?" She'd been so sure Mered was mistaken when he told her. "Surely, you don't mean Mutno, Ay's daughter—"

"At tomorrow's feast, I take Mutno as my bride." He leaned forward, his teeth clenched. "She'll watch her abbi and husband die at my hand and spend the rest of her life in the bed of a man who loathes her. Tomorrow night, everyone will know what happens to those who betray Pharaoh Horemheb." He kissed her cheek and stood. "I'll let myself out."

Anippe crumpled to the ground, trembling at his unwitting threat.

29

Mered wanted to run, to leave Egypt—at least until Horemheb was finished with his cursed vengeance. Would Horemheb's violence ever cease?

Mered sat beside an empty throne on an elevated dais, waiting for the feast to begin. Tonight would be his last official act as Horemheb's chief aid, and then—thanks to the amira—he would return to his duties as chief linen keeper of Avaris.

Mandai and another Medjay, dressed in warrior finery, scanned the room for danger while Ramessid soldiers stood guard around the perimeter and at every exit. Despite the threatening undertones, a celebrative hum rose from those gathered for Horemheb's victory feast. Mered's chest grew tighter with each breath, and each heartbeat felt like a rock tossed into sand.

Ramessid officers and wives mingled with Memphis noblemen and their Gurob wives. The women's tables on Mered's right were crowded with audacious, fleshy old women trying to feel youthful and impress young men. The scented wax cones atop their wigs had begun to melt. The perfume in the wigs and that on overscented bodies combined to fill the air with enough perfume to choke a lotus.

One table of women, however, was not chatting, cackling, or boasting. Queen Senpa stared into the distance, with Anippe and Ankhe seated on her right and left. Ay's daughter, Mutno—and Horemheb's bride-to-be—sat beside Anippe, apparently visiting the same distant land as Queen Senpa. Pirameses's wife, Sitre, sat beside Ankhe, hiding her bruised face in the shadows. Her husband had obviously discovered her indiscretions. The five women had been placed directly right-center of the throne, across from the king's table with his officers.

Several noblemen who'd been faithful to Ay also attended tonight's celebration. Some arrived by force, some by choice. Soon-to-be-king Horemheb was giving them one chance, this night, to determine with whom their loyalties lay. He'd invited as many officials as the Avaris main hall could seat—all to witness his first official acts as the imminent son of Horus.

Horemheb and Pirameses rose from their table of officers and ascended the small, elevated dais. The victorious general took his place on Tut's gilded throne—Horemheb's throne now. Pirameses, wearing his Gold of Praise collar, took the vizier's customary position, and Mandai stood as his chief Medjay. Mered sat on the platform at the right of Horemheb's feet, ready to record any notes that must be made of the night's events.

El-Shaddai, please stop this. And if You will not, then protect me—Your servant.

Horemheb's herald banged a chime bearing the king's coiled cobra at its peak. "Enter the honorable son of Sebak and son of Pirameses."

Mehy and Sety appeared at the entrance, wide-eyed and fearful. Anippe had mentioned that Sety's ummi had visited Avaris occasionally, offering the boys a chance to play together. Mered had cringed at first, remembering Master Sebak's warning about Sitre, but he was thankful Mehy had a friend tonight. Seeing the boys side by side, he noticed that Sety's resemblance to the Ramessids was striking. Mehy had definitely inherited the amira's olive skin tone and sandy-brown eyes.

Flanked by two Medjays in full battle gear, the boys peered around ostrich-plumed bows and muscled ebony thighs. The towering soldiers coaxed them with quiet whispers and even smiled during their stroll toward the throne. At the end of the crimson tapestry, the warriors knelt before their regent and pressed the boys to the same posture.

"Your abbis served me well, boys. You may rise to face me." Horemheb leaned forward, his kindness settling them, though little Sety reached for Mehy's hand. "Sety, your abbi Pirameses will be my vizier—the second-most powerful man in Egypt. What do you think of that?"

Four-year-old Sety looked at his ummi first, and then studied Pirameses from head to toe. "My abbi plays swords wif me. I wike him."

The guests chuckled warmly, as did the king. "I've never heard higher praise. I'm happy you approve."

Turning to his grandson and namesake, Horemheb's expression grew sober. "Mehy, your abbi Sebak was the bravest man I've ever known. He was murdered by cowards, who will soon pay for their treachery. You are my grandson and the son of a great warrior. I have high hopes for you."

Mehy bowed, wordless, too timid to meet Horemheb's gaze.

"Boys, you may stand beside my chief aid, Mered. I want you to see what I'm going to do to the men who killed Mehy's abbi."

Anippe covered a gasp, then lunged toward her son, but Ankhe pulled her back. Mered felt bile rise in his throat but silently reached for the boys. He could only hold them during this madness. He glanced at the women's table to see Ankhe whispering to Anippe, who had gone completely pale.

Horemheb turned to the herald. "Bring in the prisoners."

Two men were dragged to the doorway, their hands and feet bound in chains. Nassor was one of the guards tugging the first prisoner slowly up the aisle, allowing every table to assess the bald and blood-soaked man. His legs had been broken, and he hung limp between the Ramessids. His once-handsome face was almost unrecognizable except for his beaklike nose. Vizier Ay was the first spectacle this evening.

Sety whimpered, and Mehy began to tremble when more Ramessids followed with a second prisoner draped over their arms.

Mered circled their waists and whispered, "You can close your eyes but don't turn your head, or Horemheb might notice you're not watching. Make him think you're watching."

Ay's daughter, Mutno, buried her head in her hands, moaning, and Anippe leaned over to comfort her. The second prisoner was Nakhtmin. Mutno would see both her abbi and her husband die tonight—and then be forced to marry the man who killed them. Mered kept swallowing, fearful he might be sick. *El-Shaddai, keep me strong for the boys in my arms.*

Both prisoners, now hanging between soldiers before the throne, seemed only half conscious. Did they even know where they were?

Mered glanced again toward Anippe. She was shaking her head violently at him, mouthing a message. *No! No! No!* What did she expect him to do? Little Sety's eyes were now fixed on the bloody prisoners, while Mehy stood trembling, eyes closed. *El-Shaddai, give me wisdom.* Both Mered's arms were firmly planted around the boys' waists, his writing utensils at their feet.

My writing utensils.

"Victorious Horemheb, may I approach for a private matter?" Mered's words quieted every other sound in the hall. Keeping his head bowed, he waited for death or assent.

"What?" Horemheb growled, and Mered practically leapt from his cushion to whisper so only the would-be king could hear. "May I send the boys to their ummis? I can't write your judgments with them trembling in my arms."

He paused, studying Mered, but on this last day as chief aid, Mered didn't dare meet Horemheb's gaze.

"The boys will stand with my Medjays so my chief aid can record the proceedings."

Mered bowed. *El-Shaddai, please comfort the children where I have failed.*

As the boys walked behind the throne to Mandai and the king's other bodyguard, Horemheb announced to the crowd, "Ramessid boys will be warriors and must see what we do to those who betray Pharaoh."

And then his judgment began.

"The Gold of Praise is Egypt's highest military honor—one Vizier Pirameses wears proudly tonight. While fighting Hittites, we've learned of another military honor, called the Gold of *Valor*." He signaled Nassor to place a long board in front of the prisoners. The other guards held them while Nassor tethered the prisoners' right arms tightly across it. "Pirameses, take the hands of our enemies and claim your Gold of Valor."

The new vizier drew a long, heavy sword from his belt and brought it down with a sickening *thwack*.

"Nooooo!" Anippe screamed and others joined her. The prisoners writhed in their chains. Horror filled the air as the two little boys whimpered, trying to turn away, but the Medjay bodyguards held them fast, forcing their eyes to witness the savagery.

"We will bury their hands at Avaris." Horemheb sounded almost gleeful. "Sebak's estate will forever hold captive the right hands of Ay and Nakhtmin, while they wander the underworld maimed for their treachery." He stood and shouted at the terrified noblemen and their wives. "Would anyone care to join them?"

Mehy and Sety clawed at the Medjays, crying out for their ummis. Guards restrained Anippe and Sitre to keep them from their children, while the other women wept into their hands. Except Queen Senpa—her expression remained unchanged, her eyes still distant. Was she even breathing?

"Queen Senpa." Horemheb's voice resounded in the hall like a shout.

Anippe shoved a guard away, then grabbed Senpa's arm as she pleaded with Horemheb. "No, don't take her. Please. It wasn't her fault—"

The queen quieted Anippe, and the whole room grew silent as a tomb. "Death is my only escape, sister." She pulled her arm away, and two guards escorted her to stand before the throne.

Mered's hand trembled as he dipped his writing reed into water to wet the pigment. What should he write on this scroll? How could he record insanity? Ay and Nakhtmin still writhed on the crimson carpet, now dark red with blood, while a lovely young queen awaited undeserved death. Horemheb was a madman. How could he force two small boys to watch things from which even Medjays turned their faces?

"Go to your ummis." Horemheb's gruff command startled Mered's hand, scratching a black line across the papyrus. Perhaps that was the record of this night. Blackness. A record bearing a meaningless black mark amid cold details.

The boys ran behind the throne—to avoid the bloody scene before it—

and fell into their ummis' arms. Mered watched their reunion and heard three sudden *thwacks* nearly in unison. He squeezed his eyes shut, not needing to look at the scene to know what lay at the foot of the throne.

Senpa, Ay, and Nakhtmin were dead and would—according to Egyptian belief—wander the underworld without their heads.

Mered recorded on the papyrus the three names and then glanced toward the royal women's table once more. Anippe and Sitre bent over their hysterical sons, and Ankhe sat somberly eating a pomegranate. Mutno stared at the back wall—much like Senpa had done moments before.

"Mutno, come to me." Horemheb's voice, so full of hate, sent a chill up Mered's spine.

When guards reached for Mutno's arms, she fought them. Screaming, fighting, kicking, biting—like a she-jackal she battled.

And Horemheb laughed.

Escorted to the throne amid the stench of blood and vomit, Mutno was no longer Ay's daughter, no longer Nakhtmin's wife. The guards threw her to the carpet between the corpses. She lay there and wept.

"Mutno, you are now my wife—and soon will be Queen of Egypt. Dry your tears, my sweet. I'll do no worse to you than your abbi Ay did to my late wife, Amenia." He addressed Nassor. "Take her to my guest chamber, and use your cudgel to prepare her for my arrival."

Nassor bent to lift Mutno from the carpet, but Horemheb stopped him with a word. "Trust. I've trusted you with my daughter and this estate for three years, Ramessid. I know you can be kind." He leaned forward, challenging. "Can I trust you to be cruel when your king demands it?"

Without flinching, Nassor lifted a single brow. "I am worthy of your trust, my king. Cruelty is a Ramessid's native tongue." He bowed, hoisted Mutno over his shoulder, and strolled from the main hall to the sound of Horemheb's laughter.

Mered recorded the marriage for history and turned aside to vomit.

Anippe carried her terrorized son from the feast; his legs wrapped around her and locked at the ankles. Would he ever let go, ever stop shaking? Would she?

She hurried down the long corridor to her chamber, not waiting for an escort or even looking behind her. Nassor's brutality loomed in her mind. How could her compassionate protector have become a monster in a day's span? She hadn't seen him since he'd declared his love for her—and she'd refused him. When she left her chamber for the feast, another guard had taken Nassor's place. Was her refusal the reason for his bloody wrath on those prisoners? Were all men bloodthirsty jackals?

Rounding the corner, she shouted at the guard at her chamber. "Open the door!" He obeyed promptly and closed it behind her.

Anippe collapsed on the cushions in her sitting area, sobbing. She tried to calm herself but noticed a shadow in the dim lights and screamed.

"It's me, Amira," Miriam said, kneeling beside the embroidered couch.

"What are you doing there?"

The girl wiped her cheeks. "I've been praying to El-Shaddai for you and Mehy."

Anger rose like bile in Anippe's throat. "Well, your god did nothing. My son—"

Mehy lurched from her arms toward Miriam, burying his head in the handmaid's shoulder. Miriam cradled him. "Shh, you're safe now. Come, sit down. Your ummi and I love you very much."

Miriam lifted her round doe eyes, and Anippe struggled for composure. "Take him to the bathhouse. No one will bother us there."

They walked without torches along the tiled path, thankful for moonlight to guide their way. Anippe wrapped her arm around Miriam, who placed Mehy between them on a cushion under the thatched-roof shelter. His shaking had subsided in the dark stillness.

"Habibi, look at me." Anippe brushed his cheek and gently tugged on his princely sidelock.

He lifted his sandy-brown eyes. "I-I d-d-don't w-want to s-s-see . . ." He shook his head and buried his face in Miriam's side.

Stuttering? Her bright, articulate boy was stuttering? "Mehy." Her voice broke. What could she say? How could she remove the images imprinted on his mind?

Miriam cradled him in the bend of her arm, rocking and whispering. "Remember your name, Moses. You were *drawn out* of the Nile because El-Shaddai has a special calling and purpose for your life. Everything that happens—good and bad—prepares you for what's next." She paused and kissed his head, letting her words settle into his heart. "I don't know what happened in the main hall tonight, but El-Shaddai was with you—and He's protecting you, Moses. Just like He protected you when your ummi Anippe found you in the basket on the Nile—"

"That's enough." Anippe glanced over her shoulder and then up and down the river. She pulled Mehy away from Miriam, cradling him against her. "You cannot speak of his birth—ever." Her throat tight, she saw the pain in Miriam's eyes and regretted her harshness. "I know you believe in your god, and you're trying to help, but if Abbi Horem ever discovers I've deceived him . . ." She thought of Senpa lying on the floor without a head.

Mehy stirred in her arms and then met her gaze. "I w-won't ever t-t-tell my s-secret name, Ummi. I'd l-l-lose my p-power like Re, when Isis t-t-tricked him."

Anippe hugged him, laughing and crying. "Yes, habibi. You're so smart." She reached for Miriam's hand while still embracing her brave boy. "Perhaps Miriam's god has saved you for a great purpose, but we must never tell anyone else about it. Understand?" She hardened her gaze at the handmaid. "Only we three will ever speak the name *Moses*. Do you understand, Miriam?"

"I will never speak of Moses to anyone." Miriam kissed Anippe's hand but then held it, her brow lifted in challenge. "Neither will I speak to Moses of any god but El-Shaddai."

Anippe's temper flared. How dare a handmaid dictate to her?

Mehy turned to Miriam, a tentative smile playing at his lips. "The song, Miriam. Sing me the song," he said, stuttering only a little. He rested against Anippe's side, pulled her arm over him like a blanket, and placed his feet in Miriam's lap.

The Hebrew girl opened her mouth, and out came a tune that reached the heavens. "El-Shaddai is my strength, my song. He is my God, and I will praise Him, my father's God, I will exalt Him . . ."

Anippe couldn't hold back tears. Thankful for the darkness, she wiped her cheeks and stared down at Mehy. His expression was releasing the night's tension and fear. She lifted her face to the night breeze, listening to the Nile's high tide. Frogs and crickets accompanied Miriam's melody, and in the distance Anippe heard Abbi Horem's guests retiring to their chambers. She leaned over, quieting Miriam with a hand on her arm—but still heard echoes of her tune on the night breeze.

Mehy sat up, alert. "The s-slaves, Ummi. They're s-singing Miriam's song."

Confused, Anippe searched the girl's peaceful face for answers. "Why are the slaves singing tonight? I've heard them hum while working in the linen shop, but I've never heard singing all the way from the craftsmen's village."

"They sing for you, Amira—and Mehy and me. Mered went home to his wife and son earlier today because El-Shaddai answered Puah's prayer through your kindness. The whole camp rejoiced that he'll return as chief linen keeper, but they're concerned for Mehy going to school, and you and me going to Gurob. The Hebrews pray and sing to El-Shaddai for us all."

"Why would a Hebrew god help Egyptians?"

"El-Shaddai knows everyone." Miriam kissed Mehy's nose. "Regardless of our names."

Regardless of our names. Fear surged through Anippe. She'd wagered both her life and Mehy's on fooling the gods, and now there was One who knew Mehy as Moses and knew Moses as Hebrew? *Terrifying.*

Her panic subsided, however, as the rhythmic, lilting song of the faithful Hebrews continued. How could she deny its effect? Perhaps this god was real. Perhaps he wouldn't seek her destruction like Anubis or Seth. But where did he fit among her other gods?

She pulled Mehy close, resting her chin on his head. "Miriam, how long since you've seen Jochebed and Amram?"

The girl tried to smile, her cheeks quivering with the effort. "A while. Father delivered a necklace to Ankhe before the harvest festival, and Mother brought baskets to the villa shortly before sowing season."

"Go home tonight." Anippe wound a dark lock of her handmaid's hair around her finger. "Mehy and I will sleep in my chamber. I'll have two chamber guards escort you to your parents' home as a show of gratitude for the slaves' song. Why don't you go pack your spindle and wool as a gift for Jochebed. I'll get you another when you return to the villa—two days, and we leave for Thebes."

"Oh, thank you, Amira." Miriam hugged her and hurried through the courtyard and into the chamber without a backward glance.

Anippe looked down at her son in the moonlight. *Two days.* They didn't have much time to say good-bye to those they loved in Avaris. Inhaling deeply, Anippe breathed it in. Home. She would miss the dear Hebrews she called friends.

"Ummi, can we pray to El-Shaddai?" Mehy's brown eyes shone in the moonlight. "Mered and Miriam do."

Anippe knew little of the Hebrew god. "Do you think El-Shaddai would hear the prayer of Egyptians, habibi?"

"Miriam said he knows us—even our secret names."

Anippe swallowed a new wave of fear. "You can pray, habibi, but make sure the Hebrew god doesn't reveal our secret names to others."

If Abbi Horem truly became a god at his coronation, she couldn't chance divine gossip.

30

The Lord looked with favor on Abel and his offering, but on Cain and his offering he did not look with favor. . . . While they were in the field, Cain attacked his brother Abel and killed him.

—GENESIS 4:4, 8

The pink hues of dawn were fading, and Horemheb's men were already loading the king's barque to sail. Mered hurried toward the villa, prodded by Miriam's night of terror. The girl had enjoyed two wonderful days in the craftsmen's village with her family, but last night's dream roused terrified screams that awakened the households on both sides of their dividing curtain.

The moon had passed its zenith when Amram and Jochebed shoved aside the curtain, cradling a trembling Miriam between them. Aaron had peered from behind Amram, eyes wide. "My sister had a bad dream."

Puah had pushed herself off their sleeping mat. "I'll warm some goat's milk for the children." One of the Ramessid wives had given her a jug of milk earlier that evening for helping with her birth.

Amram and Jochebed guided Miriam to the single chair in the room, while the rest of their families gathered round to hear her describe the dream.

"I saw a beautiful garden. No weeds, only flowers and fruit trees and endless rows of vegetables. Flocks of sheep and goats grazed in green pastures that stretched to the horizon. One boy, my age, tended the sheep. He played a flute. A beautiful, lilting tune. An older boy, perhaps eighteen or twenty, approached him from behind and struck his head with a rock." Her eyes glistened, her lips trembled. "The older boy stood over the dead boy and laughed, and then he . . ." She shook her head and squeezed her eyes closed.

"Tell Mered, daughter." Amram patted her shoulder. "It's no small matter to be entrusted with El-Shaddai's message."

Mered shot a glance at his friend. *El-Shaddai's message?* He was tempted to chuckle—until he saw the fear in Amram's eyes that nearly matched his daughter's. "Tell me, Miriam. What happened to the laughing boy in your dream?"

She lifted her light brown eyes swimming with tears. "He was changed—and became Ankhe."

The words stole Mered's breath. He could almost envision it: the laughing boy melting, twisting, roiling into Anippe's troubled sister. The image was terrifying. But had El-Shaddai truly spoken to Miriam, or was the nightmare stirred by slave gossip about Horemheb's violent feast?

Rather than challenge the distressed girl, Mered aimed his doubts at Amram. "What makes you believe Miriam's dream is a message from El-Shaddai?"

Miriam tugged on his sleeve. "Because the voice—more like a song, really—said, 'If hope is gone, the brother becomes the sister.' And I can't get the tune or those words out of my head. They keep playing over and over in my mind."

Puah offered Miriam the warmed goat's milk, and Mered glanced at Amram. One wiry gray eyebrow lifted. "I told you it was a message from El-Shaddai," Amram said.

They'd all tried to go back to sleep, but who could rest when El-Shaddai had visited their longhouse? He'd been silent since the days of Joseph, His people seemingly forgotten.

Mered lay awake until the eastern horizon glowed deep purple. Then he leapt out of bed to accompany Miriam to the amira's chamber.

He'd never visited Anippe's chamber without being summoned, but last night's dream was reason enough to knock on her door.

"Miriam, slow down," he called.

At thirteen, the girl had grown tall and slender, her round eyes and curls transformed from cute to alluring. She'd reached the age of marriage, but there would be no match until the amira chose a man. As Anippe's personal handmaid, Miriam was under her authority—and her protection. Mered glanced toward the quay as they approached the villa's main entry and prayed the amira took precautions to protect Miriam from guards and oarsmen on their long journey.

A flurry of preparation permeated the estate. Horemheb's men loaded the king's barque and three other ships for the ten-day journey to Thebes. Perhaps Miriam would be safe with the royals on the king's barque. Mered rubbed his face, frustrated at his looming dread after last night's dream.

He and Miriam crossed the threshold and found the villa interior equally frantic. Servants bustled from kitchen to chamber to storeroom to quay.

Mered and Miriam were nearly knocked over by the cook, who never left her kitchen. "I don't know why I have to carry baskets of grain to a stinking ship." The old woman panted and huffed as she elbowed past Mered.

Miriam adjusted the small sack of personal items on her back and rushed down the long corridor. She seemed energized, embracing the duty to which El-Shaddai had called her. Was she a prophetess now, this beautiful thirteen-year-old, or did God require more than one dream to consider someone His servant? The thought brought a smile to Mered's face—until he saw Nassor posted at Anippe's door.

Unyielding and foul-tempered, the captain glared at the two Hebrews. "It's about time you arrived." He grabbed Miriam's arm, opened the door, and shoved her through a narrow opening.

"Wait, I need to speak with the amira." Mered moved toward the door.

Nassor stepped in front of him, his bulk bumping Mered back. "She's busy, linen keeper."

"But I—"

"Are we going to have trouble after the amira leaves?" Nassor grabbed Mered's robe, nearly lifting him off the tiles.

The chamber door swung open. "No, Nassor. You will not have trouble with Mered after I leave—or with any of my slaves."

Nassor released Mered and bowed. "As you wish, Amira."

The Ramessid's sarcastic tone signaled a new rift between him and the

amira. Mered had been busy with feast preparations and hadn't seen them together since he'd returned from Sile.

The amira motioned toward her chamber. "Inside, Mered. We have matters to discuss before I leave." She turned with renewed fury on Nassor. "You
may have impressed Abbi Horem with your brutality, but if you do anything
to jeopardize Avaris's linen trade—including abuse my chief linen keeper—I
assure you, Pharaoh Horemheb will find a more efficient estate foreman. You
will make sure our Hebrews are well paid, well fed, and well treated. I'll return
next year to check the accounts."

She slammed the door and whirled on Mered, Miriam, Ankhe, and Mehy,
who waited inside her chamber, transfixed. "What are you staring at?" she
demanded.

Ankhe lifted a brow. "Tell me again why Horemheb chooses your estate
foreman when Avaris isn't even his estate. Oh yes, I remember—because neither he nor his daughter respect what belongs to others."

The jealousy of Cain. There it was. Mered didn't need to know why Ankhe
felt cheated to recognize the relevance of Miriam's dream.

"I didn't take anything from you, Ankhe."

"You've taken everything, and now you're sending me to Memphis to be
rid of me." Ankhe reached for Mehy's hand. "Have you gathered your treasures
from your ummi's chamber?"

Mehy nodded, clutching a small linen sack over his shoulder. The boy's
sadness engulfed Mered like a fog, drawing him into the gloom. How would
Mehy survive Ankhe's foul humor alone? They'd always been carefully supervised during their lessons at the villa. Would Ankhe's bitter influence be tem-
pered at the Kap as well? Or would she be free to taint the boy's tender soul?

Anippe reached for Mehy and knelt before him. "I'll meet you on the
barque. We'll sail to Thebes for your Jad Horem's coronation, and then it's
another long sail before you leave Ummi and Miriam at Gurob. We have
many days together before you go with Jad Horem and Ankhe to the Memphis Palace." She kissed three dots on the back of his hand. "Remember, you,
me, and Amun-Re—always together." Gathering Mehy close, she struggled

for composure, and then released him to her sister. "I'm doing what I think is best for every—"

"You're doing what's best for you, Anippe," Ankhe interrupted.

"No. I know you wish to marry—" Anippe's breath caught, and both sisters shot a glance at Mered. Neither seemed willing to speak of Ankhe's personal desires in the presence of a linen keeper—and he was grateful.

Ankhe grabbed Mehy's hand. "Come, we'll gather a few things from my chamber and go to the barque. Perhaps the pilot will teach you how to command the oarsmen."

Mehy looked over his shoulder, waving at Mered as his aunt rushed him out the door.

El-Shaddai, protect him.

Anippe sighed and stared at the closed door. "It's been a difficult morning." She turned then and tried to smile, trudging toward her embroidered couch. "What did you wish to talk about, Mered?"

He exchanged a glance with Miriam, whose confidence had dimmed since entering the amira's chamber. "I wanted to say good-bye, of course, but there is another matter Miriam and I need to address."

Mered waited, hoping the girl would begin recounting her dream. She didn't.

"Why does Ankhe blame me for every wrong in her life?" The amira propped her elbow on the armrest and cupped her chin in hand. "I'm sending her to Memphis partly as Mehy's guardian, it's true. But it's the only place she has any hope of finding a worthy husband." She looked at Mered, pleading. "I'm not her enemy."

Mered's stomach knotted. "Amira, may I tell you a story?" Miriam stepped closer to him. He sensed she needed this introduction to her dream tale.

Anippe sat up, a wary grin replacing her furrowed brow. "What kind of story?"

"A true story—about when God created the world."

"You mean Re? When Amun-Re created all things—"

"No, Amira. I speak of El-Shaddai. He alone is God, and He created the first man, called Adam. From Adam, God formed the woman, Eve." Her frown said he was losing her, so he skipped to the relevant part. "Adam and Eve had two sons, the older named Cain, the younger, Abel. Both sons brought sacrifices to God—Cain from his fields and Abel from his flocks. El-Shaddai was pleased with Abel's offering but not pleased with Cain's."

She crossed her arms and sighed. "Mered, I have much to accomplish before the ship sails. Why are you telling me this story?"

"Because Cain was jealous of Abel, just as Ankhe is jealous of you."

The amira's eyes narrowed, examining her linen keeper for many heartbeats. "Why?" she finally asked. "Why was your god displeased with Cain's offering? Why do the gods play favorites?"

Encouraged by her thoughtful question, Mered took a step closer. "El-Shaddai was displeased with Cain's heart, the way he chose and offered his sacrifice, but Cain refused to see his own fault. He blamed Abel for his woes and was jealous of the favor God showed his brother."

"As Ankhe is jealous and blames me for her troubles." The amira picked at a snag on the armrest. "Is that the end of the story?"

Miriam stepped toward the couch and knelt before her amira, pressing her forehead to Anippe's hand. "May I tell you the rest, Amira?"

Startled, Anippe placed her other hand on the girl's head. "Of course, Miriam. Tell me."

Mered saw Miriam's hands tremble as she raised her eyes to meet Anippe's. "I had a dream last night—a nightmare, really—in which I witnessed Cain and Abel's story in my mind. Cain lured Abel to a beautiful meadow, where he struck him in the head with a rock. Cain stood over his brother's dead body, laughing, and then I saw Cain transformed into . . ." Miriam turned to Mered, took a deep breath, and closed her eyes. "Cain became Ankhe and Abel, the brother of favor, was you, Amira."

Anippe jerked her hands away from the girl. "That's ridiculous. Ankhe would never harm me." She stood, challenging Mered. "Where did Miriam conjure such nonsense? Did you help her concoct this story to frighten me? I know the slaves hate Ankhe."

Mered kept his tone level. "No one coaxed Miriam, and we aren't try-ing to frighten you. This is a message for you from El-Shaddai. Please, Amira—listen."

Anippe's olive skin turned to milk, and she slowly faced Miriam as if meet-ing death. "Why would El-Shaddai speak to me?"

"I believe it's a warning, Amira, not a prediction. He spoke to me in a song." Miriam opened her mouth and the haunting tune escaped, somehow wrapping the danger in comfort. "If hope is gone, the brother becomes the sister. If hope is gone, the brother becomes the sister. If hope is gone, the brother becomes the sister." When Miriam ceased, the words echoed in the silence.

The amira's eyes were closed. She stood utterly still. Mered dared not speak.

Moments passed in unearthly peace. Did the amira feel it too? Her coun-tenance seemed settled, far more relaxed than when they arrived. The anxiety he'd felt about Miriam sharing God's message had drained away when the girl opened her mouth. Miriam, too, stood with eyes closed, face uplifted. Mered wondered if he should leave. Perhaps he was intruding on El-Shaddai's holy ground.

With his first step toward the door, Anippe reached for his hand. "Is it real?" Fear mingled with wonder on her features. "Was I simply moved by a girl's beautiful voice, or did a god just visit this chamber?"

He cradled her hand in his. "He's real, Amira. The one true God spoke to you, and you must trust His words. If Ankhe becomes hopeless, she becomes dangerous."

Miriam's warning song replayed in Anippe's mind as she waited inside her cabin on the king's barque. Abbi Horem and the rest of the royal party paraded down the long hill from the villa to the quay amid music and rejoicing. Ankhe was on deck with Mehy. The ship's pilot had taken an interest in the king's grandson, and Ankhe had taken an interest in the pilot. Miriam had also asked to remain on deck to wave good-bye to her family and friends as the barque set sail.

But Anippe couldn't bear to watch Avaris disappear in the distance. It was home.

Avaris was all she had left of Sebak. Sometimes she wondered if she'd imagined her strong and generous husband. Their time together had been so short, but in her heart, she believed Mered when he said Sebak loved her. She might never understand why he stayed away, but he was an honorable man. Anippe had seen enough dishonorable ones now to know the difference.

If hope is gone, the brother becomes the sister. Miriam's warning—or rather, El-Shaddai's warning—drowned out the approaching royal musicians. Ankhe had never been loved by an honorable man—by any man. Did she still hope? As long as she still yearned for marriage and a family, hope was alive.

But Anippe couldn't let her settle for just any man. What if Ankhe had married Nassor? She shivered at the thought. At least they'd seen his cruelty before he'd unleashed it on Ankhe. Whether her sister believed it or not, the Kap was the best place for her. Perhaps she'd find a kindhearted teacher or an honorable soldier. Until Abbi Horem softened toward her or a man met with Anippe's approval, Ankhe would have to wait to be matched.

The doorway curtain stirred, and a shadow loomed outside.

"Hello?" Anippe called.

The figure turned as if to go and then came back. A trembling hand pushed the curtain aside. Mutno stood in the doorway, her clothing radiant, her countenance shattered.

"Mutno . . ." Anippe was at a loss.

"May I come in?"

"Yes, of course." Anippe reached for her hand to guide her, but the new queen flinched.

"Please, don't touch me. I'm not sure there's anywhere I'm not bruised."

Anippe watched as she walked—hunched—grabbing the door frame for support, lunging for the bed to avoid putting weight on her left ankle.

Sickened, Anippe tried not to think of all this woman had endured. "Did Nassor do this to you?"

"Which time?" Mutno's voice was barely a croak, choked by emotion—or pain. Was there a difference for this woman?

Mutno sat on the stuffed mattress across from Anippe, their knees almost touching in the ship's small cabin. The new queen's handmaid had decorated her well, disguising her sorrow for the royal parade. Dressed in Avaris's finest byssus, she wore a pleated robe with an enchanting sheath that shimmered in the sun. She was bathed in scented oils, and her face was festively painted with malachite, kohl, and red ochre.

From a distance, the cuts and bruises appeared to be part of the design.

Anippe leaned close, not sure who might be listening outside their door. "I can have my maid get healing herbs from the midwives before we sail."

Mutno glanced at the doorway, terrorized. "No. Someone might see."

Her heart breaking, Anippe offered her hand to a woman she barely knew—a woman in despair she could barely imagine. "How can I help you?"

Mutno drew back her hands, refusing comfort. "I think we can help each other. I'm well-connected at Gurob Harem since Abbi Ay ruled the south, and after Horemheb's victory feast . . ." She glanced at the doorway and lowered her voice. "The women at Gurob hate you. You'll find improving their outdated linen production an uphill climb."

Anippe sat a little straighter, realizing that though Mutno was a wounded soldier, she still had fight left in her. "And you have a suggestion to help me win favor among my peers at Gurob?"

"They are not your peers, and no one ever wins favor in the harem, but I have influence, and I'm willing to use it on your behalf. I know very little about spinning and weaving, but I know much about who hates who and who is sleeping with whose husband. Organizing noblemen's wives is like herding Egyptian cats. They're not like your pitiable Hebrews, who bend and bow and grovel at your slightest whim."

Anippe tamped down her rising revulsion at the life of manipulation she must abide to be successful at Gurob. "And what do you expect from me in return for your valuable influence?"

"A weekly correspondence with your abbi Horem, singing my praises. Tell him how we've become close friends, partners in the linen workshop, confidantes." She bowed her head, fidgeting with her hands, but couldn't hide the quiver in her voice. "I long ago gave up hope that any man would love me, but I cannot abide a life of hatred and abuse."

She gently dabbed bruised cheeks before lifting her gaze. "Don't ever let Horemheb give you to another husband. Marriage will destroy you—inside and out."

31

But when [Jochebed] could hide him no longer,
she got a papyrus basket for him and coated it
with tar and pitch. Then she placed the child in
it and put it among the reeds along the bank of
the Nile.

—Exodus 2:3

FIVE YEARS LATER

In less than five years, King Horemheb and Vizier Pirameses had transformed the Feast of Lotus at Avaris and Qantir into the most coveted royal
festival in Egypt. Stretching the traditional day into a full month of celebration, Egypt's wealthiest noblemen brought their whole families during the last
month of inundation to enjoy some relaxation before sowing season began.

The king's barque delivered the men to Qantir, where they engaged in
military drills and sport until the evening feasts. A short sail around the bend
took them to neighboring Avaris, where they rejoined their wives, who had
enjoyed a day of gossip and shopping in the peasants' markets and the famed
linen workshop.

Mered and his family stood shoulder to shoulder with Hebrew slaves and
Egyptian peasants, all awaiting the arrival of the Gurob Harem ship. He
scanned the sea of faces on the hillside above and below, to the north toward
the craftsmen's camp, and even south toward the new peasants' village. He
didn't see Shiphrah and Hur—or their children, Uri and Yael. The Lord had
opened the chief midwife's womb, and she hadn't been on time since.

"They'll be here." Puah elbowed him in the gut. "Hur promised he'd pick up the boys for ratting here at the quay so you could go straight to the shop. He'll be here."

Mered kept looking. They'd told the midwife and her husband where to look for them in the crowd—beside the palm tree outside the linen shop—but Avaris's bulging population made connections difficult.

"Here comes the ship." Jochebed pointed to the Gurob Harem barque rounding the corner. "We get to see our Miriam." She hugged Amram, and his eyes misted with happy tears. Even Aaron, with his wife and baby, stood on tiptoe to see the barque with its oarsmen gliding into the quay.

"Let's get closer to the dock." Ednah jumped and clapped, taking a step into the roiling crowd.

Mered snagged her hand and pulled her back. His ten-year-old daughter was fearless, having grown up in her mother and Jochebed's protective shadow. "You're staying here to help with your little brother until Hur and Shiphrah join us." Their son Heber had arrived nine months after Mered's return from military duty.

Ednah pouted, but Puah grabbed her hand and placed it on her belly. "Feel this. Your brother is kicking me again."

Ednah's pouting fled, and Mered rested his arm around his pregnant wife's shoulders. "How do you know it's a boy?"

She stretched up on her toes and whispered in his ear, "This one is more active than all three of the others combined. I'm sure he's a boy." She kissed his cheek and wiped the sweat from her brow.

Mered squeezed her tighter. His wife looked tired today. He watched her prance and giggle with Ednah, anticipating the ship's arrival. Should she be jumping like that when the baby was due any day?

"Father, please let me go back to the shop." Jered, in contrast, was completely bored. He'd known Anippe only as a summer master for almost half of his twelve years, and Mehy had ignored him since becoming close friends with Sety at the School of the Kap in Memphis. His grumpy eldest son hated crowds. "I haven't finished beading the queen's byssus gown for tomorrow night's feast."

"Take your little brother along, but don't let him play in the beads." The last time four-year-old Heber visited the workshop, he brought home an emerald and buried it.

"Here they come!" Puah squeezed Mered's arm as if she were kneading bread.

They watched the oarsmen ease skillfully up to the dock and cast papyrus ropes ashore to waiting servants, who hurriedly tied the ship to the pier. The gangplank thumped in the sand, and Nubian slaves with cubit-long staves cleared the path in front of the first gilded palanquin.

Mered covered his eyes, shading them against the midday sun. Queen Mutno sat enthroned above six Medjays' shoulders, her gaze focused uphill. The once-quaint villa had been expanded in both size and grandeur by Pharaoh Horemheb's orders. The new king had also required a row of new guesthouses built on the hills overlooking his villa. It was said even the Avaris guesthouses outshone Qantir's luxury.

Anippe followed in the only other elevated chair. Ever the gracious amira, she reached down to accept lilies and mandrakes from those who welcomed her home.

Puah buried her face in Mered's chest, tears flowing. "I'm glad she's home."

Mered noticed his wife's arm cupped beneath her round belly and wrapped an arm around her shoulders, bracing her against him. "Are you all right?" He peered beneath her bowed head to see her expression. "Puah, look at me." Tilting her chin up, he saw the pain on her face and glanced around the crowd again. "Where is Shiphrah?"

"I'm fine." Puah blew a slow breath through puffed cheeks. "I've been having slight pains all morning but nothing regular. Believe me, I know when it's time to call the midwife." She swatted Mered's shoulder, lightening the mood.

Ednah's round brown eyes mirrored Mered's fear, and for the sake of his daughter, he smiled and chuckled. *El-Shaddai, protect my wife and baby.*

The procession continued toward the main entrance of the villa, much closer now to their favorite palm tree. Finally, the amira's palanquin marched by, and Miriam followed, fragranced and jeweled like all other Gurob handmaids.

Mered clapped Amram's shoulder. "Your daughter becomes more beautiful each year. Perhaps Anippe will make a match for her while she's home this month."

Amram tried to smile, his cheeks quaking as he watched his daughter disappear into the villa. "Miriam is in El-Shaddai's hands, my friend—much like Moses after we placed him in that basket over twelve years ago. We must let God shape our children's futures."

Moses? Mered hadn't realized they'd named their baby boy drowned in the Nile. How ironic that they'd named him *drawn out*. Moses. The name sounded familiar, but perhaps it was merely similar to Pharaoh Ahmose.

Shiphrah appeared with two-year-old Yael on her hip. "I'll take Puah home to rest."

"You're finally here," Mered said.

She scowled at his unwelcoming greeting and pointed to a secluded spot near the linen shop. "We were standing over there. Hur needed to work too, so he's already taken Uri and gotten Heber from your shop. Ednah should probably go too."

Mered kissed his daughter's forehead. "You'll find Hur at the granaries, but enter the villa through the linen shop. There's too much chaos at the main entry." She pecked his cheek with a kiss and hurried toward the shop.

When Mered returned his attention to Puah, Shiphrah was examining her belly, pressing one hand on top, moving it, and pressing it again. The midwife lifted an eyebrow and waggled her head. "Maybe labor, maybe not. I'll stay with her and keep her quiet." She winked at Mered and smiled. "Calm down, Abba. We know what we're doing."

The women giggled and walked down the path to the craftsmen's village, leaving Mered to take linen orders from the fussy Gurob Harem women. This was the shop's busiest month of the year.

Anippe waited in her chamber for Miriam. This was the one area of the villa she'd refused to let Abbi Horem update or expand—her bedchamber, courtyard, and private path leading to the bathhouse. This was her sanctuary.

Memories of Sebak still lingered. The basket in which she'd found Mehy now held her most precious jewelry. Though she only visited Avaris for one month each year, it was still home.

And it belonged to her and Mehy—despite Abbi Horem's indifference to her wishes. Were it not for the weekly replies from Memphis, she might think the king cared nothing about her at all.

Anippe had begun weekly correspondence with her abbi at Mutno's prompting, but the disciplined communication had become beneficial on many levels. Mutno's standing in Abbi Horem's eyes had improved as the queen hoped, and the other women at Gurob saw her weekly scrolls as opportunity to gain the king's favor through Anippe—making them eager workers in the linen shop.

But Abbi Horem had taken liberties at Avaris beyond Anippe's approval. Building projects. Added military presence. Even an Egyptian peasant population that made Avaris more a city than a family estate.

A knock, and her chamber door opened. Miriam. Anippe glimpsed two new Ramessid guards before the door closed.

Frustrated, she lashed out at her maid. "Where is Nassor? Why hasn't he come to report on the condition of the estate?"

"He's reporting to Pharaoh Horemheb."

Anippe clenched her fists and drew in a calming breath. "I am the Amira of Avaris. Why does Abbi Horem build his own wing and hear my estate foreman's reports?"

Miriam stood with head bowed. "I'm sorry, Amira."

"Send one of those chamber guards in."

"Yes, Amira." Miriam hurried to the door and returned with an extremely young and terrified-looking Ramessid.

"Bring Mered—the chief linen keeper—to my chamber immediately." Would the child-guard even know Mered's name?

"Yes, Amira." The guard turned to go, forgetting to bow—and then realizing his error, returned with wide eyes and a hurried nod. Then he fled like a rat to its hole.

The door slammed shut, and Miriam's eyes rounded like saucers. Anippe gawked at her, then at the door—and both of them burst into laughter.

When their laughter calmed to sighs, Miriam brushed Anippe's arm, reassuring her of her friendship. "Are you willing to share what troubles you, Amira?"

Anippe moved to her feather-stuffed mattress, and Miriam followed—their usual spot for a chat. "It's not about Nassor's report. I'm nervous about seeing Abbi Horem again, and I want my visit with Mehy to go well." She stared at the beautiful Hebrew girl who had become closer than a sister. "And I know I should find a husband for you, but the truth is—I don't want to lose you."

"I'm your friend, Amira, but I've always known I must be your slave first. If you do not wish me to marry, I will not marry." Miriam turned away, evidence of her suppressed yearning.

"And because I'm your friend, I cannot deny the longing I hear in your voice." Anippe tugged Miriam's chin toward her. "Is there a young man I should choose as your husband?"

The girl's cheeks instantly pinked, and she scooted off the bed, busying her hands with unpacking baskets and arranging jars. "I wouldn't know. I saw him briefly when we returned three years ago. He may be married by now."

Anippe's heart broke. She hadn't even considered Miriam's age when she took her to Gurob. "How old are you?"

"I've lived eighteen inundations." Miriam paused, silent for several heartbeats. "Well past the age of most girls who marry."

It was true, but . . . "It's not too late."

Miriam turned and met Anippe's gaze. "If El-Shaddai wills it, I will marry. I'll leave it to Him—and you."

A knock on the door ended their conversation before Anippe could discover the name of Miriam's young man. Perhaps Mered would know.

She assumed her best angry-amira voice. "Come!" Mered entered, followed by the young Ramessid. "Thank you, guard. You may go."

She didn't know the child-guard's name and didn't want to. He at least remembered his bow this time and closed the door gently behind him.

Mered alternated glances from Miriam to Anippe, a sheepish grin fixed firmly in place. "Is someone dying? The guard said I was needed immediately."

"I called you here for a report on the linen shop, but another matter requires immediate attention." Anippe trained her features, refusing to giggle or even smile. "Miriam, why don't you go visit Amram and Jochebed this afternoon? Meet me at the quay when Abbi Horem's barque arrives for the feast this evening."

"Thank you, Amira." Miriam fled from the room, leaving Anippe alone with her linen keeper.

Anippe strolled to the chair in her courtyard—not completely private, but away from prying eyes and ears. She didn't want to be all the way down at the river alone with any man. Not even Mered.

"That was very thoughtful, Amira. Amram and Jochebed will be thrilled to see Miriam." Mered sat in the chair opposite, resting his elbows on the ebony table between them. He licked his lips, cleared his throat, and smoothed his robe. "Before we discuss your concern, I wondered if I might ask you a question."

Surprised at her friend's nervousness, her curiosity was piqued. "Of course, Mered. Anything."

"Well . . . have you considered . . ." Again he hesitated, courage flagging. "Have you considered a husband . . ."

"Have I considered a husband?" Shocked, she placed a hand over the warmth creeping up her neck. "Mered, I don't think you should speak to me about a husba—"

"No, I meant have you considered a husband for Miriam?" After he finally spit out the words, he started to chuckle and dissolved to a laugh.

Recovering from near humiliation, Anippe laughed with him until all the awkwardness melted into easy silence. "It's good to be home, Mered."

"I'm glad you're here, Amira—and just in time to welcome our new little one."

"I spotted you and Puah as my sedan chair entered the villa. She appeared to be due any minute." Mered's nod confirmed it, and Anippe let the warmth of their friendship rekindle. "I'm glad you mentioned Miriam's marriage. That was the other matter I wanted to talk with you about. Do you know who might be a suitable match for her?"

"I have an idea, but may I ask her parents before I suggest him?"

Thrilled, Anippe reached across the table and squeezed his hands. "That's a good idea."

"When do you need to know?"

"After Abbi Horem's first feast, things settle into our summer rhythm. We can talk about Miriam's betrothal and wedding then."

Mered nodded but seemed distant somehow. Was he thinking about Puah? The linen shop? Anippe couldn't read his moods as easily as before. This warming-up period was awkward each year, when her old friends felt like new friends for a few days.

"How does Mehy like school?" Mered asked.

His change of topic rattled her. Mehy rattled her. "My son no longer visits me at Gurob. He and Sety are inseparable, so he'll see me only at Avaris because Sety lives in neighboring Qantir. Our feast tonight celebrates his graduation from the Kap."

"Oh, I hadn't heard."

Good. Perhaps he hadn't heard that Mehy and Sety had become bullies at school, using Mehy's size advantage to abuse anyone who ridiculed his stuttering.

"After his summer here at Avaris, he'll begin military training under Pirameses at Sile fortress. He and Sety will be separated then, but we'll let Pirameses deal with the boys' tantrums." She noticed a shadow cross Mered's features. "It seems impossible that my little Mehy is old enough to carry a sword, doesn't it?"

"I remember when Pirameses and Master Sebak began their training. It wasn't an easy time."

Anippe's heart twisted. Was it the mention of her late husband, or that Mered knew Sebak in ways she didn't? "Tell me more about Sebak, Mered. When did you first become close?"

"Master Sebak and I grew close when his parents died from the Ramessid plague."

"He mentioned that illness wiped out many of his relatives, but I didn't know he was in military training with Pirameses at the time."

Mered paused, seeming to taste each word before releasing it. "Your husband was a good man, Amira. Pirameses and Horemheb tried to make him a monster, calling him *Seth reborn*—but he was a man, who in the end recognized his need for a God bigger than Seth, Egypt's fickle god of chaos."

Anippe still ached at the thought of Sebak's death. More than anything, she wished she could have comforted him, held him, given him the love in death he'd given her in life. Would she ever love again? Abbi Horem had asked her in repeated correspondence if she'd consider marriage to this nobleman or that retired soldier. She appreciated his request. He could have forced her. But to his credit, he respected her refusals. She wanted a man of honor like Sebak—like Mered.

A wave of grief overwhelmed her, and memories came unbidden. Ummi Amenia, Tut, and Senpa—lives taken too soon, loves lost without cause.

Mered's touch on her hand startled her. "Amira, I'm sorry. I've made you sad. This is a day of rejoicing. You'll see Mehy soon, and Pharaoh Horemheb." He offered a kind smile and a scrap of linen from his belt.

She dabbed her tears and forced a happy tone. "You're right, Mered. I must focus on the joy of my reunion with Mehy."

But she would never rejoice at Abbi Horem's return. Even after years of practiced smiles and lying eyes, she refused to feign affection for the abbi she once loved. He'd forfeited his right to her heart when he traumatized her son.

Mehy's stuttering was a constant reminder of Pharaoh Horemheb's cruelty.

32

The sun had almost set by the time the king's barque docked at Avaris. Anippe waited at the front of the crowd, Miriam behind her. Nassor stood on her right, representing the estate. Mered on her left, representing the craftsmen. The other workshop chiefs lined the quay, and the hillside was filled on both sides with slaves, peasants, and soldiers, ready to welcome the royal men from Memphis.

Mered leaned close. "You don't really think Gurob linen will ever outshine Avaris byssus, do you, Amira?"

She elbowed him—hard. Their friendly rivalry had raged for years. "Wait till you see Pharaoh's dancers."

Her focus never left Abbi Horem's oncoming procession. Piramesses, the honored fan bearer, stirred the sweet scents of the bouquets in the royal attendants' hands. Twenty priests of Seth, dressed in leopard-skin robes, followed the first tier of dancers—women dressed in pure Gurob byssus.

"Not bad for the new Gurob quality, eh, linen keeper?" Anippe couldn't hide her grin.

"Absolutely stunning." Mered inclined his head, a tribute from a master.

Tears stung her eyes. Why was she so emotional today? She'd spent most of the afternoon weeping over Sebak and Ummi Amenia, Tut and Senpa. Mered handed her a patch of linen again for her tears, and she grinned. He was the best friend she had—besides Miriam—and Miriam would soon be married.

More tears.

After the dancers and priests came the king's advisors. Then the face she'd longed for. Mehy sat astride a sleek black stallion. Sety rode a matching white steed. Both mounts were arrayed in brightly colored plumes and gold braiding. The boys threw flower petals over the crowd—though Anippe thought they seemed to be throwing them *at* the crowd. Evidently, the twelve-year-old and nine-year-old weren't happy with their assigned task.

Mehy's eyes met hers as he tossed her a fully budded mandrake and winked. Her heart melted. He was as mischievous as a prowling tomcat, but she adored him.

"Amira, look at Ankhe." Mered noticed her sister in the procession before she did. Ankhe looked worn beyond weary. "Have you received word of an illness?"

"No." Anippe felt her stomach roil at the sight of Ankhe's despair. Her sister wasn't ill. She was heartsick. Abbi Horem had informed the other royal tutors that Ankhe was the daughter of heretic King Akhenaten, making her five years at the Kap a journey through the underworld.

Now that Mehy had graduated, Anippe would petition Abbi Horem for Ankhe's transfer to Gurob. Perhaps she could find a retired soldier who would treat her sister kindly.

Anippe fell in step behind the procession, following it to the villa to greet her guests. She'd asked Queen Mutno to wait at the main entrance and welcome the royal guests until Anippe saw them safely disembarked. More guests would arrive through the day tomorrow, but the royals were here and accounted for.

Nassor escorted her up the hill. "I haven't had the opportunity to personally welcome you home, Amira. Forgive me."

She gave him a sideways glance. "I don't forgive you or Abbi Horem. I want Avaris returned to the way it was when I left five years ago."

His momentary look of panic subsided when he saw her smile. "Life was simpler then, wasn't it?"

Apparently he thought she was teasing. She wasn't, but she'd become as talented as any Gurob noblewoman at playing royal games.

"Would you be sure the chief steward places Ankhe and Mehy in guest chambers near my wing of the villa?" she said. "I'd like to visit with them both tonight, and I don't want to seek out guards to escort me across the complex to do it."

"I'll make sure their guest rooms are near your chamber, but it's never any trouble for a guard to escort you, Amira." He tilted his head, speaking for her ears alone. "I no longer guard your door, but I would respond immediately if summoned."

Her stomach lurched. The last thing she needed was an emotional confrontation. "Thank you, Nassor." Anippe quickened her step and pretended to see someone she knew. It was the safest escape.

As she watched the flurry of arriving guests, Anippe glimpsed the king's double crown disappearing into the main-hall entry, the queen beside him. Noblemen and their wives made grand spectacles of happy—and not so happy—reunions after months of government duty kept the men and women in separate palaces. But Anippe scanned the crowd for one face only.

"Mehy!"

He was already chasing Sety around the central fountain, but the sound of her voice captured his attention. "Ummi!" Both boys ran toward her. Mehy won the race—everything was a competition between them—and her son encircled her waist in a crushing hug. "Can I sleep in Sety's chamber at Qantir this summer?"

Breathless, Anippe pushed him away—and pried the invisible dagger from her heart. "Why would you stay with Sety when your home is Avaris?" She tried to keep her tone even, to make a logical argument, not an emotional plea.

It mattered little. Her son's exuberance faded, his attention fixed on a rock he kicked between his sandals. "There's n-n-nothing fun to do here. Pirameses will wake us with sword d-drills and make us run through m-m-mud pits with slaves."

Disappointment. Anger. Nervousness. These were the triggers of his stuttering.

She forced a smile and placed a hand on each sweaty boy's head, turning them toward the villa. "We'll talk about it later. Right now, we greet Pharaoh because he's waiting to see us."

She wanted to voice the thoughts of a martyred ummi—*even if you don't seem happy to see your ummi, Mehy*—but she refrained, at least until he asked about leaving Avaris again.

They entered Horemheb's new audience hall, and Mandai immediately captured Anippe's gaze. The king's chief Medjay stood on the elevated dais behind Abbi's left shoulder, his single nod filling Anippe with the warmth of his friendship. She offered a discreet smile in return and approached the throne. The chamber steward grunted and grumbled, frantic with his first day of official visitors.

Anippe bowed and silently instructed both boys to do the same. Their etiquette was flawless, a deep bow at the waist and eyes averted—never challenging the incarnate god.

"The great son of Horus has returned home," she said. "The sunshine of mankind, the radiance of the great god Re, who has brought light to the Two Lands and graces his royal daughter with his presence. Welcome great king, good god, revered abbi. My heart is overflowing at the mere sight of you."

"Rise, my treasure, and embrace me."

Guests filed into the hall, creating a low hum, while Anippe climbed the two stairs to Abbi Horem's throne. She hugged him, and glanced over his shoulder at Queen Mutno's pained smile. Despite Mehy's cool reception, Anippe's summer would certainly be more pleasant than the queen's. Abbi Horem had grown less violent but was never kind to her.

"Ummi. Ummi!" The whispered demand echoed in the hall.

Ending the royal embrace, Abbi Horem chuckled. "I believe my grandson sorely wants your attention."

Anippe turned and found Mehy and Sety elbowing each other at the foot of the throne. Hurrying down the steps, Anippe separated them, inciting an amused hum among the royals. "Can't you two behave for a moment?"

Mehy's bright brown eyes sparkled. "Ask Jad Horem if I can stay with Sety at Qantir for the summer."

Anippe sighed. Why was this so important to him? Defeated, she relinquished the hopes she'd had for a long, leisurely visit with her son and faced the throne. Abbi Horem waited, fingers tented, to hear what mischief his grandson had concocted.

"I realize Pharaoh has far greater decisions . . ."

"My grandson has turned the School of the Kap on its ear." The king chuckled, and the roomful of guests joined him. Anippe wondered how many would rather have taken a strap to her son. "He needs a strong hand of discipline, but he'll be a tenacious warrior someday. What does he ask?"

"He'd like to begin his military training early and stay at Qantir under Pirameses's supervision for the summer."

Abbi Horem's cheerfulness fled. "Mehy remains at Avaris. Tonight we celebrate his graduation from the Kap. He has one final summer to be a child. He should enjoy it. He'll thank me one day." Slamming his flail on the armrest, he addressed the audience. "I'll receive greetings from the rest of you tomorrow. My queen and I will retire now to prepare for the feast." With that, he stood and waited for Mutno to take his hand.

The queen laid a submissive hand in her husband's and shot Anippe a forlorn glance. What would this month hold for Mutno? Would she forever be the object of the pharaoh's wrath, or could he someday truly care for her?

Pirameses descended the dais and grabbed Sety's arm, dragging him away without a second look at Mehy.

Anippe watched them go, confusion pouring salt in her freshly wounded heart. "Why would you ask to stay at Qantir? Was this something you and Sety conjured up without asking Pirameses's or Sitre's permission?"

Mehy's eyes swam in unshed tears. "No, Ummi. Vizier Pirameses specifically told me to have you ask Jad Horem as soon as the ship docked in Avaris."

She pulled him into a ferocious hug while the royal guests loitered and whispered and stared. The games had begun. Mehy's military training was still a month away, but Pirameses had already started the mind-bending rigors meant to break her boy's tender spirit.

"Come, my son. We'll stop by the linen shop. Mered is anxious to see you."

But before they reached the exit, Ankhe stepped into their path. "We must talk, Anippe." She glared at Mehy. "Alone."

The sun had set long ago, but Mered lingered at his shop, having only moments ago finished the beading on Queen Mutno's robe for the feast. Amram had crafted an exquisite gold collar with intricately inlaid gemstones in a garden scene. The beading on the robe needed to be subtle, so as not to overwhelm the jewelry, and Mered had reworked it just in time for the queen's handmaid to pick it up. The musicians were playing in the main hall, the music wafting on the night breeze.

Mehy—graduating from the Kap. Where had time gone?

Miriam appeared at his shop door, breathless. "Mered, you must come home!"

Startled, he grabbed his chest and chuckled. "I just finished. I'll be right there—"

"Mered. Now!" Her face was the color of linen, and his heart swelled into his throat.

He jumped to his feet and ran. Out of the workshop, past the peasants' market stalls, around the soldiers' barracks, down the hill, and finally, finally, into the craftsmen's village.

A crowd gathered outside his door. Somber faces. Women weeping. Men looking heavenward.

Amram emerged, his eyes red-rimmed and swollen.

"Amram?" Mered stumbled toward him.

The old man braced Mered's shoulders with his hands. "Shiphrah and Jochebed are with her. They did everything they could."

And then came the baby's cry. Mered looked at Amram, confused.

Amram's chin quivered. "Puah gave you a son with her last breath. His name is Jekuthiel."

"No." Mered stumbled past those blocking his door and fell into his small home where Shiphrah and Jochebed washed his wife's body. Aaron's young wife, Elisheba, nursed a newborn—Puah's newborn. "No. Out, get out! All of you, leave us alone!"

No one moved.

Amram grabbed his shoulders from behind, then pinned his arms at his side, and shoved him through the dividing curtain to the rooms he and Jochebed shared.

Mered fell to his knees. Aaron offered him a cup of beer, but Mered couldn't breathe. How could he drink? A baby cried. Women wailed. This was a dream. It must be a nightmare. Darkness closed around him.

"Mered." Shiphrah stood over him.

How much time had passed? He glanced around the room. Amram was gone, and Mered was propped in a corner of Amram and Jochebed's room. He noticed blood on Shiphrah's robe—Puah's blood.

She crouched beside him. "I'm sorry I didn't send for you in time. Puah wanted to surprise you when you came home from the shop. Her delivery went so quickly. I sent Miriam as soon as I saw signs of trouble. It was all so completely normal . . . until—"

"Until my wife died."

Shiphrah dissolved into a heap beside him, sobbing. "In any childbirth death, there are warning signs—but not Puah. Her lifeblood drained away in moments. She was here and then gone. She kissed her perfect boy, named him, and said good-bye."

Jochebed appeared through the curtain, wiping her hands on a soiled cloth. "Mered, the men need to know if you want Jered, Ednah, and Heber to see their mother before they take the body to the caves."

Take the body? Mered resisted the urge to scream.

"I want everyone to leave us till dawn. The children may say good-bye at daybreak. Leave me alone with my wife."

Both women stared at him, mute. He stood, not waiting for their opinion or approval, and returned to his room.

Jochebed and Shiphrah slipped out the main entrance. Aaron and his wife must have taken the baby home with them. Only Puah remained.

Mered sat on a cushion beside her body. They were alone. More precisely, he was alone, and Puah had been gathered to Mother Sarah's bosom. He was alone—to raise a daughter and three boys.

How could he do it? He'd seen Heber at the quay this morning, but what did a four-year-old eat? How long must he sleep? Did he do house chores or village labor? He'd seen Ednah grind grain, but could she do laundry, make beer, or cook? Jered worked as an apprentice at the linen shop, but could he help Mered take care of their family?

The newborn—*Jekuthiel*. *"Fear of God."*

Had Puah been afraid during her last breaths? *El-Shaddai, did You deal gently with my beloved, or have I prayed to the wind these many years?* How did the Hebrew God redeem a life from death? They didn't have tidy stories of Egyptian warring gods, the underworld, and the afterlife. A Hebrew's faith was based solely on a God who kept His promises—a God who gathered His people to Abraham and Sarah at death to wait the fulfilling of His covenant. But where was the land God had promised? How much longer would Israel labor in bondage?

"Are You there, El-Shaddai?" he screamed.

No answer.

Mered stared at his wife's lifeless body and whispered, "If You're there, El-Shaddai, at least show me why You took her from me." He lifted Puah's cold hand to his lips.

Would his faith die with his beloved? Should he bury El-Shaddai in the caves with Puah? Perhaps he would decide by dawn.

33

A person's days are determined;
you have decreed the number of his months
and have set limits he cannot exceed.

—JOB 14:5

D o you feel different after your graduation feast—grown up, smarter?"
Anippe twirled Mehy's princely lock around her hand, while his head
nestled on a pillow in her lap. These were the moments she cherished, their
quiet talks in her private bathhouse.

He studied his hand in the moonlight, inspecting the familiar three dots
she'd drawn there after the feast. "I guess I feel a little grown up. I should be
able to make more decisions."

Anippe hid a smile, wondering what decisions he had in mind. "Really?"

"I think I should choose which god you draw on my hand." He held his arm
straight up, examining it at a distance. Three dots in the shape of a pyramid.

Bullfrogs croaked, crickets chirped, and an owl wondered "who." Anippe
giggled. "You see, even the owls await your decision. Which god would you
choose?"

"Ummi . . ."—Mehy spoke with appropriate adolescent disgust—"I'm
serious."

"I'm sorry. All right." She didn't care which god he chose as long as he
never tired of their special time together during these summer visits. Or this
bathhouse—comfortable, secluded, where no one intruded. "Which god
would you choose to watch over you and me?" Anippe removed the leather tie
from his lock, loosening his curly, brown hair.

"I would have Seth, god of chaos and darkness, watch over us. He's the god of the Ramessids, after all."

The proclamation came like a blow, robbing her of breath. *Seth reborn.* That title had somehow forced Sebak to stay away from Avaris, away from her and Mehy. But she couldn't speak against the Ramessids' patron god. "Hmm. May I explain the reason I chose Amun-Re and then allow my grown-up young man to make his decision?"

He sat up, straight and tall, refusing her attempt to rebraid his sidelock. "I know already. Amun-Re created all things—including all gods."

Anippe nodded. "I chose Re because he's greater than Seth. The creator is greater than chaos and darkness."

"Mmm."

She noted his knitted brow and let him continue pondering as she reached for his sidelock. He swatted her hands away.

Footsteps startled them both.

Ankhe stood on the tiled path, cheeks aflame, torch in hand. "You didn't come as I asked. I told you I wanted to speak with you after the feast, Anippe. You didn't come, so Mehy will hear what I have to say."

"Ankhe, I was waiting until Mehy was asleep. We're talking, and then I was—"

"No more excuses, and no more time to do the right thing." Ankhe marched toward them, placing her torch in the stand. "I've lived in shame at Memphis for five years."

"I know it's been difficult, but I plan to ask Abbi Horem to transfer you—"

"The other tutors treated me like a leper, Anippe, and your son . . ."

Mehy puffed his chest and lifted his chin. "I don't have to listen to you anymore, Ankhe."

"Mehy!" Anippe's heart sank. "You will not speak to your aunt that way."

Ankhe lunged for Mehy, snatching him from Anippe's side. She held a flint knife at his throat. "I'm tired of hearing what you plan to do, what you hope to do." Ankhe looked down into Mehy's frightened face. "You're the son of Hebrew slaves, yet you're treated like a prince, and I'm the slave."

Anippe stepped closer, speaking gently. "Please, Ankhe. Tell me what you want. I can talk with Abbi Horem. Do you want to live at Gurob? We can arrange it."

The knife trembled, and a small drop of blood appeared on Mehy's neck. He squeezed his eyes closed and whimpered, sending a stab of panic through Anippe's body.

"Tell me what you want, Ankhe!"

"I've been assigned to tutor a Hittite prince, Anippe. No marriage. No children. No life of my own." Her eyes blazed. "A Hittite prince!"

Mehy cried out as the blade dug deeper.

"No, please, Ankhe. Let him go." Anippe held up both hands, begging.

Mehy's eyes were wild with fear, Ankhe's wild with hate.

"You've left me no choice, Anippe. No hope."

No hope. Miriam's dream years ago—the story of Cain and Abel—came rushing back. El-Shaddai's warning: *If hope is gone, the brother becomes the sister.*

"Please, Ankhe. Don't lose hope. I'll have you removed from the Kap—whatever you wish. We have each other, Ankhe."

"I want Nassor. Make the match, or I tell the king your son's name is Moses, and he was saved from the Nile twelve years ago." She smiled then, something Anippe had rarely seen. "Wouldn't the nobles enjoy watching Horemheb's judgment on a daughter who deceived him these many years?"

"I believe the king will be interested in a whole web of deception." A male voice pierced the night, startling Ankhe. Mehy elbowed her and wrestled the dagger from her grasp.

The young Ramessid from Anippe's chamber door stood in the moonlight, sword drawn. "Drop the dagger, boy, and kick it toward me." Mehy obeyed, and the guard leaned on his sword with a superior smirk. "I followed the amira's sister into the chamber and have been listening from the shadows. It's been quite entertaining."

"I'll pay for your silence," Anippe said, clutching Mehy to her chest.

"I don't think so. Your sister seems to think you don't keep your promises, and I'm inclined to believe her, considering she's been your slave for . . . how long has it been?"

Ankhe spit on his sandaled feet, which erased his smirk.

He raised his head slowly, blood lust in his eyes. "A common-born Ramessid must find a way to distinguish himself from other soldiers. Uncovering your deception may earn me a promotion into Pirameses's fighting unit. Now, move." He pointed toward the villa with his sword. "After you, Amira."

Anippe put her arm around Mehy and lifted her chin, pausing beside the young guard. "If you're half as smart as you think you are, you'll request Commander Nassor's presence at our meeting with Pharaoh." She looked him up and down. "You'll want a witness, or the king will silence you like he would a locust."

He gulped as she walked by. Her only hope was Nassor's intervention. He could silence the guard, and Anippe would beg him to marry Ankhe. It was the only way they could keep Mehy's secret.

She couldn't bear to consider the alternatives.

The young guard whispered something to several guards on their way across the complex. She could only hope he was summoning Nassor. By the time they arrived at Abbi Horem's door, Nassor was waiting—with Mandai.

Anippe nearly wept with relief. Two of the men she trusted most in the world. Only Mered would have been greater encouragement.

Nassor and Mandai stared in silent question, and when the young guard began his explanation in the outer hall, Nassor struck him—nearly sending him to the ground.

"Never speak of the amira's private affairs where others might hear."

"Thank you, Nass—"

He lifted his hand to silence her, eyes cold and empty. Without a word, he knocked on Abbi Horem's chamber door, and a grouchy rumble sounded from within.

He and Mandai slipped inside, and Anippe's last hope rested on the young guard—who was massaging his bruised jaw and wounded pride. "Consider your report to the king very carefully. I am his treasure and Mehy his only heir. You're about to inform the King of Egypt he'll have no child or grandchild to provide for him in the afterlife. Are you sure he'll promote you for such news?"

The door flung open, and the soldier's face drained of color. Anippe prayed her threat would save them all. She grabbed Mehy's hand, pointed to the three dots, winked, and led him into the chamber. Ankhe followed, nudged forward by the now reluctant guard.

Abbi Horem reclined on a couch without wig or jewelry, and Mutno's faint whimpers rose from behind a thick, hanging tapestry. "Silence!" Abbi's face was as red as the pomegranate in his hands. He pressed his thumbs into its center, spilling out pulp all over the table before him.

The young guard stood at Anippe's right, his Adam's apple bobbing in his throat.

"Why would my daughter's chamber guard interrupt the first evening I've spent alone with my wife in three months?" He slurped the pulp-covered seeds into his mouth and let the juice run down his chin while staring at the young Ramessid.

"Because your daughter—I mean, the Amira Anippe—has been deceiving you for twelve years, great son of Horus, mighty ruler of Two Lands. The boy she calls Mehy is a Hebrew child saved from the Nile twelve years ago." He bowed, and Anippe furtively moved Mehy behind her.

Abbi Horem concentrated on his pomegranate, never looking up, scooping seeds and pulp from the rind.

During the silence, Ankhe tried to slide behind Anippe, but the chamber guard pressed her forward. "Her sister has aided in the deception from the beginning."

At this, the king grinned, lifted an eyebrow, even chuckled. Nodding, he licked each finger and then wiped them on his pure-white linen robe. "Nassor, who is this chamber guard, that he would accuse my treasure of such a conspiracy?"

The Ramessid commander turned on his subordinate, fury in his eyes. "He is a dead man, great and mighty Pharaoh."

"It's true," the guard cried. "You didn't even ask her. You—"

Nassor silenced him where he stood.

Anippe turned away, hiding Mehy's eyes. Ankhe began weeping, but Anippe knew better. Breathing deeply, she held her tears and horror in check.

She stood like stone and met her abbi's gaze without flinching as Nassor dragged the guard's body from the chamber.

"Before Nassor returns, I will ask you, my treasure. Is the chamber guard's report true? Is this boy Hebrew?"

She hesitated only a heartbeat. "Yes. It's true." Mehy grabbed his ummi's waist, but Anippe wrapped her arm around his shoulder and bent to whisper in his ear. "Look into your Jad Horem's eyes. Meet him as a brave soldier, a son of Seth—god of chaos and darkness. He will respect you for it, habibi, and we will take our punishment together."

Abbi Horem's eyes narrowed. "And did your sister conspire with you to hide the boy's identity these many years?"

Ankhe lunged forward, falling at Horemheb's feet. "Anippe forced me to silence. I had no choice!"

The king leaned over her, taunting. "You still have your tongue. What kept you silent?" Sneering, as if Ankhe's presence soured his pomegranate, he motioned to Mandai. "Feed this woman to the crocodiles."

Ankhe screamed, "No! It was Anippe!" She scrambled to her feet and lunged at her sister. "You did this to me!"

Mandai grabbed her, and Abbi Horem matched her volume. "Silence her before all of Egypt hears her yowling."

Anippe kept her eyes focused on Horemheb, gripping her son with arms of bronze. Mandai dragged Ankhe behind her, and the glee on her abbi's face told her Ankhe was gone.

Anippe felt the Medjay's presence looming behind her.

"Now we deal with you, daughter."

"Ummi!" Mehy tried to bury his face against her, but she turned him to confront the pharaoh who held their lives in his hands.

"Tell your Jad Horem you are Seth reborn. You're a brave soldier like your abbi Sebak." She shook Mehy's shoulders. "Tell him!"

"I am a b-brave soldier like my abbi S-Sebak."

Horemheb's features softened, and he motioned Mandai back to his place at the king's left shoulder. Anippe held her abbi's gaze, not daring to glance at the Medjay, her friend.

"You have always been cunning, my treasure. I should have expected you to be as shrewd with me as you were with Tut and your sister." He nodded as if convincing himself of the truth. "Mehy, come to me." He invited the boy with open arms.

Anippe whimpered for the first time, tightening her grip on Mehy's arms. Her son pressed against her, a silent but undeniable refusal.

"Please, Abbi. Mehy has done nothing wrong. I was the one. I wanted to give Sebak a child but was too afraid to bear one after Ummi Kiya's death and Senpa's miscarriages. A baby was floating in a basket near my bathhouse, and I received him as a gift from Hapi, a gift from the Nile, as I was your daughter of the Nile." She was losing control. Tears were forming, emotions rising. "Don't you see? I saved him like you saved me. I wanted—"

Abbi Horem smiled and pressed a finger to his lips. "Shh. Mehy, I said come to me." His arms beckoned. "Come to your Jad Horem."

Anippe took a deep breath, steadied herself, and then breathed out slowly. Leaning down, she took Mehy's hand and kissed the three dots. "I'm always with you. Go to your Jad Horem."

Her brave boy nodded and then walked into the arms of Egypt's brutal king. Horemheb held him at arm's length, smiling warmly. "You made the right decision, my little warrior. No one outside this room will know you are not Sebak's son. You are my grandson—a prince of Egypt—Seth reborn."

Anippe's knees nearly buckled with relief. She covered the sob that threatened her composure.

The king glanced over his shoulder at his Medjay. "Dispose of my daughter with the other bodies. Make it look like a crocodile got her in that bathhouse of hers."

Mered woke to the sound of footsteps outside his door. The moon still shone out the window. He couldn't have nodded off for long. Puah's empty shell still lay beside him. It hadn't been a dream. *I told them not to bring the boys till dawn.*

Footsteps shuffled closer, and a dark-cloaked figure with gold sandals swept aside the curtain, ducking his large frame through the doorway.

"Mandai?" Mered stood. "What are you doing here?"

The Medjay carried a long sackcloth-wrapped bundle over his shoulder. He scanned the room and saw Puah's body. "What happened, my friend?"

Emotion closed Mered's throat. He bowed his head, burying his face in trembling hands. Then, massaging his temples, he regained control and found the Medjay bent over his bundle in the opposite corner. Gently, Mandai untied the leather straps.

Indignation rising, Mered marched over. "What are you doing?" How could he intrude on a grieving husband?

Mandai unwrapped the bundle, and Mered's knees turned to water.

"Anippe?"

"Shh, don't speak her name." Mandai removed the sackcloth, lifting her arms, her legs, moving her as if she were—

"No, no, no. El-Shaddai, no. Not Anippe, too. I can't bear it. I cannot—"

"She's not dead, but she wants to be." Mandai sprang to his feet and gathered Mered's robe in his hands, then whispered less than a handbreadth from his face. "She's in some sort of trance. She can't speak. I'm not even sure she can hear us." Releasing him, the Medjay closed his eyes and drew a deep breath—the first time Mered had seen him rattled. "Horemheb discovered her deception and ordered me to kill her, but I won't. I can't. You're the only one who can protect her."

"What deception? Horemheb adores Anippe. He would never—"

"Mehy is Hebrew."

Spots clouded Mered's vision. He stumbled back, but the Medjay grabbed his arm. The men stared at each other in silence.

Mandai finally raked a weary hand down his face. "She confessed to rescuing Mehy from a basket floating on the Nile."

Amram and Jochebed's son? Mered dropped his head into his hands. Amram had said all those years ago that they placed Moses in a basket. Did Amram know Mehy was Moses? He looked at his wife, the peaceful shell of the woman he'd loved more than life. She'd known. All these years she'd kept this from him.

Pain upon pain. Loss piled on loss. He began to weep. Deep, racking sobs heaved his shoulders and shook him to the core. Mandai squeezed his arm, offering silent comfort.

El-Shaddai, if I cannot pray, I have no hope. If I have no hope, I cannot live. He'd heard the story of Job's suffering all his life, and now Mered, too, yearned for death.

But as much as he willed it, he couldn't abandon his heartbeat or halt his breaths. And, remarkably, his faith would live simply because he could not summon death. *It's all I have to offer, El-Shaddai. Faith that You hold life in Your hands.*

He raised a weary gaze to the Medjay. "You're a good man, my friend."

"I am not good. I am what my people call *nimepotea*—a lost warrior. Your Master Sebak refused to return home because he feared he'd become the dark god Seth. I too am that dark warrior. I am nimepotea."

"No one is beyond El-Shaddai's reach." Mered let the words come from a place deeper than his despair. "My one God can shine on a dark warrior."

The Medjay wiped his eyes and shrugged. "Your one God should work harder for good people." He nodded in Puah's direction and began removing Anippe's jewelry. "He should have saved your wife and helped the amira—and fed Horemheb and me to the crocodiles." He removed her gold sandals and bundled everything in the sackcloth.

"What are you doing? Why are you taking all her jewelry?"

"The king said Anippe's death must look like an accident by the river. You must burn her robe. I will not dishonor her by stripping her naked." He stopped at the doorway before ducking through the curtain. "Make her a Hebrew. No one will look for her here."

PART 3

Then young women will dance and be glad,
young men and old as well.
I will turn their mourning into gladness;
I will give them comfort and joy instead of sorrow.

—JEREMIAH 31:13

34

Amram married his father's sister Jochebed, who bore him Aaron and Moses. Amram lived 137 years.

—EXODUS 6:20

Mered sat staring at Anippe, listening to the sputtering oil lamp. Dawn was fast approaching. His children would arrive soon to say good-bye to their mother—and find the amira propped in the corner, as lifeless as the wife he would bury.

Mandai had said to make her Hebrew. How could Mered do that? Even if he kept her in the craftsmen's village, wouldn't the slaves recognize her? Mered was drowning in questions without answers.

Amram came in, head respectfully lowered. Where had he and Jochebed stayed overnight? Probably with their son, Aaron, and his wife, Elisheba. Mered remembered that when the amira's ship arrived yesterday, Elisheba was holding her new baby.

"I never imagined your daughter-in-law would nurse my son," he whispered to Amram.

Halting abruptly, Amram slowly turned, his eyes landing on Anippe. His face registered shock and then fear. "Is she hurt? Did the king discover my son?"

Amram rushed forward, but Mered stopped him. "She hasn't spoken. The king's Medjay rescued her. Horemheb discovered the deception but plans to maintain Mehy's—I mean your son's—secret. Your son's name is Moses, isn't it?"

Amram nodded.

"And Puah knew, didn't she?"

After a slight hesitation, Amram nodded again, eyes full of unspoken regret.

Betrayed. On the night he lost his wife, Mered had also lost the trust he'd placed in his dearest friends. How could they have kept this from him all these years?

"Jochebed and I felt it best not to tell you because you worked closely with the amira and Mehy at the villa." Amram squeezed his shoulder. "You are too honest to live a lie." When Mered didn't respond, Amram crouched beside Anippe. "Why is the amira here—in your home?"

"Horemheb ordered her death and will say she died in an accident. The Medjay brought her here and said I should '*make her a Hebrew.*'" Mered heard the whine in his voice and cringed.

"It's a good plan." Amram nodded, stood, and walked toward his rooms.

"Wait. What do you mean a good plan? It's a terrible plan. I have no idea how to make her a Hebrew. I'm not sure El-Shaddai hears my prayers. And I don't know how to raise a daughter and three sons." Mered was near hysteria, and the sun cast a pink glow on the eastern horizon. His children would be home very soon.

Amram settled his arm around Mered's shoulders and guided him toward Puah's still form. "Sit with me, Mered. Have I ever told you about my first wife?"

Mered glanced out the window, hoping this wasn't a lengthy story and wondering why Amram chose now to tell it.

"She died while giving birth to our first child."

Mered was startled to attention. "I'm sorry. I didn't know."

"I lost both my wife and firstborn son that day, and I vowed never to remarry. I thought El-Shaddai had cheated me, and I wanted nothing to do with God or women or children or life."

"Until you met Jochebed, right?" Mered knew how this story ended.

"Actually, no. Jochebed is my aunt."

Amram obviously needed a good night's sleep. "Jochebed is your wife."

"Yes, she is. And she's my father's sister—my aunt."

"But she's thirty years younger than you."

"Twenty-eight, to be exact."

Mered buried his face in his hands. Why did this matter? Taking a deep breath, he lifted his eyes and stared at Amram. "Why did you marry your aunt Jochebed?"

"Because she needed a husband, and I needed a wife. Anippe needs to be Hebrew, and you need help raising your sons. You're not sure El-Shaddai hears your prayers? Well, I'm telling you He does, and He answered them before you prayed." Amram rolled onto his knees, trying to stand, and used Mered's shoulders as a crutch. "Now get over there and wash off her kohl and scented oils before your children come home. Remove her wig, and I'll give you one of Jochebed's head coverings. She'll look as Hebrew as Jochebed." He patted Mered's shoulder and winked. "But not quite as pretty."

Mered was speechless. Amram was gone before he could form a thought. Puah's body lay beside him—the woman he'd loved since they were children. How could he marry Anippe? It was ludicrous. He reached for Puah's hand, but it was cold and stiff.

"You must let her go," Amram said, startling Mered. He hadn't heard his neighbor return. "Puah loved you, but she's never coming back. Your life must go on." He held out one of Jochebed's head coverings, pressing it against Mered's shoulder. "Go. You can't help Puah, but Anippe needs you."

Mered grabbed the rough-woven cloth and left Puah's side. Two steps from Anippe, he was struck with sheer panic. "Amram, her clothes."

His friend emerged from his rooms carrying a Hebrew robe.

Mered instantly felt the flush of crimson on his neck and cheeks. "I can't dress her—"

"I'll wait at the door for Jochebed or Miriam. One of them can change Anippe's robe. I'll turn away anyone else who comes, but you start washing her face."

※

Anubis, take me. My heart died when they stole Mehy. My body breathes without permission. Take me. Anubis, search for my heart to weigh on your scales. You will not find it—a heart melted in sorrow weighs nothing at all.

A cold cloth on her cheeks. Icy hands. Trembling fingers.

Let them kill me. Please, whoever you are, let darkness come.

"Anippe, can you hear me?"

No. I will not hear you. Leave me to die.

The cloth, now warm, stroked her forehead and pressed against her eyes. "If you can hear me, know that you are safe. Mehy is safe."

Mehy? My son, my son is safe.

"That's right. He's safe. Your eyes fluttered. You can hear me."

She didn't want to hear unless it was Mehy's voice. Strong arms jostled her, lifted her, moved her. She leaned against something soft yet firm. The scent of ben-tree oil and hard labor.

A sudden chill. Her head exposed. Gasping, she thrashed.

"Shh. Shh. Relax. Relax."

Lips against her forehead. A cloth over her head.

"I'm going to lay you on Miriam's sleeping mat for now."

Miriam. A husband for Miriam. Miriam should marry.

The warmth shifted. Arms beneath her, carrying her away. Falling, she was falling.

"Shh. I've got you. You're safe, Anippe. You're safe."

Safe? Her chest tightened, tears threatening. *Anubis, please hurry, before I weep or wail.*

Children's voices. Gasping, she called, "Mehy?"

Eyes open, she stared into the startled face of—Mered. She clutched at his robe and then pushed him away, pressing against his chest, squirming out of his arms. Why was he carrying her?

"Wait. Wait. Let me set you down." He lowered her to a sleeping mat in a low-ceilinged room she'd never seen.

"Where am I? What are you doing? Why am I here?"

"You're in my parents' rooms." Miriam stood behind Mered with a rough-woven robe in her hands. "I'll help you put this on."

Children's voices came from a room beyond a tattered curtain. "Who's that?" Anippe asked.

Mered stood over her, dragging his hand through his hair, eyes tightly shut. "My children. They're saying good-bye to Puah."

"Mered, not now." Miriam knelt beside Anippe. He left without a word.

Anippe began to tremble uncontrollably, teeth chattering.

"Are you cold, Amir—" Miriam shook her head, seeming frustrated. "Are you cold?"

"No." Anippe submitted to Miriam's dressing—as she'd done a thousand times before, though never in Hebrew cloth. Pride bowed to Anippe's fear. "I don't remember how I got here or what happened after—" What was the last thing she remembered?

Miriam's round, brown eyes glistened in the early shades of morning. "Are you sure your questions can't wait until you've rested?" She brushed Anippe's cheek with her hand. "I'll sit right here while you sleep. I won't leave you."

Anippe felt bone weary, and the confidence of her friend's presence might allow her to sleep. "Would you sing to me, Miriam?"

The girl nodded and rested Anippe's head on a piece of lamb's wool. Soft but strange after sleeping on a neck rest all her life. Miriam opened her mouth, releasing the haunting tune that washed away every sound and thought. Anippe settled into her weariness, listening to the words.

"El-Shaddai is my strength, my song. He is my God, and I will praise Him, my father's God, I will exalt Him . . ."

❧

"I should tell her," Mered whispered.

Miriam made sure Anippe was still sleeping beside her. "I can tell her if you'd rather. I've delivered other startling news to her at Gurob. Your plan to marry her will be a bit more than startling, but she'll accept it—I think."

Miriam's flagging confidence fueled Mered's doubts. Anippe was Pharaoh's daughter. Why was he even considering Amram's advice?

Anippe's eyes fluttered and opened. She smiled at Miriam, furrowed her brow at Mered, and then noticed her surroundings and jumped to her feet. "Where am I?"

Miriam gently tugged at her hand. "Come. Sit. You're in my parents' room in the craftsmen's village. Sit down with us."

Anippe folded her legs beneath her and sat stiffly on the reed mat. She stared at Mered.

"How are you feeling this afternoon?" he asked.

She directed a panicked glanced at the single window. "Afternoon? What happened to morning?"

Miriam cradled her hand, patting and soothing her. "You have many questions, I know, but we have one for you—and it may be very hard. Tell us everything you remember about last night."

As if she were a bird in a fowler's snare, Anippe's every move seemed anxious. Each sound startling, every blink a change in focus. "I remember . . ."

"Go slowly." Mered kept his voice low. "We have all day."

"All day? Why aren't you at the linen shop?"

He couldn't hide a grin. Of course, her first response would be practical. "King Horemheb declared a day of rest."

Anippe sobered at his name. "Abbi Horem . . ."

She studied the packed-dirt floor. Silence lingered. The first signs of memory came with uneven breaths that tensed to rapid gasps.

"Mehy. He took Mehy from me and . . ." She shook her head, emotion twisting her features.

Miriam rubbed her back. "Take your time."

"Abbi ordered Mandai to kill Ankhe and said my death should look like a crocodile attack." The words came out on a sob as she alternated panicked looks from one Hebrew to the other. "An accident. You must make my death appear an accident. How will you do it?"

"We're not going to kill you," Mered said. "We would never hurt—"

"But you must. If Abbi Horem discovers another deception, he'll kill Mehy."

"He won't discover the deception." Mered's tone broached no argument.

Miriam took her hand. "Anippe is dead. They found her—pieces of her body—this morning at the river near her bathhouse. Crocodile attack."

Confusion and shock alternated on Anippe's features as she stared at Miriam and then Mered. "How? Whose body did they find?"

"I don't know," Mered said, "but Horemheb has declared a three-day mourning period for his daughter. We'll hide you here with us—in plain sight."

"No, Mered. He'll know. Abbi Horem is a god. He'll know."

"He isn't a god," Mered said, cupping her cheeks and wiping away her tears with his thumbs. "There is only one God, and He brought you to us for safekeeping."

Her expression changed to that of a lost lamb, and her cheeks grew warm beneath his touch. When she dropped her gaze, he withdrew his hands, wishing he could hold her.

She spoke in barely a whisper. "How can you hide Pharaoh's daughter in a Hebrew village?"

Mered inhaled deeply, praying for wisdom. "Do you remember anything after Horemheb's death sentence? Do you remember who brought you here or anything before this afternoon?"

Anippe shook her head, more tears falling. "No, and it terrifies me. Why can't I remember?"

Miriam patted her knee. "Perhaps El-Shaddai is protecting you and comforting you by helping you forget those frightening moments."

"Do you want me to tell you what happened?" Mered peered beneath her bowed head, capturing her gaze. She nodded but didn't look up. "Mandai couldn't obey Horemheb's order, so he brought you to our long house—into the room where I was grieving my wife. Puah died giving birth to our fourth child last night." Mered's voice broke, and Anippe's head shot up.

"Mered, I'm sorry." Her face twisted with pain. "It seems we both lost our families last night."

Mered reached for her hand. "Mandai left, and Amram came in as I wept in despair. He offered a solution that can hide you safely and provide my children with a mother." He searched her eyes for a spark of recognition. "You really don't remember any of this?"

She shook her head but didn't speak, her cheeks growing pink.

Still holding her hand, Mered closed his eyes, his heart pounding like a herd of Pharaoh's stallions. *El-Shaddai, give me the words to convince this woman we need each other.*

When he opened his eyes, the woman before him was no longer Egypt's royalty in sheer linen. Her rough-spun robe covered the details of her form, and her sandy-brown eyes held compassion for his loss, giving him courage to say her name. "Anippe." The sound of it on his lips made him brave. "I want you—I need you—to be my wife."

She didn't laugh—that was promising—and she didn't remove her hands from his grasp. She did stop breathing, which was concerning. But it was her unbroken stare that grew awkward. He drew breath to explain more fully, but she broke the silence first.

"I think you should kill me instead."

Miriam giggled, but Mered saw no humor in her words.

"Wait, I didn't mean—" Anippe's face burst into brilliant crimson. She'd evidently realized she'd placed death above a lifetime with him.

"Perhaps you're right," he countered. "How shall we do it—sword, dagger?"

Mered tried to pull his hands from her grasp, but she tightened her hold. "I'm sorry. I'm honored you would ask me—especially when I know how you loved Puah. What I meant by my choosing death is that you would be safer, Mehy would be safer, Jochebed, Amram, Miriam—your lives could be normal if I were dead."

He reached to brush her cheek, but she turned away, looking at Miriam before ducking her head. Miriam's presence as a friend had been essential to calm Anippe, but to embrace her as a wife, he must speak to her intimately.

"Miriam, please give us time alone." He lifted his hand when the girl drew breath to refuse. "You can stand outside the curtain if you like, but I will speak with Anippe alone."

When the curtain drew closed, he tilted Anippe's chin up, capturing the wide brown eyes he now examined freely. "None of our lives would be normal without you. We have shared a deep friendship, you and I, so we will enter this marriage truly honest. My heart still belongs to Puah, and your heart yearns for Mehy. Our marriage will be a ship in a storm. Let's sail together through grief's waters and see what waits beyond."

35

The man said,
    "This is now bone of my bones
        and flesh of my flesh;
    she shall be called 'woman,'
        for she was taken out of man."
That is why a man leaves his father and mother and
is united to his wife, and they become one flesh."

—GENESIS 2:23–24

Yes? I said yes? Anippe watched Mered walk through Jochebed and Amram's doorway and heard him announce their marriage.

Miriam rushed in, concern etched on her features. "Are you all right? Are you sure about this? I'll be as close as our rooms at the villa—only a curtain separating us."

Anippe nodded but felt numb. Would she ever be all right again? She surveyed the room and saw three ornate baskets, two partially finished. *That's right, Jochebed is skilled in basketry.* Dirt floors. Reed mats for sleeping that also served as movable dining space. A grinding stone and sieve. Well-worn baskets stacked with dried fruit, dried fish, and nuts.

"Just like the villa, Miriam."

Jochebed drew back the curtain, and Anippe felt her cheeks flame. She'd taken this woman's son without conscience and then sent her back to the craftsmen's village. How long had it been since she'd seen Jochebed—since Jochebed had seen Mehy?

Jochebed's abiding peace entered the room with her. She cupped Anippe's elbow and led her to a floor mat. "We must talk about your name, dear. We can no longer call you Amira, of course—or Anippe."

Why must her life revolve around a name? "Call me anything you like. I was a decoy for the gods as Meryetaten-tasherit, adopted by Horemheb as Anippe, and I became Amira when I married. None of it mattered."

"A name matters very much to El-Shaddai." Jochebed rose from her mat and began rummaging through one of the ornate baskets. "Our God has even changed a person's name to represent the character within the soul. Now where is that . . . oh, here it is." She produced Anippe's bronze mirror, holding it aloft. "Miriam brought this basket from the Gurob ship yesterday and planned to return it when she reported to your chamber this morning." She returned to the reed mat and held the mirror up to Anippe. "Look at your face while I describe who I see. Then we can choose your name."

Grudgingly—almost fearfully—Anippe peered into the polished bronze. A stranger stared back. Arched, brown brows perched over wide-set brown eyes ringed with thick black lashes. Her olive skin was dry in patches, needing an oil-and-salt scrub. Her lips, too, were chapped and pale, missing the familiar red ochre. The head covering rode high on her forehead, exposing thin patches of hair usually covered by her wig.

Jochebed patted her shoulder. "I see a Hebrew bride, lovely but frightened."

"Lovely, no. Frightened, yes." Anippe tried to rid herself of the mirror, but Jochebed pushed it back in place.

"All right then, dear. Tell me who you see in the mirror."

With a defeated sigh, Anippe looked again, and this time saw Ankhe's reflection staring back. She squeezed her eyes shut as memories of last night assaulted her. If only she'd summoned Ankhe right after the feast. If only the guard hadn't followed Ankhe to the bathhouse. If only . . .

When she opened her eyes, Anippe saw her reflection again. The stark absence of paints and a wig made her feel naked, as bare as her life. "I'm no longer a sister. No longer an ummi. No longer a daughter." Emotion closed her throat.

Gathering her into a warm embrace, Jochebed soothed her. "You've told

us who you aren't, but who will you become? As long as El-Shaddai gives us
breath, we have reason to hope."

Hope. The word tortured Anippe. "I stole Ankhe's hope when I refused to
make a marriage match for her."

"That's not true." Miriam grabbed Anippe's arm, startling her. "Hope
can't be lost or stolen. Hope is a choice we embrace for ourselves each day."

"But wasn't it your dream that warned me against Ankhe losing hope?
Cain and Abel—if hope is gone, the brother becomes the sister?" Anippe's
voice rose with each word, regret and sorrow warring.

Miriam released her arm and softened her gaze. "El-Shaddai spoke through
that dream to warn you of danger, not to hold you responsible for Ankhe's
choices. Please don't blame yourself because Ankhe *chose* to live in despair."

Anippe clutched her middle, trying to squeeze the pain away. "I blame
myself because Ankhe kept my secret—and now she's dead."

"Blame and guilt serve no purpose," Jochebed said, turning Anippe's chin
toward her. "I'm sure you'll miss Ankhe in the days to come as we'll miss Puah,
but make no mistake—El-Shaddai saved your life for a purpose. And we'll
work with Him to protect you."

Shame mingled with confusion, hushing Anippe's voice to a whisper.
"Why? Why would your god save me?"

"Why did He save Moses?" Jochebed said, wonder in her tone. "Why does
He save any of us from the slave master's lash? The plans of El-Shaddai are yet
to be revealed."

Miriam pointed to the dividing curtain and the growing chatter beyond.
"The people in this household will become your family if you allow it, Anippe.
You'll be an ummi, a sister, and a daughter again."

"We're all daughters of El-Shaddai." Jochebed said, patting her hand. "He
spun every thread of our inner beings and wove us together in our mothers'
wombs." Her eyes suddenly went wide. "That's it. Your new name will be
Bithiah, daughter of God."

"Daughter of God?" Anippe whispered. The words pierced her. She'd
been daughter of Akhenaten, sister of Tut, wife of Sebak, and again Pharaoh's

daughter—but never the daughter of this Hebrew God. "I can't. I'm not." She sniffed back tears, afraid she'd ruin her kohl—"I'm not wearing kohl." Startled at the new freedom, she looked again in the mirror and blinked, purposely sending a tear over the edge of her lashes.

Jochebed was delighted. "Yes, we Hebrews can cry all we want."

Mered poked his head around the curtain. "Are you ready to meet my children? Jochebed, have you settled on her name and story?"

Anippe's heart skipped a beat. "What story?"

"Hurry, the boys are restless, and Amram is ready to give the wedding blessing." Mered disappeared, and the curtain fell into place.

The wedding blessing. Anippe felt as if she'd swallowed a boulder.

Miriam started toward the door. "I'll help Mered settle the children until you're ready to join us." She offered Anippe a final glance over her shoulder. "Welcome home, Bithiah."

Anippe's—Bithiah's—throat went dry as Jochebed began explaining. "Puah's death was a great loss to both Qantir and Avaris, but slaves aren't allowed a formal mourning period. It's understood that Hebrew men with children must remarry quickly to manage their households—though this marriage is a bit quicker than most." She lifted a brow and added, "Many single women will want to know why they weren't considered in the choosing."

"Oh." Anippe covered her face. Had she traded the backbiting, competitive nobility for a nitpicking, clucking village?

"Miriam and I decided we can tell the others you came with her on the Gurob Harem ship—which is true. You were born in the king's household—also true—but you displeased him and have been exiled."

"True but understated," Anippe concluded.

"So, are you ready to become Bithiah?" Jochebed pushed herself to her feet and then extended a hand.

Anippe stared at it a moment, wondering if Mered's offer of death by sword or dagger was still available, and then accepted the help to stand. Still a bit woozy from her lack of food, she squared her shoulders and faced the dividing curtain. "I am Bithiah."

Waiting on the other side of the curtain were Amram, Miriam, and

Mered's three older children—Jered, Ednah, and Heber. Miriam's brother, Aaron, held a newborn as did another woman. Had Puah delivered twins?

"Mered?" She whispered his name, this moment surreal.

Mered rushed toward her, gathering her hands in his. "Are you all right? You look pale."

He smelled of ben-tree oil and honey. Her heart raced, her breathing labored.

When she didn't answer, he turned to those waiting. "My bride needs more rest—"

"No, it's all right." She squeezed his hand, refusing to let go. "Please, I want to meet everyone."

Panic shadowed Mered's features until Jochebed arrived at her left side. "I'll introduce Bithiah to my husband, Amram. Miriam knows Bithiah from their time together at Gurob. Our son, Aaron, married last year and lives in the long house with his wife's family. This is their firstborn, Nadab."

Bithiah nodded to her old friends, each one pretending they'd just met.

Mered placed his hand at the small of her back, guiding her toward the only woman she didn't know. "This is Aaron's wife, Elisheba. Their son is only two weeks old, so she volunteered to nurse my son Jekuthiel. She'll keep him overnight until he's ready for goat's milk but will bring him back to you for care during the day—and, of course, stop over regularly for feedings."

Elisheba glared at her suspiciously. "You won Mered's heart quickly, Bithiah. Many women in camp will be disappointed."

Thankfully, Mered nudged her toward his older children before she had to reply. "And this is Jered. He's twelve. Ednah, ten. And Heber—"

"I'm 'dis many." Heber held up four chubby fingers, and Bithiah's heart melted.

Kneeling before him, she said, "You are such a big, strong boy. Would you help me carry water in the morning, Heber?"

"Sorry, I can't. I help my mama carry water."

The whole room gasped. Bithiah stood quickly. Her head swam, and Mered steadied her, whispering against her cheek. "It's all right. He forgot. He's a little boy. It will take time."

She stood trembling while Mered reminded his son, "Heber, your mama Puah is resting in Sarah's bosom. She won't come home to draw water, remember? Bithiah will be your new mama."

"She's not our mother," Jered croaked. Anippe closed her eyes, refusing to see if it was puberty or grief that changed his voice.

Mered met Jered toe to toe, eye to eye, crimson creeping up his neck. "We all know that, and no one misses your mother more than I. But Ani . . . any . . . thing you could do to make Bithiah welcome would be appreciated."

The near slip of Anippe's name doused Mered's anger—and left Jered confused. Mered returned to her side and cradled her hand. "Amram, we're ready for your blessing, my friend."

Amram cleared his throat, unrolled a yellowed papyrus within its leather protective skin, and began reading. "A man must say of a woman, 'She is now bone of my bones and flesh of my flesh; she is called Woman, because she was taken out of Man.' Therefore a man leaves his father and his mother and holds fast to his wife, and they become one flesh. If this is your intention, Mered, son of Ezrah, I bless this marriage."

Mered faced her, held both hands, and looked into her eyes. "You are Bithiah, daughter of God, bone of my bones, flesh of my flesh. I will hold fast to you above all others as we become one flesh."

Bithiah . . . flesh of my flesh . . . hold fast to you. The man before her was so familiar and yet a stranger. Her best friend, and yet she knew so little of his life. Mered needed her, wanted her, had promised to protect her. *As we become one flesh.* This moment was meant to be the most perfect in a woman's life— but it came in the wake of Anippe's most devastating life events. No words could describe her jumbled emotions, but somehow she felt safe looking into the eyes of a man she thoroughly trusted. Even if for only that moment, Bithiah was born into one flesh with another. The reflection of herself in Mered's eyes was enough.

"Kiss her." Elisheba's crass intrusion ruptured the dream, sending Bithiah's heart into an erratic beat. "I don't plan on nursing Jekuthiel for three years. Surely you two can produce a child before that."

The familiar terror of childbirth consumed her. Mered appeared nearly as frightened when he leaned down for a kiss, Bithiah bolted for safety behind Miriam's curtain, leaving her wedding guests staring after her. Shaking uncontrollably, she backed into a corner and slid down the wall, listening to the commotion she'd left behind.

"Well, I didn't mean to frighten her. I was teasing. Can't the woman take a joke?"

Anubis, take me. My body breathes without permission. Take me. Anubis, search for my heart to weigh on your scales. You won't find it, for a heart melted in sorrow weighs nothing at all. Deliver me from this world of pain and confusion . . .

❧

Elisheba's guilty conscience moved her to invite Jered, Ednah, and Heber to spend the night with her and Aaron. She was still apologizing for sending the sensitive bride fleeing when she left with the children.

"Are you staying in our rooms, or would you like to collect your wife?" Amram's grin softened his message, but he was no doubt exhausted. Late-night jewelry preparations for Mehy's feast, Puah's burial, and a wedding—Amram had earned his own bed.

"I'll get her." Mered shoved aside the curtain and found his bride mumbling and staring, much as she'd been when Mandai had brought her last night. *El-Shaddai, what do I do?*

He walked toward her, and she curled into the corner, fighting hysteria. *What was this?* "Shh, stop. Stop this." He knelt beside her trembling frame and grabbed her arms, forcing her to look into his eyes. "It's me, Mered. Why are you so frightened?" Her eyes were tightly shut, so he shook her gently. "Look at me—Bithiah."

Her struggling eased, then ceased. Her eyes opened slowly and studied him. Fear—no, terror—was in their depths. "I don't want a baby. I'll die. Like Ummi Kiya. Like Puah. They died."

He lifted her to her feet, tucked her safely beneath his arm, and guided her into their rooms—giving Amram, Jochebed, and Miriam silent permission to leave them. When they were alone, he sat her on their reed sleeping mat.

"Elisheba was insensitive and will apologize to you personally—I'll make sure of it—but you'll come to realize she's an ox with sharp horns and a soft heart."

He moved to sit beside her, and she skittered away like a shy lamb. Frustrated, he stood and lifted her into his arms, marching toward the only chair they owned.

"What are you doing?" She kicked her legs. "Put me down."

He plopped down on the chair and held her securely in his lap. "Is this position sufficient proof that I intend to talk with you tonight—only talk?"

Her cheeks pinked instantly, and her neck turned splotchy. She crossed her arms in a huff. "Then talk."

He rested his forehead on her shoulder. *El-Shaddai, thank You for this infuriating woman who knew and loved my Puah as I did.* Tears threatened to undo him. Puah wasn't what he planned to talk about, but he was exhausted—physically and emotionally. Both his and Bithiah's hearts had been ground like grain. Could they ever sift out enough flour to make a real life together?

"Mered, I'm sorry." She brushed his hair with her fingers. "I've been afraid my whole life."

A deep breath, a nod, and then he wiped his nose on her shoulder.

"Oh, stop that!"

He chuckled. "Do you know how to grind grain?"

The look on her face was priceless, appalled. She'd probably never touched a sieve either.

"I didn't think so. Do you know how to collect water with Heber—like you promised?"

She crossed her arms over her chest again. "No, but I knew it had to be done."

"Bake bread, cook lentils, dry fruit?"

"No, no, and no." She stared at the sleeping mat for a moment, her gaze distant. "How will we convince anyone that I'm Hebrew, Mered? Elisheba will know within a single heartbeat, and she'll tell all those disappointed women in the village who are lining up to take my place."

"The king has declared a three-day mourning period for Anippe and closed the linen shop. While you were sleeping this morning, I asked Nassor to place Miriam under my supervision since she's no longer needed as the amira's handmaid."

Bithiah's gaze grew distant again. He assumed she was thinking of Mehy and Ankhe.

Drawing her chin toward him, he searched her eyes and issued the challenge. "That means Miriam and I have three days to make you Hebrew."

"My son will grow up without his ummi or abbi."

"My children will never hear their mother's sweet voice again." Mered let the tears come and watched realization dawn on Anippe's features. "I will trust you to love my children, and you must trust me to keep close watch on Mehy's progress—as an Egyptian soldier, yes, but more importantly as a man of integrity."

Tears pooled on her thick, black lashes. "You'll see him in the summer at the linen shop, but I'll never see him again."

He brushed her cheek. "Never is a long time. Only El-Shaddai lives in eternity. We live today." He stood abruptly, catching her before she toppled to the floor.

She squealed and clutched at his robe. "Don't drop me."

He righted her and held her a moment longer than needed. "I won't let you go." Her cheeks flushed the color of roses. *Thank You, El-Shaddai, for providing a friend to share my grief.* He cleared the emotion from his throat. "I'll get Miriam. We can start your lessons tonight."

36

All my longings lie open before you, Lord;
my sighing is not hidden from you.

—PSALM 38:9

THREE YEARS LATER

Bithiah pressed the grinding stone around the grooved wheel, crushing and conquering the last kernels from her second basket of grain. Three-year-old Jekuthiel knelt beside her, poking at the bread dough Miriam was trying to knead.

They'd turned it into a game. Miriam leaned into the dough, shoving her hands deep into its middle. Jeki poked his finger into the squishy glob, trying to pull it back before Miriam caught him. His giggles and squeals made for more enjoyable chores but kept Miriam from the linen workshop too long.

"Shouldn't you be helping Mered by now, Miriam?" Bithiah asked.

The Gurob Harem ship and king's barque would arrive any day for the annual royal visit, and Mered had worked late every night for a week to prepare extra byssus robes.

With a casual smile, Miriam continued her kneading. "Your husband said I should help you this morning instead."

Bithiah felt her cheeks warm. *Mered sent her to help because I'll never be capable of caring for his family as Puah did.* She swallowed back tears, keeping her head bowed to the task. In the early days after Puah's death, they'd all grieved her openly. Stories of her warmed their hearts as they sat by the cook fire late at night. But no one grieved Ankhe. Anippe alone felt the hole in the world left by the girl no one had loved. Mered had heard Anippe crying on her sleeping mat a few times and tried to comfort her, but there was little time for sentiment in the Hebrew camp. If she'd learned anything in the last three years, it was that.

Once Mered and Miriam had started her training on their wedding night, Bithiah's hands had burned as if with hornet stings for a month. Blistered and bleeding, she'd worked through it, determined to learn, firm in her commitment to raise Mered's children. Jered and Ednah had been helpful but missed their mother terribly and resented Bithiah's intrusion. She'd begged Mered to let them work at the linen shop, finding it preferable to deal with blisters rather than the children's bitterness.

She inspected the hard, yellow calluses at the base of each finger, her dry and cracked knuckles, and remembered the feel of olive oil massages and salt scrubs.

"Are you all right?" Miriam had stopped kneading and sat back on her heels. "I don't mind helping, you know." She tousled Jeki's hair, leaving his black curls coated with flour dust.

The floodgate of Bithiah's tears burst then, and she tried to wipe them away before they dripped into her grain.

Miriam reached over and stopped her hands on the wheel. "Talk to me, Bithiah."

"I'm Anippe." The name came out like a curse. Slowly she raised her eyes to the handmaid she'd known long ago. "Some days are easier than others to pretend I'm Bithiah. Today I'm Anippe." She wiped her eyes and nose on her sleeve. Disgusting, but who had time for a dainty cloth? "We still have clothes to wash, water to gather, grain to parch, and beer-mash to sieve. Let's not talk about things that don't matter."

"You matter." Miriam returned to her tasks. She worked at twice the pace and accomplished three times as much.

Bithiah poured finely ground grain into a bowl, but as quickly as she ground it, Miriam added a splash of water, stirred, and kneaded another batch of bread. She had several rounds of bread cooking on the hot stones and still had time to entertain Jekuthiel.

"Will Amram find a husband for you . . . since I never did?" Guilt still clawed at Bithiah for taking Miriam to Gurob during her marriageable years. She could have been baking bread for her own husband and children by now.

"Since father's falling sickness started last year, I care for him while mother makes baskets for the villa. Add in my work at the linen shop, and I have no time for a husband." Miriam's rhythm never slowed. Stirring. Kneading. Baking. She sounded so brave, so sure.

"Don't you ever want to be held, Miriam? Yearn for a man's touch?"

"Don't you?" Miriam leveled her gaze at Bithiah, a spark in her eye. "You've been married three years, and Mered's never touched you." She pointed to the separate mats in their small room. "Ednah told me she sleeps with Heber on that one, Mered and Jered sleep on the roof, and you and Jeki sleep over there." She went back to kneading. "Why does your husband sleep on the roof? Mered is the best man I know, Bithiah. You're blessed to have him."

Was Miriam jealous? Did she want Mered? His family? "Miriam, I . . . we . . . Mered and I have an arrangement. I needed a place to live, and he needed someone to care for his children. He loves Puah—"

"Mered loves you, my friend. Can't you see it?"

"No. No, he can't. He doesn't." Bithiah jumped to her feet, distancing herself from Miriam and her wild imagination. "Perhaps you love Mered and are simply jealous."

Miriam leaned back on her heels, a slow, sweet grin on her lips. "I do love Mered."

The words stole Bithiah's breath.

"I love him like a brother, but there's another who holds my heart."

Relief swept over Bithiah like the Nile's cool waves. She returned to kneel beside her friend. "Who, Miriam? Is it the man you spoke of when we returned from Gurob? The one I hoped to match for your marriage?"

"El-Shaddai holds my heart, Bithiah. He's the One I adore. I feel His presence when I sing."

"Oh, Miriam." Disheartened, Bithiah ached at the girl's loneliness. "A god could never fill the longing for your one true love."

"No, Bithiah. A man can never fill the longing for my one true God."

Mered sat at his workshop desk, head buried in his hands. The rhythmic hum of his Hebrew brethren couldn't dull the pounding in his head. Nassor's threats had increased as the arrival of their royal guests drew near. The estate foreman had always been brutal toward the Hebrews, but whatever monster dwelt within him was unleashed after Ankhe's and Anippe's deaths. Violence alone no longer sated his amoral cravings.

Nassor now demanded a percentage of all linen production—his private wages to supplement a foreman's woefully insufficient pay. He also took percentages from the bakery, brewery, and every other workshop at Avaris. The bread and beer Nassor shared as bribes with his underling guards, but the other goods he stockpiled—waiting to use the Egyptian peasants as salesmen when the royals came to visit each year.

Nassor's coffers had grown fat on the villa's free production, so his greed had turned to human fare. He offered Hebrew women to his guards as incentives, payments, and rewards, and Nassor had his eye on Miriam.

Mered was running out of excuses to keep her away from the shop.

Jered and Heber had noticed Mered's caution. That morning, seven-year-old Heber had asked why Miriam didn't walk to the workshop with them anymore. Jered, the ever-sage older brother, had explained that she cared for Amram now that his falling sickness kept him in bed, his fits of shaking making him unable to work. Mered was thankful he didn't have to answer. He'd told Miriam he needed her to help Bithiah with little Jeki and the chores. All excuses, but effective in keeping her away from Nassor's hungry eyes.

"What are you doing, Father?" Jered's deep voice startled him. The boy grinned and plopped down on a pile of uncut flax stalks. "Do you need help?" He pointed to the unfurled scroll Mered had been pretending to read.

"No, no. I'm just going over some figures."

"Really? Because I was sitting with the bead workers—making sure Heber learned the craft without pocketing the beads—and you haven't looked at that papyrus scroll since you sat down."

Mered sighed and rolled up the scroll. His son was growing up too fast.

"I'm thinking about Bithiah." It was partially true. He always thought about Bithiah.

"Do you ever think about Mama anymore?" Jered's tone had an edge as he examined his sandals.

Mered jostled his son's shoulder, trying to draw his gaze. "Of course. I think of your mother every time I hear a baby cry. She loved assisting Shiphrah at births." He forced his son's chin up and met his sad eyes with a grin. "And I remember what a fine cook your mother was every time poor Bithiah tries a new recipe."

Finally a chuckle from his firstborn—quickly gone. "Do you love her? Bithiah, I mean."

Mered's heart hammered in his chest. He'd been wondering that himself lately. "I think so."

"I need to know because—" Jered raised his chin, almost defiant. "I think I may love someone."

"Well." Mered nodded, stalling for time. He wasn't prepared for this conversation. When had his son grown dark whiskers on his chin? "Well."

"You said that already."

"Yes, well."

Jered lifted an eyebrow and glared. "Father, don't you want to know her name or why I love her or when we plan to marry?"

"Plan to marry? You're not ready to marry, Jered. I don't even know who she is."

"I'm fifteen years old. Aaron was married and had a child by fifteen."

Mered scrubbed his face, frustration mounting. "Aaron moved in with the girl's parents and became apprentice to his father at the metals-and-gem shop— only two years before Amram's illness."

"What does that have to do with me?"

"Both Aaron's and Elisheba's parents sought El-Shaddai's counsel, and Aaron began preparing to take Amram's place in the shop. Everyone watched for God's active confirmation during the process, Jered. You've decided to marry, but have you considered El-Shaddai? Have you asked His opinion?"

"Not everyone hears from God like you do, Father."

Another male voice stammered an intrusion. "Am I interrupting an imp-p-p-ortant conversation?" Master Mehy offered a sheepish grin from the workshop doorway. "Hello, Mered." He gave Jered an awkward nod.

Nassor stood beside the master, glaring at Mered, but the linen keeper ignored him.

"Master Mehy, welcome home."

"Yes, welcome, Master Mehy." Crimson rose on Jered's neck. "Father, I'll keep an eye on Heber at the beads." He fairly ran down the long center aisle. Jered and Mehy, while so close growing up, now seemed like a pigeon and a dove—not natural enemies, but certainly belonging in different nests.

Without subtlety, Mehy turned to his estate foreman. "Thank you for the escort, Nassor. You may leave us now."

"But Master Mehy, I—"

"Thank you, Commander. Leave." Mehy's three years of military training had honed his authority and lessened his stutter.

Nassor shot Mered another warning glance before marching away.

Mehy stood with his feet apart and hands clasped behind his back, accenting his well-muscled shoulders. "Let's talk beneath our palm tree."

Mered directed Mehy out the door into the noisy world of Avaris's bustling Egyptian peasants. Their market stalls lined the pathway to the quay, tainting the view from their favorite tree. But it was still the most private place to talk. Their conversation would be lost in the commotion.

Each year since Mehy's military training had begun, he'd returned home with Pirameses and the other Ramessids from the Sile fortress. Mered noticed Pirameses's troop ship conspicuously missing from the dock and realized Master Mehy had come home early this year.

Mered leaned back against the rough trunk and waited for his young master to bare his heart, but silence stretched into awkwardness until Mered could stand it no longer. "Has something in particular brought you home from Sile earlier than expected?"

More silence. Concern laced with dread tightened Mered's chest, but he wouldn't ask again. This young soldier must open his heart when he was ready.

They watched geese fly overhead and skate across the Nile. A bennu heron waited on the shoreline for its prey to swim past. Mered's left arm was in the sun, so he scooted over to find shade.

When he glanced at the master, Mehy was grinning. "Comfortable now?"

Laughing, Mered pointed to the small space between them. "Well, if your shoulders hadn't grown a cubit since last summer, I'd have more shade."

Mehy's laughter faded as he pulled a braided leather cord from beneath his brass-studded breastplate. He wrapped it around Mered's wrist and then lifted the linen keeper's hand to his forehead—a sign of respect. "I win this award for you each year, Mered. You're the only family I have left."

Mered choked out his thanks, wishing he could embrace Mehy—but no slave would be so bold. Though aching to tell him Bithiah kept the previous two years' awards beneath her sleeping mat, Mered kept silent. The deception gnawed at him, but lives depended on it. "I'll keep it safely hidden with the other two."

"I won't be winning any more training honors, Mered." His tone was cryptic, haunted.

"Of course you will. You're Sebak's son. Master of Avaris."

"When the king's barque arrives for the Lotus Feast next week, Jad Horem, Pirameses, and the royal advisors will plan a new offensive against the Hittites."

The news landed like a rock in Mered's belly. "Pirameses can't send you to war yet. You're fifteen years old with barely three years of training."

"He's sending Sety with me—without any Sile training." Mehy turned his head slowly. "He said he'd train his son on the b-b-battlefield." His tongue tripped over the final word, evidence of his fear.

Anger, fear, and disbelief combined to steal Mered's words. What could he say to a terrified boy? Every instinct as a father wanted to protect him—as Amram would if he could. But Mered couldn't protect himself—or Bithiah or Miriam or anyone else he loved. As Amram had once told him, they were all in God's hands.

Steadied by the reminder, Mered asked, "Why now, Master Mehy? Why launch an attack on the Hittites during sowing season?"

With a wry grin, Mehy seemed to ponder Mered's question. "Ah, yes. Strategy. Pirameses says Egypt's sowing is the Levant's harvest—something about we'll live off the fruit of their land and not run low on supplies like they did when Jad Horem led the attack years ago."

Mered nodded, contemplating how much to confide about his days as supply chief in Horemheb's army. Did this boy realize the level of depravity he was about to encounter? "Does Vizier Piramoses ever talk about your abbi Sebak, the role he played in the battles fought with your Jad Horem?"

Mehy turned slowly, his cheeks white as natron powder. "What do you know of Abbi Sebak's role in battle, Mered?"

Mered's heart broke. "I was the supply chief who helped get needed provisions to King Horemheb's army the last time they marched on Kadesh."

The boy returned his gaze to the quay. "I am the son of Sebak, Seth reborn. I know what is expected of me on the field of battle, Mered."

El-Shaddai, please, no. Mered grabbed Mehy's shoulders, shaking him. "You are not Seth reborn, and your abbi was a kind and gentle man. He was plagued by demands, tormented by his choices. Men are not gods, Mehy. There is only one God, and His name is El-Shaddai."

Mehy shrugged off Mered's hands and sniffed back tears. "Sit back, Mered."

The linen keeper pressed himself back against the tree. He waited, head bowed, for his master's verdict. Had he gone too far?

"I go to battle representing my ancestors, Mered. Abbi Sebak and Ummi Anippe will be watching from the underworld. Jad Horem will remain in Memphis to implement his Great Edict and ensure the rebuilding of Egypt, so I am the only member of our family that can fight. I must bring them honor. I must be Seth reborn." He reached for Mered's hand and squeezed it gently. "I must be who they've trained me to be, my friend."

Anger, guilt, and submission churned in Mered's belly. He yearned to tell Mehy the truth. *You're the son of a faithful Hebrew who loves El-Shaddai and trusts Him with your life.* Instead, he wiped the moisture from his cheeks and tried to ignore the deep ache inside. "Of course, Master Mehy. I will pray to El-Shaddai for your protection—just as I prayed for your Abbi Sebak. Is there any way I can help prepare for your journey?"

"I want to see Miriam."

Startled, Mered tried to imagine a benign reason a handsome fifteen-year-old soldier would want to see a beautiful twenty-one-year-old slave girl. "Of course. She works for me in the linen workshop. You can see her there any—"

"No. She must come to the villa . . . to my bathhouse. Tonight."

Mered swallowed his rising panic. Master Mehy's interest would be worse than Nassor's—if he intended what most Egyptian men intended when they summoned a Hebrew slave girl. Did Mehy know she was his sister? As an Egyptian prince, did he care?

Before Mered could form a well-phrased question, the master stood and offered his hand to help his linen keeper stand. "Make sure she arrives before dusk. I'll have guards escort her home when I'm finished with her." Mered accepted the proffered hand, and Mehy pulled him to his feet, pointing to the gifted leather braid around the linen keeper's wrist. "I will make you proud when I fight the Hittites, Mered."

He walked away, his broad shoulders and powerful stride reminding Mered of a younger Amram. "El-Shaddai, protect your handmaiden, Miriam," he whispered.

"Protect Miriam from what?"

Mered whirled to find Jered's face clouded with anger. He lifted his hands to explain—or at least form a plausible half truth.

But Jered forgot Miriam when he saw the braided leather band around his father's wrist. "Where did you get this?" He glanced down the hillside path, where Master Mehy was just entering the villa. "Mehy gave you this? Why does Bithiah have two of these hidden under her sleeping mat?"

"How do you know what she has hidden under her mat?" Mered was indignant at his son's snooping but also anxious to divert his intuitive mind.

"I may sleep on the roof, Father, but I'm a part of this family, and I know more than you think about what does and doesn't happen on Bithiah's sleeping mat." Comprehension dawned on his features—at first gentle like the early inundation and then the flood of his fury. "Bithiah is the amir—"

Mered clamped his hand over Jered's mouth, grinding out his threat between clenched teeth. "If you are the grown man you claim to be, you will consider the many lives at stake—and you'll never speak those words again."

37

Do not fear, for I have redeemed you;
I have summoned you by name; you are mine.

—ISAIAH 43:1

Bithiah had been awake most of the night, waiting for Miriam's return and worrying about her two youngest boys. At times like these she missed Ankhe. She would have woken her and chattered on about her fears. Turning to cuddle with three-year-old Jekuthiel, she whispered into his dreams. "You will not plug rat holes at dawn, my precious boy—and neither will Heber."

The moon was well past its zenith, and she still wasn't sure how she'd keep that promise. The plan would undoubtedly involve deceiving Mered, since he'd refused her repeated pleas to exempt their boys from the task.

"My children will do their duty like all other slave children," he'd said.

Well, other slave children didn't fill the hole in her heart as Jeki and Heber did. She'd cried until she was sick when Heber had helped Hur previously. Tomorrow would be the first time Jeki was old enough to share in the awful task.

A heavy-footed pair of soldiers drew near their outer curtain and halted. Bithiah lifted Jeki's sleep-sodden arm from her throat and eased off her mat in time to meet Miriam at the doorway.

Miriam gasped. "Why are you still awake?"

Bithiah grabbed her arm and led her back outside. "I wanted to hear what happened with Mehy." She refused to believe Mehy would harm Miriam—as Mered feared—but Ramessid training changed people. Bithiah peered into Miriam's troubled eyes. "Are you all right?"

"He wanted me to sing for him."

Relief came like a wave, and Bithiah pulled Miriam into a fierce embrace. But the girl was shaking. Bithiah released her. "What happened? Something's wrong."

"Mehy also asked me about El-Shaddai, and—"

"He wants to believe in the Hebrew God?"

"His questions were only about the Hebrews, Bithiah. Mehy asked if I knew his Hebrew parents. He asked me about the day you found him on the Nile." Tears pooled on Miriam's lashes, and Bithiah swallowed her rising panic.

"What did you tell him?"

"I told him his Hebrew nursemaid, Jochebed, was his mother—and mine. I was the sister who followed his pitch-covered basket among the reeds until he was safe in the arms of Pharaoh's daughter." Miriam blinked, sending a stream of tears down her cheeks. "He ordered me to leave—and then he begged me to stay." She hugged Bithiah again, sobbing quietly into her shoulder. "He's so alone, so confused and afraid."

Her heart breaking, Bithiah held her and remembered the three dots she used to draw on Mehy's hand. How she wished she could reassure him of her presence now and tell him of the Hebrew God that Mered said was greater than Re. "He's not alone, Miriam. Did you tell him?"

She nodded. "Of course. I told him El-Shaddai had preserved his life for a purpose, but he laughed and said the gods had better hurry with their purpose because he'll surely die before seeing his eighteenth inundation."

"Die?" Bithiah pushed her away, holding her at arm's length. "Why does he think he'll die?"

"Mehy must walk in Sebak's sandals and become Seth reborn when Pi-rameses engages the Hittites next month. He told Mered when he gave him this year's training award—"

"The Hittites?" Bithiah felt her face drain of color.

Miriam's furrowed brow lifted in dawning regret. "I'm sorry. I thought Mered told you. I'm sure he just didn't want you to worry."

Bithiah's trembling began in her legs and crawled up her spine. Mered had come home from the workshop with Mehy's braided leather around his wrist—

joyful and winsome, but weary from a long day. He'd gone to bed early. She should have known something was wrong.

Why had she stayed awake half the night, worrying about her intended deception? At least her lies would protect Mered's children, not send a son to battle. "Should I try to see him, Miriam? Would it help Mehy to know he's not alone?"

"Mehy was furious when he discovered I'd kept the secret of his Hebrew parents from him. I don't know how he'd react if he found out you and Mered have deceived him too."

The truth burned in Bithiah's chest. Her presence now would only intensify Mehy's pain. And what if he meted out his wrath on Mered and the children? No, for everyone's sake, she would continue as Bithiah—and for Jeki and Heber's sake, she would deceive her husband. She couldn't prevent Mehy from going to war, but she would keep her little boys' arms out of rat holes.

She squared her shoulders and offered her hand to Miriam. "Come, dear one. You need some rest. We caught up on most of our household chores yesterday, so you can accompany Mered to the shop in the morning."

"I don't mind helping you, really. I could—"

"No, I insist. Mered came home especially worn out tonight. I think he needs help preparing for the Lotus Feast next week."

Miriam laced her arm through Bithiah's. "All right. I'll go with Mered, but I enjoy helping you. In fact, I think I prefer our quiet days at home."

They entered Bithiah's dark room, the sounds of sweet snores and heavy breathing assuring them the children were still dreaming.

"Good night, Bithiah." Miriam slipped beyond the dividing curtain to her family's rooms.

It would be a good night only if Bithiah could devise a plan to keep Heber and Jeki from ratting.

Dawn finally cast its lavender glow through their single window, and Bithiah untangled herself from Jeki's sleeping form again. Tiptoeing to the rickety ladder leading to their roof, she climbed up and peered over the palm-covered mud-brick rooftop. Mered slept under one canopy and Jered under a second. Her husband stirred on his mat, and she ducked down, heart pounding. With a calming breath, she popped her head above the roof again and reached out to touch his foot.

Mered jumped to his feet, bumping his head on the canopy, and saw her at the opening. "What's wrong?" he said, loud enough to wake the gods.

"Father?" Jered sat up on his mat.

Bowels of Anubis, he's awake. Bithiah pressed her finger against her lips and then ducked out of sight, hoping Mered would reassure Jered.

"It's nothing, son. Go back to sleep. I'll wake you for breakfast." Mered approached the opening where Bithiah waited, pulling his robe on over his tunic.

Bithiah hurried down the rungs, feeling her cheeks warm. She'd never seen her husband in his undertunic. Flustered already, she waited by the curtained doorway and fled outside the moment he saw her. He followed, as she'd hoped.

Mered slipped around the curtain and stared down at her with pleasure. "You wanted to talk alone?" He took a step nearer, his hands sliding down her arms, stealing her breath.

She shuddered, part cool morning breeze, part nerves.

He pulled her into a gentle embrace, sliding his hands up and down her back. "You're shivering. I can go back in and get our wool blanket." He pressed his lips against her ear, his nearness making her head swim. "I'll go to the roof and wake Jered. He and Ednah can collect dung chips for the fire. We could watch the sunrise from the roof. It's beauti—"

"The boys!" Her words echoed in the stillness.

Mered jumped as if she were a viper and he, just bitten. "What about the boys?"

"My boys are too tired to help Hur with ratting after digging trenches in the garden yesterday." She was still shivering, and her delivery was less than convincing.

He leaned against the doorjamb, crossed his arms, and grinned. "Your boys?"

If he wasn't so annoyingly handsome, she would be angry at his swagger. "All right, our boys are not teasing cobras with a dead rat on a stick and then shoving old linen into their nests. It's ludicrous to place children in such dan—"

His lips were on hers, silencing her. He cradled her head gently but firmly. Sudden and decisive. And then he released her. "Thank you for loving our sons."

She had no response. Three years, and he'd never kissed her. And then he picked today, when she'd decided to deceive him? Of course, she loved their sons.

He brushed her lips with another kiss. "But they are Hebrew children, and they must take their turns at ratting like other slave children. It's scary and unpleasant, but we trust El-Shaddai with their lives." He shoved aside the curtain as if the conversation was over.

"How can you entrust them to a god who sends my son to battle the Hittites?"

He halted midstride, his playfulness gone like the morning mist. Slowly, deliberately, he faced her—no kiss this time. "I'm sorry I didn't tell you about Mehy. How did you find out?"

"Miriam told me last night when she came home."

His concern deepened. "Is she all right? What did Mehy want with her?"

She glanced right and left to be sure no one else would hear. "He was curious about his Hebrew heritage. He questioned Miriam, and she told him the truth."

Panic flooded his face. "About you?"

"About her and Jochebed. Mehy doesn't know you and I continue the deception." She saw a web of unspoken thoughts cloud his eyes.

His hands fell from her shoulders, and he stepped away, the distance between them making her shiver. "How did he react to the truth?"

"Miriam said he was hurt, angry."

Mered stared at his bare feet for a moment and then cradled her elbows, drawing her near. Bithiah thought he meant to hold her again, but he merely bent to whisper, "I think we should tell him, Bithiah—about you, about us. I hate deceiving him when I believe El-Shaddai could use the truth to encourage him."

She stood like a pillar, confusion warring with longing. Everything within her ached to see Mehy again, but what would he do when faced with the truth? She'd seen what Ramessid training did to a man. What if Mehy had become like them?

"No, Mered. I couldn't bear it if he hurt you or one of our children."

He tucked a stray hair behind her ear, his tenderness wringing her heart. "If fear robs us of truth, faith never has a chance to grow. Trust El-Shaddai, Bithiah. He saved your life and ours when He brought you to me." He leaned down for a kiss, but she turned away.

"You mean trust the god who took Mehy from me and killed Puah in childbirth?"

His affection withered, and he scrubbed his face with both hands and gave her a hard stare. "Someday, El-Shaddai will prove Himself to you, but until then, I will trust Him for both of us. Jeki and Heber go ratting at the villa today, and I'll wait to see Master Mehy's mood to determine if today is the day we reveal our secret." He stood glaring down at her, waiting for her challenge.

She wanted to scream. She wished she could rant and demand he change. But Mered's faith was the bedrock of the man—and the man was the bedrock of her life. She would simply follow the plan she devised last night. Her children were not poking at snakes or reaching into rat holes today, and according to Miriam, Mehy's mood should keep Mered at a distance.

Lowering her head, Bithiah pretended submission. "I'm sorry I don't share your faith in El-Shaddai, but our sons need rest. Jeki and Heber are exhausted after helping Miriam and me prepare the new garden site for sowing season. Please, let them sleep this morning, and then I'll ask Shiphrah to take them to the villa for ratting when she takes Uri. She won't mind."

Mered lifted her chin up, searching her eyes. "If you say Shiphrah will deliver them to the villa, I believe you."

Without flinching, she held his gaze. "Perhaps I'll put on a wig and byssus robe and take the boys to the villa myself—and appear to Mehy as Anippe, raised from the dead." She meant to tease, but her humor fell flat.

"Such a reckless deed would kill us all." Mered pulled her into his arms again and laid his cheek atop her head. "When we tell Mehy the truth, we'll do it gently. He'll understand why we've kept it from him so long, and he'll be relieved to know his ummi is alive."

Could Mehy really be relieved? She hadn't anticipated anything but anger and feelings of betrayal.

Mered brushed her cheek with his fingers and released her. "We'll let our little boys sleep. You start the fire, and I'll get Ednah and Jered to help me gather water." He leaned down and kissed her gently, thoroughly. "I love y— your way with our children."

Breathless, Bithiah hurried inside before Mered noticed the heat in her cheeks and before the fire in her veins betrayed her. *Did he almost say, I love you?* For three years, she'd kept him at a distance. Still terrified of childbearing, she would rather deny him than confront her deepest fear.

She couldn't risk loving Mered, but loving his children gave her another chance at being *Ummi*—the one name in her life she'd loved more than any other. She'd been terrified as *Meryetaten-tasherit,* betrayed as *Anippe,* and abandoned as *Amira.* Bithiah could never deceive Mered, but as *Ummi,* she could do anything to protect her children.

Mered let the morning sun warm his left shoulder, purposefully wading through the receding shoreline of inundation's last days. Jered, Ednah, and Miriam walked ahead of him, silent and pensive, as was he. These morning walks to the workshop gave him time to think—of El-Shaddai, his family, and the woman he called Bithiah. Would she really ask Shiphrah to take their boys to the villa?

He blew out a deep sigh. *Can I ever trust her fully when our marriage is based on a lie?*

In the early days, he'd grieved Puah deeply and felt relief at Bithiah's coolness. Now he wondered if a lie was more comfortable than the truth for Bithiah. How would she respond if he told her his feelings were changing—deepening? Sometimes sharing the truth seemed harder than living the lie.

He watched Miriam splash in the muddy waters ahead of him. She'd been deep in thought all morning. Had she come to the same conclusion? Now that she'd shared the truth with Mehy, had she forfeited what little bond existed between a slave and master? Their lies to Mehy were intended to protect him in the beginning, but in the end, he felt vulnerable and betrayed. How would he feel when Mered told him about Bithiah? *El-Shaddai, forgive our piteous efforts to control our circumstances.*

Jered stopped at the hilltop, where the path diverged to the three-building linen complex. "Father, do I release the night workers or assign new designs to the weavers?"

"You release the night workers. I need to speak to one of the weavers about a flaw in yesterday's design."

Jered started walking away before Mered finished talking. He'd barely met his father's gaze since realizing Bithiah's identity yesterday. Another relationship tarnished by deception.

"What about us?" Ednah sidled up to Miriam, obviously thrilled the older girl was with her. "Can Miriam and I work together today?" Her voice was nearly swallowed by the growing din of the Egyptian peasant market. Standing by Miriam, Ednah looked entirely too grown up. His thirteen-year-old daughter was nearly as tall as the willowy twenty-one-year-old. Though youthful freckles still dotted Ednah's cheeks, she was of marriageable age for Hebrew girls. *What if both Jered and Ednah want to marry soon?*

"Father?" Ednah placed a hand on his arm. "Are you all right?"

"Yes. You stay with Miriam, and both of you remain close to me today." Mered cast a wary glance around. He needed to warn Miriam of Nassor's dangerous interest, but how could he, without frightening Ednah? "Though Ramessids seldom intrude in the linen shop, the estate foreman has visited every day, Miriam." A lifted brow and tilt of his head would hopefully imply his concern.

Miriam drew a deep breath and patted Ednah's hand. "Nassor sells Hebrew girls to the highest bidder. You must never meet his gaze and never speak directly to him. Keep your head covering low on your forehead and wrapped around your lovely curls." She loosened the girl's belt. "And never show your curves."

Mered's mouth was instantly dry. So much for subtlety. He searched his daughter's face for signs of fear. Before he had a chance to address Miriam's candor, the older girl closed her eyes, and Ednah followed her lead.

Praying. The girls were praying. While Mered inwardly fumed, these completely vulnerable young women offered their fear to El-Shaddai. Miriam opened her eyes and waited for Ednah to do the same. Their serene smiles reached their eyes, and Mered realized his little girl had not only grown into a woman's body but also into a personal faith.

Choking back emotion, he brushed Ednah's cheek. "Are you frightened?"

She glanced at Miriam and then back at him. "Yes, but Miriam and Jochebed have taught me that fear is the most fertile ground for faith."

Mered laughed aloud. "So it is. I'll have to share that wisdom with Bithiah." He tucked her under his arm and opened the workshop door.

"I've been waiting, Mer—" Mehy's gruff greeting halted when he glimpsed the girls. He offered Miriam a cold stare but softened when he saw Ednah. "And who is this?"

Nassor loomed behind his right shoulder. "If she pleases you, I can have her brought to your chamber."

Mered stepped in front of Ednah. "She is my daughter, Master Mehy. She's only thirteen."

Mehy remained silent, glaring at Mered until the linen keeper thought his knees would give way. "They both please me, Nassor. I want them both marked as mine so neither will be passed among the guards while I'm away. Is that understood?"

"Understood." Nassor's jaw muscle danced. Evidently not the answer he'd hoped for.

"In fact, you can bring them both to me tonight." Mehy shoved Mered aside and brushed Ednah's cheek with his hand. "Miriam can sing while I get to know the younger one."

Ednah winced, and Mered grabbed Mehy's forearm. Nassor buried his cudgel in Mered's gut, doubling him over.

"Enough." Mehy's single word stopped his foreman from further violence.

Miriam and Ednah huddled together, weeping. Mered straightened and met his master's gaze. "You are master of Avaris, son of Sebak, an honorable man. I pray you can look in the mirror tomorrow and still be all those things."

Mehy turned on his heel and stormed from the workshop. Nassor followed, casting a wicked grin over his shoulder as they crossed the threshold.

Miriam and Ednah were immediately at Mered's side. "Are you all right?" Miriam asked.

"Come sit down, Father." Both girls led him to his desk as if he'd been wounded in battle.

"I'm fine. I'm fine." He waved off their concern but captured their attention. "I want you both to stay in the linen shop today. No breaks or walks to the quay." He glanced at the doorway leading to the villa's garden. "Nassor will more than likely come here to collect you for the evening with the master. I want you both to be tired and dirty when he sees you."

38

Their venom is like . . .
that of a cobra that has stopped its ears,
that will not heed the tune of the charmer,
however skillful the enchanter may be.

—PSALM 58:4–5

I'm hungry," Heber whined. He and Jeki sat around a mat, playing their fourth game of pick-up-sticks.

Bithiah took the last piece of bread off the oven, placed it in a basket, and covered it with a cloth to keep it warm.

"Mama, Heber cheated. He touched one stick and then pulled another from the pile—"

"I did not. Jeki doesn't know how to play right."

"I'm big. I know how to play."

"Boys, enough." Bithiah's emotions couldn't abide bickering tonight. She walked toward the doorway, where Jered was watching for his father.

He raised a disapproving brow. "They're hungry. Father said he and Ednah would be late tonight. Why not let them eat? When Father hears you hired a snake charmer instead of sending Heber and Jeki ratting with Hur, he'll be angry no matter who's sitting at the table."

Bithiah leaned close and whispered, "Do you hate me because I'm your father's wife or because you discovered I was the amira?"

Silence was his only answer.

She sighed, too weary to fight Jered and prepare for Mered's fury. "I'll feed Heber and Jeki, but will you at least defend me when I explain the miracle El-Shaddai provided?"

Jered sneered. "Don't try to blame El-Shaddai for your deception, or Father will be even angrier."

Bithiah ladled Mered's favorite stew into bowls for Heber and Jeki and cut a fish cake in half. "You boys may eat. There's nabk-berry bread after you finish your soup and fish."

"I wish the snake charmer came every day," Jeki squealed.

"Father's coming." Jered ran to the fire to ladle his own bowl of stew, and Bithiah huddled behind their three boys.

Mered pushed back the curtain and let it fall closed behind him. He looked weary. "What's this?"

"Where are Miriam and Ednah?" Bithiah asked.

"Master Mehy asked them both to attend him in his bathhouse this evening."

Bithiah raised a hand to her throat, fear silencing her.

Jered's back straightened like a measuring rod. "If he touches my sister, I'll—"

"I've made your favorite meal." Bithiah laid her hand on Jered's shoulder, hoping to silence his fury in front of the little ones.

Jeki held up his fish cake. "Mother said we could have fish cakes every time she hires the snake charmer."

Mered's eyes narrowed. "Snake charmer?"

Bithiah's cheeks flamed—not exactly the way she'd planned to inform Mered of the day's events.

Before she could answer, her husband growled at their boys. "Take your meal to Jochebed and Amram's while I speak with Bithiah alone." Jered quickly herded his brothers through the adjoining doorway, drawing the curtain behind them.

Mered trembled head to toe, the cook fire's flame reflected in his angry eyes. He covered the space between them in two large strides, and his hands gripped her arms, fingers biting deep. "When I left this morning, was I at all unclear?"

She set her jaw. "No. You were quite clear."

"So you deliberately deceived me."

"I was desperate to protect our boys. I prayed that El-Shaddai would send a snake charmer, and when I walked them to the villa this morning—"

"You walked to the villa?" He shook her, and she felt the first stab of fear.

Swallowing hard, she considered her words carefully. He was beyond fury, almost desperate. "Not all the way to the villa. When I reached the top of the hill, I saw a skiff at the quay with a strange-looking man getting out of it, so I asked one of the Egyptian merchants who he was. A snake charmer. Mered, your god brought me a snake charmer on the very day I needed—"

He lifted his hand, and she squeezed her eyes shut, ready for a blow that never came. When she opened her eyes, his back was turned. Of course, Mered would never hit her . . . would he? Every man she'd known had become violent when pushed too far.

Mered dragged both hands through his hair. "How did you pay the charmer, Bithiah?"

"I used the trinkets hidden under my sleeping mat."

"Mehy's honor braids?"

"No. I would never—"

"What then?"

"A turquoise clasp and a silver ring from my days as amira. Miriam brought a basket from the Gurob ship when she was still my handmaid and never had the chance to return it, so I buried them in the dirt floor under my sleeping mat."

"What if Nassor discovers the snake charmer can do Hur's job more efficiently and sends Hur to dead-man's land?"

"Hur worked with the charmer," Bithiah said. "It was only the children that were sent home and worked in the village."

"What if Nassor asks about the Hebrew woman with Egyptian jewelry? What if the guards assume your husband stole it from the villa? Or perhaps the Hebrew girl, Miriam, stole it when she visited Master Mehy last night."

"No!" Bithiah shouted. "It was a simple transaction with a traveling snake charmer." She peered over his shoulder to be sure the children weren't peeking through the curtain. "Who are you to chastise me about deception? You didn't tell me about Mehy going to battle—and besides, we live a lie every day."

Mered moved closer but didn't touch her this time. "You're right. I should have told you about Mehy, but the truth burns in my belly every day. That's the difference between you and me. That's what frightens me. You don't just lie. You're a deceiver who's lived a lifetime of lies, *Anippe*."

She flinched as if he'd slapped her. "Don't call me that name."

"When you act like the deceitful amira I once knew, I can't call you anything else." With a few angry strides, he was gone.

Anippe. Alone in the empty room, life became suddenly clear. Mered was right. Everything about her was a lie. Jochebed had named her *Bithiah,* but she was not a daughter of the Hebrew god. She'd been a fool to think El-Shaddai heard her prayer for a snake charmer. The Hebrew god was like all other gods—playing with human hearts.

Mered could call her whatever he wanted; in fact, they need not speak at all.

She filled her bowl with lentil stew and climbed the ladder to the roof. She tossed down Mered's and Jered's personal things, pulled up the ladder, and placed the thatched covering over the roof access. No one would bother her here. Mered could tend the children tonight, and Jered could sleep on her mat with Jeki. Miriam and Ednah would return from Mehy's chamber, and life would go on.

Without Bithiah's comments. Without Anippe's interference. Without her lies.

For her heart's protection, for her sanity, she would breathe, live, and work. That was all. Never again would she spend her treasure on Mered's sons, and Mehy's name would never again form on her lips. Drastic measures for a desperate woman.

It was all too clear—the gods were angry with her. Was it because she lived among the Hebrews or because her pain amused them? It didn't matter. She would be silent. Invisible. Nameless.

Nameless rolled to her side, sensing a heavy dew on her face, hands, and arms. A chill ran through her. She bolted upright.

A screech owl perched on the long house across the path and clacked its beak. Something stirred in the nearby Nile waters, thrashing, fighting, submitting—dying. Pulling her rough-spun robe tighter, she shivered in the fading darkness. Dawn was approaching.

Life is relentless. She must face her first day with no name.

Gathering her bowl from last night, she straightened what would become her space. A three-sided canopy of palm branches suspended by several poles, it provided shade in the day and protection from birds at night. A small piece of lamb's wool made an adequate headrest, and a woven woolen blanket helped turn away the night chill. It was more than she deserved.

Jered's canopy lay empty opposite her. Wasted space in this new sleeping arrangement, but she'd use it for storage so Mered and the children would have more room downstairs. Or perhaps Miriam would come up and sleep under the second canopy.

No! I refuse to need anyone. She squeezed her eyes shut, reminding herself of her vow. *Breathe, live, work. That's all.*

She rocked to her feet, removed the thatched opening in the rooftop floor, and noticed the cook fire already flaming, lamps already lit. *Why would someone be awake so early?* She stepped down the rickety acacia-wood ladder, not yet accustomed to the climb. Safely on the packed-dirt floor, she was startled to find Heber and Jeki sharing her sleeping mat. Jered and Ednah were awake with the adults—all standing in a huddle near the table, staring at her.

Had they decided to put her out? Her mouth went dry. "What? What is it?"

Mered stepped toward her, hands extended as if approaching a shy filly. He tried to reach for her hands, but she backed away, bumping against the ladder. "It's Miriam," he said. "She's alive but badly beaten."

She saw Jochebed, face buried in her hands, sobbing. Amram comforted her. Ednah, too, was weeping, but Jered stood with his arms folded across his chest.

She looked to Mered for answers. "Who beat Miriam?"

"Bithiah . . ." His tenderness was unnerving. Last night he wanted to feed her to the crocodiles, and this morning he treated her like Persian pottery.

"Who hurt her?"

"Mehy."

The single word was like a nightmare replaying in her mind. She blinked but kept hearing her son's name. *Mehy. Mehy. Mehy.*

Gentle hands shook her shoulders. "Bithiah, look at me. Look at me." Mered's face was less than a handbreadth away. "Ednah was with Miriam when it happened. She's shaken, but she said Mehy had to do it. He saved Miriam's life."

Confused and overwhelmed, she shrugged off his hands. "I don't understand. Why would Mehy hurt Miriam? I know he was angry when he found out Miriam was his sis—" Panic seized her when she realized Jered and Ednah—even Amram—might not know Mehy's true identity.

"It's all right. Everyone in this room knows Mehy is Moses."

"Is that why he beat her?" she asked on a sob.

Mered pulled her into his arms, quieting her. "No. It's why he saved her."

Jered's anger erupted. "You're why he beat her."

"That's not true, Jered," Amram intervened, cradling the boy's shoulders. "I'll not have you laying blame."

Nameless tried to free herself from Mered's embrace, but he held her tight. "It wasn't your fault," he said. "I know you were trying to protect Heber and Jeki."

Understanding dawned, and panic overtook her. She flailed in his arms. "It was the snake charmer, wasn't it?"

"Stop fighting me." His strong arms held her fast, quieting her thrashing. "I'll tell you everything if you'll calm down. Rest, Bithiah. Rest in my arms. Shh."

His mercy was inescapable. Her strength vanished, and she crumpled to the floor.

Mered held her, speaking softly. "The guards noticed the snake charmer in the villa was assisting Hur instead of the children, and they grew suspicious. When they questioned the charmer, he showed them the jewelry he'd been given as wages. The guards took the pieces of jewelry to Mehy, who recognized them as his mother's."

She began shaking her head before Mered finished speaking. "But Mehy knows Miriam wouldn't steal those things. He wouldn't—"

"Miriam confessed to stealing the jewelry." Mered's tone was even, deliberate.

"What? No. Why would she do that?"

"Because if she denied it, Nassor would have searched the craftsmen's village—and found you."

A wave of nausea nearly overwhelmed her. Ankhe's final words haunted her. *You did this to me!* Would Miriam scream the same? No, Miriam would do far worse. Miriam would forgive her.

She kept swallowing the bile and with it regret, shame, and self-loathing. Surely, if she had a name, she would be darkness itself. Had her darkness tainted her son?

Not Mehy. Mehy is good.

She lifted her gaze to Ednah. "Why didn't Mehy let a guard punish Miriam?"

"He did it to save her." Ednah's voice was shaky but absent the judgment in Jered's gaze. "After Nassor landed the first blow, Mehy took away the foreman's cudgel and dismissed all the guards. He told Miriam he must make the beating look real—but he would leave her alive. And then he did this." Ednah knelt beside Bithiah and Mered and held out her forearm, revealing a fresh burn in the shape of the Avaris estate symbol.

Nameless covered a sob. "Why? Why would he torture you?"

"Master Mehy said the brand would keep Miriam and me safe from other guards while he was at war. It marks us as his. He said Pirameses has started marking some of his slaves." Ednah looked up, her eyes swimming in tears. "He hurt us to save us."

The smell of burnt flesh was too much to bear. Bile rose in her throat, and Nameless ran out the door to vomit.

A tender hand pressed against her back, rubbing and patting, and then she heard Jochebed's voice. "Love forces us to choose, Bithiah. I chose to protect Moses in a basket on the Nile. You chose to protect Heber and Jeki, and

Miriam chose to protect you. If our motives are truly pure, the result is in God's hands."

Shame kept her head bowed. "I don't deserve your forgiveness, Jochebed. Leave me alone."

The older woman disappeared inside, and the one with no name stared at the brightening sky. *Life was truly relentless.* She would breathe. She would live. She would work.

Inhaling deeply, she returned inside to the averted glances of Mered and his firstborn. Amram and Jochebed had disappeared with Ednah into their adjoining room.

"Ednah will help Jochebed tend Miriam and Amram today," Mered said. "I've asked Jered to help you with household tasks."

Nameless crossed the room and scooped a cup of rough-ground grain into a pot, adding a pinch of salt. "I don't need help."

"Regardless, he's staying. I'll send Heber and Jeki to stay with Shiphrah. They can play with Uri and Yael until it's time to help prepare the fields for sowing." Mered reached for the pot of gruel and hung it over the fire to cook.

"Whatever you wish." She bowed her head and tensed as his hands rested on her arms, his tenderness scalding her.

"I'll stay home instead of Jered if you need me."

"No. You must prepare for the Lotus Feast. Please go."

Only a moment's hesitation before his hands fell away. "I'll come home later to check on you."

"I'll get water at the river." Jered grabbed a water jug and was out the door before they could answer.

She lifted her eyes, forcing herself to speak. "Please take him to the shop with you. I can't deal with his hatred today."

"He doesn't hate you." Mered's eyes were pleading. "The truth is, he's so angry at everyone right now, I'm afraid to have him at the shop or near the villa. Please, Bithiah. He must stay home today."

She bowed her head, nodding slightly. *Breathe. Live. Work.* "As you wish, Mered."

After gathering two more jugs of water, Jered plopped the last one on the floor and started toward the roof ladder.

"Where are you going?" she asked.

He didn't answer, didn't even acknowledge her question.

She grabbed his arm and whirled him around. "Jered, please. I need your help making this week's beer." Of all the household tasks, making beer was the one she hated most—even more than cleaning waste pots.

He rolled his eyes, but didn't refuse.

"You can have the rest of the nabk-berry bread if you help me," she said.

Bribery seemed to work. Within moments, they were settled into a deserted clearing behind the first row of long houses. *Breathe. Live. Work.*

She held the sieve over the flavoring vat, while Jered lifted the large amphora of fermented mash. "Pour slowly," she said. "I don't plan to wash robes for three days, so no splashing."

He started pouring. "I don't hate you."

She raised an eyebrow but didn't respond.

"And it's not your fault Miriam was beaten. It's Mehy's. He could have found another way to punish her."

Again she remained silent.

"Even if he did have to beat her, he didn't need to be so brutal. You should see her." Jered poured faster as his fervor increased. "How could he do that to his sister? If you love someone, you don't hurt them."

She shook her head and scoffed at his youth. "Those who love us hurt us most." A huge lump of mash plopped into the sieve. "Slow down, you're splashing."

He ignored her, the mash pouring out with his words. "But I love someone, and I would never hurt her. Father won't even let me talk about marriage until I hear from El-Shaddai."

"Why are you in such a hurry to get married? You've only seen fifteen inundations."

"I've been a skilled craftsman in the linen shop since I was twelve. I can support a family with wages in grain and linen."

She looked away from the sieve of soupy sludge and found Jered's chest puffed, chin raised. He wasn't interested in dissenting opinions.

"Is the girl ready to manage a household?" she asked.

"She is of age, from the tribe of Judah, and her abba is a metal worker. Her family's women are respectful to their husbands, and most have borne sons."

Jered listed her qualities as if they were workshop supplies. Did he think building a marriage was as simple as making linen? "A man will do what a man will do."

"Exactly. Men choose a wife, and women bear children—as El-Shaddai intended when He created the world."

His comment sliced her to the core. If bearing children was the purpose of women on earth, why did she still draw breath?

"Speak to your father, Jered. I have no answers." Her throat tightened around the words, emotions blurring her view of the rapidly filling vat.

"I've tried, but he says I should seek El-Shaddai. What does that mean?"

Crumbled loaves clogged the sieve. Soupy, smelly goo rose to the top, overflowing.

"Wait, wait!" she cried.

Too late, the lovesick boy righted the amphora—leaving Anippe's arms and lap soaked in mash. She stood, dripping.

Wide-eyed, Jered whispered, "Bithiah, I'm sorry."

He was sorry. What did he have to be sorry about? He was young and reckless, ready to love and live a real life. Nameless deceived others and lived only lies—and her life smelled like the mash that covered her.

"I'll wash at the river. You clean this up."

"Yes, I will. I'm sorry."

He was still apologizing as her feet kicked up dust, fleeing to the river. Fear, anger, and guilt clung to her like the mash on her robe. Too many people cluttered the shore near the long houses, so she ran farther down the bank among the reeds. Checking for crocodiles or water serpents, she saw none and waded into a secluded spot.

Waist deep. Chest deep. She walked until the water rose around her neck.

Why should she live? To Mehy, she was already dead. To Mered, she was a vile deceiver, and she'd nearly cost Miriam her life. Jered, Ednah, Heber, and Jeki would be better served by a real Hebrew mother. Perhaps one of the many village women who hated her for snatching the handsome linen keeper so soon after Puah's death.

Jered's profound declaration, *"Men choose a wife, and women bear children,"* had answered her lifelong restlessness. Now she knew. She had no purpose. When she refused to bear children, her life held no meaning, and the gods fought against her.

She held her breath, took another step, and her head dipped below the water. She waited for death to come.

And waited.

Her lungs convulsed.

Sudden panic turned her legs into sling shots, flinging her up from a watery grave. Relief was fleeting as the current, like a rope wrapped around her legs, robbed her of her footing. Gasping for air, she slapped the water wildly, gulping great mouthfuls of the river as she tried to keep her head above water.

"Bithiah!" a voice called, and then an arm surrounded her. "Stop fighting me! Stop fighting. Just stand."

A strong grip pinned her arms at her side, holding her steady. Still gasping for air, she fought sobs and turned, clinging to her savior. Shaking uncontrollably, she buried her face in his shoulder, the smell of ben-tree oil as calming as the arms that held her.

Mered lifted her and held her close to whisper against her wet hair. "What were you doing out there?" His voice broke, and he fell onto the shore, pressing his cheek against her head. "You can't leave me, Bithiah. Please, you can't leave us."

Waves of shame rolled over her. *He knows. He knows what I tried to do.* She rolled away from him and buried her face in the sand. "Take me to Nassor. Tell him you found me in the village. You'll be a hero. I'll be dead. Please, Mered. Please . . ." Tears robbed her of her voice.

"Shh. Quiet, now."

He lifted her into his arms and began walking. She closed her eyes and hid her face against his chest, shame clinging to her like her wet robe. Voices called Mered's name, but he continued his march, silent, leaving unanswered questions in their wake. Was he taking her to Nassor as she asked?

"Is she all right?" Jered's voice was panicked. "I thought she was washing off the mash."

"I need a dry robe and cloths to dry her. Bring them to the roof." Mered entered their home and set her feet beside the ladder. "Climb," he told her. It wasn't a request.

Numb and quaking, she obeyed, and he followed.

"Father can we come? Is Mother all ri—"

"Heber, you and Jeki return to Shiphrah and have her tell the village women that Bithiah is all right. Your mother needs rest today."

Your mother. The name was a lie. She was neither their mother nor Mehy's.

Clutching Mered's robe, she pleaded through sobs. "Let me die. Please, let me go."

He wrapped her in a ferocious embrace. "You are Bithiah, daughter of God, bone of my bones, flesh of my flesh. I will hold fast to you above all others." He kissed the top of her head, pressing his cheek against it. "I will never let you go."

Her knees turned to water, and he caught her as she fell, then carried her to the canopied reed mat. She turned her back, unable to face such kindness.

Footsteps approached. "Here, Father." Jered's voice. "Bithiah, I'm sorry if I upset you. I . . ."

She heard his hurried retreat as she curled into a tight ball. Did he think her despair was his doing? "It's not his fault. Don't let him think it's his fault."

Mered sat beside her. "Miriam cried and pleaded the same about you this morning." He made her sit up, facing him. Gently pushing off her headpiece, he stroked her cheek as he moved to her belt.

Panic rose, her breathing ragged.

"Bithiah, I'm just going to help you change into a dry robe." He cupped her cheek and then started untying her belt.

"Please, please, Mered, no," she cried, trembling violently. "I don't want to die in childbirth. I can face a sword, but please, Mered, I can't have a child."

He pulled her close, held her as she poured out years of fear and pain.

"Ummi Kiya. She left me. Babies die. Ummis die. Senpa—so much suffering. Abbi cut off her head. Puah—good and lovely Puah. They die, Mered. They all die. If I love you, I'll die, Mered. If I love you . . . I'll die."

He rocked her and cried with her until they could cry no more.

39

And without faith it is impossible to please God,
because anyone who comes to him must believe that he
exists and that he rewards those who earnestly seek him.

—HEBREWS 11:6

Mered sat on his roof beside his wife's sleeping form, watching the once-quaint estate of Avaris whirl and spin in preparation for the Lotus Feast. He'd asked Jered to take over at the linen shop for the rest of the day. The boy would have chewed pottery if he thought it would help Bithiah. "Father, I don't know what I said to upset her. I only mentioned my love for Sela and our hope to be married." Assuring him that he wasn't at fault, Mered had sent him to the workshop to focus on linen. It had always helped Mered when his heart and mind ached.

Guilt seemed a heavy load in their small household. Mered winced at the memory of calling his wife *Anippe*. He'd chastised her more harshly because he'd been burdened by his own deceptions. How he wished he could remove his words from her memory. But words spoken were like the Nile—ever-present but washed clean by a new season. *El-Shaddai, let it be so.*

Bithiah stirred, long lashes fluttering. She was so beautiful.

She bolted upright. "Why are you still here?"

He tucked a strand of hair behind her ear. "Because I sent Jered to the shop—and because I love you."

She shook her head and scooted farther away, putting an arm's length between them. "Mered, no. Don't."

"I already do, and I apologize for the words I spoke in anger."

Silence lingered. She kept shaking her head, sniffing from time to time.

He peeked beneath her silky, black curls. "May I ask you one question?"

She laughed through her tears, finally looking up. "Ask me anything now. I blurted out things I've never told anyone else." She bowed again, still shaking her head.

"Remember that day when Ay's ship docked at the quay? If his troops had come ashore, and one of the soldiers had tried to take Mehy, what would you have done?"

Her head stopped shaking, and she slowly lifted her gaze. "I would have stopped him."

"How? You're a woman. He was a soldier. He would have had weapons."

"I don't know, but I wouldn't let him have my son."

"Would you have died to save Mehy's life?"

She didn't answer. She stared intently at her fidgeting hands.

"What if Nassor came into the craftsmen's village and started beating Heber or Jeki?"

"You said only one question."

He chuckled and repositioned himself beside her. Shoulders touching, he leaned in close. "Answer this one, and then no more questions."

She relaxed against him. "Then, yes, I would reveal my identity to Nassor and try to save Heber and Jeki."

Mered whispered against her ear. "How is giving your life during birth so much different?"

His wife was quiet. Moments passed. She shed no tears. She seemed lost in the commotion of Avaris's preparations at the quay. The king's barque and the Gurob Harem ship would arrive soon.

But she was peaceful. *Thank You, El-Shaddai.*

"The gods taunt us, you know." Her tone was laced with bitterness. "In a perfect moment like this, I look at the quay below and remember our lives will be invaded too soon. They give a moment and then snatch it away."

Mered felt her shoulders tense and the slight tremble of her body. He laid her on the mat, hiding the world outside their rooftop. "Help me understand how Egypt's gods taunt, and I'll explain how El-Shaddai remains faithful in good days and bad."

She tried to turn away. "Never mind."

"I do mind." He lay at her side, careful not to trap her but intent on loving her. "We will never again live at a distance, you and me."

She swallowed hard. "What if I'm still afraid to die? What if I'm still afraid to love you?"

He nuzzled her neck, letting silence console her as he prayed for wisdom. Had Meryetaten-tasherit ever been loved without condition? Horemheb had adopted Anippe to gain power, and Sebak had married her to bear children. Even Mered needed her to care for his children. She believed every man demanded something from her in return for his love. Could he truly love her without demands?

"I will love you, Bithiah, until I draw my last breath—even if we never consummate this marriage." He kissed her deeply, thoroughly, and felt her body relax beside him. Breathless, he pulled away before his passion took him too far. "But can you control *your* desire?" He chuckled, teasing her with a bounce of his eyebrows.

With a slight moan, she laced her fingers through his hair and pulled him into a hungry kiss. Sudden passion nearly scorched them both, memories of the marriage bed fanning to flame every caress.

"Wait, my love, wait. Are you sure?" he asked.

His caution was answered by her desperate embrace and whispered "*I love you*"—words he drank in like a desert wanderer. The world below them forgotten, Mered and his bride enjoyed the tender awakening of newlyweds and tasted of love until morning.

Dawn tinged the eastern sky in brilliant pinks and orange. Bithiah lay in the bend of Mered's arm—yes, *Bithiah.* Nameless no longer, she felt like a daughter of God. Why? How had Mered's love assured her of El-Shaddai's care?

She listened to her husband's steady breathing in the morning stillness. Steady—that was Mered, and somehow she knew El-Shaddai was steady too.

The gods of Egypt were fickle and changed with the teller of the legends. But El-Shaddai didn't change. He was mysterious, to be sure, but the solid faith of Mered, Miriam, Jochebed, and Amram was more certain than the flowing of the Nile. When had Bithiah ever known certainty?

Not until Mered. If any of her children were in danger, she would certainly give her life for theirs. She pressed her hand against her stomach and drew in a deep breath. If a child grew inside her, she would willingly give her life to see its first breath. Mered's reasoning had calmed her like the voice of El-Shaddai. Fear still threatened, but it didn't consume.

Only once before had she given herself to a man without first taking the precaution of herb bundles. Her wedding night with Sebak had been both terrifying and exquisite. He hadn't forced her, but she'd had no choice, really. To deny her groom on their wedding night would have shamed Anippe and her family.

Sebak. Her heart constricted. Had she betrayed Mered by thinking of her previous husband after sharing their first night of intimacy? Mered's tenderness had overwhelmed her, healed her, revived her. How could a man be strong and yet so gentle? She draped her arm over his chest to feel the slow rise-and-fall of his breath as he slept.

He turned and wrapped his leg over her. Entwined. "Bithiah." Her name came in a sleepy whisper, and he smiled.

Relief washed over her. Until this moment, she hadn't realized she was terrified he might whisper Puah's name in his sleep. Tears came quickly though she thought her eyes had run dry. Trying to wipe them away before soaking his arm, she woke him fully.

"What? What's wrong?" He instantly hovered over her, cradling her head, his countenance stricken. "Why are you crying? Are you afraid? Should we have stopped? I'm sorry, Bithiah."

She laughed through her tears. "You didn't call me Puah."

Confusion replaced his concern. "Why would I call you Puah?"

"Puah was so good, so pure and loving. I'm afraid I can never be—" Tears choked her, and she tried to turn away, the familiar wall of shame building inside.

Mered laid his lips against her ear. "And how can a linen keeper compare to Egypt's premier soldier?"

Startled, she turned to meet his gaze as he smiled down at her.

"We are blessed and cursed to have known each other's spouse so well. Let's focus on the blessing." He kissed her nose, each eyelid, and then her mouth, slowly. "The night Mandai brought you to me was the night I realized Puah had known of Mehy's secret heritage all along. You know things about Puah I never knew, and you can share them when you're ready. Likewise, I can tell you things only I knew about Sebak." He kissed her forehead. "I believe he experienced victory in death, by the way."

"Victory in death? That's a strange phrase."

"Horemheb and Pirameses had convinced Master Sebak that he must be Seth reborn to honor his ancestors, but his gentle spirit rebelled and the violence tormented him."

"Miriam said they've told Mehy the same thing." Bithiah's heart ached at the thought of her sweet boy's torment.

Mered brushed her cheek. "Yes. But I assured Mehy that I would pray to El-Shaddai for his protection as I prayed for his abbi Sebak. Before Sebak was sent to kill the Hittite prince, he and I talked about my belief in El-Shaddai— and his. I can't know with certainty that Sebak waits for paradise in Abraham's bosom, but our God is merciful. If Sebak believed in El-Shaddai's promises, I will see my friend again."

"Tell me more—"

"Father!" Jered appeared at the rooftop entry. "Nassor sent guards. Oh, sorry. I didn't mean to interrupt . . ."

Mered donned his robe and met his son at the rooftop entry. "Bithiah and I will be sleeping on the roof from now on, Jered. What were you saying about Nassor?"

Bithiah made sure the linen sheet covered her completely—including her flushed neck and face—and then tried to focus on Jered's report.

"Mehy demands your presence to correct a problem with his byssus sheath for the Lotus Feast. The king's barque arrives today."

"Tell the guards I'll report to Mehy's chamber at once."

"Yes, Father."

"Jered, wait. How's Miriam this morning?"

"Jochebed said she's drinking clear broth and sitting up now. She can't sing yet, but she'll walk again."

The world came crashing back, shattering the dream Bithiah and Mered had created, but somehow it wasn't quite as overwhelming.

Mered returned to her side, sat down, and removed the sheet covering her. "I must leave you now, beloved, but we no longer hide behind anything. Nothing separates us. No lies. No fear." He kissed her gently and turned to go.

"Wait, I'm going with you." She stood and reached for her robe.

He helped her put it on, concern etched on his brow. "I'm sure Miriam will be glad to see you, but make sure you rest some today."

"No, I mean I'm going with you to meet Mehy."

The fear on her husband's face matched her own. "No, not today, Bithiah." He cupped her cheeks and stared into her eyes, barely a handbreadth away. "Not when you've been through so much. We'll tell Mehy the truth when you're feeling stronger."

She traced his furrowed brow, loving this man for his concern, his integrity, and his faith. "I'll feel stronger when we tell Mehy the truth. It's one less lie we must live."

Mered dropped his hands to his side and turned away. What was he thinking?

She slid her hands around his waist and laid her head against his back. "I want to tell Mehy I'm alive before Abbi Horem arrives. It's easier to trust El-Shaddai before the son of Horus comes to Avaris."

El-Shaddai, protect those I love.

Mered walked the long corridor toward Mehy's chamber alone. He'd made the right decision to leave Bithiah at the workshop with Jered. Nassor was waiting beside the master's chamber and would be the only Ramessid who might recognize Bithiah. He'd been utterly devoted to the amira and grieved her death violently.

"It's about time you got here. Master Mehy has been waiting since dawn." Nassor rapped his spear on the door and escorted Mered inside. "He's at the bathhouse."

The estate foreman pointed the way, and Mered continued down the tiled path alone.

Mehy lounged on faded pillows under the shabby three-sided enclosure. Evidently, the master didn't spend much time here. "How's Miriam?"

"She's much better this morning. Sipping broth. Jochebed says she'll walk again."

Mehy covered his face, shoulders shaking. When Mered took a step toward him, Mehy waved him away. The linen keeper stood awkwardly beside the boy who'd made a man's difficult choice.

"You did what you had to, Master Mehy. Ednah told us what happened. She explained the brands on their forearms too. Thank you."

Regaining some composure, Mehy wiped his face but still didn't look at his friend. "You're thanking me for marking your daughter with the symbol of a concubine?"

Mered bowed his head and knelt near Mehy's couch. "I'm thanking you for saving Miriam's life and for finding a way to keep both her and Ednah safe while you're away."

Mehy shook his head. A single tear rolled into his wig, the kohl around his eyes wiped away long ago.

"Master Mehy, I need to confess another hard truth. I risk many lives in the telling because it will certainly cause you more pain." Mered swallowed hard. "But it must be told."

The young warrior pushed himself off the couch, towering over his linen keeper. "Do you really want to test my anger right now?"

"No, I don't want to at all. In fact, I'd rather dance with a crocodile than tell you this now, but to wait any longer would betray our friendship." Mered stood, meeting him eye to eye. "Like Miriam and Jochebed, I have kept a secret from you in order to save lives—yours and others."

Mehy's eyes narrowed. "A true friend keeps no secrets."

"When you were a child, we kept secrets to protect you, but you're a man now. Secrets will never separate us again." Mered peered around the shelter to ensure no one else would hear. "Your ummi Anippe is alive."

Mehy didn't flinch; he offered no sign that he'd heard. His eyes remained fixed on the willow tree by the bathhouse.

Mered cleared his throat, inspected his sandals, and even adjusted his gold-braided belt. Still no response. "Did you hear me, Mehy? I said—"

"You're lying." Mehy's cheeks quaked. "Jad Horem ordered Mandai to kill her. A Medjay never disobeys an order. I saw him kill Ankhe."

"Ankhe is dead. Your ummi is not."

His eyes sparked. "She's not my ummi. Where is she?"

Mered hesitated more than a heartbeat, stoking the young master's anger.

Grabbing Mered's throat, Mehy nearly lifted him off his feet. "I said, where is she?"

"Only if you promise not to harm her."

A moment of decision crossed Mehy's face, and he loosened his grip. Mered gasped for breath while Mehy stared at him, expressionless. "I can't promise that." His eyes glistened, and he turned away. "I didn't mean to hurt Miriam so badly. Sometimes, I can't control it."

Mered's heart ached for the boy he once knew—and the man Pirameses was breaking. "Only one God can help you, Mehy. Your ummi has found safety and peace in El-Shaddai. Mandai brought her to the Hebrew village that night—the same night Puah died. Anippe became my wife, and her name is Bithiah."

Mehy laughed—a harsh, mirthless sound. "Go, Mered. Go, live with *Bithiah* in your safety and peace, and leave me to my gods and wars."

"Mehy, please. El-Shaddai can give you that same peace—"

"I said, go!" Mehy whirled, his eyes blazing. "Don't make me prove I'm Seth reborn."

Mered stood without flinching, feeling no fear—only pity. "She misses you desperately, Mehy, and we love you very much." He took two steps and held the boy's face in his hands. "Please, find a way to see her, but be careful. Nassor might still recognize her."

He kissed Mehy's forehead and walked away.

40

I am a foreigner to my own family,
a stranger to my own mother's children.

—Psalm 69:8

ONE MONTH LATER

Bithiah watched her husband sop up the last bit of gruel with his nabk-berry bread. He loved their daughter's cooking. Since Miriam's beating, Ednah had taken over the cook fire, and both households were eating like Pharaoh himself.

Jochebed sat by Amram, helping him slowly spoon up the gruel when his hand shook too violently to lift it to his mouth. Mered's boys were the exact opposite, slurping their gruel ravenously. Jered would join his father at the linen shop, grumpy as usual, still impatient to marry Sela. Heber and Jeki sat on Bithiah's right and left—her constant helpers and companions as sowing season grew near.

Bithiah felt like the only unskilled worker among them. She could grind grain, haul water, and make beer, but she had discovered a week ago she couldn't make a baby. Her red flow had come as usual, bringing a strange mixture of relief and sadness. For most of her life she'd been terrified of getting pregnant. Now that she loved Mered so thoroughly and had begun trusting God more fully, she dared to hope. Perhaps she was past childbearing.

Mered shoved his bowl away and pushed to his feet. "Come, Jered. We can't be late today. The noblemen's wives pick up their orders, and the troop ships . . ."

His words died as every eye turned to Bithiah.

Tears threatened instantly. "I know Pirameses's soldiers need their war kilts before they sail today." She tickled Heber and Jeki, earning their squeals and giggles. "We can't have Pharaoh's soldiers fighting without any clothes."

Their laughter soothed her melancholy, and her husband's kiss bolstered her courage. "Mehy knows the truth now." He leaned down to hug her. "We've done all we can. The rest is up to him—and El-Shaddai."

She nodded, but emotion tightened her throat. Mehy knew she was alive yet had made no effort to see her—and now he was leaving to fight the Hittites. Would she ever see him again?

"Mama, don't cry." Jeki patted her shoulder. "Heber and me will be good today."

Bithiah squeezed her three-year-old tight. "You're always good, my big boy. Now go get our special jar so I can draw your three dots."

Mered pecked another kiss atop her head, and Jered waved before they both slipped through the curtained doorway.

"Time for my nap." Amram tried to rock to his feet but required Jochebed's help to stand.

"Come, I'll get you settled before I start weaving my next basket." Jochebed's gentle spirit amazed Bithiah. She showed the same gentleness with her daughter.

Miriam still hadn't recovered sufficiently to join them for meals, but she was steadily improving. Shiphrah visited daily, teaching Miriam the healing herbs and midwifery. The girl would need a skill if she and Jochebed hoped to remain in the craftsmen's village. Amram still worked on jewelry in their home but could no longer work at the metal-and-gem shop.

Jeki appeared with the jar of henna and a small stick. Bithiah dipped the applicator into the reddish paste and smeared three dark-red dots on his right hand. Heber remained seated beside her, hiding his hands.

Bithiah raised a brow. "And what is this sudden aversion to our dots?"

Head bowed, avoiding her gaze, he mumbled, "I've seen seven inundations. I'm too old for dots."

One son going to war and another refusing his dots. She kissed his forehead and stashed the jar, gathering Jeki's dotted hand and Heber's undotted one. "El-Shaddai is always watching over you, whether your hand has dots or not, but the dots are there to remind you." She pointed to the first dot on Jeki's hand. "Who is this one?"

"Jeki."

"And this one?"

"Mama."

"And this one?"

"El-Shaddai . . ." Jeki spoke the name of God as a whisper, reverent and holy.

Bithiah's heart squeezed. "That's right, little one."

"I'll remember, Mama." Heber patted her hand, gazing intently at her. "I don't need dots to remember Him."

She pulled them both into a ferocious hug. "Let's get started on our day. I promised Shiphrah I'd grind some herbs for her. If there's no breeze, we can do it outside." Both boys shouted and bounced, nearly toppling over the gruel pot. "All right, all right—let's clean up our dishes before we celebrate."

With morning chores complete, the three of them left the confines of their one-room home and walked the alley between long houses toward Shiphrah's doorway. Bithiah called through her curtain, "*Shalom* . . . Anyone here?"

No answer. She shoved aside the curtain and saw two bundles of herbs—mint and dill—placed on Shiphrah's single table near the grinding pestle and stone.

"She must have been called away for a birth and left these for us."

"Can we help grind?" Heber picked up the bundle of dill, sniffed it, and wrinkled his nose.

"You and Jeki can help by going back to our house and getting two small jars. I'll need something to hold the ground herbs when I'm finished."

The boys ran off, Heber way ahead of his little brother.

"Stay together," she called after them. "I'll meet you under our favorite tree."

Bithiah left Shiphrah's home and walked down the path toward the Nile to a single willow tree. This area had been flooded last month when the Nile's waters brought rich black soil from the south to nourish their crops. Now thick, lush grass grew around the trunk, so she propped herself against the tree, closed her eyes, and tried not to think about Mehy going to war.

Like the waters of the Nile, her fears had seemed to ebb during the past month. Not because her circumstances had improved or changed, but because she trusted more in El-Shaddai. She'd realized the despair that drove her into the Nile that day was the same hopelessness that had haunted Ankhe all her life. Her sister had seen nothing but the offenses, the fear, the pain of life. Bithiah's heart broke for the little girl who never knew a father's love, a man's love—and never knew of El-Shaddai's love. None of the people Anippe had loved—Amenia, Tut, or Senpa—knew of El-Shaddai's power to heal a broken heart and restore shattered lives. How she wished she could tell Mehy of that God someday.

"Mama!" Heber's panicked scream brought her to her feet.

"Heber! Jeki!" She ran toward her sons, who were being marched in front of four Ramessid guards.

The boys grabbed her knees, and she reached down to cradle them against her. They were trembling and crying, and it stirred her fury. "Why must you frighten little boys? Have you nothing better to do than—"

"Yes, this is the woman." A male voice startled her, causing her to look up as the four guards parted.

Mehy stood beside Mandai, both threatening her with their stares.

Her mind reeled, tying her tongue.

Heber sobbed into her robe. "Mama, the master saw Jeki's three dots and got angry. Are they going to hurt us?"

Indignation replaced her fear. Bithiah moved her sons behind her and lifted her chin. "Can't a Hebrew mother place three dots on her son's hand?"

"It proves you are the woman I seek," Mehy said, stepping closer. "You are Bithiah, aren't you? I believe you once lived at the villa. My chamber and bathhouse have recently been restored and need a thorough cleaning. I want someone who knows the master's chamber and is careful to maintain my treasured past." Mehy took another step closer and lowered his voice. "I knew when I saw the boy's three dots I'd found my ummi's favorite chambermaid. Ummi Anippe used to put three dots on my hand." He bent down to show Heber and

Jeki his gold wristband and then removed it, revealing three henna dots beneath. "My ummi used kohl on my hands, but I use henna under my band because it lasts longer."

Bithiah's breath caught, and she covered a gasp, quickly bowing her head to hide her reaction. *He remembers the dots—and still paints them.* Grasping at composure, she lifted her head. "Yes, I'm Bithiah, and I would be honored to clean your chamber, Master Mehy. May I take my sons to their father in the linen shop?"

"They can follow us to the villa, and my Ramessids will escort them to the shop." Mehy turned to Heber and Jeki again. "Tell your abbi Mered I'll stop by to see him before my troop ship sails this afternoon."

The boys bobbed their heads, eyes wide.

"Follow me."

He walked away, and the Medjay grabbed Bithiah's arm as if she were a prisoner. Heber and Jeki followed, the guards falling in step behind them.

When they walked through the narrow alley between long houses, Mehy tossed a question over his shoulder. "Do you live in one of these houses, Bithiah?"

"Yes, our family lives through that doorway, there." She pointed, and Mehy took note. Was he simply curious, or did he have other motives?

As she watched her son's confident stride, she was startled by a revelation: she knew Mehy as a boy, not a man. Though he was still only fifteen, his body was a man's and his military training had matured him too quickly. She looked over her shoulder at Heber and Jeki. She must guard her little ones from the son she once knew.

Every Ramessid, Hebrew, and merchant took note as they paraded from the long houses, up the hill, and toward the workshops, market, and villa. Whispers and pointing—sure signs of speculation of their crimes. What might they have done—a Hebrew woman and two little boys—to require four Ramessids, a Medjay, and the master to apprehend them?

Halting abruptly at the villa's garden entrance, Mehy turned to the guards. "Take the boys to the chief linen keeper, Mered, and then return to the king's delegation. I have no further need of you."

"Wait, I——" She reached for the boys, but the guards had already herded them in the opposite direction.

Mehy grabbed Bithiah's arm, nearly lifting her off the tiles. Hurrying toward his chamber, he kept his voice low. "You look terrified. I think you convinced them."

"What do you mean *convinced them*? I am terrified. What if they hurt my children?"

He lifted an eyebrow and lowered his voice. "Would you protect every Hebrew child as your own, Ummi?"

Startled, she wasn't sure if he meant to tease or condemn her. Bithiah glanced over her shoulder at Mandai, who still followed closely. As they approached the master's chamber, she saw Nassor ahead. "Mehy, no. He'll recognize me."

"Keep your head bowed. Mandai will lead you in." Mandai grabbed her other arm as Mehy quickened his pace toward his estate foreman. "Did Pirameses find you, Nassor? He was looking for you this morning."

Bithiah ducked her head as Mandai lead her toward the door, opened the latch, and——

"Wait. Who is——" Nassor gripped Bithiah's arm, and her heart leapt to her throat.

"I asked you a question, soldier. Have you spoken to Vizier Pirameses?" Mehy's tone allowed no argument or delay. "Why do you care about a slave woman cleaning up the construction mess in my chamber?"

"I'm sorry, Master Mehy, I . . . uh . . . no. I haven't spoken with the vizier this morning."

"Find him. I won't suffer Pirameses's temper because you can't follow orders." Mehy stormed past him.

Mandai had already pushed Bithiah through the open door when Mehy entered and calmly closed it behind him. The young master motioned them toward the courtyard but directed his comments at the door so the chamber guards would hear. "Clean the bathhouse first, and then you can begin on my chamber."

He joined Mandai and Bithiah at the bathhouse, hands braced on his knees, chuckling. "That was too close."

Mandai congratulated him, but Bithiah stood in awe of the enchanting place where she and Mehy had once confided fears and laughed at bullfrogs. The bathhouse's three-sided structure was covered with newly placed palm fronds, which fluttered in the breeze. Brightly colored pillows decorated a long, built-in couch.

"Just as it was when Ankhe and I played with you here." Tears clouded her vision as she whispered the words to her son. Memories—good memories—of Ankhe flooded her heart.

"He did it for you, Amira." Mandai nodded toward Mehy, whose jaw was set like a flint stone. "He finds words hard sometimes, but he's a good man— like his abbi Sebak."

The Medjay turned to walk away, but Bithiah caught his arm. "Thank you, Mandai. Thank you for saving my life."

His arms came around her in a hug, hiding her in ebony muscle. "You make a lovely Hebrew, Amira."

She squeezed him tighter but felt him let go. He stepped back, and she turned to find Mehy just a handbreadth away.

"Sebak was not my abbi." His eyes glistened. "I'm sorry I—" He hid his face, his shoulders shaking, and Bithiah gathered her strong son into her arms.

"My life could be full of regrets, Mehy, but making you my son will never be one of them." She held him tightly, suddenly aware of his scented lotions and her unkempt body. Would he be repulsed by her? He hadn't seemed to notice or care. So much about her had changed—nothing more drastic than her faith. She'd prayed for a moment to tell him of El-Shaddai . . .

"Sebak wasn't your abbi, Mehy, and he wasn't Seth reborn. In fact, Mered told me that during Sebak's last days, he may even have believed in the Hebrew God, El-Shaddai."

Mehy quieted in her arms and slowly pulled away. "Mered told you that they've trained me to take Sebak's place, didn't he? He told you what I've become." His countenance was stricken, shame hanging on him like filthy rags.

"I don't know everything—about you or Sebak. But I knew Sebak's heart, and I know my son. Neither of you is a god, and neither of you is darkness and chaos. You were created by El-Shaddai, who loves deeply. He created you to love deeply too. I've seen this love in you—and I saw it in Sebak. You feel compassion, and you protect the weak. Sebak was that man, and you are that man." She looked at Mandai. "Tell him. Tell him about the Sebak you knew."

The Medjay nodded with a knowing grin. "I've already told him these things—many of the exact words, Amira."

"But I must obey Jad Horem and Pirameses. They're my commanders." Mehy spoke like the little boy she remembered.

"You are a man first, a soldier second," Mandai said. "Remember what we discussed. I will defend you with my life, but you must make your life worth defending."

Bithiah's heart beat faster. "Mandai is your personal guard now?"

Mehy nodded. "Jad Horem made his best Medjay my protector. I'm Pharaoh's only living seed, the only one to provide for him and Amenia in the afterlife."

She held her son's face between her hands, peering into his confusion. "You are not Horemheb's seed, and there is no afterlife with Egypt's gods. They are myths and legends, my son, meant to keep you in chains. El-Shaddai is your only hope for freedom in this world and the next."

He pulled away. "Why do you people always talk about your god?"

She grinned—almost giggled. "We people?" Had he really just called her a Hebrew?

His cheeks turned pink, like her sweet, gentle, Hebrew boy.

Bithiah's gaze wandered beyond the bathhouse to the river, to a spot now overgrown with reeds. "That's where I found you," she said, pointing.

Mehy's expression was a strange mix of emotion. What was he thinking? How was he feeling? "Miriam said she stood in the bulrushes, watching me float in a basket until you drew me out. That's why you used to call me Moses."

Bithiah nodded, and they watched the spot together—as if another basket might float by.

"Is Miriam all right?" he asked. "Recovering from her injuries?"

"She's healing well. She spends most of her time with her ailing father—" Bithiah covered her mouth, watching the realization dawn on Mehy's face.

"Our father is ill?"

She reached for his hand, and he didn't pull away. "Amram started with a falling sickness last year. Jochebed cares for him at home. She still weaves baskets, and Amram does some jewelry work, but he's seen over seventy inundations, Mehy. If you ever hope to see your true abbi again, you should come soon."

He squeezed her hand and lifted it to his lips. "I'll think about it."

Every fiber of her being wanted to press him to see Amram today. To make him believe in El-Shaddai. Suggest he marry. And she hadn't yet told him what to tell Pirameses about this *Seth reborn* nonsense. But in the quiet corners of her heart, she felt the gentle reins of El-Shaddai.

"Would you like me to clean your bathhouse or your chamber first, Master Mehy?" She kissed his hand and winked, hoping she saw love with the sadness in his eyes.

"I want you to go home and enjoy a quiet afternoon." When she started to protest, he added, "I'll have Mandai escort you."

41

Because [his brothers] were jealous of Joseph, they sold him as a slave into Egypt. But God was with him and rescued him from all his troubles. He gave Joseph wisdom and enabled him to gain the goodwill of Pharaoh king of Egypt.

—ACTS 7:9–10

THREE YEARS LATER

Bithiah tossed and turned, vaguely aware of a raucous commotion in her dreams. And who had lit a torch? Why was it so bright?

She shaded her eyes against daylight—and then sat up with a start. How could she have slept past dawn? Mered's place beside her was empty, and Avaris buzzed with activity. She could have slept through a war—

War. Mehy was returning today on the medical barque. Avaris had buzzed yesterday with the news from a royal messenger that both Master Mehy and Master Sety were injured in the Hittite battle to regain Kadesh and they were returning home. There was no report on the severity of their injuries. *Please, El-Shaddai, let them live.*

She grabbed her robe and hurried toward the ladder, but had to hang on to the canopy pole when she felt lightheaded. Why hadn't Mered woken her? She wanted to be at the quay when the barque arrived to catch a glimpse of her son. Would he be walking or carried on a palanquin?

Steadier now, she started climbing down the ladder in bare feet to the comforting sound of her husband's voice.

"Go back to the roof. I was about to bring your gruel."

Bithiah peeked down into their one-room home. Jochebed winked at her while stirring the pot over the cook fire. Miriam sat at the table with Amram, Heber, and Jeki. Bithiah still missed seeing Jered and Ednah there. Would she ever grow accustomed to her chicks leaving the nest? It helped when Jered's wife, Sela, brought their new little one over to visit. Who would have imagined Bithiah a grandma?

"Up, up, up," Mered coaxed, her clay bowl in hand. "We need to talk before I go to the shop."

She hurried back up the acacia rungs, Mered close behind, wondering at her husband's impromptu breakfast chat. "Will you meet the medical barque at the quay and find out about Mehy's injury?"

Please, El-Shaddai, give Mered a chance to speak with Mehy about You.

"I'm afraid to be seen at the quay, my love. You know Nassor resents my relationship with Mehy. I can't seem overbearing, or life gets hard for me and my linen workers." Mered placed the bowl of gruel between them, and the smell made her nauseous.

She nudged it away. "I certainly don't want you to put yourself or your workers in danger, but if Mehy's been injured, he might be frightened and more willing to hear the truth about El-Shaddai. Promise me if you get the chance you'll talk with him, you'll tell him about your final talk with Sebak. Make Mehy believe so he'll be in paradise if—" The words caught in her throat, the thought of what her son had been through too frightening, too dreadful to bear.

"Bithiah, I can't make Mehy believe. I can't even talk about El-Shaddai unless he's willing to listen. Sebak was open to my prayers." He brushed her cheek, a smile on his face. "I will speak to him about El-Shaddai if he'll listen."

Tears came unbidden. Why was she crying? "I'm sorry. I guess I'm more upset about Mehy's injury than I realized."

"Remember what we talked about last night. They wouldn't have sent him on the medical barque if he hadn't been well enough to sail."

She nodded, but the tears wouldn't stop. She shrugged and pointed at her wet cheeks. "What is wrong with me?"

Mered chuckled, picked up the bowl of gruel, and waved it under her nose. Bithiah gagged, almost retched, and her husband started laughing—laughing!

Humiliation turned to anger. "It's not funny. Why are you . . ." Realization dawned, and her heart nearly leapt from her chest.

"That's what I wanted to talk to you about." He kissed her gently, a grin still on his lips. "Your stomach has been upset, and you've been extra sensitive to smells recently."

She didn't respond.

"And you've been sleeping longer than usual in the mornings. Have you been extra tired or simply lazy?" His eyes danced with mischief.

"If you want me up at dawn, you should jostle me when you rise."

He chuckled. "Bithiah, how long since your last red flow?"

"I can't be pregnant, Mered. We're grandparents."

"It doesn't matter. If God grants it, we'll have a child."

She began figuring the courses of the moon and realized she had skipped last month's flow.

Mered scooted closer, slid the bowl aside, and pulled her close. She curled into him, letting his warmth repel the returning chill of fear. "The child that grows within your womb is our child, wife. You and El-Shaddai will protect him until he greets the world. In this single act—the creation and sustaining of life—a woman and El-Shaddai share a special bond, one that a man can never know." He kissed her forehead. "Treasure these months, and I will cherish you and our child forever."

"What will we tell the children?"

He laughed again, and she giggled. "Since Ednah told us last week that she and Ephraim are expecting, we can tell them our grandson will have an uncle to play with."

"Or our granddaughter an aunt to play with." Bithiah snuggled closer into his chest, the weight of the truth growing heavier by the moment. "What if Shiphrah and Miriam are busy at Ednah's birth and can't help me? What if my body's too old to deliver a child? What if—"

"What if we have ten more happy, healthy babies before we age to one hundred and ten and die at perfection?"

She shoved him away. "I haven't even had this one, and you want ten more?"

With a roar, he rolled her onto their sleeping mat, laughing, playing, loving, wanting, adoring. She saw it in his eyes. All she'd ever hoped for.

"If I am to bear your child, Mered, I must ask one thing." She grew serious and combed her fingers through the gray hairs at his temples.

"Anything, my love. Name it."

"Heber and Jeki sleep on the roof, and we get the main room."

He smiled wryly and glanced down at the bustling quay. "All right, but I'm going to be late for the workshop this morning." He buried kisses in her neck, and the bowl of gruel was forgotten.

EIGHT MONTHS LATER

Mered walked the aisles of vertical looms, inspecting the fibers, the weave, the designs. Forty men now stood or sat at their craft, deftly working the warp and weft. Someday Jered would manage this alone. How would Mered know his son was ready?

Bithiah was due to have their first child any day, and he'd readily trusted her pregnancy and delivery to El-Shaddai—even after losing Puah in childbirth. Why then was he so hesitant to entrust the linen shop to his firstborn son? The question plagued him. Maybe he loved his work too much and trusted his son too little. Or was it deeper?

El-Shaddai, could I trust You if You asked me to give up everything—as Anippe did?

The thought was staggering and made him yearn for his wife. Her transformation had been remarkable. She was remarkable, because she'd learned to trust in El-Shaddai completely. Mered realized it was time to give Jered more responsibility at the shop—because he must trust El-Shaddai completely.

Feeling God's pleasure, he wiped away tears and raised his head. Nassor stood before him.

"I didn't want to interrupt." Disdain tinged Nassor's voice. "Since you were weeping like a jilted maiden."

"How can I help you?"

"Master Mehy will see you in his chamber." Nassor spoke the words like a curse and shoved Mered toward the door. "Your linen sales are down. Perhaps he'll finally send you to the mud pits where you belong."

Mered kept walking—past the garden and down the corridor—using every drop of restraint to stay silent. Linen sales were down because Nassor had stolen more linen this year, selling it in the peasant market to line his own pockets. He settled on a bland reply. "I'm thankful we have a gracious master. Aren't you, Nassor?"

A sudden blow, and Mered found himself on the floor. A kick to his side, and he rolled into a ball, covering his head for protection.

"You will never address me as an equal, Hebrew. Is that understood? We helped the amira long ago, but don't imagine we're friends." Nassor kicked him again. This time Mered heard his fingers pop, and he cried out. "Get up, linen keeper, and straighten your robe." He grabbed one of Mered's arms and jerked him to his feet.

Mered stood on wobbly legs, walking and blinking away black spots in his vision. Hand throbbing, he paused at the master's door while the estate foreman knocked with his spear and ground out a threat.

"If you breathe a word of our scuffle, your sons will be in the mud pits by dusk."

Trying to straighten to full height, Mered smiled when Mandai answered the door. The Medjay took one look at his stooped form and opened the door wider. "Master Mehy, perhaps you should see how efficiently your estate foreman obeys your commands."

Nassor's grip on Mered's arm tightened, and the linen keeper tried to stand taller, but his ribs were almost certainly broken.

Mehy sat on his couch, expression unchanged. "Nassor, I could use a man like you at my new post. When I'm finished meeting with Mered, you and I will talk about your future."

The estate foreman shoved Mered through the door and puffed out his chest. "Thank you, Master Mehy. I'm honored. You won't be sorry."

Mandai supported Mered with one arm and closed the heavy door with the other. "Don't speak until we get to the bathhouse." He kept his voice low and supported Mered's left side.

Mehy led the way and quickly cleared pillows off the bathhouse couch. Mered noticed the large scar across the boy's left shoulder, well healed but evidence of a serious gash. He'd only seen the master once since the injury, soon after his return to the estate.

"Your shoulder wound has healed well, Master Mehy." Mered's voice was breathy. Each word pained him.

"I'm in better shape than you are at the moment." Mehy lowered him to the couch. "I'm sorry, Mered. I thought assigning Nassor to escort you directly here would keep him from touching you."

Mered waved off his concern with his good hand, and Mandai eyed his broken fingers.

"These don't look so bad." Mandai yanked them into place, and Mered screamed. "You see? They're straight again."

Mehy pulled some reeds from the river and handed them to the Medjay. "Here, use these to wrap them." Mandai went to work, and the master clapped a hand on Mered's shoulder. "Wrap some linen around your chest when you return to the shop to support your ribs. Nassor is a brute. He'll leave with me and Mandai in the morning on the troop ship to Nubia."

"Nubia? Why are you going to Nubia?" Mered thought of his pregnant wife at home. She wouldn't be happy about her son going so far away.

"Jad Horem is sending me to Nubia for my protection." Mehy waved away Mered's concern. "Back to Nassor's transfer. Do you know of a more trustworthy Ramessid officer to replace him—one who could manage the estate and treat the Hebrews fairly in my absence?"

Mered considered the few Ramessids he knew who were both honest and kind. Most men of higher character served as military officers or noblemen. "There is one man, Gadiel. He oversees the peasant market and to my knowledge has never taken a bribe."

"Gadiel. I remember him." Mehy nudged Mandai aside, winding the last reed around Mered's hand. "When our friend here leaves, send for Gadiel. I'll inform him of his new position as estate foreman. He has much to learn before I leave for Nubia tomorrow."

Mandai stood over them and laid a hand on Mehy's shoulder. "You should tell the linen keeper about Nubia. Perhaps Mered's one God can help us. I've seen his prayers work before."

Mehy sighed and rolled his eyes, but Mered noted a slight grin. "Even my Medjay speaks of El-Shaddai."

"Perhaps you could start by telling me about your injury," Mered suggested. "I've heard stories from my linen workers, but I'd rather hear the truth from you."

Mehy tucked in the end of the reed, securing the wrap around Mered's hand. He sat on the ground beside the couch and sighed again, seeming weary beyond his years. "The stories are undoubtedly grander—and happier—than the truth, my friend. Mandai was commander over both Sety and me. We encountered heavy Hittite resistance along the coastal route. Sety lost a chunk of his thigh to a Hittite swordsman. I tried to pull him to safety, but the same warrior slashed open my shoulder. Mandai rescued us both." He recited the story like a merchant reading a supply list.

"At least you're alive, Mehy, and your courage to help Sety sounds remarkable."

"Vizier Pirameses doesn't think it so remarkable. He blames both Mandai and me for his son's injury. Sety will walk again but never fight. Jad Horem made him high priest of Seth's temple in Qantir, and his ummi Sitre chose a bride. They marry within the month. Pirameses is furious."

His countenance faded into resignation. "Jad Horem named me Son of Cush—governor of Upper Egypt. I think he meant to remove me from Pirameses's fury. Instead, he stirred it further because Pirameses—who was vizier over both Upper and Lower Egypt—is now my equal. That's why I leave tomorrow for the Nubian fortress of Buhen with Mandai as my bodyguard." He laughed without humor, too cynical for a boy of eighteen. "And Nassor will become the new *Seth reborn*. He's more suited for the role than I ever was."

Mered could only stare at the miracle before him. A Hebrew babe, saved in a basket, reared a prince, and raised to Pharaoh's right hand. "Do you remember any of the stories Jochebed or Miriam told you growing up?"

Mehy tilted his head and grinned. "That's an odd question. I remember a few. Why?"

"Do you remember the story of Joseph? His Egyptian name was Zaphenath-Paneah."

Mehy's geniality fled, his face suddenly pale. "I know Zaphenath-Paneah's policies allowed migrant Canaanites—Hyksos—to rule Lower Egypt until the Ramessids expelled them." He stood, signaling their meeting's end. "Don't ever mention his name again. Jad Horem has protected me from Pirameses thus far, but if you compare me to this Joseph, no one can save me."

Mandai patted Mered's shoulder and then pointed to his hand. "Change the reeds each day, and rest your hand. It should heal in a few weeks, my friend."

"Thank you." Mered pushed himself off the couch, gaining a little help from both men. He turned to Mehy and squeezed his shoulder. "I won't mention the Hebrew's name to you again, Master Mehy, but I will never stop mentioning your name to El-Shaddai. May my God bless you and keep you and be gracious to you. May His face shine on you and give you peace."

He turned to go, praying his last words would seep into the boy's soul on his long journey to Nubia.

Bithiah sat in the only chair they owned and measured her growing hips by how much they hung over the seat. She felt like a hippopotamus and almost certainly looked like one—though she couldn't be sure since Mered had hidden her bronze mirror the day he found her crying at her reflection. If persistent swelling, constant burping, and endless sweating were previews of childbirth, Shiphrah should simply drown her in the Nile at the first contraction. Her fear of death had been consumed by abject misery.

"Mama, where should I put the parched grain?" Ednah stood at the curtained doorway with her cute round belly, two heavy trays of grain in hand. How could anyone be so lovely while pregnant?

"Set it by the cooking pots. We'll shuck it when we're finished making beer." She appraised her daughter's youth and grace and wondered again why El-Shaddai had allowed her—a grandmother—to conceive a child. Since she no longer believed in Egyptian gods or their tricks, she must trust in El-Shaddai's good plan. "Did your father say when he'd be home?"

"Oh, I forgot to tell you. He sent Jeki with a message earlier. They're working late to prepare kilts for a troop ship leaving tomorrow."

Bithiah's heart skipped. "A troop ship? Did he say what troops or where they're going?"

Ednah's features fell, and she waddled over to kneel before her mother. "I'm sure if Mehy is involved, Father will tell you when he comes home. Let's stay busy so we don't think about it." She reached for the flavoring vat and sieve. "Here, you hold the sieve, and I'll pour the mash."

Bithiah would gladly stay busy as long as she could sit in the chair. Positioning the flavoring vat at her feet, she picked up the sieve and set it on the vat, bracing her forearms on her knees to relieve her aching back. Not an easy position when a pyramid pressed on her insides.

"Ready, Mama?" Ednah held the heavy amphora aloft, waiting for Bithiah's signal to pour.

"All right. Pour."

The chunky, fermented sludge was almost more than Bithiah could stomach, especially in their stifling one-room home. She much preferred doing this chore outside, but her swollen legs and added bulk made squatting impossible.

"Are you frightened, Mama? About the labor, I mean."

Ednah's words raked Bithiah's heart like a hackling comb. What could she say? *Yes, it's been the single paralyzing fear that's ruled my life.*

"No, of course not. We'll be fine. Shiphrah and Miriam are excellent midwives and have delivered hundreds of healthy babies."

"You're not even a little frightened?" Ednah's voice was small, breaking down Bithiah's defenses.

She'd considered before that both she and Ednah had lost their mothers in childbirth, but Bithiah had never asked her about Puah's death. Had the girl witnessed it?

"The truth?" She looked away from the sieve for a moment, and Ednah nodded. Sighing, Bithiah braced herself to relive it. "I was five when I watched my ummi die trying to birth my little brother. Neither of them survived. I've been terrified of childbirth most of my life, Ednah." She fell silent while the girl kept pouring. That was all she could say about Ummi Kiya. "What do you remember about Puah's death, habiba?"

After a moment's hesitation, Ednah spoke, her voice gravelly. "I didn't see Mama die, but I heard her cries—and then I heard the silence." Tears glistened like gemstones on her dark lashes. "Is it terrible that I'm scared?"

Bithiah wanted to drop the sieve and hug her precious girl. "No, habiba. It's not bad. You're not bad, but fear—unchecked—can make you do wrong things. Fear can overwhelm you and imprison you—as it did me all my life."

"How did you stop?" Ednah reached for a stick to clear a chunk blocking the sieve. "Stop being afraid, I mean?"

"El-Shaddai has worked from within, growing my faith with every kick of this baby in my womb. Egyptian gods of gold or stone are external and can't work within to give me peace. If I lose my life while giving life—well, I've felt God's pleasure. And that's enough for me." Bithiah heard her words as if someone else said them. "I don't think I knew how I felt until I spoke it out loud."

Ednah smiled and propped the amphora against her belly, using a stick to dislodge a few more clumps. "I've felt joy at every kick and hiccup as well, but I'm not ready to die yet, Mama." Her voice broke. "I don't want to die."

Before Bithiah could comfort or console her daughter, a sudden gush wet the chair beneath her. "Ednah, stop!"

Eyes wide, the girl placed the amphora on the floor. "Did I spill that?"

Bithiah felt her first contraction and breathed as Shiphrah had instructed. It passed quickly, and she grinned at Ednah. "I think you should find Shiphrah or Miriam and tell them my water broke." She shoved away the vat of beer—just to be safe—and then stood, sending another gush of liquid to the floor.

"I'm going!" Ednah rushed out the door, leaving Bithiah alone.

She examined her home as if seeing it for the first time—or perhaps it would be the last. Would she die as she'd always feared? Though the thought gave her pause, she still felt the peace she'd described moments ago.

Miriam appeared with Ednah on her heels, took one look at the floor, and giggled. "I'll get Shiphrah. We're having a baby today."

Miriam disappeared again, but Ednah came in and gently cradled Bithiah's elbow. "What do we do now?"

"We pray to the one God." Bithiah brushed the girl's cheek, trying to ease her tension. "I was Pharaoh's daughter and King Tut's sister—daughter and sister to supposed gods. But I watched them face death, habiba, and neither of them displayed the peace I feel now. Only one God offers freedom from the fear of death."

Ednah's eyes widened. "You're not afraid? Even now?"

Another contraction seized her, doubling her over this time. Breathing wasn't helping. Bithiah ground out words through gritted teeth. "I'm not afraid, but I want your father here—now!"

Ednah released her and ran out the door, leaving Bithiah grasping for the chair. *El-Shaddai, I'm not afraid, but I am asking for help. Please bring Shiphrah and Miriam quickly. And Mered. I don't want to deliver my baby without my husband's calming presence.*

42

One of Mered's wives gave birth to Miriam,
Shammai and Ishbah. . . . These were the
children of Pharaoh's daughter Bithiah, whom
Mered had married.

—1 CHRONICLES 4:17–18

Shiphrah's face was grim, and Bithiah's contractions layered one on top of the other with little relief between.

"Please, I need Mered." Wild with panic and pain, Bithiah squirmed on the birthing stool and pressed against Miriam's chest. "Find him before I die. He needs to know I love him, that I believe in El Shaddaaaaahhhh . . ."

The urge to push overwhelmed the searing pain, and Miriam rocked forward with Bithiah over the bricks. A steaming bowl of hot water sat beneath her to ease delivery.

It wasn't working.

"Gently, Bithiah. Push gently." Shiphrah's calm and tender voice grated on Bithiah's nerves.

"I'm going to rip out your tongue!"

Miriam shushed her, but Shiphrah chuckled. "Yes, my friend, most women feel that way about now."

A wave of nausea swept over her, and Bithiah retched into a bowl Shiphrah had placed beside her. "Please, make it stop," she said, wiping her mouth. "I don't want to have this baby."

"Your labor has progressed quickly, Bithiah." Shiphrah exchanged a concerned glance with Miriam and pasted on a smile.

"Aaaaahhhhhh!" Another urge to push robbed her of dignity.

"Gently, Bithiah, gently." Shiphrah patted her knee.

Ednah burst through the doorway, supporting her belly with both hands. "He's coming. Father's coming."

"Shiphrah, check on Ednah." Bithiah's contraction was starting again, but she saw pain on her daughter's face. "Ednah, are you all riiii . . ." She bore down uncontrollably.

Mered slapped aside the curtain and limped toward her, his right hand wrapped with reeds. *He's been beaten!* Near hysteria, Bithiah reached out for him amid her pushing, begging him to come nearer.

"I'm here, my love. I'm here." He knelt beside her until her pain lessened and then quickly replaced Miriam as Bithiah's back support. Months ago, when Mered told Shiphrah he planned to assist with the delivery, she'd refused. But he had explained the milestone of faith this birth represented for his wife. Hesitant but understanding, Shiphrah agreed.

Shiphrah pierced him with her gaze. "What took you so long? She's progressing too fast."

"She's fine. She's going to be fine." Mered whispered in his wife's ear, "I'm here now, my love. You're fine. We're fine."

"What happened? Who hurt you-oouuuu . . ."

Another pain overtook her, and Mered rocked forward. He sucked in a deep breath, his pain as evident as hers, but she couldn't stop to ask him more. Ednah huddled in the corner with Miriam, panting through a contraction.

"Aahh, El-Shaddai, help those I love," Bithiah cried out as the contraction ebbed.

Shiphrah chuckled and patted her leg. "That's the first time I've heard that from a laboring mama." She looked at Mered and lifted a brow. "We'll tend to you after we welcome your baby into the world. Care to tell us what happened?" Another pain overtook Bithiah, and Shiphrah began her instructions again. "Lean forward with her Mered. Push, push, push, Bithiah. With all your strength now that Mered's here."

She'd already been pushing with all her strength, but she was weakening.

She could feel it. Falling against Mered when her contraction eased again, her head lolled against his chest. "Please, how's Ednah? Please."

Mered's strong arms cradled Bithiah as the urge to push seized her once more. His whisper strengthened her resolve. "Push, my love. Miriam will care for Ednah, and El-Shaddai will give you strength to deliver the baby He created. You were born for this moment—to deliver this baby. Our baby. Push, Bithiah. Work with your Creator. Bring our child home."

The urge, still painful, seemed less foreign now. When the intensity passed, she relaxed into his strong chest, resting in the security of El-Shaddai.

Shiphrah nodded at Mered, glowing approval from the weary midwife, and then patted Bithiah's knee again. "Bithiah, on the next push, listen carefully to Mered."

As the pushing continued, Shiphrah's voice became indistinct droning. Bithiah melted against Mered's chest, counting his heartbeats until the next urge seized her.

His words came quick and clear. "Gently at first, wife. Now harder— Shiphrah is guiding the head. Now harder, harder . . ."

With her last bit of strength, Bithiah pushed a new life into their world and fell back into her husband's arms.

"It's a boy!" Miriam squealed and then tied two clean strips of linen to the cord, four finger-widths from the babe. She withdrew her small flint knife and severed the cord, passing the little one to Shiphrah, who waited to rub him with salt and wine.

Laughing and crying, both Mered and Bithiah reveled in their miracle, while their squalling boy announced his objections to his new home.

"I can't explain it, but I know El-Shaddai delivered our son." Bithiah brushed her husband's cheek, looking over her shoulder at his weary expression.

"You did it, Mama." Ednah appeared at her side, beaming, cradling her baby brother. "He's the most beautiful baby I've ever seen."

Bithiah reached for the babe. "He can be the most beautiful until yours comes along."

"Which will likely be tonight or tomorrow," Miriam said, poking her head over Ednah's shoulder. Ednah winced and grabbed her belly. Miriam walked her around the crowded little room, coaching her breathing, encouraging her to relax.

Joy and wonder filled Bithiah as she laid their new son on her chest, letting him nestle, skin against skin. The sensation was indescribable, unforgettable—but she'd felt it before. She'd held another squalling babe against her naked body eighteen years ago. Bithiah looked across the room at the young woman who'd appeared to her first as a little girl with riotous curls and round brown eyes, following a basket on the Nile.

Mered knelt beside her. "We haven't talked about a name yet. Hebrew mothers usually name their children."

Smiling, Bithiah felt the nudge of El-Shaddai's blessing. "Good. I have an idea."

Shiphrah paused in her cleaning and called over Ednah and Miriam. "Choosing a child's name is like forming his future. It must be right."

Bithiah's heart seized at the truth she knew too well. With tears in her eyes, she held out her hand to Miriam, calling her close. "His name will be *Miryam*, like the little girl who delivered my first child in a basket on the Nile, for he is *beloved* and *wished for* as the name implies."

Tears glistened on her friend's lashes as droplets of the Nile had beaded on her curls that day so long ago. Miriam leaned down to embrace her but hesitated. "Give little Miryam to his father so I can hug my friend."

Chuckling, Mered lifted the babe from his mother's chest. When Bithiah had received hugs from all three women, she found her husband cooing to their son.

"You are loved. You are wished for. You are a miracle, our little Miryam."

AUTHOR'S NOTE

Finding Pharaoh's Daughter

When writing this biblical novel, I began with a central unquestionable fact, grounded in God's Word. Exodus 7:7 tells us Moses was eighty years old when he returned to Egypt as God's human instrument of deliverance for Israel.

Scholars quibble, argue, and flat-out rant about the date of the Exodus; however, two dates emerge above the rest. Both 1450 BCE and 1250 BCE have merits and pitfalls, but 1 Chronicles 4:17–18 helped me decide on 1250 BCE.

> One of Mered's wives gave birth to Miriam, Shammai and Ishbah the father of Eshtemoa. (His wife from the tribe of Judah gave birth to **Jered** the father of Gedor, **Heber** the father of Soko, and **Jekuthiel** the father of Zanoah.) These were the children of **Pharaoh's daughter Bithiah**, whom Mered had married. (emphasis added)

Notice this scripture mentions no daughters, but the biblical record seldom lists women in genealogies. Realizing it was possible that either or both of Mered's wives had daughters, I added Puah's daughter, Ednah (from Hebrew meaning *"pleasure"*), as a fictional character in the story.

But why does this scripture point to 1250 BCE as the date of the Exodus? Because if I chose 1450 BCE, my story must somehow depict the famous Egyptian Queen Hatshepsut as the woman who drew Moses from the Nile. Hatshepsut—the woman who reigned as pharaoh for twenty years, and whose tomb is possibly the most extravagant in the Valley of the Kings. I couldn't conceive a plot in which Queen Hatshepsut would marry a Hebrew slave and bear him three sons.

So I went with 1250 BCE—as did Cecil B. DeMille and Walt Disney.

With the date of the Exodus established, and Moses's age given in Scripture, it should have been an easy process to establish which king ordered Hebrew baby boys to be killed. Simply add eighty years to 1250 BCE—right?

According to Ian Shaw in *The Oxford History of Ancient Egypt,* the reigning pharaoh in 1330 BCE was—drumroll, please—King Tut.

Wait! Tut had no daughters. In fact, he died before he and his sister-wife had any children. Ankhe-Senpaaten's (Senpa's) miscarriages are historically accurate. So how could Pharaoh's daughter pull Moses from the Nile when Pharaoh had no daughters?

Because King Tut had a sister, who would have been Pharaoh Akhenaten's daughter—Meryetaten-tasherit. I fictionalized her adoption by Horemheb to create an important connection.

Keep reading. You'll love the way Egyptian history and God's Word fit together.

Finding Moses

The walls of Egypt's Great Hypostyle Hall tell us much about the New Kingdom's pharaohs and their military campaigns. On the northern exterior wall, Pharaoh Sety is accompanied into the Libyan and Syrian campaigns by a "group marshaller" or "fan bearer" named *Mehy.* But this mysterious character has no recorded genealogy or burial among a civilization of meticulous record-keeping. How can it be?

Further confusing Egyptologists, biblical scholars, and hobbyists, *Mehy's* name and likeness were rubbed out and in some places replaced by Sety's son, Rameses II. Of course, other pharaohs were known to replace the name of a previous pharaoh on monuments, but why would Rameses II try to erase a simple fan bearer or commander?

When I discovered *Mehy* was most likely a nickname for Horemheb (also from Ian Shaw's book, *The Oxford History of Ancient Egypt*), I knew I could link Moses to Pharaoh Horemheb and needed to link Tut's sister (Moses's Egyptian mother) to Horemheb as well. Thus, the fictional adoption of Anippe.

But Mehy isn't fiction, and neither is Moses. Are they the same man? Only God knows.